Heirs

in the

ICE

Heirs
in the
ICE

C.H. WILLIAMS

ISBN: 978-1-7333569-7-8

For Elsie.

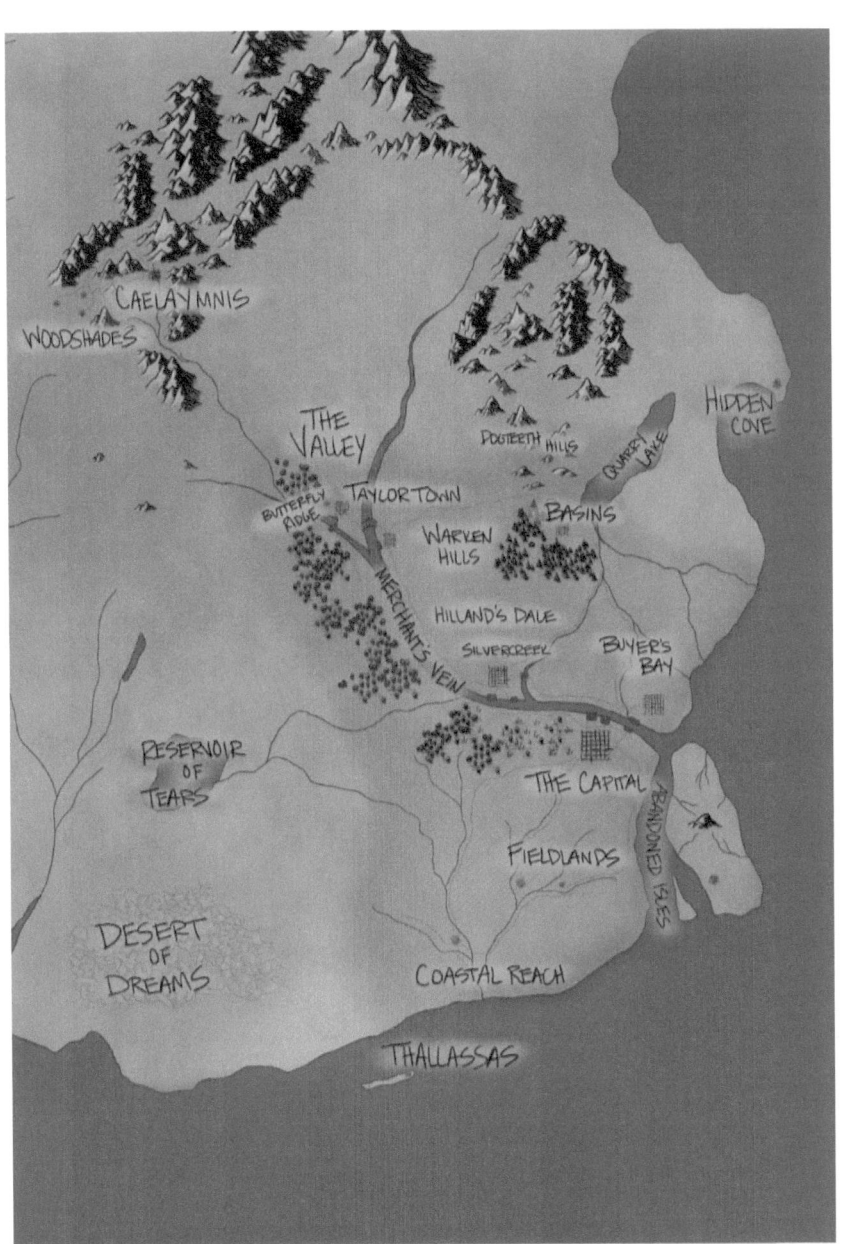

PROLOGUE

I have lived in suspension between page and pen. My passing moments are well-worn books, and each breath is the liminal space between inked letters.

It is said that the gods built this world with nibs and inkwells.
It is said that only the gods bleed stories.

We are watching the world crumble around us as we nurture our little scraps of faith. I don't know what victory means, anymore.

And still, I search for the endings.

That's the fate of my ink and paper soul. Endings, and nothing more.

THE PASSINGS

We are not living in the same world anymore. Was it just this summer that Fletcher arrived in a wave of magic? And now we are well into winter.

The scheme has folded itself over time and again. We saw that the daughters of the merchants were dying, but now, it is clear this was part of larger treachery. It was no plan to bring the Merchants down, but a ploy to find our dear Elsie, for, it seems, she is the Heiress to the Hidden City, the great sanctuary of magic for humankind.

I acquaint myself with the myths of the gods, of late.

With Cora, God of Death, supposed progenitor to our dear Elsie. With Kiran, God of Life, who has been set against Cora in every legend and myth I can find.

With Lucia, God of Chaos, mother to the kobalde like our dear Chim.

With Stell, God of Ice, protector to Caelaymnis. With Hadri, God of Darkness, she who commands the night sky.

With Natali, God of Order, mother to the adpare, who leave order and organization in their wake, and gods know we could use one of those around. With Ignata, God of Flame, whose lamps guide the lost.

With Asa, God of Healing, they who gave way to Healers like my beloved Theodore.

~SAM ALDERTON,
EXCERPT FROM A LETTER DATED JANUARY 23RD

CHIM

"There's magic in you yet, child. That's what my
Granma told me her mother would say to her, and her
mother before, and so on, and it was this inherited
familial belief that despite all our sins, we had a little
spark of something good. I don't know if she was right. I
hope she was, though. I hope she was."

~Theodore Alderton

In a distant village at the foot of the mountains, nestled just beyond the reaches of the wood, sat a cottage. It was ordinary, as ordinary as any cottage might presume to be in a world freshly-made and brimming with magic. Within this decidedly un-ordinary cottage dwelt a decidedly un-ordinary little girl and her mother. It is of consequence to note that the mother, despite being steeped in a world of the fantastic, had managed to remain unequivocally and unquestionably plain.

Being an oddly ordinary woman, and lacking the generally cautious instinct most parents find imbued in their being upon the arrival of their child, she had developed the unwise habit of sending her little girl on errands through the wood, wherein lay the ailing grandfather. The grandfather belonged to nobody in particular, having dwelt beyond the village since before there was a village to dwell beyond. Unimpeded by this unsettling detail, the mother resolved to care for the old man by way of her daughter.

Armed with a basket of bread and a bright red cape, so that she might not disappear amongst the green of the wood, the daughter was sent down, down, down the winding path from the safety of her house to the grandfather's cottage in the woods.

It was a boring path, by all accounts. Dusty and brown, with ruts from the rain, the little girl's eyes remained fixed on the ground, for she did not dare to take her gaze from where her feet carried her. But as she followed her given path with fervent devotion, she paused not to consider the folly of her habit. Dangerous was the familiar road.

Not long into her ill-fated journey, she happened upon a wolf. And the most un-ordinary wolf it was, too! Having once been a mortal man tempted, it had left all trace of its former self behind. With a mangy coat of gray fur dripping off the creature's bones, and a flaring ridge of menacing spikes rising along its back, the little girl could not help but to stop and stare.

With a grin, the wolf beckoned the little girl forward, scenting her unease and thinking her a tasty morsel. But the little girl was wary, and kept her distance.

"You need not fear me," the wolf said, thinking quickly. "I simply wonder what might bring such a sweet little thing into the woods on such a beautiful morning?"

"I am bringing bread to the grandfather in the woods," the little girl explained.

An idea came to the wolf. "That is all well and good," the wolf nodded, "but have you brought the flowers, too?"

The little girl stopped to think. No, she realized, she had been a rude little girl. The grandfather was ailing, and Mother hadn't sent along flowers? It was no wonder Grandfather was so displeased.

Thanking the wolf for his help, she skipped merrily off the path towards the meadow, very pleased with herself, for children know no greater joy than realizing their mother has erred. The little girl, collecting a nosegay for the grandfather, began to wonder what else her mother might have forgotten. She had forgotten to tell the little girl not to talk to strangers, the little girl thought. And she had forgotten to tell the little girl to be home by dark. And now that she thought about it, the little girl realized that her mother had not instructed her to collect berries to accompany the fresh bread in her basket. So, flowers tucked neatly in her apron, the little girl set out to pick some berries.

The wolf, all the while, had run ahead to the grandfather's cottage. To the wolf's dismay, though, he had died, leaving naught but a pile of dust upon the bed where he'd lain. Undeterred, the wolf dusted off the nightcap, pulled the curtains about the bed, and waited for the little girl to arrive.

When at last the sun began to sink beyond the mountains, the little girl came knocking at the grandfather's cottage.

"Grandfather, I have brought you bread," the little girl called out, wandering through the open door. Her mother ought to have warned her of that, too, she supposed. But the oughts and naughts yielded no thoughts, and the little girl wandered in, anyway.

"Come closer, dear," the wolf purred, belly growling with hunger.

"Why, Grandfather," the little girl gasped, pulling back the curtains, "you look dreadful!" Grandfather, the little girl thought, was not usually so mangy.

"You speak the truth," the wolf conceded. "Give your Grandfather a kiss, my child, so that my spirits might be lifted."

Leaning in, the little girl made to obey, when with flashing fangs and foul breath, she was swallowed up whole, basket and all. The light departed from the world, leaving an impermeable darkness in its wake. The joy and hope of the meadow had gone, and the little girl began to cry, wondering why the grandfather would have gobbled her up, flowers and all.

One must think the girl in the red cape had a truly terrible grandfather not to notice a wolf had taken his place.

The little girl waited in the belly of the beast, sobbing, until a very peculiar thing began to happen. Perhaps it was the darkness around her. Perhaps it was the hot, foul odor that permeated her senses. Or perhaps it had been the apparent betrayal that had gotten her swallowed up. But whatever it was, the little girl found that at last, she had used up her tears. Her eyes would cry no more, and she was left with nothing to do.

The days passed, and the little girl had grown bored and hungry. She had devoured the berries and the bread. But they were not enough. So she began to devour the beast, too. Her teeth grew sharp, all the better to chew through the sinewy flesh. Her eyes grew black, all the better to pierce the darkness. Her memory began to fade, all the better to forget her careless mother and the village.

But before the girl could consume the beast entirely, at last the day came when a great blade sliced through the beast.

It was Fate.

Heartbroken by Volition, she had torn through the cosmos, her knife rending the sky itself asunder, the stars shattering, the velvet night tearing, and as she tore the universe apart, so she slit the beast's belly, releasing the little girl.

It was there, the beast should have died.

But in the wake of the slices left through the cosmos, Desire came crawling through after Fate, and the little girl hid in the bushes and watched as Desire mended the beast and claimed it as his own.

The little girl was furious, for Fate had deprived her of her vengeance. Fate, though, cared not, for she had driven her dagger into the earth and vanished.

It was then that the little girl found a new mother. A better mother, one with a taste for Chaos, and together, they plotted their revenge.

Mother Chaos sent her child into the woods each day, and together, they searched for the wolf that had tried to eat the demon child.

Desire, Mender of Beasts, had taken the old wolf under his care as he himself searched for Fate. But a new beast, untested and young, had risen to take the old one's place in the wild, and not knowing what dangerous things roamed the woods, the new beast approached the little girl, thinking her a delicious morsel.

"Hello, little girl," the wolf said, "I wonder what might bring such a sweet little thing into the woods on such a beautiful morning?"

The little girl stopped her searching, staring at the creature. "Perhaps I might tell you."

"Perhaps you might," the wolf conceded, preparing to pounce.

"Then again," the little girl said, "do you think it wise to talk to strangers?"

The wolf paused, thinking over the query. "And why do you ask?"

"It can be dangerous," she warned.

The wolf only laughed, looking her over. Her red cape made her easy to see, her only weapon a nosegay of wilted flowers in her apron pocket.

The laughter only made the little girl angry. In a fit of rage, she began to stomp her feet on the ground with such ferocity that the mountains themselves began to shake, the trees began to tremble, and the wolf became afraid. Leaving the little girl, the wolf bolted, disappearing into the woods and through one of the slices in the cosmos carved by Fate's dagger.

Determined to seek her revenge, the little girl tried to follow after the beast. She would track the wretched wolf to the ends of the universe, for Fate had carved the path to follow.

Chim, chim, chim, went her knife against the whetstone each night as she sharpened her blade, always ready for the wolf.

Chim, chim, chim, whispered the folds of her red hood as she searched the world, determined to exact her due.

The little girl followed the paw prints through where Fate's dagger had been driven into the earth, ripping slices through their world and into another.

What a tremendous blade with which to exact vengeance!

What a beautiful knife with which to carve the wolf down!

But the gods warned of the dagger. No mortal should toy with such a dangerous weapon, such a relic of destruction, and thus, with their blood, the eight young gods sealed it away, untouchable. The ward that protected the dagger could only be undone when their blood—and their lives—were given.

And so it was, the little girl watched and waited as countless souls tried and failed to exhume the dagger. She watched and waited for her wolves to return, watched and waited as the world began to awaken, and Chaos abounded, fresh and ripe for the taking.

FLETCHER

"Much is the burden we don't wish to carry, and
light are the trials we have asked to bear."

~Dradan Proverb

A heavy self-consciousness weighed on Fletcher as he strode down the bright palace halls—the weight brought, in part, by the circlet set atop his head, silver, a teardrop sapphire cold against his forehead.

Heir Apparent to Caelaymnis.

Even in an empty hall, he felt the eyes of the mountain city on him. He'd always been a prince. But he was the third child in a secure monarchy, he'd been beyond the heir and the spare—he'd been almost ordinary. Caelaymnis wasn't the great expanse of the Guild, they were simply a city—admittedly a somewhat large one, sprawling through the mountain valley—but he'd been able to brush off the titles and privileges and disappear into the crowd when he wanted to.

All that had changed, though.

The people of Caelaymnis were in the midst of a torrid love affair with Elsie.

They adored her—and by consequence of his relationship with her, they loved him, too.

It was such a valiant story. Bowyer's evil children had kidnapped a helpless human—hilarious, Elsie was anything but. They twisted their sacred religion in her torture—that was true, what Augustus and Cam had done was an affront to the gods themselves. Then Alva, the holy mystic daughter had freed Fletcher, and the two of them, crusaders against the night, had stormed the house of darkness and saved the girl, and that...that was technically correct, though it made Fletcher scoff and roll his eyes.

It'd been friends, trying to look out for each other. Trying to protect each other. Loving each other as best they knew. That was all.

But the Drada were, at heart, a dramatic people.

The Drada, and their gods-damned ribbons that were strung up on Fletcher's once-discrete wrought-iron fence. Some had sent boxes of them—which was simply lazy, Alva had loudly professed—but most had taken to tying them to the fence, in lieu of tying them to the girl herself.

It was a tradition as old as dirt, and probably as idiotic, too. His mother had told him it was so the gods could find the wounded and bring them peace. Someone else had once said it was from the ancient healers, who would bind wounds in colorful swaths to ward off the demons that sent them sour.

Whatever the reason, though, as Elsie lay recuperating in the upstairs bedroom, the Drada had done their very best to help.

A few folks *had* made it upstairs. Rodion. Mia. Isa, frequently. They'd offered ribbons, too, now braided and tied in a beautiful bracelet around her wrist, and she was on her feet again, so what the hell.

Maybe there *was* something to it.

He hadn't minded being in the public eye—he'd been in a position of prominence since birth—but Heir Apparent was an entirely different matter.

Once he'd taken that on, privacy no longer belonged to him. His moments were the moments of his people. Bowyer's decisions were no longer the uncomfortable orders of a father-slash-king that Fletcher could disobey as he saw fit, they were teachable moments where he could demonstrate for his son how to rule their realm.

He had not wanted this. Had not planned for this, had not prepared

9

for this. The days after he'd carried Elsie from the dungeons below Cam's house were waxing to weeks, and when he had walked from that house with her in his arms, he had not paid thought to where the crown would pass.

But the treason of his elder siblings was an unforgivable crime.

Fletcher pressed into the General's Hall, taking his place among the crowd at the back. The triumvirate interrogations were going in full force, the Senate determined to unearth the truth—or at least enough of it to keep the city from rioting.

Augustus himself was standing before the panel in rough-spun clothes, shackled and chained. He glanced back once, when Fletcher came in, doubtless recognizing his brother's footsteps, but a second later, his eyes were fixed back on the floor.

Despite the public thirst for justice, access to the triumvirate had been restricted today, for at last they had reached the point of interrogation most critical—and most dangerous, for they'd be discussing restricted knowledge Bowyer was unwilling to make public. Even so, many had turned out.

An elderly Drada, a senior official, folded his hands, eyes fixed on Augustus as he prepared his question, lips twitching. "Barghest and dhacrym are the tools of one man. Anscip Xavishia. And his practice is tenancy—controlling a forebearer through the blood of their kin. In its true form, a kinsman would give their blood so the Insidiae could intervene when the antecedent strayed. For *obvious* reasons, this has been negotiated away in the Treaty. We gave up a number of manners of magic to secure a peaceful future. Magic yielded the war; take away the magic—at least, the dangerous parts—no more war. And yet," the official pressed, "and *yet*, you think you're the exception."

Augustus said nothing.

"At first glance," the senior official pressed, "it appeared that something was afoot in the Guild. Commander Praequintelya, your brother, argued repeatedly for intervention. He identified a pattern-killer with an increasingly long list of victims, he voiced concerns about how they died, he identified that the dhacrym and barghest were at play, he came to you and said that the children of the merchants were dying, and with evidence of barghest and dhacrym, we assumed the culprit was vying for control of the merchants themselves."

Fletcher had to swallow a snort. It was greedy, the way they'd laid claim to his own theories, as if he hadn't faced the very real consequences of voicing them.

"That brings us the arrest."

And there it was.

At last, they'd gotten to Elsie.

The crowd bristled, angry already, for between their prince and the mysterious human girl from the Valley, it would be no contest.

"She didn't have any magic!" someone shouted across the crowd.

The elderly man whistled, silencing the room with a scowl. "We will *not* be taking questions. This is a formal proceeding. You are witnesses *only.*" He turned his gaze back to Augustus. "You...issued a warrant for Elizabeth Mirabeau. It was technically lawful—humans are not permitted to breach the city perimeter, and she did. The problem was, she breached it under your watch—and more than that, with your permission. When Commander Praequintelya protested, you arrested him too, for bringing her to Caelaymnis." Displeasure was carved in the man's brow. "Where was the treason, General? Was it when she voiced her desire to stop a murderer? Was it when she risked her life, coming here to provide information to you and Commander Praequintelya about your primary suspect—"

"It was technically treason," Augustus breathed, but his words were cut off.

11

"Treason? You think, had she come to this triumvirate herself and said, *I know I break your laws, but I fear for the safety of us all, for blood is being spilled, sacrilegious and terrifying,* that we would have thrown her in a cell?"

Elsie would've never done such a thing. She'd try to fix it herself—and if she'd been backed into a corner enough to ask for help, she wouldn't have used such lilting and poetic words.

"She is of Death," Augustus pressed, "Death, an invaluable armament on the battlefield—"

"Tenancy controls the lineage. You openly admit to using this mortal girl to seek control of the gods?"

Augustus looked horrified at the accusation.

Fletcher did not linger to hear the rest—nor to watch the crowd grow increasingly unruly. He had no need to hear the outlandish rebuttal his brother would present. Augustus had let his faith carry him too far, and none would look kindly on how his crimes made a mockery of the gods.

~ • ~

Fletcher paused just outside his father's private council chambers.

He didn't know if he was ready for this.

But it wasn't like he had any other choice. It was why he'd come here today, in truth, and he'd hoped that listening to Augustus would've bolstered his anger, his confidence, but it just made him painfully sad.

The palace had been his home until 16, when he'd been swept by both his parents into study at the Acadamae. His childhood friends went off to hone their magic, to learn to hunt in the wild mountains, or to weave textiles on the enchanted looms, or perhaps to pour spirits at their mother's tavern, or to pursue any number of professions. Isa themself had been the child of potters. They might've spent their life throwing clay, Fletcher had once bitterly pointed out as all of them had sat round Rodion's table, drinking and bemoaning their poor choices.

12

Yet, the Acadamae had called them, willing or not.

Two years of training and work, and then, a rightful commission. An upgrade from *cadet* to *officer*, and the move to a different set of barracks, and they'd all been honed to fight.

Sort of.

Augustus definitely had been. He was young for a general, but he'd spent five years living and breathing in the militaristic air of the compound, and before that, he'd wasted his youth dreaming of the insignia.

The rest of them had just gotten good at pretending that the violence didn't slowly erode them.

And like it or not, that same violence had coated the King's throne in blood—blood that would become Fletcher's burden, in time, if things kept on in the direction they were. The irony had not been lost on him, that spilling blood in the name of the crown was not seen as heinous, whereas spilling the blood of innocent people in the name of the Master's crimson magic was an egregious crime. Both acts of bloodshed were to cement power, and nothing more.

With a heavy sigh, Fletcher slumped against the wall.

This palace had been built by an ostentatious man who had sought to make his people proud. The first Praequintelya had built this place up on the heels of crushing defeat. Originally, it'd been a library, a kitchen, and an arboretum—a place of preservation. To save learning, to save lives, and to save beauty. The stone called back to the Dradan ways, to the familial stone homes now ruins in the mountain tops, and before that, to the caves.

Now, it was nothing more than an expanse of pale stone and posturing.

The echoing halls were draped in tapestries to soak up the sound, the floors covered in mats to conceal the echo of steps, and the whole thing was trying to be something it wasn't.

The door to the King's council chambers slid silently open, an aide beckoning Fletcher in with two fingers.

Bowyer had draped himself in his high-backed seat, brow furrowed. He looked, to Fletcher's eyes, a man who was coming apart. His own circlet was dangling off one of the ornamental knobs on the top of his chair, his stole in a crumpled pile on the floor, his ordinarily braided hair let loose, a shimmering sheet across his shoulder.

Senator Cormalum, Cam's husband, was sipping a small cup of herbal tea as he looked painfully out the window.

"Father." Fletcher gave a slight bow, apprehensive.

"We were just discussing the predicament with your elder siblings." Cormalum turned from the window, thin lips poised, pale eyes chilled.

"And I was expressing my continued disbelief at Cam's decision to partake in these unfortunate events," Bowyer sighed. "Augustus? This does not surprise me. The boy has always been headstrong, and ignorant to strategy. He was a thoughtless child, and a careless leader. But Cam?" He clicked his tongue.

"Father, Cam was harboring a production ring in their home. Whether she partook or not, she was complicit. Some have come forward—Augustus himself confessed she wished to dethrone you—"

"Lies!" Boywer sat up straight, glaring. "She was a sweet child. She would not forsake us this way—"

"She did," Cormalum hissed. "And you are a fool if you swallow her lies."

Fletcher cleared his throat, knees weak. The crackle of the fire coupled with the *flick-flick-pink-flick* of the storm against the windowpanes sounded to his ears like the departure of snow before an avalanche.

Gods below, do not bury me now.

14

Cormalum was going red in the face, his tirade gaining momentum. "How do you expect your people to regain their trust in this family when you so blatantly disregard the treachery—"

"That is, er, actually what I had hoped to discuss with you both," Fletcher edged, tentative. "I...can't do this."

The King's brow crumpled, eyes falling with disdain upon his third child. "Do what?"

"Lead?" Fletcher's voice was hoarse, his mouth dry. "I—I can't. I'm not cut out for this." He closed his eyes, reciting the words he'd practiced in front of the mirror what felt like a thousand times. "I...wasn't cut out to be a commander, either? I love the realm, but I—I can't send my friends to die on behalf of it. Especially not—not after..."

"Not after Elsie," Cormalum filled in softly, his voice gentle. His pitch hair was slicked back into a knot, and yet his pale eyes still looked chilled as he glanced between Fletcher and his father. "Sentiment has shifted in her favor, you know. They would not balk to see her at your side, when the time comes. She may even bring peace to the Woodshades, precluding you sending your friends to war—"

"I'm not made for this. Meetings, and strategy, and—and what about when public opinion swings back, and the Woodshades attack again?" Fletcher cast a worried look at his father. "This trust they have in us isn't real. It's fragile."

"Alva cannot assume your position." Bowyer's words were angry as he rose, robes whispering. "She has taken the cloth—"

"Cormalum can, though. And should." Fletcher crossed his arms. "When they wed, wasn't one of the conditions making him a Titled Prince? As long as he was a Senator he would hold his own family name and district, but if he resigned, he would take our name, as well as the title granted to him by marriage?"

Bowyer's expression was inscrutable, eyes flashing between them.

"I...that is a gross overstep," Cormalum muttered, rubbing his jaw. "I cannot step in. And I am not free from criticism, my wife—"

"There were plenty to see you condemn her," Fletcher said quietly. "Forget the officers in the house, who I am sure were quick to tell the rest of her betrayal of you. You marched her through the street. That is a more lasting source of confidence than any I hold. They love Elsie. But they have not seen her hardly at all as she recovers."

"Out of sight, out of mind," Bowyer considered.

The room was still for a moment.

Then, the King rose, attempting to straighten his robes. "I would find this to be an acceptable compromise."

With an exhale of relief that felt like it reached through the floor and into the earth itself, Fletcher tipped the circlet off his own head with shaking fingers and laid it carefully on the table. "Thank you, Father." He turned to leave without another word, tears of gratitude prickling in the corners of his eyes.

"Fletcher?"

He paused, his name foreign on his father's tongue.

"You understand what this means. You know our name is no longer yours."

Fletcher glanced back. "I know, Father."

"But you know you will always be my son? And I will always love you for that."

He nodded, swallowing hard even as the room began to flood with tears.

He was no longer Prince.

He was no longer Heir Apparent.

No longer anything.

Just Fletcher.

ELSIE

*"Mess is evidence we live. Perhaps that's why we try
to clean it—to erase ourselves from this world, and thus,
find peace."*

~ Theodore Alderton

Whisps of steam curled up from atop the hot bath, dancing in the evening light.

The sun may have been a liar and a coward, teasing at warmth through the last vestiges of frozen daylight, but it had sworn no fealty to the mortals. Its only task was to rise and fall, and even that inclination shifted with the seasons.

It owed them nothing.

The heat of the bath soaked into Elsie's bones, a gentle vanguard to the winter chill, and she was reluctant to rise. She savored these moments of peace and rest—and they were still few and far between, even as days waxed into weeks, and *better* was a word starting to be thrown about.

Elsie had not confessed to anyone that she preferred the company of solitude to the presence of her living, breathing family. She couldn't say when she'd began to mistrust them, exactly. She'd longed to be near them, but once safe in their harbor, their kid gloves pained her, their placating words infantilized her, and their sugar-coated, affected manners made her want to hurl.

They tried her patience, more and more with each passing day. It was not that she wasn't relieved to be free of Augustus, nor could she say she had regrets about how it had come about—heads would certainly roll for what they'd done to her. But she disliked the delicacy with which she was being handled, the way she was treated like a child, as if she, on account of her hurts, was incapable of comprehension and decision.

In the back of her mind, she'd begun to wonder about the dhacrym.

It was true that the draught of fear had put her through her paces. It was true that the phantoms it conjured had tormented her endlessly, that the havoc it wrought on her mind and body alike was brutal, and yet...yet, she missed it. She missed the kernels of truth she'd found there.

No one was honest with her anymore. They wouldn't admit that she wasn't alright, that she wasn't going to be alright, that alright was something she could only dream of.

She was irked at herself for the thought, and knew others would be too—did she really want to be afraid all the time?—but her waning patience was evidence that *something* had to be done.

Risa, as her advocate, advised time and patience.

But Risa was being pulled in too many directions as it was. Playing healer, student, and advocate, she was already unraveling, and the uncertainty of what to do—about Elsie, about the Hidden City, about the Chancellorship, about the Master, about Clark—it was too many variables with too little information.

Dripping wet and leaving the bath water to groan and moan as it circled the drain, Elsie grimaced at the fogged mirror, running her hand over it, leaving messy lines of water droplets as she tried to clear it enough to get a look at herself.

She didn't look like the descendant of the God of Death, and she sure as hell didn't look like the Heiress to the Luminary Chancellorship—the best of the two Chancellorships, Risa had said, like *that* was reassuring.

It didn't really matter, though. Without her locket, she wasn't anyone.

It'd gotten lost, the night she'd been arrested, and it'd yet to surface. Just as well—Elsie wasn't exactly interested in the repercussions that came with that damnable thing. She might as well wear a sign that said, *Hey, look at me, I'm the daughter of a political enemy, and maybe a little divine! Come kill me!* But even still, it was the only connection to her mother Elsie ever had, and that made it difficult to brush off the loss as a casualty of battle.

The mantle clock chimed.

Her hour of solitude was over. They'd send a search and rescue up to the second floor of Fletcher's Caelaymnis house if she was not down for dinner for fear the bath had done her in, she thought bitterly.

Bathed, irritated, and ready to argue, Elsie headed downstairs—and nearly tripped over Sam, who was sitting on the floor in the hall across from her door. His legs were stretched out, ankles crossed, a small piece of sewing in his hands as he glanced up. He'd taken to a slightly more informal affect, only wearing belted pressed trousers and a button-up tunic with sleeves folded neatly to his elbows.

"Excuse me, what are you *doing*—"

Sam quirked an eyebrow, rising. "I said I'd be just outside if you needed anything."

"That's an expression, you gods-forsaken tart," Elsie snapped, "not a literal commandment—"

Sam put his hands up in surrender, still holding his sewing in one of them. "Talk to your brother. I was sitting happily downstairs, in an exceedingly comfortable armchair, minding my own business until he interfered."

"You've never minded your own business a day in your life." Despite her anger, a faint smile tugged at the corners of her mouth.

"Consider this the exception." Sam gave her an apologetic smile. "I'm

19

sorry. I'm sure you're suffocated, with everyone fussing."

"It's driving me mad." Elsie turned to head down the stairs. "But I also don't know what I would do without you," she added quietly, an afterthought. It was true. They were sending her batty, but she couldn't imagine being *alone*, either. Truly, a cursed way to be, she reflected.

Unable to stand those around her, unwilling to send them off, desperately desiring a taste of the fear that sent her tumbling into this turn in the first place. Utterly, undeniably cursed.

Fletcher's house, at least, was more spacious than the Taylor Town apartment her brother and Sam let. Seated close to the center of Caelaymnis, it gave her purview across the mountain valley—at least, it did when she took refuge in the window seat in their bedroom—and otherwise, the accommodations had allowed her brother and Sam to stay close as she recovered.

The kitchen was crowded, though, the sounds of utensils clacking, food sizzling, and conversation bubbling making quite the din, for the house had also acquired a number of honorary residents in the last few weeks. Risa, for one—though she did seem to be splitting her time between Caelaymnis and the City, a harrowing decision for someone already at their breaking point—and of course, the host of elves Fletcher rightly called friends were never far.

A host of elves? A flock? Elsie made a note to ask what they were called in multitudes as soon as Fletcher returned.

The smell of garlic and meat danced on the air, and something cinnamon too, and the wash of sensation was temporary relief, but relief all the same, as Elsie joined the throng.

Teddy was talking quietly with Isa and Risa as he sliced some sort of pale blue vegetable with a furrowed brow, Isa all the while pouring glasses of wine as Sam joined them.

Mia, a fellow soldier with short, strawberry blonde hair, was leaning on the counter, watching Rodion stir some sort of sauce. She was occasionally tossing herbs and spices into the pan as he did so, talking loudly about how only fools had faith while Alva protested, glaring. The youngest Praequintelya and holy mystic Listener, she took issue with Mia's assertions, being of the faith herself—and she wasn't shy about matching Mia's volume to express it, either.

Rodion merely nodded wisely as they both argued. His dark curly hair had been pulled back, his tawny skin beginning to glisten as he stood above the stove. He'd been caught in an argument he wanted no part in, that much was plain, but the sauce simmering before him kept him rooted where he stood.

The elves heard their friend before Elsie did. That frustrated her, the way Isa kind of cocked their head to the side, the way Mia rolled her shoulders back, bitter words falling abruptly off. Fletcher was *her* lover. She should've known when he came home.

The front door slammed, and a moment later, Fletcher walked in, door swinging behind him, warm hazel eyes absolutely alight—

"Well?" Elsie tapped her head, nodding to him, a gesture to the circlet.

"It's done." Fletcher was grinning. "I am officially out. You are looking at Commander Fletcher Nist, who has no claim whatsoever to the Caelaymnic throne."

Whoops of excitement filled the kitchen, celebration overtaking them all.

~ • ~

Elsie picked at the third helping of starchokes and elk as she sat, listening to the quiet conversation unfolding around the kitchen table. Her celebratory mood had been short-lived, and as always, the conversation had turned back to *what happened.*

Not with Fletcher, of course—with her. All roads led back to her pain. Fletcher had abdicated any claim to the throne, and he'd done it *for her.* He'd never say it outright, but of course, they both knew it. He didn't know what she was going to do about the City, he didn't want to jeopardize her claim, he didn't want to be another Praequintelya that took away something from her, and invariably, though none of it was said directly, the conversation drifted back to *what had happened.*

"It's curious," Sam was saying, "that Elsie is so center to this. They have no qualms with Augustus running around, kidnapping the children of merchants and Woodshades alike?"

"Apparently," Fletcher said with some irritation. "They are offended he makes a mockery of their faith. My faith."

"Oh?"

Fletcher glanced at Elsie, brow knit. "He claims she is of Death. You heard Elsie say the same—though that he admitted it openly, in front of the triumvirate, is concerning. He says he wishes Death to walk with his warriors, nothing more, though plainly when tenancy is concerned, there is a great deal implied. Controlling a god—and through a, what, 20th-generation descendant?"

A faint smile tugged at the corner of Elsie's lips. Hilarious.

"And tenancy, that's what this Xavishia fellow's expertise is," Sam pressed. He had the air of someone discussing a fascinating newspaper article, and that sat badly with Elsie. That he could talk about it so academically, as if he didn't have a care in the world that she'd lived it—couldn't *stop* living it, if truth be told.

"Tenancy is an Insidiae talent, that's correct," Isa said, nodding. Soldier, medic—and history buff, Elsie had learned, listening to them talk fervently about centuries past. "They're very private, but it seems to have something to do with the familial magic they possess generally. They have this—this connection with each other. They're bound to each other. They always know where the other is, what they're doing—what they're thinking, if you believe some accounts. Anscip and Almarin are all that is left—and actually, all there ever really was—of both the Insidiae and the Xavishia."

"I can't imagine it. One of two ancient beings, watching what are essentially the lives of mortals passing by," Teddy said quietly. "That'd be enough to twist anyone, I think, no one was meant to watch the eons pass so."

"It's not really any wonder that they're renowned for tenancy," agreed Isa. "For so long, they lived in a world where blood magic was common and accepted. Then, on top of that, they have this magic that runs between their family, that's entirely based on connecting a family—no, think about it," Isa pressed, "it's this magical ability to know where your family member is at all times? To know what they're doing, to know what's in their head? That's right down the street from controlling a person entirely. It was only a matter of time before they tied them together."

Rodion quirked an eyebrow. "An interesting theory."

"And one substantiated by thousands of reports," Isa countered. "Anscip Xavishia is a man with a calling card. He's got barghests, he's got dhacrym, and he *always* has something to do with reports of tenancy."

"It's called peace-keeping, Isa, open a gods-damned book—"

"That's my point! We can debate the morals of the Coalition's system of government—alleged system," Isa added pointedly, "as it's all hearsay, aside from what we know of the end of the Clash six-hundred years ago, but it's all there. Relegation is as far as anyone else has taken it—"

"Mm, come again?" Sam gave Isa a pleasant look, gesturing to them to repeat the phrase with irritating casualness.

"Relegation is when you give one person's magic to another,"

Fletcher put in, leaning over to explain it to Sam. "Like in the Woodshades. When, um...when they drain an elf," he went on, obviously aware of the discomfort spreading across the table. "They take the elfmagic that person had. They consume it. Use it. But they don't possess that elf's grandfather or anything. As far as I know, only Anscip Xavishia has been able to use blood to walk up someone's family tree like that."

"Relegation, as in assigning out, tenancy as in occupation," Sam muttered, nodding. He considered the point, taking a bite of chicken. "And you're certain when Augustus said he wanted Death to walk with him on the battlefield, he meant it literally?"

"He's an idiot." It was Teddy who cut in, much to Elsie's delight. "Sounds like they're crediting him with far more strategy than he had. He's a kid, and a careless one at that. Twenty-one?" He scoffed. "I doubt he was trying for anything so heretical. He probably thought you, Elsie, had some ability to prevent death, mortal though you undoubtedly are," he added. His gaze lit on her, warm and attentive. She liked that, when he talked *to* her—not just about her, like everyone else did.

Elsie was always partial to her brother's condescension—that was, when it was directed at anyone but her—and now was no exception. He was careful, thoughtful in ways many weren't, and an admonition from him would cut deeper than anyone else's. It was grounding, hearing Teddy say that Augustus was not some mastermind who had crafted a clever scheme too complex for them to see.

He was an idiot who got caught up in something he didn't understand.

And dinner went on.

Elsie had not bothered to even finish her first helping of winterbean soup—if she'd wanted to eat paste, she'd simply fetch a bottle from the supply closet for a snack. It was tragically a Caelaymnic tradition, a part of the religious fasting that happened in the winter months. Devoid of flavor, its purpose was ascetic.

"It's quite bland, isn't it," Alva suggested, giving Elsie a small smile. Seated beside her, Alva had been a quiet conversation partner most of the evening, seeming to sense Elsie's preference to be unbothered.

"Exceedingly flavorless," Elsie agreed with a grimace.

Alva glanced across the table to Fletcher. "It was Augustus's favorite."

Damnable man was inescapable.

"A man as tasteless as his soup," Sam muttered under his breath. "Apologies, but…"

"Why apologize? You're right," Elsie put in, stabbing a slice of steamed starchoke. "At least the soup hasn't tried to arrest me."

Faint, but forced laughs echoed about the table. It wasn't funny.

Tension was building, the warm atmosphere across the table chilling as the conversation died out to silence.

"Has there been any new information? Is there word about the Master, about his aims? New schemes, anything?" Elsie glanced around the table, glaring. *"Anything?"*

Silence.

She asked the same question every night, and every night, she got the same answer.

Teddy was looking down at his hands, folded neatly in his lap, brow furrowed in discomfort. She knew that look, too, that was the worst part—he was just waiting for this to be over. Waiting for her anger to ebb.

Fletcher made a sound to say something, but only shook his head.

"There's nothing? You talk for hours each night of what happened, and you have *nothing*? There is a man out there persuading princes to do his dirty work! There is a man out there using magic that targets specific families, specific bloodlines, and he went after me! Am I still in danger? Is he going after anyone else? How can you tell me there is nothing when there are so many questions left to answer!" There were tears in Elsie's eyes as she stood, table clattering. "What is it you've all been doing? It's been weeks!"

"Elsie." It was Rodion who spoke, even and calm. "We have no answers. That does not mean we have not been working. We talk for hours each night because there's a great deal to unravel, and we strategize together. You know that the interrogations of Cam and Augustus yielded nothing, and that leaves us to piecing field reports together like puzzle pieces, which is lengthy work. I don't know if you're still in danger. I don't know if he's going after anyone else—"

"Then figure it out!"

"You're not the only one that got fucked over, you know," Isa frowned, staring at her with dismay. "You're angry—fine. But I don't think it's fair for you to act like you're the only one who cares about righting this mess. I am to appear before a disciplinary triumvirate where they will decide whether to toss me in a cell because my boyfriend—"

"Ex-boyfriend," Teddy corrected quietly.

"Yes, because my ex-boyfriend is a traitor to the realm! Don't act like you're the only one shouldering this," Isa clipped.

Risa clicked her tongue. "She's shouldering more than anyone else, I don't think we need to minimize that—"

"And what have *you* done," Elsie bit, glaring at Risa. "You play advocate, but you've got your own agenda! You claim you're on my side, but you've worked with Clark for gods know how long, reading letters, conspiring about a whole dossier" —she shot a pointed look at Sam— "and plotting away! This is your fault, yours and his! If Clark hadn't left that letter, if he hadn't left that—that stupid locket—if he hadn't been conniving, meddling, then—then none of this would have ever happened! I hope he dies! I hope he keels over and *dies,*" she cried, "it's no less than he deserves!" The world was pressing in around her as she stormed off from the table, leaving whispered murmurs behind her as she stomped up the stairs, nose bleeding profusely, tears still pink against her sleeve as she tried to dry her eyes.

RISA

*"One lie. That's all it takes. You convince yourself of
one single lie, and the world will twist before your eyes,
all the truth gone."*

~Advocate Adrian Lynch

Risa tapped her pen impatiently against her fingertips, waiting, as she
had been for the last hour.

Her conversation with Asher some two weeks prior and the
disastrous dinner with Elsie had haunted her, haunted her right to Cele,
right to scheming, and ultimately, right into this carriage house, vial of
clear liquid in hand, eyes on the liquor cart and heart pounding.

But of course, Clark would be late.

Cele Carson sat perched on the edge of the desk, her skirts draped
elegantly over her crossed legs, her maroon blouse stylishly low-cut, the
lacy collar high against her jaw. "He does this," she muttered, checking
her wristwatch with a sneer of irritation. "You know how he is. Obsessed
with his childish games." Her eyes flicked to Risa.

Clark Carson had played puppet master long enough.

Adrian was fond of saying that right and easy weren't the same thing,
and each mountain in your way was a test of who you are. Of course,
Adrian didn't know where his lackey had gone, tonight.

The fewer who knew, the better.

"You'll pardon me," Clark was saying, closing the carriage house door
behind him. Suspenders were slipping out from beneath his vest, his
crisp-collared shirt looking a bit wrinkled. "I'm afraid matters with the

Guild are consuming most of my time, these days, after the City has left us absolutely fucked." He moved towards the bar, graying hair askew. "Risa, you need to bring trade negotiations back to the table."

"Excuse me?" Risa raised an eyebrow, trying to keep her voice steady. "What part of 'you're cut off' didn't you understand? The Hidden City could not have been more explicit. They're done with Aerdela."

"Then why are you here?" Clark turned, decanter and empty snifter in hand, the brandy the only liquor that had been displayed on his silver bar cart. "Why, Risa? Why are you back?"

Her eyes flicked to the decanter for a split second before she brought them back to him. "Just because the City has walked away doesn't mean the Rescindants are not interested—"

"And can they deliver medical supplies, bring innovations as we progress down this road of industrialization—"

"No, Clark," Risa sighed, exasperated, watching him at last dole out the liquor with a sense of mixed foreboding and relief. "You know that. Our resources are limited. What we can do is bring people into the City. We can offer a couple Healers to the Guild, on loan, in lieu of medical supplies. But that's it." Risa exhaled deeply, trying to fight the unease of tension in her chest.

Clark perched himself on the arm of the sofa where Risa was sitting, beetle eyes glistening deviously in the lamp light. "I want that City, Risa. I was supposed to sit beside Elizabeth as she ruled. Mentor her. Guide her." He clicked his tongue in disgust. "Find another way to make this happen. Gods forbid any difficulty should befall that *dear brother* of yours."

Risa ground her teeth, seething at the threat. "There's nothing you can do, Clark. He's not here. He's rightfully with Elsie, beside her sickbed in Caelaymnis."

Clark merely raised an eyebrow. "Ah. Yes. If only we had some sort of political alliance with the mountain city, some agreement to ferry in medical supplies—oh wait. We do," he mused. "You need me, Risa, if you and Adrian have any hope of political ambition in the City—or any hope of security with your new-found family, which is not entirely unrelated to the former."

"Security—you're kidding, right? You paraded Teddy—and Elsie, for that matter—out at the masquerade to twist my arm, Clark, and it might've worked before. But these are different circumstances." Her eyes locked on his, icy. "For one, Teddy and Elsie know me, now. They trust me. I don't need your dossier—we don't need Sam's letters—and we certainly don't need you." Rising, she moved herself for the bar. "I'm not some wide-eyed first year interning for Adrian anymore, tripping over herself for a chance to get back to this gods-forsaken district." The brandy splashed into her snifter, the color a soothing amber, the scent of alcohol fire on the air.

"And yet, you continue to deceive your brother," Clark breathed, a smile on his lips.

"I—you—mind your own business!" Angry, she was watching him with bated breath, waiting for that moment when the crystal glass would touch his lips—

At last, with a look of victory at having cornered her into childish retorts, Clark took a sip of brandy, smacking his lips. "You think so little of him that he would so quickly betray the ones he loves?"

"No. I think so little of *you*, playing people to commit sins on your behalf." She glared, discarding her own snifter of brandy untouched with a *clunk* on the side-table. "You paraded Elsie about with that ridiculous locket, whispered about her to your little flocks of birds to inflate your own value—but then the Factionists got word, and burned her gods-damned house down. You told her that locket would buy the City—and fuck, Clark, all it did was hold her hostage to an impossibility.

And look what you've done to those around you—you've held them hostage, too. Cele and I were just talking about what a good man Sam is, and how you manipulated him into believing your deviance was his desire, and that his friends were worth betraying for you. Elsie is sharp, and you pulled out all the stops to make sure she was on the path of implicit trust in you, where each stop would have gutted the faith she had in the people she loved. And me." Risa scoffed. "I walked right into your trap. I had this idealistic dream, and you played on that. I…" Her voice began to break. "I lost so much of myself to your dreams that tied me to my past, that I didn't know what it was I wanted. And now, I am lost."

Clark choked on his brandy, face going red. "You—you are," he coughed, eyes alarmed.

"I have denied my own life, and denied it to my brother's face," Risa said softly, a terrifying realization rising. Clark had used Teddy as leverage for the last time.

But the Commissioner waved her off, face deepening towards burgundy. His snifter fell to the carriage house floor, shattering, and little flecks of saliva, white and frothy, were starting to blossom at the corners of his mouth.

Cele rose from her perch on the desk, watching him with interest. "Cheers, Daddy," she murmured softly, and he fell to his knees, gasping. Gently, Cele stooped down, watching him the way one would a small child playing in the dirt. "Your time is over. You were devious and clever and horrid, and the world is changing, Father dearest. It is time to begin anew." A smile was curling on her lips, now, watching him collapse onto the rug for a moment before her eyes flicked up to Risa's. "Any words to the soon-to-be late Commissioner, Advocate?"

Risa shook her head, anger burning inside her chest, fear coiling close behind.

What have we done?

Cele clicked her tongue, glancing back to her father, spasming and jerking about on the rug, clawing at his neck. "Very well. Give Death our regards." And with that, she rose, brushing off her hands. "Good riddance." Her eyes flicked to Risa. "You should go. I'll write to Sam shortly, but it would be best if you were not here when I call for assistance. After all, what would they say, finding an advocate of the Hidden City here, moments after he's had a horrible heart attack?" Her eyes went soft, mockingly mournful. "Why, Risa darling, they might say he was murdered."

Risa's knees were weak as she rose for the door.

Murdered.

Oh, gods.

What have I done.

EZRA

"Run, run, run, boy, run on round the bend,
Under weir and over hedge, run to River's End."

~Valley limerick

Out of breath, Ezra hugged the wall, listening.

"He went that way!"

Feet were pattering down the alley beyond, and he loosed a breath.

Gone.

They were gone.

For now, anyway. They were never really *gone*, hadn't been for years, but there were moments when they were looking somewhere else, moments where he could catch his breath.

Ezra peeled himself from the factory wall, heart slowing as he looked around.

This would do.

Not quite abandoned, so it wouldn't be the first place they looked, but not busy enough where he'd get caught, least not right away. He'd bunk in the rafters—move a few boards around up there, it'd be cozy as anything—and food...

Gingerly, he kicked a shard of glass with the toe of his dangerously thin canvas shoe.

Bipart's Boil'd Potatoes, a peeling label read.

Well.

It was better than nothing.

~ • ~

It was probably a mercy the Capital wasn't colder, this time of year.

As it stood, though, it wasn't warm, and Ezra pulled the thin blanket-sometimes-turned-knapsack tighter around him.

The boards in the rafters weren't soft, but they weren't hard, and there weren't rats up here, so that was kind of nice.

The potatoes hadn't been good, but they hadn't gone bad, so he remained more or less full, which was something he hadn't felt since leaving Nan's house almost three years ago.

He missed her, tonight more than most.

I always wanted a baby boy, she'd said. But her husband had gone off and died long before Ezra had been born, and she'd been an old woman, then, anyway. All the same, he'd been left, and though he didn't know if it was true, how sad she'd been before, Nan never let a dark cloud sully her mood, at least in the years he knew her.

Nan wasn't her real name.

It was Mary.

Mary Hollick.

Keep your chin up, she'd've said, on a night like tonight.

They'd had some rough times, the two of them. Nan and Ezra Hollick.

Nan had a little piece of land south of the south-east quarter. Not much, but it was enough for her to tend her gardens and the beehives therein. She'd sell most of it, and the rest she nearly always gave away, because that was the kind of heart she'd had. A couple years before the fire, she'd run out of money, though, because her good-for-nothing husband who'd up and died didn't think she was stubborn enough to live to see sixty, which was absurd, because *anyone* who knew Nan knew she'd do anything to spite her late husband, even if it meant she had to go

34

right on living without a copper to her name. Nan had started taking in laundry, which was hard on her back, but she did it anyway, and Ezra was pretty much done with school, so he'd started taking odd jobs—sweeping, selling papers, running for the merchants, at one point—and they did okay.

They never starved, anyway.

'Course, that was all before the fire.

He'd snuck out, because that was the kind of thing kids his age did, they *snuck out*, even though Nan always knew. He'd gone down to the river with his buddies, took a few drags of someone's cigarette, skipped some rocks across the bay, talked about girls—there was one, in particular, the one who brought by the butter each week for Nan, she was quite pretty he thought—and they talked about boys—the butter girl had a brother, who one of Ezra's friends had first go at—and when he'd started to get tired, he walked back.

Ezra rolled over on the rafter planks, eyes drifting to the shadows beyond the fogged factory windows below.

The people who'd burned down Nan's house kind of looked like that.

Vague, dark shadows.

They'd only just lit the place up when Ezra'd come up the road.

And they'd seen him, as he'd shouted for help, thinking it was neighbors, thinking it was neighbors right up until one of them threw a bottle of something through Nan's window and it exploded into a plume of flame.

He didn't know why he ran.

Maybe he'd been afraid.

He told himself it was because he was going to get help, that he was going to find someone that would help him chase away the hooligans who'd killed Nan and burned her house down.

That didn't really feel true, though. Not anymore.

It'd been a long time since he'd been back here. In the city. In the Capital.

It stank of too many people packed into one place, even in the winter. He had not missed that smell.

His fingers were digging into the planks beneath him as he fought back tears.

Don't cry. Don't. CRY.

If he started, he would never stop. Because he *had* missed this place. He missed the bakery just a block down from here, he missed his friends by the river, he missed the girl that delivered the butter for Nan, he missed every last piece of it.

And it was gone.

It'd been easier not to think about when he was someplace else. The Coastal Reach had been nice. A good district, with good people. And good peaches, too, he thought wistfully. He'd snagged a good many from the drooping branches as he'd helped harvest them this summer. It'd been a good year for peaches—such a good year, it'd been easy to find work picking them, no references needed.

An easy summer.

They'd found him, eventually, like they always found him. It'd been a close call, too, not unlike tonight, but three years, and he'd gotten good at running.

He wouldn't be running much longer, though.

Living on the streets, a man *heard* things.

There was a place.

A place where people were *different.*

Where people had a knack for things, things people didn't usually have a knack for.

Ezra was going there, too, day after tomorrow.

He had to survive two more days, and then, he'd start a new life. He'd find a new name, find some menial job, keep quiet, and start actually *living.*

A few pinprick stars were visible through the slats in the roof, shining brighter than the lights of the city beyond to peek through into the factory below.

And as Ezra drifted off into uneasy sleep, he found his thoughts on the girl who brought the butter.

There'd be other girls, in this place beyond imagining.

He just had to make it there.

Two days.

He could survive two more days.

ISA

"What kind of lover believes destruction is coming,
and leaves you behind?"

~Festival of Frost

The disciplinary triumvirate Isa had spoken of so sharply to Elsie at their dinner several nights past was waiting in the anteroom of the General's Hall. For all intents and purposes, it was not really a Hall, in the traditional and most elven sense, but rather a row of offices occupied by the top military leaders of the Dradan Royal Army.

Where the older halls were rich with tapestries, the stone worn from the ages and almost soft in the rare places it was still exposed above woolen threads, this room was stark, baren, echoing uncomfortably in the shuffle. The anteroom made the three senior officials at the table look desperately out of place, too.

Ears pointed to delicate tips, fingers lengthy, nails like talons, eyes that glowed like a wolf's in the night, and their nature-rending magic— none of it belonged here, in this gray, unfamiliar hall.

The elves before them should've been before a great forested tapestry with gods and mortals alike locked in a moment of storytelling for the onlooker, with layer after beautiful layer of silken cloth belted about them.

But the King willed otherwise.

Isa's uniform felt uncomfortably tight, around the neck, their binding too stiff across the chest, stealing their breath.

Too tight.

Anxiety, another voice seemed to whisper.

It was liable to be both, truth be told.

Isa replayed their argument at the dinner table, as if imagined retorts were a sufficient distraction as they waited. Elsie had been furious—and Isa had been, too. It was Augustus. Resentment wasn't in short supply in his wake. Even so, it had been poor behavior, particularly as they were supposed to be celebrating Fletcher and his abdication.

Standing before the panel, Isa tugged at the jacket sleeves, a would-be gesture of well-to-do-ness, except that they'd done it several times already, hands unable to stay still.

"The matter," a rather elderly man sighed, lacing his fingers together where he sat behind the table, "is the current commission of Captain Isa Mirestva."

A door clicked open behind them all, and Isa turned to see Fletcher, looking uncomfortable at the interruption, working his way quickly over to Rodion, who stood with a handful of others waiting to the side.

Another *ro* with graying hair to the right of the man clicked their tongue, pale eyes on Isa. "Do you have anything to add before the review begins?"

"No, *praela,*" Isa said, gaze flicking to the floor.

The woman to the man's left snapped her fingers, and an aide brought forth a piece of parchment. "On or around the summer four years past, Isabella Mirestva became acquainted with one Augustus Praequintelya. All reports suggest that communications during approximately the first two and a half years remained adjacent to scandal and solely professional."

"Is this necessary?" Rodion scoffed, glaring. "Every damn one of us would have called him our friend—"

The elder *ro* slammed their hand on the table, rising. "Enough, Commander. The realm was taken in, we see that clear enough. The heart is a different matter, though, so unless you, too, can profess your love for the ex-general, *sit down.*"

Rodion growled, taking a step forward. "I did love him, we all did—"

"Commander Kastarae, that is enough!" The *ro* was glaring, cold eyes flashing. "It is admirable that you are defending one under your command. But the circumstances call for an examination. Mirestva walked back on their decision to part ways with the ex-general. We must ask *why*. There is too much at risk. We must inquire why they did not *immediately* seek to apprehend him, upon seeing the den beneath the sister's home. Why they did not come to you, for that matter, the moment it became clear what was happening! Instead, they lingered, waiting—"

"She asked me not to leave," Isa cut in, angry tears in their eyes. "*Praela*, she was scared to be alone. And—and I do not see how you can't understand that. He..." Their voice broke. "He *tortured* her. She was delusional with poison. How was she to know I would come back? She was *dying*—"

"All the more reason to seek aid," the elderly man put in.

"I did—"

"Sending a *kobalde* on an errand does little to cast you in good light, child," the *ro* put in, tucking a strand of graying hair behind their ear.

"I am *not* a child, and I will not be talked to as if I am a first-year cadet with no training—I have fought at your side, *praela*, I see—"

"—very little, I am afraid," the woman cut in sourly. "You *are* a child, dear. You are twenty-one years old, and arguing like a lovesick babe. We have granted you ample leash, Captain, interrupting after you have already declined to submit additional information for the review."

"What she means to say," the *ro* snapped, "is mind your place, you unconsecrated fiend, or your head will roll."

Isa's breath would not catch.

Their heart gave a jolt, room shifting out of focus for just a moment as the words pounded in their ears.

Or your head will roll.

They found Rodion's dark eyes across the room, and he shook his head almost imperceptibly.

It was the closest thing to comfort he could offer, at the moment.

Fletcher looked deeply disturbed, arms crossed as he grimaced.

Isa's teary eyes found the panel. "I...apologize," they said softly, voice steady. "I loved him. That was no secret."

The elderly man nodded, folding his hands once more. He glanced to his right, then to his left. "Though you offered no immediate objection, I think perhaps we could dispense with the reading of the review. It...is cruel, I think now, to relive the betrayal once more. And betrayal, it was." His eyes lingered on Isa, though, unbreaking. "But I will warn you, child. All of this city is watching you. One misstep. One. And you will meet your lover again. Only this time, it will be beneath the earth."

ELSIE

"Face your fears. It's what we tell little children. And so, I only did as I was told. I faced them.

I faced them."

~Elizabeth Clement Faulise

Elizabeth Faulise.

Her name had turned into a promise. A promise for revenge. A promise for power.

At least, that was what she told herself. The alternative was to admit that her name was a taunt of something that could never be. It was a reminder that things could've been better if the world had been kinder.

Today, she had woken with a hunger, deep in her bones.

It was the kind of hunger that could shatter mirrors. The kind that couldn't be mended by sweetrolls over a counter or porridge in bed, the kind that had been blossoming for weeks, entrenching itself into the spaces between her ribs, working its way into the bloody, quivering mass pounding in her chest, splintering its way through her aching muscles, the kind of hunger that haunted, waiting.

The hunger of the almost-dead.

Elsie paused, finding the stilled city corner.

Right, for four-ish blocks, and their house would be on the left. Their house, with the wrought-iron fence of ribbons and easy cobblestone walk to the painted door and the narrow-but-tall windows that let the light flood into the bedroom in the morning and the sitting room in the evening, and it was left that Elsie went, turning down the familiar street.

Walking nowhere had a way of making her feel like she was at least going somewhere, but today wasn't like the other days, the other walks, the other attempts to escape beneath the blue sky in the bowl of mountains.

Demons had been awoken in the dark of that cell, lies and memories dogging her every footstep, unseen shadows even here, in the morning light.

Clio was waiting on the bridge across the Weir, the water roaring half-frozen beneath.

He was unassuming.

The kind of man to pass by unnoticed, unless one was in the habit of noticing.

"Morning," she nodded, leaning up against the stone, not sparing him a glance. It was an historic bridge, carved during the War by the first Praequintelya, a veritable shrine to Fletcher's family name, a mark of what great leaders could do in a moment of necessity.

She disliked it.

It was gaudy. Ostentatious. Full of self-pretention.

With the casual air, Clio withdrew a vial from his cloak. "Just as you asked for."

She gave him a wary side-long glance. "I very much doubt that." Then, taking the vial, she popped the cork.

It was thick, a deceptively deep burgundy that *almost* glowed black in the morning light, and he must've taken her for a fool, thinking she wouldn't be able to spot the difference.

Her eyes flicked to his, and not breaking her stare, she let the contents fall sluggishly into the river below.

"No—"

"Don't fuck with me, Clio. You know what I wanted, and it wasn't this half-stewed swill of a wine from the back of your cellars." Shaking out the last of the drops, she tossed him back the empty vial. "One word, and the Commander will *shut you down*, now do you have it, or not?"

Frowning, Clio pocketed the glass, trading it for another. "Just, eh, making *sure*. Can't be dolling that out to just anyone, now, can I..."

Holding the vial up to the light, she searched for any tinge of red in the thin concoction clinging to the sides.

Nothing.

Perfect.

Her gaze flicked back to him. "This'll do."

"If you don't mind, it's an odd amount you're asking for," Clio edged, pale eyes darting between her and the vial. "I can get more, that isn't a problem—"

Turning, she pocketed the vial, not bothering to answer.

"Now, wait just a moment," he scoffed, trailing after, "that wasn't the deal—"

"The deal is that you do as I ask, and my lover won't shut your whole operation down," Elsie shrugged, picking up her pace.

"I told you my price—"

Turning on her heel, she met him face-to-face. "And I told you mine," she snarled. "Now leave me alone."

There were fears to face.

And for that, she didn't need company.

~•~

Beyond the icy windowpanes, big fat snowflakes drifted down, joining their cousins in a woolly blanket across Caelaymnis. The walls of the bedroom were draped with tapestries of pastel blue and soft lilac, dark threads of black and gray seeming to soak into the walls themselves, carrying the mountainous landscape from the distant frosted glass into the silent room. A massive fireplace glowing orange and pink threw off a preternatural heat, the soft rugs drinking in the sound of footsteps, and this place...it was peaceful.

Elsie wanted to become this place.

Wrapped in a deep purple cardigan that had been belted at the waist, fleece-lined leggings tucked into gray socks, she could pretend to be someone else.

Someone who wasn't breaking.

Someone who was a barrage.

A cloudburst so strong it swept all else aside, and in the wake of reckoning, a new beginning.

But only gods wrote the beginnings.

The draught of fear oozed beautiful and dark into the teaspoon. Dhacrym, she'd learned the practitioners called it. She knew this poison well. It had permeated her. Seduced her. Made her a convert to the terror. She hadn't cared that it was antithetical to kinder magics. Didn't care that it inhibited healing, that it made travel that much more painful—what was the loving touch of her brother the Healer or the nauseating golden sparks of her lover, when she had truth as a companion, now?

It seemed to caress the silver, and in the pool of black, she could see her reflection, distorted in the mirrored lake of poison.

"What are you," she breathed, balancing the spoon over the bathing room sink.

Silence hung heavy in the air.

As if it hadn't answered back a thousand times.

Fear.

It was fear.

Every fear she'd ever had, every worry left unspoken, every doubt

45

that was fermenting, even now, in the recesses of her mind.

There was truth in fear.

She trusted fear. Trusted the hidden secrets it betrayed, the little weaknesses it whispered in her mind, and now, more than ever, she craved it.

Craved the words no one else would dare to speak.

It was hardly anything, in the teaspoon.

Augustus—he'd given her bottlefuls, but this, this was just a taste. Just a spark. Just enough to conjure the wretched magic, but not enough to lose herself entirely, and certainly not enough to tip her hand to the others.

Fletcher would lose it to know that they'd drawn her from those dungeons only for her to seek this swill.

In her, the dhacrym had awoken a flicker of resistance, dark and terrible and if she had to follow the fear to find it, then so it was. The trust of fear, traded so she might grate against this world, and that had to be a better deal than most got, in the end.

It met her tongue, acrid and bitter and *familiar.*

The teaspoon clattered into the sink and she took a step back, letting herself slide down to sitting on the tile, letting her eyes close as it overtook her.

At last.

Peace.

TEDDY

"Possibility is folded in the pages of books. What we wish, beyond all else—I promise it can be found in ink and parchment."

~*Theodore Alderton*

Teddy paused, shaking his hands out as he met the second-floor landing.

It was funny, how quickly a place could become home. Fletcher's Caelaymnic house had been cold and more or less empty a few weeks ago. But Alva and Sam had quickly rectified the situation, turning it into a cozy enclave against the frigid winter.

It kept Teddy's heart well, all the people he loved clustered safely under one roof. Sam, his husband, albeit secretly, for their marriage had been a private one. Elsie, his sister, back safely under his watch. Fletcher, a mentor in magic, Isa, another soul radiantly uncontained and ready to mend, Risa, his...friend, he supposed, though his suspicions had grown strong that *sister* might be a word she used, too, though she would never admit it.

His knuckles met Elsie's door with a soft *tap tap tap.*

No reply.

"El?" Tentatively, he pushed the door open. "Elsie?"

"Coming." Elsie was hurrying out of the bathing room, eyes red. Her dark hair was pulled into a tight braid that fell lazy over her shoulder, the sleeves of her purple cardigan pushed up passed her elbows.

"Everything alright?"

She made a small sound of annoyance, looking at him askance as she pushed past him. "Everything's fine."

It wasn't fine. He knew that.

Weeks of shouldering the draught of fear from Augustus's hand, of drowning in that wretched poison, and she wasn't fine at all.

The dhacrym had interfered with Teddy's ability to heal her, among other things. He'd sat with her as she slept and bled, and never in his life had he felt so helpless. He was a Healer. He had a knack for this sort of thing. But it broke his heart that there was nothing to do but let time work its own magic.

The living room found Fletcher and Sam, waiting. There were a few gifts wrapped in colored paper piled onto the coffee table, a platter of sweet treats balanced precariously atop the piano, fire crackling merrily.

In lieu of Elsie's birthday—a date unknown, as was the consequence of babes left on doorsteps—they had Leaving Day. The day she'd been left.

Of course, Elsie had spent her last Leaving Day in a dungeon and in the company of a barghest. Hence, the modest make-shift celebration in Fletcher's living room.

Teddy had found himself wanting to make up for lost time, and Sam would not let an excuse for a party pass.

"Isa and Risa aren't coming?" Elsie asked, voice flat.

"I—I thought it would be nice to just have us—just the family—"

Elsie shot him a murderous glare. "They. Are. Family."

Teddy ruffled his hair, giving her a shrug. They were, both of them. But things were more than a little fucked between him and Risa at the moment, and anymore, the back and forth between them exhausted him. Maybe a month ago, it'd given him hope. Now, though? It was crushingly childish.

"Isa's hearing was today," Fletcher said quietly, "they're at home,

48

packing up their things to move back to the barracks. They'll be by later."

Elsie sank down on the sofa, eyes distant.

"Sorry," Teddy breathed, perching beside her. "I tried."

Her emerald gaze flicked to him, and her expression softened. "Thanks." She gave him a small nudge, scooting closer. "I'm sorry. I'm just feeling off today." The forced smile on her lips was confirmation of this.

"That's alright, El." He smiled back weakly, crossing his arms. It wasn't alright. But these were the lies they told.

Sam reached for the red parcel on the coffee table, rising to pass it to her across Teddy. "Here. Start with this." He was grinning as he sank down onto the arm of the sofa, watching with glittering eyes.

Elsie took it, untying the string with deft fingers, eyes blank. "Ah." She crumpled the paper, letting it fall carelessly to the floor, and held up a silk scarf.

"I saw one of the elves with scarves braided into their hair, she kind of looked like you, I thought—"

"It's really lovely. Thank you." Elsie's voice was tired, already exhausted with this exercise.

Sam's smile faltered. "Anytime, El."

Teddy leaned back into the sofa, eyes trailing up to the ceiling. *Gods, below.* "El, if you don't want to do this—"

"No. It's like you said. It's just the family, and if others are stopping by later..." Her words were clipped as she reached for the next parcel.

A knock at the door interrupted the reveal of what would've been a frostsheep woolen sweater, and Teddy swore quietly, straightening up. Fletcher was already moving to answer, but before he could, a note flitted beneath the door. He stooped to pick it up, frowning. "It's...for Sam." Raising an eyebrow, he turned it over once, twice, three times in his hands as he walked back to the living room. "From Cele. They must've lent the Carsons a courier, as part of the Commissioner's deal."

Sam met him half-way and took the letter, slitting it open. "Cele?" His eyes flew across the paper, a look of displeasure growing on his face. "No." The word was a pained whisper, his brow creasing. "That's simply not possible."

Teddy's heart sank, and he swore softly under his breath.

He recognized the look of despair on his husband's face.

"Sam?" Elsie's placid expression had been shattered, her hands shaking slightly as she rose, watching him.

Teddy moved, slaying the distance between them in a few easy steps. *I am a mountain, and I will shelter you.* That much, he knew how to do, anyway.

But Sam moved, pressing the letter to his chest, a glare carved into his brows. "Clark is dead," he breathed, taking a step back away from Teddy. "His heart, Cele says."

"Oh, Sam—"

"Don't." Sam's eyes were welling with tears, his face reddening. "Just...I..." He shook his head, a silent push for space, and with that, he turned on his heel and disappeared around the corner.

"Well, fuck." Teddy blew out a breath, glancing back to Elsie. "You okay?"

She gave a small nod. "Yeah. Good riddance."

"El—"

"No, it's true! Don't expect me to mourn this—"

Teddy crossed his arms. "I'm not shedding any tears, either, it's not like it's not for the better, but—"

"What the fuck is wrong with you?" Sam's voice was tear-soaked and icy behind them, and Teddy turned, eyes wide. "I can still hear you, you asshole," Sam clipped, running his hand against his cheek to wipe away the tears. "I'm just down the fucking hall!"

"Sam, I didn't mean—"

"No, you meant exactly what you said! Both of you!" His damp eyes flicked between Elsie and Teddy. "I know you hated him! I know you hate what he did, and who he was, and—and my relationship with him, but for fuck's sake. Let me have this." And with that, he turned, this time stomping up the stairs, decidedly out of earshot.

Teddy pinched the bridge of his nose, exhaustion, above all else, starting to bubble up.

Another mess to clean up. Another heart in crisis. Another life, touched undeniably by pain.

SAM

"For it is in death that we find the love we wish we didn't feel, the regrets we tried to dodge, and the anger that feels wrong, standing beside the casket."

~Sam Alderton

Clark is dead.

Reason for his melancholy. His jubilation. His tears and his silence, his laughter and his relief.

Clark is dead.

The bath was steaming, on the verge of overflowance. This was a modest arrangement, residing as guests here while Elsie was on the mend, though the view, he thought, glancing out the window, was befitting of the gods themselves.

Great snowcapped peaks, mauve in the low light, pierced the topaz sky as the sun washed out Caelaymnis in sepia.

Cora Lucia Stell Hadri

Kiran Natali Ignata Asa

Fingers fumbling with the tunic buttons, Sam caught his own eye in the mirror, holding the gaze.

A patchwork person.

Golden hair. *Flaxen,* the fairy tales would've called it.

And his eyes, which had been lovingly called cinnamon or amber or sugared or any number of such sweet things. Brown. They were simply brown. Others saw what they wanted, but they were an anomaly. Valley born and raised, with hair as fair as his, they were supposed to be blue.

But like the rest of him, his eyes had rebelled.

Beneath his sun-kissed skin lurked the shades of roses. Others there, they would darken from pasty pale, like toasted almonds in the summer fields, sinking into shades of taupe, a sort of sickly crisping of their skin, like it craved the sun but had never quite shaken off the gray of winter.

And gods, would they burn first.

Teddy's skin was prone towards the blistering red before it could give way to the tan he carried through to fall.

Sam, though...even now, as January waned, there was something carnelian there, a sun-kissed glow like he'd spent the day taking in the summer sun.

The thin chain sat golden around his neck, the band resting on his bare chest.

He watched the reflection of his fingers brush the band, lingering on the braided gold.

They called him beautiful.

All of them.

He wished they wouldn't.

Because what they meant, when they called him beautiful, was that he had managed, for another day, to put himself together enough so that they didn't see how badly he was hurting. What it meant was that he'd managed, for another day, to pass for something more than an ashen heart.

In his youth, he'd been carved of some sort of sardonian marble. Exercise regimes, an almost vain adoration of his own body, a strict diet, it'd kept him strapping to the highest degree, and though nobody would've called him bulking, he'd been left with an exquisitely muscled frame.

His eyes traced the memories in the mirror.

Teddy's hands had followed the same lines, years ago. Had swept down his waist only to trace the *v* at the top of his trousers, eyes lost in desire.

The recollection was a sweet one.

He'd watched Teddy, *felt* him, the soft touch of his hands, the quiet smile, and it'd been verging on miraculous, the witness of realization. It was more than watching someone fall in love.

It'd been watching someone be remade.

Redefined.

And he'd been happy, in those moments, that he'd kept himself strong for others. But his definition had been on the terms of everyone else.

Letting go was supposed to taste sweeter than this.

I am not beautiful.

The thought came, unbidden.

It felt true.

Clark is dead.

And I cannot be beautiful.

The water sloshed over the edge of the tub as he lowered his aching body in, the heat swarming, prickling sweetly against his skin.

Elsie would be fine.

He should've been a better friend, been a better brother, been willing to stand with her while she was so transparently struggling, and he just couldn't.

Clark is dead.

He did not understand these feelings, in the wake of the Commissioner's death.

He'd wished Clark dead, once.

And Mattie and Cele, and all of them, and suddenly, that juvenile wish felt so pathetically powerful.

The last vestiges of sunlight tumbled in from the hazy window, and he closed his eyes, letting them drape across the tub in long, warm almost-shadows.

Even now, he could feel the warmth resonating in the steady swaths set gently through the window as the sun began to set.

The door to the bathing room clicked open, and Sam didn't bother to open his eyes, lest he break the spell cast down by the sun.

"Are you okay?" Teddy's voice was still tinged with annoyance, even through the soft timbre.

Sam hadn't seen okay in months.

Some days it didn't feel like he'd seen it at all, but he must've, once, for the sake of comparison.

What will you tell them, Sam? That you sought comfort in the arms of your mentor? That, in a world unfamiliar, in the throes of adolescence, I ushered you into manhood?

No.

No, he wouldn't dare sugar such things. Wouldn't dare couch them in tangled words like that.

Not anymore.

It'd been a shameful fumbling, saying them once, and if he was being honest, he'd never tell anyone again, if he had a choice.

He hadn't been sure why he'd even told Teddy, at the time, because it seemed so pathetically trivial, so decidedly un-romantic, and yet, some part of him had been compelled to wade through the words.

He'd been sitting with Teddy on the sofa in his apartment, legs curled beneath himself as he'd watched those ocean eyes, daring the words out. Late. It'd been so late, and he'd been a little bit drunk, and Teddy had, too, and they'd been figuring it out, the two of them together.

It feels good, Teddy had said quietly, fingers laced through his own. *Holding your hand. Sitting in your arms. Just...feeling you.* His eyes had flicked up, then, finding Sam's.

There'd been a deep sadness in them, the kind of sadness of someone who'd spent their life treading water, finding solid land for the first time. Not relief. Regret.

Like he knew the simple act of not drowning was no victory.

Like he knew there was more to it all than keeping his head above water.

I wish... Teddy had looked away, then, and it'd sounded like his voice had been on the edge of breaking. *I just like it, that's all. It's so simple. And it feels so damn good, and...Sam, you need to know that I will never stop liking the way this feels, because it is so different from everything else I know.* And then he'd whispered it. Under his breath. Three words.

It doesn't hurt.

Those weren't the three words new lovers were supposed to tell each other.

I know what you mean. Sam had said the words before he'd meant to, because it was his *friend*, sitting there, confessing, and that was what they did, trading these hurts back and forth. *I, um...look, I just—I want you to know...*

Teddy had glanced up, alert.

So, Sam told him.

Told him all about how much he used to watch the shadows flickering on the carriage house floor. About how loyal he tried to be. How much he had loved Clark, loved him badly, and had tried to be everything to him. Everything, like Clark had been to him.

And it'd felt so mundane, so wretchedly ordinary, so useless, right up until the moment it didn't.

"Sam? Are you okay?"

His eyes snapped open, a glare etched on his brow. "No. No, I'm not okay."

"Excuse me—"

"My father *died*," Sam snipped, sitting up, knuckles going white where he held the lip of the tub, "and you have the audacity to ask me if I am *alright*, moments after I catch you telling Elsie how you're glad he's gone?"

Teddy crossed his arms, a look of deep displeasure across his face. "He wasn't your father—"

"No. No, you don't get to do this. You don't get to storm in here and interrupt my grief just so I know you feel vindicated!" Sam rose, stepping out of the tub, snatching a towel with almost violent determination off the rack. "Great, you hated him and everything he did, wonderful, now get the fuck out and just let me mourn!"

The slamming door behind his husband was the only answer.

CORA

"Gods have spent their lives trading relics back and forth. It is all in an effort to pretend they are infallible, that they are not simply serving whims like the rest of us mortals."

~Blaine Liss, Coalition Representative

Cora, God of Death, Cutter of Threads, Keeper of Souls, was enjoying the heat being thrown off the ghostly brazier nearest her throne in the Hall of the Departed where she kept court every Thursday evening.

The dead were people too, and as such, she had reasoned that unlike her predecessor, she ought to be hearing what they had to say.

Yara, First Soul, had joined Cora, basking in the heat of the brazier, passing her a cup of tea with misty, opalescent hands. "For you, love."

"Thank you." Cora balanced the saucer on the arm of her obsidian throne, one leg crossed lazily over the other. Few had come today. Few, in truth, ever came, for Cora had provided many comforts for those who had left the Land of the Living.

Thus, she was accordingly startled when the doors to the Hall of the Departed were thrown violently open, clattering as they slammed into the walls, and a bedraggled figure strode forth across the hall.

In her alarm, Cora's teacup fell to the floor, shattering with all the aplomb of divine dishware as the god herself rose abruptly.

Clark Carson strode angrily across the hall, a look of unholy anger on his face. A curl of blood was at the corner of his mouth, his suit mussed, his hair ruffled to death—

"You." Cora frowned, taking the steps down the throne in quick succession. "Explain yourself."

"Explain myself? *Explain myself?* I'm dead, you wretched woman—*oof—*" Clark had been caught with a ghostly arm across his chest, Yara stopping him from going further.

"I assumed as much, given the locale," Cora frowned. "Why the dramatics? You would have been welcomed with the rest—"

"With the *rest?* You think that's all I deserve? I've carried out your errands," Clark hissed, struggling against Yara's arm, "I've done your bidding—"

"As a favor to your old friend and doubtless with the aim of putting wealth in your own pocket—and when a God of Death comes knocking, I would advise you not pretend compliance to be an act of altruism," Cora admonished, anger rising. "Explain this display—"

"I was *murdered!*" The fury of his screech echoed off the gilded black tiles.

"Murdered." Cora pinched the bridge of her nose. "My condolences, but why is this my problem, exactly?"

"You are the God of Death—"

"My patience is waning."

"My own daughter," Clark snarled, "this, I expected of her—she has always been ambitious, but Theresa? Theresa was in my pocket! She owed me her life—"

Cora wrinkled her nose, taking a step back. "Hardly. At best, she owes no one, and at worst, she could extend a bit of gratitude to me. But you? No. No, no, no."

"No? *No—*"

"I said it four times, do you need me to say it again," Cora snapped.

59

"No. You'd have let that girl simply die if I had not burdened you with another babe. Just because you fancied yourself clever, trading the children, doesn't mean that she owes you a lick of gratitude, much less your life."

"They would have found Elizabeth if I had not—"

"Oh, I'm sorry, Clark, did you want me to applaud you for doing your fucking job?" There was a mocking tone to Cora's voice. "Fieldson did something similar in the Capital with the boy. And do you know why you both summoned such cleverness, Clark? Because you don't fuck with Death, that's why."

"You—"

"I'm done, here." Cora turned, heels clicking across the tile as she snapped her fingers. "My mood is soured. *Out.*"

An unearthly yowling in the distance heralded the ghostcat. Clark's shrieks had turned from promises of vengeance to cries for mercy.

"You—you could stop this—I know he's here!" Clark screamed in panic. "You know I helped put him here—"

Cora paused at the door to leave the Hall of the Departed. Though she did not look back, she heard the ghostcat hiss, its massive paws padding across the floor.

A relic of Cora's predecessor, one that had served the Underworld well.

"Kiran," Cora breathed, "is unfit to do more than sit in chains. As such, there he will stay."

"They're after you, you know! They're hunting for you—for the gods, you will all pay—"

The sound of a struggle was music to Cora's ears as she closed the door behind her.

What a gods-damned bastard.

~ • ~

That evening found Cora sitting before the tapestry.

A great colorful weave of threads, it represented Reality. Each thread—each soul—wove in and out of others, and together, they created a beautiful depiction.

Well.

A *mostly* beautiful depiction.

Cora sat at the Present, staring at the tangled mess.

It started with one soul.

One thread that had been cut...and retied.

One soul survived, and it spawned chaos, for it preceded thousands upon thousands of threads that had been retied together, making the once-orderly tapestry a knotted mess.

One soul survived, and whatever it was they died for meant that thousands would live.

Yara's footsteps heralded the arrival of the First Soul.

"Did he find his way out," Cora asked dully.

Yara sank down onto the tile beside her, sitting cross legged. "With the help of the ghostcat, he did. Good riddance, I say. Foul man." Her fingers brushed Cora's arm with the touch of a once-lover. "I thought I'd find you here."

"He said they're hunting for the gods," Cora said quietly. With a heavy sigh, she leaned her head on Yara's shoulder.

She knew this day would come. She knew that her reign would not be forever.

Imposters could not walk in the shoes of a god for so long unimpeded.

And more than that, it had only been a matter of time before the slice had been found once more, and the relic locked beneath it, coveted by

61

anyone wishing to claw their way through the worlds.

"You really think this is about the slice, and the quays," Yara asked in an undertone. As First Soul, she knew Cora's heart, could anticipate the thoughts before they happened.

Cora was silent, moving to run her fingers across the threads.

How could it not be.

Elizabeth's thread was severed, knotted again, like a mistake—except the tapestry didn't have mistakes. These were souls. Souls didn't just get snipped off by accident.

"I think," Cora said softly, at last breaking the silence, "that someone is collecting the gods to open the quays. Why, I cannot say. But Alder tried once before. He stole the iaculus and murdered gods, and his failure doesn't mean others can't succeed." Her eyes flicked to Yara's ghostly gaze.

The Tapestry could not claim prescience, and threads were ever-shifting as decisions were made and steps taken, but it could gesture towards a vague future.

Cora closed her eyes.

Though it had been six-hundred years behind her, she could still see it. She'd found Alder, over the bodies, blood soaking into the floor, the stone groaning and clacking together as the ancient locks undid themselves.

He had done what so many wished.

He had slain the gods.

Two of them, anyway. Two quays open, six still left sealed. Without all eight quays opened, at least the relic was safe. That was what mattered.

Alder had taken a new name—Kiran—and she had taken the moniker of Death, and the mantle too, and the secret of the two open quays—and the two dead gods—had been kept.

To her predecessor, she'd vowed to protect the mortal spawn of indiscretions.

To Alder—to Kiran—she had made no such promises.

Cora had guarded her predecessor's heirs, put Alder in chains, and prayed no one learned that two of the quays had been unlocked, for resealing one meant going back on her word.

It meant one of the heirs had to die.

Cora's eyes drifted to Elizabeth's thread again. Cut, retied. Dead, but very much alive. Heir to Cora's predecessor, one she'd sworn to protect when Margaret Faulise had arrived at the gates of Death, beseeching the god to save her children.

Little do the mortals know their gods have already fallen.

A realm and religion, built on nothing but lies, and Cora was left with a tangled tapestry as the Present thrust itself upon them.

Cora's fingers brushed another thread. *Theresa.* A woman who had tangled with Death and won—more than once, it seemed.

Arrogant mortal, and one with answers.

A faint smile curled at the corners of Cora's lips.

"I have to go," she said softly. "It's time to introduce myself to the person who decided to make Clark my problem once again. The cutting of such a thread cannot go unaddressed, now, can it."

Yara gave a wistful smile. "No, ma'am. It cannot."

THE BEAST

"Wisdom is in the ears of those who listen and the minds of those who dream."

~*From 'Tales of the Recently Revived: A Sequel'*

The Master stared into the fire, his eyes glowing in the shadows.

Something was amiss.

The Beast stretched, spines flaring as it arched its back, setting to prowl about the house once more while the Master brooded.

Three, three, three, the servants whispered, agitated, and three keys could not open eight locks.

The Master only had three.

Three of the vials, three of the gods, three wells of deep and ancient magic at his disposal, and the Beast knew something had gone awry.

Chaos. Order. Fire. These, the Master had in tow, these, he would tote out like a parlor trick.

Death.

Death had been on the docket for ages, and the Beast bristled, padding up the stairs, agitated that the feast had been for naught. The Beast and its brothers had feasted on Death in service of the Master.

Death had been afraid. The Beast had consumed her fear. Of her fear were borne shackles, blood with which the Master might chain the gods.

And yet, the Master had not conquered Death.

The Warrior who had promised to vanquish Death, Death who had slain so many allies, but in the end, the Warrior had succumbed to *cowardice*. He had stumbled in his doubt, faith wavering, and now...

The Beast let out a low grow.

Now, they would have to undo the Warrior's folly.

THE WAKING

Where we collectively should be grieving, nobody else seems to care.

I am trying to mourn for my father, and I get nothing but ridicule. I should not love him, they say, and they do not understand that his violence against me did not make me love him less. I hate that it did not, I hate that my heart aches, and I cannot stop it, and they do not understand!

We are all uneasy. Caelaymnis seems precarious, the Guild is now in flux with my sister, Cele, assuming the role of Commissioner...

And still. I write.

~SAM ALDERTON,
EXCERPT FROM A LETTER DATED FEBRUARY 2ND

ELSIE

"I knew what I needed to do. I needed to prove that I
was alive. That I would not give into his fear. That it
was my fear, and mine alone, and I controlled it. How I
felt it. When I felt it.

I wish I'd known then what horrendous lies those
were."

~Elizabeth Clement Faulise

There was an empty space where the locket should have been.

Empty space between her fingers where she should've worried it idly. Empty space upon her chest where it should've lain, dormant and warm.

Elsie's eyes flicked to Fletcher as they waited just beyond the door.

Down the hall, a cell.

Singular.

A prison for someone too dangerous to warrant the contact of other living souls.

A prison for someone whose crimes were too abhorrent even to risk the contamination of other criminals.

A prison for Augustus Praequintelya.

"Commander—er, I mean—" The guard looked uncomfortably at Fletcher, unsure.

"Commander Nist," he nodded firmly.

In the wake of his abdication, and subsequent loss of the Praequintelya name, he'd taken his father's family name in its place.

"Ah. Commander Nist," the guard echoed. "Well. If I might, I'm sad to see you depart the family. Always did think you were the most sensible of the bunch."

Fletcher merely sighed. "Do you mind..." He gestured to the door before them.

"Wait." Elsie's voice was loud in the reverberant stone, her eyes finding Fletcher's. Little splotches of mud on a field of moss, mountain through-and-through.

"If you don't want—"

"I need to see him alone," she cut in.

Fletcher rolled his shoulders back uncomfortably, shifting beneath the uniform. "You...need to?"

She nodded, turning for the door. "He has to know I'm not afraid of him. He has to know that—that I'm still a fighter. That he didn't break me into cowering behind his brother."

His hand was on her back, a soft touch of reassurance.

I will be right here, it seemed to say.

With a nod to the guard, the door clanked open, and swallowing, Elsie took a step across the threshold.

Augustus's head snapped up, eyes flashing as they found her.

The cell was bright, a silvery-black mesh dividing the room in half, and it was unfair, the comfort he'd been afforded.

The cot, neatly made, a thick blanket tucked into sharp corners beneath the mattress. The warm air, funneled from where, she couldn't say, but deep below the earth, it was utterly unnatural. A discarded bowl boasted what must've been a hot meal, and it must be a prince's privilege, she thought, that warranted such generous accommodations.

Perhaps he was dangerous.

71

But that wasn't evidently an excuse to suffer.

It was a long while before he spoke.

But she waited all the same.

Hands in her pockets, she didn't break his gaze.

Waiting.

I am going to kill you, some day.

I will make you pay.

She'd never seen him out of uniform, but here he was, in the rough-spun garb of a Dradan prisoner, pacing the floor with bare feet, and it was easier not to fear him like this.

An animal caged.

But feral beasts like him were so much more dangerous in their cages, so it was an irrational un-fear.

"You came alone," he growled, at last breaking the silence, "though you did not have to."

"I did," she countered softly.

"So I would think you do not fear me." He paused, still watching her. Then, scoffing, he sank down on the end of the cot, the wood groaning beneath his bulk. "But you do," he whispered, frowning. "And you should."

"Is that a threat?"

"It is a fact. You should be afraid of me. It's the reaction of a fighter." His eyes narrowed. "Are you still a fighter? Or are you unafraid?"

"Don't," she hissed, taking a step towards the bars. "Don't act like you've done me any favors. Don't act like because you showed me terror itself, you made me into a warrior like you." Her nose was almost against the grating, now, and he was rising, rising to meet the challenge, to set her down— "Everything I am, I owe to the people who picked up my pieces after you'd finished with me. You're a gods-damned page ripper. You destroy. You hurt. You—"

"Elsie." Augustus's brow was creased, expression shifting as he met her at the fence.

Her name on his lips brought her to a halt.

"You have no right," she breathed, chest tight. "No right to—to use my name, like you know me—"

"You're bleeding."

She brought her hand to her face, fingers coming away damp and glistening red.

Swearing, she fished the rag from her pockets, pressing the crumpled white cloth to her nose as she turned away.

His fingers drummed against the grating, a metallic pulsing filling the cell.

"Fuck you," she bit, voice muffled and nasal as she pinched her nose, head tilted up.

He sighed, and the tapping dwindled away.

Back to the prisoner, she dared a glance at the door. *Fletcher's just on the other side.* The grated bars played the role of something delicate, but it'd take more than Augustus had to break through them.

Pocketing the rag, she turned, meeting his stone-cold eyes. "What happened to my locket? The night you arrested me?"

He bore into her, frozen. "You're still bleeding."

Don't engage. He's trying to distract you.

"The locket."

"Why are you still bleeding?"

"Tell me where the locket is. *Now.*"

Augustus paused, eyes narrowing. "I'm a dead man," he breathed, leaning forward against the grating. "You can't walk in here and demand answers. You have all the leverage, Elsie—and I have nothing to lose by holding my tongue. This is a basic interrogation. *Negotiate.*"

He was right, she realized.

A fundamental tactical flaw.

"What is it you want," she asked coolly.

The seconds of silence were a lifetime, swimming with what-ifs, her head screaming the thousand things he could say, the ways he could taunt her, how he had her up against a wall, there was nothing they could give, not really, and they *need* what he had, and this was failure, naivete, inexperience at its fucking finest—

"Tell me why you're not better yet. Tell me why you still bleed."

"Why?" The demand had tumbled off her lips with a glare.

"Six weeks." He gave a small shrug. "Should've been plenty long to clear it from your system."

"And then what?"

"I'll tell you what you want to know."

"Anything," she pressed, tucking a strand of hair behind her ear.

"I'll do you one better. *Everything.*" His voice was lethal, his eyes flashing as they followed her.

Scoffing, she began to pace, eyes skirting the room. "I'm bleeding because a coward was chasing religious delusion in a sea of a people he hated more than death itself," she said softly. Her fingers moved to grab the locket that wasn't about her neck, the phantom touch of metal against her fingers. *Not irretrievably gone,* she told herself.

"Liar."

"I'm bleeding," she pressed, ignoring him, "because we were friends, and you betrayed me. You were going to help us. I trusted you, I—I even *liked* you, and you repaid my kindness with poison."

"No!" His voice barked across the room, and he was straightening up off the bars, now, shaking his head. "No, I did not *ask* why you bled the first time, Elsie! I asked why it is that you still bleed now, and you won't answer, because you're still *afraid.*"

"I—"

"You're *afraid*," he snarled, gripping the grating with clawed hands. "Don't play the fool with me. I watched you at its mercy for weeks. I don't know how you found it, but I know you're dosing yourself, and I want you to tell me *why*."

Why she'd been dosing herself with teaspoons of dhacrym.

It was difficult to stand on her jellied legs, with the words echoing through the cell, and she'd found the wall, had let her hands slowly guide her to the floor against the smooth stone, and there it was again, the metallic tang of iron in her nose, the saltwater on her cheeks.

Why, indeed.

~•~

The hard stone wall was making Elsie's back ache where she sat, watching him unblinking, eyes damp.

Augustus leaned against the grating, brow knitted, pale eyes studying her, flicking to the door for just a moment before moving back. "Why," he breathed, voice low.

Get up get up get up

"Answer me, Elsie, and my information is yours. Anything you want to know."

Breathe. It was Isa's phantom voice whispering in her ear, like it had a thousand times before. *Breathe. In. Out. Nice and slow. And again.*

In.

Out.

Slowly, she rose, still leaning heavily against the wall, but standing, nonetheless, panic abating.

It was reasonable, falling apart. Look at what he'd done to her. Look at who he was.

It is reasonable, falling apart. Look at the lie he caught you in.

She shook the voice from her head, finding Isa's voice.

75

In.

Out.

"Are you alright?" he asked softly, watching her.

Her head snapped up to meet his gaze. "Do you really care about the answer?"

"A question for a question. Tell me why, and I am yours to command."

She pushed herself off the wall, glaring. "You," she hissed. "Not a word. I tell you, and you tell *no one.* I have my reasons. Very good reasons. And you've done enough, so don't go running to Fletcher, thinking you know best—"

"They're always very good reasons, aren't they," he cut in.

"Not a *word.*"

He gave her a small nod, putting a hand on his chest. Atop his heart that didn't deserve to keep beating.

Exhaling deeply, her fingers found her hair, started unbraiding the already falling-apart mess. "It...sparked something," she said slowly, choosing her words carefully as she paced the cell. "Something deep inside. Like part of me was resonating with it. Like it—it was the only thing capable of truth." Combing out the tangles with her fingers, the headache pounding in her temples eased faintly, letting her hair fall down about her shoulders. "I owe myself the time to tease it out."

Silence overtook them, the scuffling of her boots against the stone the only sound in the cell.

Her steps were a timekeeper, counting the seconds.

The minutes.

At last, shaking out her hands, she set to work, putting her hair back into a braid. Some semblance of neatness, otherwise there'd be questions. "I saw my worst fears," she murmured at last, weaving the strands together as she walked. "And...it was terrifying. But there was something honest about it. About being afraid. There's truth, watching the visions scream. Truths about me. About where I'm weak. It's like walking with the parts of my mind too cowardly to show themselves most of the time. They shift, too. They're never the same. They speak their peace, but they're just me, just my own fears, and I...I think the things they say are more true than anything else I've heard. I think the world might be a lie, and the only thing that's true is fear."

Tossing the braid over her shoulder, she dared a glance behind the bars.

His pale eyes were glistening, unblinking as he watched her without really seeing.

"Your turn," she said coolly, raising an eyebrow. "We made a deal. You promised everything I want to know."

"I meant it." He turned, voice rasping, and she saw him move to bring a hand to his face before his back met her. He sniffed, shaking his head, making for the back of the cell, like he couldn't quite face her. "When I asked if you were alright, I meant it."

"Oh, fuck you—"

His head snapped back, eyes red. "I meant it," he growled.

"Bullshit. You don't get to pretend like you give a damn—"

"I made a tactical decision, Elsie! I was a general. I was charged with protecting this realm, and I had to decide whether to trade one for hundreds of thousands, and I am sorry that it was you, I am *sorry* that it cost so much, I am sorry that my realm is going to crumble because of it, I am sorry that I was wrong, and I would do it again, because I thought I was doing the right thing! But amity isn't loyalty! What you were subjected to for weeks—and you came in here, facing me alone, still fighting, and so when you collapse against the wall, I'm going to ask if you're alright. What happened," he breathed, coming to the grating, "in that—that place, in that cell...that was a general executing strategy—"

77

"Take some responsibility," she snarled, meeting him at the bars, fists clenched. "*You* did that. Nobody else. *You—*"

"I *am*. This *is* me taking responsibility. I don't deny what I did. I'm telling you that I did not allow my decisions to be swayed by personal feelings—"

"Well, maybe they should have been!"

She held his stare, her words snapping across the stone.

Then, eyes damp, he took a step back, shaking his head. "Loyalty before amity," he whispered, falling to sit on the edge of the cot. "I did as I was told."

"And what were you told?"

"That you were the daughter of Death," Augustus breathed, "that her blood ran through you, and that above all else, we needed you to evoke her. To evoke Death herself, your predecessor—"

Elsie's patience had snapped. "The locket. Where is it."

"Your *iaculus* is with the rest of your possessions. In my quarters— not the barracks," he amended. "At the palace." He looked down, unwilling to meet her gaze. "A relic like that was to be treated with reverence. By all means. Go retrieve it."

FLETCHER

"Brother dearest, brother mine,

Brother I am soon to find,

Lay me down, my soul to keep,

Rest eternal in earth so deep."

~Valley limerick

The cell-room door slammed shut, and Elsie stepped into the hall, face flushed. "Fuck." She tucked a strand of black hair behind her ear, and slumped against the door.

"What happened," Fletcher breathed, moving to meet her from where he'd been himself leaning against the wall. "Are you alright?" His fingers met her jawline, eyes flicking over her, assessing. It was hard to tell, with those dhacrym eyes, but it looked like she had perhaps been crying, and there was a crust of blood near her nose where she'd messily blotted it away—

"I'm fine." Elsie cut the thought off. "Apparently my locket is in his room at the palace." She made a small noise of discomfort, brushing his hand away where it lingered on her cheek before she herself ducked under his arm.

Her heartbeat was a panicked *da-dum da-dum da-dum* reverberating in the small stone corridor, her breathing still ragged as her lungs cleared, and nothing would ever be the same again.

How could it be.

How could she claim to be fine when she oscillated between numbness so catastrophic she disregarded all sensation, and incendiary pain at the softest touch of amity?

The problem with *fine* was that it was an ideal. An unobtainable ideal, and none of them ever would be fine, because they were all broken in their own ways, which made the lie all the more irritating. *I am better than the rest of you*, it seemed to say. *I can carry more than you and I am superior for it.*

"Commander?" The guard was watching them with a worried look. "You be leaving?"

"Yes," Fletcher snapped, annoyed.

"Without interrogating the other one? She's bound to be dismayed you didn't."

Fletcher glared, folding his arms across his chest. "Dismayed? Guard Tepre, she is being held on accusations of partaking in an obscene treason against the realm, she doesn't *get* to be dismayed anymore. She's no longer giving orders. And she hasn't been for a while, I'll kindly remind you that she has been retired from service for two years."

The guard only shrugged.

Swearing, Fletcher glanced at Elsie, who was watching them both with an inscrutable glare. "Fancy a visit to my sister?"

She quirked an eyebrow. "Fine."

There it was. That word again.

Maybe it pissed him off so badly because it was another way of saying *I don't trust you with this catastrophe.* Like she was accusing him of not being built to shoulder her feelings with the competency of other people, and that stung.

Fletcher's pained gaze locked on her emerald eyes, and he lost his words. It'd become an easy out, where he could hold her stare the way she loved so much and she expected no words—it had become quintessentially a moment of understanding. A faint smile twitched at her lips, and for the blink of an eye *fine* became the moment, but not as a lie this time. It was a tiny microsecond of refuge. In the space of a heartbeat, they were fine. In the next, the world crumbled.

So it went, these days.

Fletcher broke her gaze, eyes turning to the floor. Elsie found his hand, though, and laced their fingers together, her skin dry and rough from the harsh winter air and the perpetual washing of blood from her still-bleeding cuticles. He gripped her hand tight, breath catching.

There were a lot of noble reasons he'd given, relinquishing the family name, and he wished they were true.

He wished he were a hero first and in love second.

But the truth was that his life with El would always come first. He didn't know, precisely, what she was going to do about the Hidden City—the City that rightfully belonged to her—or what the future held, but he knew that carrying the mantle of a Kingship he didn't want would tear them down eventually.

The rest—the morality of it, the obligation...it was an afterthought.

The guard's keys clanked as he walked down the hall and hung a left. Cam had asked for an interrogation. Had threatened her own dismay if the answer was no. Cam Praequintelya, in Fletcher's experience, was someone who knew how to toe the line. Augustus would tumble right over it, Alva had probably danced across it without notice, Fletcher himself would avoid it if he could—though he would often cross it inadvertently, as a means to some other end—but Cam...Cam was clever, and her strength had always come from knowing her limits.

"Your brother's a right mess, if you'll permit me to say," the guard mused, fiddling with his keys. "Refuses his food—or else hurls it at whoever's come to retrieve the tray, he's belligerent..." He clicked his tongue. "The Princess is ever her courteous self, though. I reckon her husband stuck her in here for some other purpose, if you take my meaning."

Fletcher frowned. "You're insinuating Senator Cormalum had his own wife arrested because of, what—an unhappy marriage?"

"All due respect Commander Nist, but that's Prince Praequintelya now, isn't it?"

"Will you just cut the bullshit?" Elsie glared, dropping Fletcher's hand to put hers on her hips. "How can you possibly think she's innocent?"

The guard mulled the question over, thoughtful. "I didn't say that, now. But I'm just saying, I'd be quick to question why he was so keen to get rid of her. It was his house too—though it's unpopular to say. And I'm not implying anything," he added quickly, "gods know I've seen his denouncement..."

Elsie glanced over, sharing a meaningful look with Fletcher.

The guard unlocked the door with a loud *clack* and pulled it open. "All yours, Commander."

Fletcher heaved a sigh. This had not been on the agenda today. He straightened his gray jacket, and with Elsie right behind him, strode into the cell, bracing himself.

Buried deep into the stone and suspended across the cell as bars, thin strands of metal that had been ripped from the darkest caverns of iaculia hung taught. He could feel his own magic seeping away, the prickling of the pull subsiding into nothing more than a distant fatigue and emptiness as it dampened his own preternatural abilities.

"Ah." Cam was lounging lazily against the iaculic bars, her pale hair pulled into a severe knot, flashing eyes watching them both. "It's about time."

"What do you want, Cam?"

"They tell me you have forsaken the family name and abandoned my title to my husband." Her eyes flicked to Elsie. "And you let him!"

"I am not my companion's keeper," Elsie sneered.

"Did you beckon me here to chastise me, Cam," Fletcher glowered, crossing his arms. "I'm not a sixteen-year-old cadet anymore, fumbling through my first year of the Acadamae."

"No. You're twenty, so you have it all figured out, right?"

"He's got it down better than you did," Elsie put in coldly. "At least Fletcher knows when to step away."

Elsie's sharp defense sent a jolt of something warm through Fletcher's chest.

Cam pushed herself off the iaculic bars. "You let him take my crown."

"Augustus gave a statement against you. He said that you conspired together. You had your wine cellar converted into a prison, for fuck's sake! If we had any evidence against Cormalum, Cam, he'd be behind bars, too. But he's been nothing but cooperative. He even suggested we take him into custody while we clear his name, which we did. And I was there when Rodion arrested you, Cam! He was livid!"

"He took no part in the ring, nor did I—"

"You did, Cam!" Fletcher felt tears prickling at his eyes. His elder sister. The one who'd taught him how to climb a tree and who'd run with him on the beaches of Thallassas and who'd taken him under her command when he *had* been a foolish boy of sixteen at the Acadamae and this was what had become of her. Of Augustus, too.

This was watching his family rotting from the inside out. Siblings, traitors, his mother waxing into nothing as her illness took her, his father capitulating, because Cam was right, objectively this was folly, and this was no interrogation.

It was a debriding.

ISA

"Loss comes in waves. We feel it swell and ebb, and this, I believe, is one of the tides of life. To grieve."

~Sam Alderton

The dawn was silent, beyond the walls of Caelaymnis.

A soft gray sky waited, calm above the high plains, puffing out fat snowflakes down to be drifted by the brutal winds that would inevitably charge off the mountains behind them. Massive trees, dormant and crooked, held their branches to the sky in the distance, marking a small creek that would lead to the mass of dugout homes known as the Woodshades.

Isa ran their hands across the triage vest. *Bandages, cruor tonic, anesthetic, knife, salve, bands...*

It was going to be a hell of a first day back.

Isa had previously been granted the privilege of running the medic's tent that stood just within the city walls, but today, they would linger at the back of the battalion. They would fix—but they'd also fight if need be.

Rumors of an attack had reached the compound, whispers that some of the Woodshades were planning to use the cover of the storm to set in motion another assault—and with officers down, the Caelaymnic numbers had been diminished to a desperate degree.

Augustus's legion had been pulled, the whole lot of them intoxicated with blood magic. Fifty, under his command, forget the countless others who had died, and the lot of them had been restricted to quarters until they'd sobered up, and even then, would not be permitted on the front lines. *Gods forgive them, they knew not who they followed*, but then again, surely they must have.

Augustus had pulled no punches. *Loyalty before amity.* He'd been clear that he would do anything for Caelaymnis.

Commander Fohella was poised, still as they listened. Their dark brown skin was beaded with sweat of concentration, two braids framing their face as they studied the landscape. Then, with a two-fingered gesture, they vanished in a whorl of golden sparks, the signal to move.

Isa had been reticent, being reassigned—Commander Rodion Kastarae was a fair leader, and a good friend. But Commander Fohella was *ro*—albeit consecrated, unlike Isa—and there was a kinship amongst the uncontained. With a deep exhale, Isa followed Fohella's lead, evanescing deep into the sickly grove along the river.

The battalion was small, even by recent standards. Fifteen of them, and this time, Isa had hugged their mother farewell. Augustus—he was wrong. What he had done was wrong, objectively, horribly, wrong in a twist-your-darkened-heart unflinchingly bad sort of way.

But at least the Drada in his legion had stopped dying by the dozen.

The ordinary magic of Drada had become coveted by the Woodshades. Drada were kidnapped, their blood drained like common forest game, and through a ritual of fermentation and distillation, what was left behind was a grotesque echo of elfmagic, dangerous and difficult to control. The Woodshades were mostly humans forgotten by time and treaty alike, but when they dosed themselves with what they'd stolen, their violence became scarred into the memory of thousands.

Dradan tactics brought steel and magic together, the former very much reliant on the latter, for shielding and lucents in advance of a swinging sword made for a powerful adversary. But the Woodshades, with their stolen elfmagic tainted by blood, could easily subvert a shield, absorb the blow of a lucent, and gods, what they could conjure in turn—Isa had seen more than enough in the medics' tent to know that the gods had not intended this sort of suffering.

Augustus had seen it too, firsthand. He'd watched a wretched lucent the size of a dinnerplate tear through the gut of his aide, Epherias, he'd absorbed blows that caught fire to bone, had watched magic wild rip right through a man, guts spilling as human hands touched storming clouds of lightning, and he'd broken.

Any one of them could've, and many had. Just not in the way Augustus did. They'd stolen magic first, that was what he claimed. That they'd taken the elfmagic, and he wanted it back—with interest.

Dradan magic, taken in blood and twisted by the Woodshades, and in turn Augustus took their lives and their families in tow, and Isa had heard rumors of the battles Augustus raged in, whispers of the terrible things the Drada had done.

Dhacrym, to agitate the blood and provoke fear.

Barghest, to consume the fear and provoke the magic.

With dhacrym and barghest, one could draw the magic painfully, fearfully from another.

And with the help of a Xavishia, it was possible to control dynasties—something Augustus seemed to be keen on ignoring, Isa thought bitterly.

The heart of the settlement pieced itself together, but Isa knew better than to trust their eyes. Evanescing was sensory hell, even more so if you thought to trust your eyes above all else. The first feeling—magic. It guided Isa along, and was the first thing to anchor them down. Then, feet on the ground, the air in your lungs, and the eyes...

Well. They were the last to see.

But when they did, Isa wished they hadn't.

Someone had already been here. Carnage had already torn through this temporary shelter. The snow was marred with blood, muddy puddles the resting ground for bodies that had been ripped limb to limb, and in the snow, humans lay dying.

Commander Fohella held up a hand to wait, but of course, it did little good.

Isa was already moving for the fallen. Because fuck whoever had done this. Fuck whoever had come into this place of protection from the winter winds and destroyed it. Maybe it was one thing when they charged onto a field of battle—and even that, Isa wasn't so sure of—but one look around, and it was clear.

This had been no place of violence.

This had been a home.

"Commander Mirestva, I gave the signal to wait—"

"Then censure me."

Caelaymnis had already been here. This battalion had been sent to finish them off. There was no battle to be won. Only vengeance to be sought by senators and generals kept far from the blood and the hurt.

Isa fell to their knees into the snow beside a man gasping for breath. It had been one thing to tend to the wounded Drada, pretending their people were the victim. And maybe they were, sometimes, but that did not excuse this merciless slaughter.

But you consented to this.

From the moment you put on your uniform this morning and kissed your mother goodbye, you agreed that if they asked it of you, you would enact this violence against the innocent.

A cry of anger echoed through the woods behind Isa, and they turned, hands covered in blood.

It was a trap.

Training had become instinct, and the shield was up in the blink of an eye, but the man decimated it with a single sparking fist against the wall of magic. Debris went flying, and Isa's serrated blade was in hand, the other holding up a block against the bits of stone and spear tips and branches flying through the air. An arm behind them locked Isa into immobility, and a moment later, Isa's blade was in their captor's gut.

And still, the wounded lay dying in their snow.

Whether they'd been put there by a Caelaymnic hand or by one of their own, it was impossible to say.

But watching their captor fall into the snow to join her friends, Isa didn't much care how any of them came to be there.

Anymore, they only wanted to go home.

CHIM

"We forget our parents were mortal. We forget they
lived, erred, died—and yet, we raise them up like the
gods that, to our eyes, they were."

~Sam Alderton

A prick on her finger, a bit of blood spilled, and Mother Chaos had sworn Chim to silence.

Do not speak of the Master.

Do not tell anyone of how I called to you to come before him. Do not confide in your mischief with the beluae—and do not repeat such deception against him.

Sucking her bleeding finger, Chim had sulked off, bitter. This spoiled her plans wretchedly.

Mother Chaos had never bound her children with blood pacts before. Pacts were serious. They dealt with souls themselves, and Chim had tried to test the boundary, but when she'd gone to tell her hearth, she found she could not.

On pain of death, she could not.

The screams of children playing and the sound of laughter drifted up out of the mouth of the cave.

Chim grinned her fanged grin, skipping happily into the darkness, her red cape fluttering along behind her, a bag of candy tucked neatly into her apron pocket. The hearth was nice—but this was nicer.

This was playtime.

There was nothing quite like the frolicking of demonic chaos-children to really make her feel like a true *kobalde*.

Kobalde nests were most often shared by three or more *kobalde,* but always an odd number.

This one boasted at least 19, perhaps more, if Chim judged correctly. There were little piles of crunched-on bones, which were ever so delightful to gnaw on after a long day of fomenting destruction, little nests of paper and feathers and shiny things on which they would dream of more chaotic futures, and a brazier in the back that served as a make-shift hearth, for it was the command of Mother Chaos that they all bring the fire.

A shriek split the air and Chim was tumbling back in a mess of shadows and fangs, and she was giggling, clawing away, pleased, for it had been too long since she had been welcomed back among them. The tang of blood and magic filled the air, and clawing her way out of the heap of *kobalde,* she was grinning ear-to-ear.

"You're back!" Jazmyn whooped, eyes pitched black as she scampered from the pile, orange frock almost fire incarnate. Her assertion was met with a rousing chorus of high-pitched squeals.

Ryo jumped up and down, his little tunic coming untucked from the neat britches. "What ploy did you bring! Will we string up the merchants by their itty-bitty ears? Or perhaps by their biggly-wiggly pockets?"

"She's been *hearthed!*" The squeal came from Emalee, who had not joined the fray, and instead elected to sit by the fire and sip on her stew. Gingerly, she picked an ear out of the bowl, then delicately began to eat at it, talking all the while. "Smell her! She smells of pine and affection!"

There was a clattering and clamoring all around as questions began buzzing.

"Do you have a hearth? Is it true?"

"Are they humans? Are they murdery, like everyone says they are?"

Chim only smiled her devious smile. "Where is Mother Chaos?"

The chittering fell silent.

"She has not been back in weeks," someone called out.

Chim carefully drew her bag of sweets from her apron, pulling out a shard of ribbon-candy—though not before hissing at an encroaching *kobalde* keen on the sweets. "Longer than that," Chim whispered.

"Not true," another yelled, and the *kobalde* began to simmer, egging on the argument.

The whispers flowed freely, but they had not come from Mother Chaos. Oh, no.

"I would inquire of all of you," Chim mused. "How many have been called upon by Mother Chaos to enact the will of the one known as the Master?"

A handful of voices assented.

"Our Chaos is not to be bought and sold. Mother Chaos told us this, and yet instructs us to pledge cacophony to a mortal?" Chim scoffed. "I hope I was not alone in defiance!"

"But Mother—"

"She has only come back to instruct us into the employ of one who uses the covenant of the blood," Chim chimed in her sing-song voice. "I have even gone so far as to take a hearth, what good that does." Her black eyes glittered, surveying the mass. "We must invoke the Below and Above. Something is wrong with Mother. And we must find out what."

There was a clamoring of excitement, for there was little that the *kobalde* loved more than a chaotic web of treachery and lies, and if Mother had in fact become woven in—well. That *would* be a thrilling adventure, then, wouldn't it.

And to invoke the Below and the Above...

Chim gave a squeal of glee.

~ • ~

The Above had been vacant for many years, it seemed.

Chim's buckled shoes *click-clacked* along the pale gold floor, frowning as light spilled in from every window into the warm hall. A film of dust coated the braziers, motes startled into the air by Chim's steps, and this place...it had been built on light.

Kiran, God of Life, had crafted these halls from sunlight itself, a place of revelry and laughter, and it was the sound of laughter that guided the souls through the dark unknown. If Cora took the souls with sorrow, then Kiran let them dance—if she cut the threads with scissors of shadow, then Kiran was the one who'd spun the thread with light and life.

Chim had always been fond of Kiran, because he'd had a knack for chaos. He'd sown laughter and light amongst the mortals, and as it was when gods mingled with those below, it caused a certain amount of unpredictability. But that was what he did.

Souls are born in the fire of joy, she had once heard him say. As such, he set fire to all the mortal world, as best he could.

But this place had been long-since abandoned, and though he had not kept court here often, there were such things that were best kept beyond reach of those below. The spindle, in the corner, undisturbed, for each thread of life was spun of pure sunlight. There was supposed to be a sewing box, too, but there was no sign of it anywhere, and so, he had probably taken it with him wherever he had gone.

Chim frowned.

The game had begun.

The pieces were in place, and it had started, the sun moving behind the clouds and shadows whispering lies.

~ • ~

The Below was deathly still.

"Miss Cora?" Chim called, voice echoing through the darkened throne room. Carved of shadow itself, this place was ornate, darkness whirling beyond the windows. Where the Above had the memory of laughter, here, there was only grief.

Grief, and quiet.

"She is not here." A ghostly woman Chim knew for a fact was named Yara strode silently across the hall, her ancient armor shimmering. "Why do you cross the plain? What business do you have with the dead, *kobalde?*"

"What business does Death have, traversing beyond the realm," Chim mocked with frustration.

Footsteps met the hall, the shade of a mortal moving from her spying place. "What business do any gods have, besides arrogance and folly." Her wheat eyes bore the resentment of a life cut too short, and Chim thought this was very good of her, holding onto that bitterness.

"I need Auntie, this is very important," Chim scowled, "Mother is not herself, hearths are at stake—"

"Not herself," the mortal shade snapped, "when has she ever been herself? Your *Auntie* is a liar and an imposter—a forgery, a fake—"

The ghostly soldier named Yara was dragging the soul away. "Beca, enough. Child of Chaos," she added, looking back, "I do not know when Cora will return. You best go."

With a stomp of her foot, Chim let out a scream, the darkened hall shaking with reverberations.

Death had no business outside the realm.

Not when the Master had begun shackling the gods to his will.

ELSIE

"That's what is dangerous about belief. It clings to doubt, of which there is much in this world."

~ Tristan Praequintelya, Second King in the Age of Quietude

"Gods *damn* him." Elsie kicked a piece of ice down the walk, glowering. Hands stuffed in her pockets, she thought back to the mystery of Caelaymnis, when she'd first been snuck in to plan and scheme in secret. Those were the easy days, she reflected, back when she'd bantered with Augustus and tiptoed around in a cloak about the compound with Fletcher.

Caelaymnis felt more ordinary these days, with its chilled streets full of vendors and shop windows and elves running about doing painfully mundane tasks like picking up supplies at the corner shop and bumping into friends on the street corner.

"As disturbing as they are, at least his motive seems consistent with your recollections," Fletcher frowned.

"He clings to his lore, that's for certain." She sighed. "He thinks I'm the descendant of Death herself. He's lost his marbles."

"If he ever had them to begin with, which I don't think he did." Fletcher bit his lip, stopping to look at her.

Elsie had a glare still etched on her brow. She was starting to shiver, lingering in the cold.

"Here, let's—let's sit down." Fletcher gently took her hand, nodding to a tea shop at the end of the lane.

The rush of warmth as he opened the door was welcome, gentle music filling the air as a little magic music box cranked away on the counter while elves moved gracefully about the shop, making tea, serving tea, drinking tea. It was a beautiful little shop, too, with bright pastel panels of wool on the walls, the fire roaring, the smell of yeast and fruit filling the air as a waft of steam rose up from an opening oven door at the back.

Fletcher moved for a table by the window, far from a group of gray-haired elves gossiping up by the front.

"Do you think Teddy was right?"

"About what? Augustus being stupid? Very much so," he said, gently laying his gray cloak over the back of his chair.

"He said he was trying to evoke Cora." Elsie pursed her lips. "It was such a line, Fletcher. You should've heard him. Those words weren't his. He was clinging to rhetoric."

Fletcher sank down, quirking an eyebrow. "I'm hardly surprised he ended up being such a pasty."

"Do you mean patsy?"

"What's the difference?"

"Pasties are for dancers at the merchant clubs." Elsie gestured across her chest. "Patsy is someone who is easily taken advantage of."

"If Augustus is attached at the teat of anything, it's idiocy. The latter is what I mean." Fletcher grimaced. "It's this Master that concerns me. I think Teddy was right, that Augustus got caught in something he didn't really understand. The Master, though?" His displeasure was evident, eyes troubled.

"The barghests and the dhacrym are damn fine pieces of evidence. My parents are dead, and their parents..." Elsie's voice faded to nothing. It was perhaps the one time she was glad they were gone, so they could not be trapped in this awful scheme.

Fletcher's gaze lingered on her from across the table. "You," he breathed. "You're the one who's different. Whatever Augustus thought he was doing with you..."

"My line, the—the Faulise, the Chancellors, are said to be descended from the God of Death." Elsie frowned. After Clark's note naming her thus in the days of her recovery, she felt little use in keeping the secret. Before Augustus had taken her, when it had been games and dreams, that had been different—but now? Now, after the Factionists had almost certainly left their calling card at the Mirabeau farmstead, an unmistakable warning? Now, after Augustus had taken her, poisoned her, bled her nearly dry? She would need all the help she could get, navigating this uncertain future.

Fletcher let out a small sigh, glancing out the window. "The Master is Incidiae. We know this. You saw him, named him as Anscip Xavishia. He is a man even *I* have read of in the history books," he pressed, "he *is* the master of tenancy. And for some particular reason, he wanted *you*. I cannot make sense of it. His history is bloody, and at times violent, but you have done nothing." The look in his eyes said it all.

"The Master goes after me with blood magic that targets my family line," Elsie recollected, pinching the bridge of her nose in exasperation, eyes squeezed shut. "Only, my family line is of the Hidden City and supposedly stems from Death herself. Fuck, Fletcher, I don't like that at *all.*"

Risa had been a font of information, supplying copious amounts of lore—both about the City, and about Margaret Faulise and Jon Clement. Truth and legend were muddled, but one thing had been clear. *Death* and *Faulise* and *Chancellor* had all become synonymous.

Quiet fell between them.

"That's a terrifying thought."

"Summoning the gods? I can't even imagine what would possess someone to try. I pray they're wrong—or if they're not, I pray they're unsuccessful," Fletcher nodded firmly.

Elsie leaned back. "And if they're not, who are you praying to, Fletcher?"

"That is between me and whichever poor mystic has the task of easing my crisis of faith."

Reaching across the table, Elsie took his hand, giving his fingers a squeeze. He answered with a tiny smile, one tired and effortfully given.

He had been so good, these past weeks. He was losing everything, piece by piece—his brother, his sister, his crown, his name—and still, his heart was so gentle, the anger pointed where it belonged, namely, away from her.

That been her biggest fear, waking up outside the cell.

She'd screamed, tears streaming down her face, when she'd seen him in the cell—and again, when she'd seen him beside her in their bedroom. The fear had lied to her. It had conjured figments of him, shouting nasty things she had taken to be truths, and of all the things she'd seen, that remained the worst.

That he could fall out of love with her so easily, and more than that, that he could come to resent her.

That she was so awful, so wretched, so unlovable that even the gentlest of souls could be soured by her.

"I am very partial to you," Elsie said quietly, still holding his fingers tightly. "And I think there will never be a day where I am not grateful for your love."

His smile brightened, spurred on by her words. "I feel the same, El. I love you dearly."

One of the elves who had been busy at the counter at last circled by, not bothering to take their order but instead placing two very large cups—bowls, really—of tea before each of them, along with a plate of intricately iced cookies.

"I didn't order this," Elsie interjected, pointing at the cup of steaming pink tea. It smelled strongly of rosehips, globs of honey still pooled at the bottom.

The Drada merely winked, leaving with a garish little twirl.

"You don't make requests here," Fletcher clarified with a faint smile. "The brewer just...knows."

Elsie leaned in, taking a sip. It was mild in flavor, gentle on her agitated stomach, the sweetness warming her bones. Some of the anxiety in her chest began to ease, lungs taking in the aromatic shop air in slower, deeper breaths. *"Oh."*

Fletcher was grinning, watching her. "Not bad, eh?"

"Not bad," she conceded with a smile that faltered a moment later. "Clark is dead."

Fletcher's shoulders sank. "He's dead."

"I was awful about it with Sam."

"It's understandable. You're going through a lot."

"Yeah, but I was still awful about it," she frowned. "And Leaving Day. Teddy tried so hard, I just—Fletcher, how am I supposed to pretend like everything is alright? Leaving Day has come and gone, we are firmly into the first month, how does he expect me to pretend—"

"I don't think he expects you to pretend. I think that he was just sad that you weren't there to celebrate with him, Elsie."

She grabbed a cookie, breaking off a piece. "Well, for me, it's just another reminder of how fucked it all was."

More silence.

"Are you going to his funeral, though? Clark's?"

"No." Elsie almost snorted into her tea. "I said it before. Good riddance. I don't need to be there to witness all that grief. I don't doubt Sam's is real enough, but the rest?" She rolled her eyes. "They should be counting their blessings that he's out of the way. It's a small miracle that the dead can't make waves."

RISA

"What's in a name? Someone once told me a rose by another name smells as sweet—but I always wondered why they never talked about the poison thorns all roses bear. By another name, a rose is most certainly Death."

~Cora, God of Death

The dawn was gray and listless in the Hidden City.

What have I done.

Huddled up against the wall beneath her tiny bedroom window, Risa stared blankly at a point in the distance, eyes red and puffy.

I did this for my family.

I did this because there is a Factionist sympathizer in the ranks of the Guild, and when they found Maggie's child in the Valley, they burned down her home and killed her adoptive parents.

I did this because he has weaponized my brother and me against anyone and everyone.

She was grateful, at least, that Cele had given her those justifications as they'd lingered over Clark's body. It was something to cling to. Some pathetic justification of how two wrongs really did make a right, of how she was an objective executer of justice, of how she was good and right and deserving to make the call of who lived and who died.

What have I done.

A preternatural cold was beginning to crawl into the small City apartment.

Clouds were shifting beyond the window, darkening the sun, and

Risa was almost grateful.

Maybe it'd rain.

Maybe the sky would share in her dismay.

"Ah." A soft voice cut like a hot knife through the cold apartment.

Risa started violently, head snapping to the door.

"I wondered who I would find here." A woman stood leaning on the doorframe, arms crossed. She was wrapped in a dark shawl, little roses embroidered along the hem, closely-tailored trousers tucked into leather boots, her pitch black hair falling across her shoulder, dark eyes glittering in the light. Empty foreboding seemed to nip at her heels as she took a step forward.

"Who are you." Risa was on her feet, an empty well of nausea sitting heavy in her stomach.

"I was curious," the woman mused, straightening up off the frame. "I wanted to meet the gods-damned piece of work that sent an insufferable prick straight to the gates of the Underworld. I see so many souls," she went on, "and as you could surely imagine, I have seen distress and despair and anger, and yet, I cannot say that I have ever had someone march to my hall and deliver perhaps the most scathing indictment of malfeasance I've had the pleasure of hearing. It has been a fair while since I had the privilege to drag such a soul out of the Hall of the Departed and toss him to the shadow wolves buck naked and yowling of injustice." The woman crossed her arms, eyes sparking as they met Risa's. "I am Cora, God of Death, Cutter of Threads, Keeper of Souls. And I am here to meet the one who ended Clark Carson."

~•~

Risa watched the woman named Cora, numb. And there were a thousand things that should have been running through her mind, a thousand names that they gave the God of Death, a thousand stories behind the legend...

"God of Death, as in...the Foundress?" Risa said quietly, brows gently furrowed.

You should be begging for mercy. Questioning this woman, standing before you. Running, perhaps, running far away.

Cora shifted, smile faltering.

Risa swallowed hard. The Foundress had taken on a legacy of destruction, once upon a time. She built the City, had herself helped draft the infamous Treaty that cordoned off the continent, and she had acquired many monikers when she chose the many over the few.

But one stuck above them all.

Death.

She was Death.

Tears welling in her eyes, Risa slumped back against the wall. "Fine." Her voice was choked with regret, gaze fixed on the woman's shoes. "You want the one who killed him. It was me. Now, just—do whatever you're gonna do, okay? I knew there'd be consequences when I did it. I'm ready."

Risa's cheeks were damp, heart aching violently. *Will Teddy mourn for me as the sister he seems to so clearly know I am. Will he withstand a second round of grief.*

She'd been going to tell him.

She'd been ready to confess. Her and Cele, they'd rid themselves of the liability that was Clark, and somehow, Risa had decided this meant it was time. No more games, no more denial. No more masks, either.

"Wait." Risa wiped her eyes with a shaking hand. "I have to know, first. Did you find Cele, too?"

"Why would I do such a thing," Death frowned, cocking her head to the side.

"She..."

"She what? You supplied the poison. You yourself dumped it into the snifter, did you not? And besides. Daddy expected his baby girl to rebel," Death cooed, a faint smile on her lips. "But you? You were bought and paid for, darling. He thought he *owned* you."

"Bought and paid..." Risa scoffed, tilting her head back against the wall. Tears blurred the room once more, hot and sick. "Fuck. Guess it was borrowed time anyway, right?"

Cora said nothing as she took a step forward.

Then, with a deep sigh, she unwrapped the shawl, revealing an easy red blouse beneath, pearly black buttons gleaming about her wrists. She shook the shawl out, lips pressed into a line, with the air of someone preparing to act.

"Just be quick," Risa breathed, saltwater raw across her skin. "Please."

"I'm afraid it is not so easy," Cora said softly, eyes glittering. "After what has transpired?" She clicked her tongue.

A sob escaped Risa as she hugged her middle, shaking. "I'm ready, please, just make it fast—"

Cora moved, and Risa closed her eyes.

Gods, forgive me.

Risa felt Cora sink down beside her.

There was an arm around her shoulders, the *swish* of fabric as Cora placed the shawl across them both.

"Regret and grief are unmercifully slow," Cora said quietly, pulling Risa into her arms. "Death is not the fatal blow of a sharp end. It lingers, on and on, my poor dear. Trust me."

And Risa dissolved into painful sobs, cradled in the arms of Death.

TEDDY

*"Trust me for the sake of my own merits. To trust me
because you have no alternative—that is the highest
insult, for it strips us both."*

~Adrian Lynch

Tense silence filled Teddy and Sam's room in the house in Caelaymnis as morning sliced through the windows, bringing on the day.

Rubbing his eyes, Teddy sat up, the spot beside him in the large down bed empty. Sam, it seemed, had fallen asleep in tears, curled in one of the window seats. His golden hair was rumpled, warm in the sunlight, his robe slightly askew, brow furrowed, arms crossed, and Teddy felt a pang of guilt for letting him simmer alone through the night.

But Sam had been clear.

Leave me alone. Let me have this grief.

Though, the desire had not, it seemed, been strong enough to provoke Sam to leave entirely, to take a night back at his apartment in the Valley. Teddy groaned, rolling out of bed. Everyone grieved in their own ways, and everyone found sadness and anger at different intersections, and he tried to remind himself of this as he made for where Sam was tucked into the corner of the seat.

He needs a place where he can rage about. He needs to defend his grief, because he's conflicted, too.

Of course, knowing this didn't make it any less aggravating that Sam felt the need to go on the attack, all the while refusing to take the space he claimed he needed.

But of course, when Teddy sank down on the narrow strip of bench left vacant beside Sam, sidling up beside him, the frustration seemed to dissipate. Sam was warm, his belly soft as Teddy wrapped an arm around him, the smell of soap and lavender mixed with the tang of tears long-since dried lingering, and he did wonder, even if just for a moment, what kind of magic there was in moments like this. Forget the Healing and the lucents and the massive shimmering shields and the way some men could move mountains—this was sufficient.

Sam groaned, squirming in half-wakefulness, cinnamon eyes tired as they blinked back the sunlight. "What..."

"Morning." Teddy leaned his head against Sam's, sighing quietly. "I'm sorry."

Sam only sniffed, gently moving himself to sit fully upright. "'Ts fine," he mumbled. His hand found Teddy's and gave it a squeeze. Then, wincing, it looked like the memory hit him. "Oh, shit."

"Yeah." Teddy tensed, bracing himself.

But Sam just let his forehead fall softly to the window pane, eyes looking down to the street below. "I stood with you when you mourned your parents," he said softly. "As you still mourn them. I didn't turn around and tell you all the reasons *I* wouldn't be doing the same. And gods know I had reasons, Teddy."

"I know—"

"And I know Clark was a sonofabitch." Sam let go of Teddy's hand, drawing his knees to his chest. "You don't know the half of the guilt, okay?"

Teddy shifted, moving over to the other side of the bench to face Sam. "Then tell me," he said softly.

"I don't have to prove my pain to you," Sam said dully.

"I'm not asking you to—"

"You are. And fine, maybe it's unfair to ask you to carry the weight of pretending not to feel righteously vindicated in his death, but..." Sam trailed off, glancing over. "I did love him, Teddy. I was deeply invested in my life at the manor. So please." There were tears in his eyes as he begged. "Please. Tell me it's okay to hurt like this."

~ • ~

Bags were packed, the briefest of farewells had been said, and it was with reluctant silence that Teddy found himself once more at the Carson manor.

He adjusted the leather satchel on his shoulder, frowning as he watched Sam meet Cele in a somewhat awkwardly cold embrace in the foyer. Exhaustion pressed in on him, as ever, and he vaguely wondered if everyone simply drudged through life feeling like they were on the cusp of crumbling. But it sort of made sense, as that seemed to be the lot of mountains, to watch the tragedies of the world and stand idly by, helpless—and make no mistake, he *was* a mountain.

The beating heart of magic running through his veins gave a twinge at that, bristling.

Lovingly named the Thread, his magic disliked the notion of inaction. It burned for interference in ways he himself never had.

A young merchant man was gliding idly down the stairs, fingers sweeping the banister as he went. "Ah, you have arrived safely, I see," the man bristled, soft eyes locked on Sam and only Sam. A dapper suit, sandy brown hair neatly parted, a perfectly worried mouth with concern that did not reach his eyes, it had to be—

"Mattie." Sam let his satchel fall, and he met Mattie with a hug.

"I'm so sorry," Mattie breathed, "it was so sudden—are you okay?"

"Not in the least—Mattie, this is Theodore." Sam pulled back, putting a hand on Teddy's shoulder. "Teddy, this is Commissioner Matthew

Fieldson, he's the late Commissioner Fieldson's son—from the Capital, of course."

A spark of jealousy flared as Teddy took Matt's hand. "I've heard a lot about you."

"And I, you," Mattie said casually.

To Cele's credit, she scoffed. "Because Sam's a shameless gossip." Her dark eyes flicked to Teddy. "I do wish to catch up with my brother? Perhaps my husband can show you up to Sam's room."

Teddy gave a small nod, but before moving to follow, he couldn't stop himself from giving Sam a conspicuous kiss. In fact, it took more restraint than he cared to admit not to flaunt the word *husband* around, or to try his hand at a few catty remarks aimed at Master Fieldson, because Mattie—Mattie was just one more person who broke Sam's heart.

"That was nice of you to give your darling a kiss farewell," Matt remarked quietly as they reached the second-floor landing.

"I dunno what to say. I'm fond of him."

"He is a terribly nice young man."

"And deserving of so much better," Teddy breathed, incredulous.

Mattie paused, turning to face Teddy where they stood in the lavish hall. The rich burgundy-and-gold carpet seemed to bring out the heat clearly rising in Mattie's face, the striped wallpaper a fine window-dressing for the tart. "I am sure you are more than an adequate partner for Mr. Alderton."

"It is an unfortunate refuge to cloak malice with wit," Teddy quipped, glaring.

"I didn't know you were fond of Dechanty." Matt's smile faltered. "Her work is quite dense—"

"Look. I've never met you, but I know enough about you not to like you."

"And I've never met you, but I know that Sam has loved you deeply for a very long time, and while Sam and I have a storied past, I would never presume to interfere," Matt said quietly. "I fucked up, okay. I get that. And I get that you were probably the one picking up pieces then, too."

Teddy crossed his arms, prepared to argue.

But a small voice from down the hall cut shrill through the moment.

"Daddy! Daddy!" Chim bolted towards Teddy, catching him in a big hug around his legs, smiling sweetly.

Matt's eyes went wide, surprise poorly concealed. "Oh. I...didn't realize you—"

"Oh, my Papa told me about you!" Chim cut in, looking to Matt. Her eyes were bright, curls pristinely set, pink smock smooth and clean. "He said...well, I don't remember what exactly the words are, but something about 'eat your heart out' and—"

Teddy stooped over, scooping her up onto his hip.

"Your, er...daughter is very sweet," Mattie said stiffly, smile not reaching his eyes. With a look of annoyance, he turned, glancing at his pocket watch. "Oh, look at the time. I'm afraid I must be going soon. Come, Sam's room is in the South wing."

Chim hissed at Matt as he walked away, fangs gleaming and eyes darkening for a split-second before she resumed her ordinary self. "What did he do to Sam," Chim whispered in Teddy's ear as they walked.

"He agreed to marry Sam, but had already signed a contract of proposal with Cele and Clark to be executed when Cele came of age the following year," Teddy whispered. *He lied to try to get Sam in bed.*

"Should I eat him also?"

"*Also?* Chim." Teddy glared. "We don't eat people." His eyes flicked to Matt as they followed at a distance for Sam's room. "At least, we don't discuss it so conspicuously."

EZRA

*"Trying to understand the world is like trying to see
the back of your head. We can, with tricks and mirrors,
but it's never quite what the rest will ever see. And how
infuriating, thinking you've managed to capture a slice
of reality, only to watch it slip away beneath your
fingers."*

~ From 'Tales of the Recently Revived: A Sequel'

Sunlight streamed through the rafters of the cannery, cold in the early morning, and Ezra had found consciousness with the dawn.

The gold coins glistened as he counted them for the thousandth time.

Eighty-six.

His heart was pumping viciously, his hands shaky. What if this time, he was wrong? What if this time, he was a coin short?

Eighty-seven.

What would he do when he got there? This was it, this was the life of Ezra Hollick, lined up in a gleaming yellow row in the rafters of an abandoned factory, and when it was gone, he'd have nothing but himself.

Eight-eight.

And he wasn't a whole hell of a lot.

Not remarkably handsome, by any accounts, he wasn't specifically clever beyond what his daily life required. He had no trade, no skills to peddle, so what came next?

Eighty-nine.

Hunched over, huddled beneath the thin blanket, he set the coin atop the stack.

Tomorrow, he'd be somewhere else.

Tomorrow, he'd be in a city beyond imagining, and...and what then?

The plan had seemed simple, a few days ago, but today was a different sort of day, the kind of day where plans didn't really feel like they were going to go like they were supposed to go, and there was a chance he was going to be swindled out of what little hope he'd been clinging to and left gutted in an alley somewhere.

Ninety.

A magic city.

It was the kind of thing Nan would've told him about before bed. *A city beyond imagining,* she would have whispered, a big grin splitting across her wrinkled lip. Her eyes would've gone wide, and her hands would've taken to the air, gesticulating the story in time to her words.

A whorl of dust motes was stirred into the air in the draft.

He missed her.

She was the closest thing he'd had to family. Was, past tense, which was sort of the worst tense, because it meant that by the time it'd been said, it was all over.

Someone else had already written the ending, and this part—it was just the telling of it all.

"Don't....move."

Ezra jumped, startling the gold coins lined up along the board, watching in horror as most of them tumbled over the edge, clattering down to the factory floor below.

Something cold was pressed against his neck, a hand yanking his head back by a handful of dark, overgrown hair. "No funny business, boy."

"H-How..." His own voice was choked, though, hoarse from disuse.

When was the last time he'd spoken to an actual person? A week? Two?

"You're not in a place to be asking questions," the man growled. "Now listen, and listen carefully."

~ • ~

The house of the person his captor only called the Master stood at the east end of the Capital in the Merchant's district, backed up against a large swath of forest that was undoubtedly a part of the estate, the front facing a moderately busy through-way that led to the ports.

Ezra had been led inside, down a narrow hall, past a table decorated with miraculously fresh flowers, and into a drawing room where an etiolated man with red eyes and lardish hair sat tapping his fingers on the armrest of an upholstered chair.

"Ezra Hollick." The lard-haired man sighed, cocking his head to the side. "You look *exactly* like her."

"Like...who," he edged, uncertain.

"Your sister. She's a bitch, and her friends are cowards, and you...seem cooperative, don't you, Ezra?"

"I don't understand what's happening."

"Many, *many* things, Ezra." Rising, the etiolate held out a hand. "I am Anscip Xavishia, Insidiae of the Coalition." His eyes flicked to Ezra's captor, the grouchy, worn-down man who even still was holding Ezra's arm tight, brow furrowed. "This is your uncle, Asher."

"My...uncle? I don't have an uncle, I'm an orphan—"

"Quiet, you stupid boy," Anscip sneered. "I have deigned to intervene on your behalf. You are trying to get to the Hidden City, no?"

A wave of relief flooded into Ezra. "Yes! Yes, I am—"

"Very good. But the price has gone up." A faint smile was tugging at the corners of Anscip's mouth, amusement in his apple-red eyes.

"Gone...up?" As quickly as Ezra's heart had lifted, it fell once more. "I can't afford any more, it's taken me three years to save what I have—"

"I'm not asking for money. Keep your gold." Anscip's gaze flicked to Asher. "I'm going to tell you a story, Ezra."

Ezra swallowed hard, nodding.

His heart was racing painfully, anxiety making his thoughts swim.

I just want to be free.

I just want to be safe.

More than anything, I want to stop running.

"Once upon a time," Anscip drawled, looking amused, "there were two brothers. The elder brother was well-loved. The younger brother was not. One day, the younger brother took up a cause against the elder brother. He killed his elder brother and his wife, and swore to murder their twin babes, too—only, the gods favored the elder brother, and interceded. On that day, the younger brother swore that he would do anything to fulfill his mission and take revenge against his brother's family. He heard whispers that the children might someday return, and kept a watchful eye. He heard whispers that somewhere, there was a man who sought those same children, and he swore himself to the cause." Anscip's eyes flicked to Asher. "Of course, ideology and passion are fine, but he rather bungled everything, because he did not realize why the gods had favored the elder brother and his children."

"Why," Ezra asked, in spite of his worry. He glanced back to Asher. *Uncle Asher.*

"The gods favored the elder brother because he had taken the granddaughter of Death for his wife, and his babes themselves carried the blood of the gods." Anscip snickered, turning to pour himself a cup of tea. "Fucking fool."

Asher let out a guttural groan of anger. "You watch your mouth—"

"You tried to kill your own niece and nephew," Anscip drawled, quirking an eyebrow. "If you had not been stopped, irreparable damage might have been done. But...credit where credit is due." He turned back to Ezra. "Your uncle has...repented. Realized the error of his ways. And it's because he knows that the gods can be conquered, Ezra." Anscip's voice was oily, and it made Ezra feel sick.

"I don't get it. You're insinuating that I'm, what—the descendaf a god?" Ezra at last jerked his arm from Asher's grip, glaring. "I'm not an idiot—a lot of people think that, but I'm not—"

"No, you are not."

A gentle voice, soft as lambswool, cut in behind them, and Ezra turned.

Winking at Ezra, he wore a jovial smile, and shooing Anscip away from the teacart, set about fussing with the accoutrements. His sandy brown hair was set perfectly in a side-part, his jawline cleanshaven, his waistcoat probably fashionable and expensive, though Ezra couldn't really say for certain. He was clean, though, and smelled sweet, warm even. "How do you like your tea, Ezra?"

"Two lumps and cream," he said weakly. He couldn't remember the last time someone had offered him a cup of tea.

"I think we can dispense with these dramatics. Both of you, shoo."

"But, Master—"

The Master only shook his head, looking amused. "He is a sweet young man, to my observation polite and very, very tired. Much less of a threat than either of you, and I do mean that as a compliment to everyone, my darlings."

From then on, the Master ignored everyone but Ezra.

He fussed Ezra into a chair by the fire, worried if the cup of tea was alright, and when Ezra asked if he was still going to be able to go to the City, the Master laughed gently, saying he could if he wanted to, but that

113

he didn't have to.

"What do you mean, I don't have to," Ezra asked, cradling his now-lukewarm tea.

The Master leaned back, smiling warmly. "You wanted to go there to procure safety, did you not? But the Capital is your home."

"It is," Ezra agreed. "And I just...I don't want to run, anymore." Desperation and exhaustion were beginning to press down heavy on his heart, and tears were once more pricking at his cheeks.

Don't cry.

"Oh, my poor dear." The Master leaned over, face crumpling in worry. "All I mean to say is that you may stay in the Capital—here, if you wish. I just need one thing in return. Mr. Xavishia explained to you the unusual predicament you're in, of course. Being rather stranded, awash in a legacy that nobody thought to tell you of, caught between the feuds of the gods and mortals. I will shield you from this, if I can."

"What do you need, then," Ezra asked, voice breaking. "I—I was told I could keep the coin I saved—"

"And you many. All I need is a bit of your blood."

ELSIE

"He accused her of the most base violation of nature.
Or, this was what I saw at the time. He dropped her
down to be his equal, sinning right along with him. If I'd
loved her, I would've accepted her sins. Instead, I put her
on an impossibly high pedestal, so high I couldn't see the
help she was asking for."

~Fletcher Praequintelya

Past the arboretum that boasted a summer harvest even as snow pressed in at the glass above, beyond the massive library with towering mahogany doors and rows of tomes and scrolls filled with a script she was learning to read, Elsie strode through the halls of the Caelaymnic palace, trying to imagine. Surely, Fletcher and his siblings had run through these halls in a childish game of chase. Fletcher must've paced these corridors, a lovestruck adolescent, pining. And eventually, he must've walked through them as he prepared to depart for the Valley, intent to disobey in the name of halting the production ring manufacturing the darkest magics.

"Wait up!" Isa's voice echoed behind them, accompanied by soft leather footfalls. Their damp hair was pulled back into a topknot, their black civilian jacket half-buttoned, the cowl sitting cozy about their neck. "Sorry, I only just got your note, I..." They trailed off, shaking their head, a slice across their cheek and their bandaged hand boasting the reason they'd been late.

"How did it go," Fletcher asked darkly.

Isa just shook their head, expression dour.

"If you aren't up for this right now..." Elsie trailed off, frowning.

Isa raised an eyebrow. "What's the alternative, here? The three of us go sit at Fletcher's and speculate about it?"

"You look tired," Elsie said softly.

Isa only gave her arm a gentle nudge. "So do you."

It was probably true. How could she *not* look tired, between the dhacrym and the strain of recovering and the whole gods-damned world falling apart around her.

The door to Augustus's room was the last one in the line of doors, tucked into a dark corner at the end of the hall. A whitewood door with a silver handle and a matching lock, it felt lonely, away from the rest. Fletcher's room, and Cam's and Alva's, they all sat at the other end of the corridor, and perhaps it had just been the unfortunate architecture, and the unpredictability of future generations, but the long space of wall between their doors and his made Elsie sad.

It was alone and isolated, and though she knew he had not necessarily been—she knew of his friends, that he had been loved, by and large—it still must've been upsetting, having to slink off to the door in the dark corner, away from the others.

We do not thank the page-rippers.

But we can mourn for them.

Mourn, against her better discretion, because Augustus was a man who had been afforded every opportunity and every sympathy already, and her grief should've been saved for someone better.

Fletcher fumbled for the key, and unlocked the door with a small click.

The room was indiscernibly dark, and Elsie lingered on the threshold. "Can...one of you..."

"There are no fucking sconces," Isa swore, already hidden in the

116

black. Lucents bobbed to life a moment later, though, shedding warm, shimmery light across the room.

"El, catch," Fletcher called, under-handing her one.

She caught it, cradling the soft membrane in her hands as she stepped inside.

The room was a nest of memories, that much was apparent. Clothes were spilling out of the wardrobe and onto the floor, like they'd been gone through a thousand times. The bed was unmade, the imprint of where someone had slept still visible, blankets tossed back. The desk was stacked with personal effects, Elsie realized, fingers grazing the papers as she ventured further inside. Commendations, letters from his mother, knick-knacks that looked like they'd been accumulated over years—a seashell, a small slip that might've been a theater ticket—

A gold chain peeked out from one of the half-open drawers, and Elsie's heart caught, fingers darting for it.

The locket.

She pulled it around her neck, the tang of blood welling in her nose as her heart lurched.

Elsie reached for the chair to steady herself, but her fingers met silk, and the lucent had been left hovering in the air as she lifted her emerald gown from the masquerade off the back of Augustus's chair. There was a massive slash through the side, where he'd split the seam to let it fall.

"El." Isa gingerly lifted a mask from a nest of crumpled paper heaped onto a side-table, gems sparkling in the lucent light.

Frowning, Elsie tossed the gown aside.

The side table was a mess, like someone had sat in bed, distraught, tearing page after page from a diary—pages she couldn't help but unfurl, now, morbid curiosity getting the best of her.

If there was a drop of suffering in those pages, an ounce of grief, she wanted to revel in it.

To her disappointment, though, all she found were Vernacular lines, scratched out again and again and again.

~~I needed to~~

~~It wasn't like I had a choice~~

~~People are dying and I can't take it anymore~~

~~I had to make this stop~~

~~Make it stop~~

But one sheet lay, untouched.

I hope your soul shines brighter than mine ever will.

"What is this," Elsie frowned, kneeling in the mess.

"Fuck." Fletcher punched the bed, sinking down onto the edge to glare at the pile of discarded notes. "Fuck him—"

Isa knelt down beside Elsie, picking through the crumpled sheets. "When someone dies, you can put your final prayer with them on the pyre. You arm them, so that they can fight through the darkness and take their place among the stars. Vernacular, too, these were...well." Their eyes flicked to hers, the rest left unsaid. *These were intended for you,* that's what they'd been going to say.

"He thought I was gonna die," Elsie said quietly. She'd known this. But then why didn't he stop it, instead of drafting funeral prayers for her on these slips of paper? "If he was so sure that having my Ruby Tears was going to end the killing, why did he let you follow him into the cell?"

Isa's expression was stony as they watched her. "I do not know. He's a more than adequate strategist." They were smoothing out one of the sheets, and their eyes flicked down to the words.

Elsie scooped up the untouched sheet, parchment rough against her fingertips.

I hope your soul shines brighter than mine ever will.

Isa sighed, going through the notes. "Loyalty before amity."

"What was that?" Elsie glanced up.

"His endless mantra. Loyalty before amity."

Elsie's eyes flicked down to the note. "Curious kind of loyalty."

"Curious kind of amity," Isa mumbled.

That it was, indeed.

AUGUSTUS

"Sister, sister, by the bay,
far too old to come and play,
Sister dearest, sister mine,
killed the king and left behind
Something gray and something old
the fever that then was foretold."

~Valley limerick

The forty-six days since Augustus's arrest provided ample time to reflect. To sober up. To pray.

And Augustus had come to one conclusion.

Right or wrong, in pursuit of futility or justice, lives saved or no, his head had to roll.

The cell door clanked open, and Augustus rose from where he'd been brooding on the foot of his cot.

Seeing Elsie had been a relief, the first time, and he was absolutely shit for thinking so. She had been on her feet, mostly, voice decisive, eyes determined, and he'd said a quiet prayer, because he had never intended to extinguish that in her. But he was a gods-damned page ripper. And the accusation had wormed its way under his skin.

He was only relieved to see her because it was a way to justify himself.

To say it wasn't so bad, or else she wouldn't be here.

And that was why he had to die, he'd decided.

"I retrieved my locket." Elsie crossed her arms, pacing the length before the silvery iaculic bars. "Your room was a mess, by the way. Which surprised me, because everything I knew about you made me think you were organized to the point of minimalism. Isa and Fletcher and Rodion and Mia tell me how you always barked *no more, no less* to remind them of their obligation to live neatly minimal, and then I find your private quarters trashed."

Augustus was silent. Nausea was rising again in his stomach, the iaculic bars of the cell dampening his magic.

"You called it a relic, last time we spoke."

"It is," he breathed, quoting sacred prayers, "Cora, marked by Death, a heart of gold full of conflict, for fair intentions mean foul weather—"

"Enough!" Elsie's chest was heaving, anger in her gaze. "Don't parrot your religious bullshit back at me—"

"It is not religious bullshit, it is my faith! I believe that Cora, God of Death, was bestowed with a relic called the iaculus, I believe that she is the Scribe of Ends, that one day, she will go head-to-head with Kiran, God of Life, and she will end our world, only for him to begin it again—"

"You think you're so holy," Elsie breathed, looking at him with disgust. "You think your fight is sacred, that you're above the gods."

"At least I do not doubt the gods—"

"You know, I forget that you're my age." Elsie was pulling something out of her pocket. "I am so perpetually a child in my brother's eyes, and I forget that you and I—we are practically peers. You're two years my senior, are you not?" Gently, she unfolded a piece of parchment. "*I hope your soul shines brighter than mine ever will.* What really got me were the other notes. The ones that were crossed out or tossed in a rubbish pile. You tried to pass the blame, and every time you penned your absolution, you knew it was wrong."

"It was not immoral. It was inaccurate." Augustus turned, bitter.

"Well, that's bullshit, because you know they were both."

Her words echoed into silence as the seconds passed.

"I want so badly...to understand," Elsie went on, after an interminable moment. Her boots scuffed against the stone floor as he listened to her pad over to the bars. "And that's on me. That's the way that I'm broken, I think. I want to understand, because I want to believe that I was capable of such acts. If, in your shoes, I would have enacted such violence...then it feels forgivable. I want to believe that you got broken so badly that anyone else would've done the same. It needs to be inevitable. But it can't be. Because then who am I, but the inevitable victim in a game I could never win."

Augustus's jaw clenched, and he glanced back to look at her, a painful stabbing in his gut.

"I hope this breaks you, too," she whispered, eyes cold. Then, quirking an eyebrow, she began her pacing once more. "We need to find the Master—Anscip, he called himself. Of course, he was the one Fletcher was chasing. The one killing the pastries. And now, I know he killed them because he was looking for me."

Augustus grimaced. "Anscip Xavishia—the Insidiae? He is not the Master. He's just another lackey." His pale eyes lingered on her, brow furrowed. "And who are you, specifically," he asked, voice a low growl. "Besides Death."

"I am Elizabeth Faulise, heir to the Luminary Chancellorship in the Hidden City."

Augustus swore quietly.

Heir to the Luminary Chancellorship. The truth hit him hard.

The Chancellors were descended from Death herself, if their claims were to be believed. The fall of Margaret Faulise had been historic, her babes nothing more than rumor—so of course, when the Master had gone searching, he'd looked in the homes of merchants, in the homes of her political allies, in the homes of those of comparable status.

"Stell's left ball," Augustus breathed, "When he said you were the daughter of Death..."

"Death, the supposed foundress of the Hidden City," Elsie bit sarcastically, her fear of truth cloaked in disbelief.

Augustus shook his head. "I dislike that."

Elsie shot him a skeptical glare. "What, is your preference not seeing the forest for the trees?"

"No, I dislike that this reeks of political interference. I assumed that this was...a...holy thing." His voice was hardly a whisper. "This was a matter of the gods. I sought Death, to have her walk with my soldiers— your blood, it would've...protected my soldiers against dying, but this? Having Caelaymnis take down the heir to the City? That is not holy, that's—that's outsourcing an assassination!" He scoffed. "And in such a typically deceptive manner. Humans, they think our faith is nothing but a joke, exploiting—"

"I have no sympathy. When you choose to eschew a world of fact, you face consequences."

But anger was bubbling up in Augustus's chest. Gods, to punch something. Anything. The gods and their power were not something to be mocked, diminished through such dark motives and magics, and the Master had weaponized his metaphors.

Elsie's eyes lingered on him, thoughtful and distant and furious.

"What," he spat.

She crossed her arms. "We have to find the Master."

Augustus ran a hand across the back of his head, glaring. "Well. Your best bet is certainly your supplier." His flashing eyes flicked up to hers. "You're using, so I assume you know Clio."

Elsie's face was inscrutable.

"You know Clio," Augustus sneered. "The man who oh-so innocently grows an illegal hallucinogenic berry in the small glass house behind his border-edge home—berries retrieved undoubtedly from far beyond these mountains—that he discretely brews into the draught of fear that you would know as dhacrym?" He snorted. "Elsie, cut the bullshit. You're a clever woman. I'm sure you're already leveraging Fletcher's position to your advantage. Clio is a known distiller, and he's probably the first one that Fletcher even talked to the instant it became apparent there was a ring here, in the city of lights."

"Fine. But he's not going to tell me anything. He's already wary."

"No, he's not going to talk, because if he thinks he has nothing to lose, then he's got no reason to." Augustus frowned, coming up to lean on the bars. "How do you feel about being a bit of a bastard with him?"

Elsie's eyes were distant, finding his. "I don't think I feel much of anything, anymore. Least of all, sympathy. Tell me what to do."

SAM

"Dead and buried is not quite the same as over and gone. Not the same at all, in fact."

~Rebeca Alderton

It was a bitterly cold morning to bury the Commissioner.

Sam blew out a breath, glancing about the crowd that had congregated in the gated family plot some distance from the manor. "Everyone and their dog came crawling out today," he muttered, tugging at the wrist of his gloves. *Not that I have any right to be bitter at the crowd congregating. Top-tier hypocrisy from someone screaming about grief and mourning.*

Teddy raised an eyebrow, arms crossed. *I dunno what you expect me to say,* his gaze seemed to say. He looked vaguely uncomfortable, standing there in his suit. Fidgeting would've been the better word for it.

Black just *might've* been his color, though. It seemed to set his hair burning copper in the morning sun, his eyes the sharpest shade of sky-blue Sam had quite possibly ever seen.

Edging a hand around Teddy's arm, Sam moved a bit closer, grateful for the warmth. It was good, not having to do this alone.

Even if Teddy would've had every reason to refuse this wretched display.

Oh, darling. If you only knew the half of it.

There was much to critique of Clark from the public view, but even Sam had no love of rehashing his private sins—and there'd been plenty.

But at the end of the day—and this *was* the end of Clark's day, make no mistake—he'd been a parent to Sam, as much as anyone ever had been. His funds had provided a degree of stability, his rare praise had been a source of joy, and it was with trepidation that Sam gave Teddy's arm a squeeze, letting go to stand before them all.

Cele was perched in wait, eyes on him, unreadable, Mattie standing beside her, his hand on her shoulder.

The burial box had been gilded, visages of wheat and honey engraved into the gold. It had been set on the frozen ground atop neat braids of hay, a Valley tradition retold differently from everyone. Teddy's family, the Mirabeaus, said it was to cushion the soul as it moved from the sullen rest in the dirt into freedom brought with the blossoms of spring. Mrs. Mulligan, Sam's former employer at the dress shop, insisted it was to keep the soul warm, for the dirt was very cold and souls often had a long time to wait. In the end, it was as most things were in the Valley—sentiment disguised as practicality.

The mourners took up much of the field. Sam's social expertise, his merchanted training...they wore thin today, he found, for when he stepped up to the burial box, he was nervous, ungodly nervous.

"Clark and I had a—a varied relationship." Sam cleared his throat, voice threatening to break, and he wondered if it carried far enough. He exhaled, trying to steady himself. "As with all family, we had the misfortune to see each other at our lowest lows. I could list his faults, and we would be here for weeks. But I could do the same with his successes. I hope, at least, he would've counted me as the latter." Tears pricked at his eyes, hot and painful. "I wanted him to be proud of me. I wanted him to love me. And I think he did, but..." Sam trailed off, looking at the saltwater-stained crowd. To Teddy, standing there, brow invariably furrowed, hands crossed neatly before him as he watched his husband. *Don't I owe them a bit of truth?* "I think he loved me. Just not enough. He fought for me, but not in the ways that mattered. You...you

126

were all there, I am sure," he pressed, tears on his cheeks, gesturing to Mattie, to Cele. "Clark Carson was not a man you could count on, and I had the misfortune to rely on him for too long. You knew him as a clever man, an insidiously persistent merchant. I knew him behind closed doors, when he was a pitifully jealous man who loved to be loved. You knew him when he was seducing secretaries, I knew him when he was seducing me. You knew him to chase contracts, I knew him to break them. I did love him, though, despite all that, because when—when he was there, he was *there.* When he committed, he committed. It didn't matter whether it was a trade deal, a social maneuver, or dragging me into his bed, when he was determined, there was no stopping him. A gift and a curse, and one cannot be separated from the other."

The crowd was uneasy. Someone gave a derisive laugh, another loudly swore, but mostly, they waited.

Carrion, all of them, wanting it first-hand instead of in the paper tomorrow. They want to say they heard it from Sam Alderton's very mouth.

"As we lay him to rest, I—I suppose I ask you all to think about commitment." Sam swallowed, reaching for his handkerchief, drying his eyes at last. His cheeks burned where the tears cut into them. "Are you giving enough to the ones who matter? Or are you hitching your cart to a horse that's going nowhere?" He sniffed, glancing at the burial box one last time before returning to take his place beside Teddy.

Cele was a bird of prey, swooping in with her black cloak snapping at her heels, her high-collared white lace dress betraying her animosity beneath. She said nothing, taking perch before her father's burial box, just as Sam had, eyes scouring the crowd with silence. She would have the final say, and it seemed that after Sam's eulogy, she had decided this display had carried on too long.

"We are gathered here today to remember a man." Her voice was soft and cold across the grounds, like mist seeding beneath a closed door, reeking of foreboding. "My father."

A murmur of condolences swept through the crowd—

"Silence!" Cele's eyes were hungry for blood, skimming the skittish mourners. Then, not taking her eyes from them, she withdrew her hand from beneath the cloak, and at the snap of her fingers, a pair of mercenaries emerged from the mausoleum, dragging with them a very plump, very frightened merchant.

Sam stole a glance at Teddy, trepidation rising. *What the fuck?*

"Many of you know Commissioner Johannsen," Cele was saying, gesturing to the pale lump of a man quivering like jelly in his patent-leathers. "He was a self-professed ally of my father—and after looking at the ledgers, I can confirm he so generously cheated both the district and the Guild time and time again." Her eyes snapped to Sam. "My father was a degenerate fraud. He played the game," she said, and the words weren't for anyone else, they were for him, and him alone, "he played, and he *lost*, because he was weak and foolish and blinded by his own hunger. That is not a mistake I will make."

With lethal smoothness, she withdrew a blade from beneath her cloak, the silver catching the morning light.

Sam gave a sharp inhalation, eyes going wide, and he felt frozen where he stood.

"Commissioner Johannsen approached me, not an hour ago." She was turning the blade over, studying it carefully. "This imbecile" —she thrust the dagger towards him— "offered me a singular opportunity to betray this district. A silent coup of a district that *does not belong to him,* dressed in quiet assistance for a grieving daughter. Despicable."

Two steps, and she was behind him, the knife at his neck, her eyes scanning the crowd.

And with a single, clean gesture, she slit his throat.

Johannsen's suit was painted in blood, and Sam felt nausea rising, a sick feeling coiling in his gut, and yet he could not tear his eyes away from the dying man, nor from Teddy, somehow already gone, somehow kneeling beside the crumpled mess, from Cele, watching with disturbing calm as Teddy rolled the body over, checking for a pulse—

Teddy glanced to Sam, then to Cele, shaking his head. His hands were coated in bright red, eyes dark.

"If you cross me," Cele said, and her voice was hardly a whisper, deadly and quiet across the crowd, "you will *pray* for an ending as quick as this. I serve the district. I serve the Guild. And if you do not serve me, I will end you."

THE BARGAINS

I don't know what to say. This feels dumb, but I know that Sam is the one who has been chronicling things.

Or, he was.

I've been visiting Augustus. I feel like we're walking in circles, trying to find the root of this bullshit. But I haven't seen Risa in a while, Teddy and I are feeling our own kind of grief, and it feels like this world is gonna swallow me whole.

~ELIZABETH CLEMENT FAULISE,
EXCERPT FROM A LETTER DATED FEBRUARY 4TH

THE BEAST

*"There is great sadness, to be cast out when what you
expected were open arms."*

-Isa Mirestva

"No!" An end table went clattering, and the Master's face was red, sandy
hair mussed. "I refuse to accept it!"

"Ani, do something." The Fearless One was sitting in a nearby
armchair, one hand resting quietly on the soft bulge around her middle.
Despite the knitted brow, she seemed deeply uninterested in what had
transpired, her voice unconcerned. Even so, she shared a look—and the
word, *Ani*—with the Insidiae, seated beside her.

"Johannsen was an ally, my aide in this search, in establishing cover
for my quest," the Master hissed.

"And for *my* rings," the Insidiae frowned, "but we make do. He's
hardly necessary. She is young and rash and attempting to cement her
new regime, I can't fault her for boldness—"

"Impossible! Johannsen was in the pocket, you—you and your bitch,
you sit there—"

The Insidiae frowned. "Careful, boy." As if to cement the threat, the
Fearless One gave her belly a rub. *I carry the Insidiae's child,* she seemed
to say. *He will protect us above all else.*

The Master seemed humbled by the threat.

The Beast was fond of the Fearless One, as much as the Beast could
recognize fondness. She did not shirk at the Beast, did not, in fact, feel
the slightest notion of terror or discomfort, and the Beast found it odd

that she wasn't afraid, for *everyone* feared the barghests.

The Fearless One transcended survival.

The Beast knew three things. Fear. Eat. Survive.

And now, get scritch-scritches under the chin from the Fearless One as they sat by the fire.

Fear. Eat. Survive. Get Scritches.

The Beast padded over to the Fearless One, curling up at her feet.

The Master raged, kicking over a small glass cabinet full of undoubtedly expensive trinkets in lieu of further threats. "She *cannot* be onto us—"

"Why do you care, when you possess the gods themselves?"

"Because," the Master whispered, livid, "because if I have to bring the gods against her—I cannot afford a battle on two fronts. I have little of the blood left—Lucia's heir gave so little..." He stormed to the cart, fixing himself a drink. "I must have my full strength—our full strength—to take on the mystics atop the Dagger. They will not give up their post so easily, not even against the gods they claim to love."

Something terrible twisted inside the Beast.

"Who's a good puppy," the Fearless One cooed, reaching down to give the Beast a little pat-pat on the head.

And for the first time, the Beast doubted the Master. A creature of the Insidiae, the Beast had been loaned out for fear and blood, and perhaps it was the Insidiae's own caution as maker of the Beast, or else the Master's own raging, but the Beast felt a twinge of mistrust for the young man storming about.

"No matter." The Insidiae rose, smoothing his hair to silky slickness. "No matter. Heir and a spare, that's the phrase, isn't it? Well, we found the spare, as far as Death is concerned."

"I tire of incompetence." The Master's face turned sour. "Perhaps I tolerated these *minor* inconveniences in the name of higher aims, but no longer. I will accept nothing less than ultimate and unequivocal control."

"You," the Insidiae drawled, apparently amused. "Despite your moniker, you are master of nothing, boy. In lieu of the trail of bodies—stupid to leave behind, mind—I allow you more efficient tools. I arrange for dhacrym to be supplied, to agitate blood and elicit fear. I bring my barghests, to consume the fear and agitate the magic. I linger here, still, supplying my talent with familial magics so that you yourself can possess the gods. I will permit you the gods in timely order. I don't care what you do with them. Play with them, use them—but know your place. You will accept nothing less than what you're given, unless you wish to go back to murdering boys behind barns and boiling their blood like the novice you were. How long did it take you to summon Ignata, God of Fire? How many fell?"

The Master grew silent, stewing.

"You have as much love for bodies falling as you do for playing puppet with the gods," the Insidiae snapped. "How many pastries did you drop, searching for Death's girl? And how many of them wronged you, eh? How many of them insulted you, rejected you?"

The Beast set its head on the Fearless One's knee, panting happily. This conversation was of no interest.

Now, good pats...

Those were of *great* interest.

"What will you do," the Insidiae pressed, "when the pantheon is yours? Perhaps you are stalling because you know it will not content you to wield the relic. Maybe you do not wish to see this through, because then you will have little excuse to continue this regime of torture and death you seem so partial to—"

The Master at last rose, storming out of the room in silence.

"Fool," the Insidiae whispered, eyes flicking to the Fearless one. "He suspects."

The Fearless One stroked her belly thoughtfully. "Maybe. Maybe not. But he can do little to stop you. He's fragile. It will take little to wrestle the gods away from him."

"Volition willing," the Insidiae breathed. He glanced to the Fearless One. "Be careful. He cares not for you."

"That is his loss."

"All the same—"

"Ani. I have not grown adept in my talent with blood to be scared by a man too arrogant to learn these methods for himself. He outsources to you, and to Lys," the Fearless One admonished, "where I? I have always done the dirty work myself. Let him whine. Hell, let him send his gods after me. He will regret the day he does."

AUGUSTUS

*"Grief takes many forms, and it changes us. I don't
pretend the changes are necessary or good, but we can't
ignore we are different, after loss. The problem is that
many mistake difference for somehow being less. We
change. We shift. This is no sin."*

~Sam Alderton

Prayer, Augustus was beginning to feel, was only of consequence when the gods deigned to act.

He'd done a lot of praying, in his life. He'd done even more since arriving in this cell. At first, he prayed that his immortal soul might be wiped clean of the stain that he had brought upon it, but as he'd sobered up from the blood magic he himself had imbibed before and during Elsie's imprisonment, that desire diminished and he discarded it as the self-absorbed wish that it was. If the mystics and the gods alike preached penance, then he should bear that stain. He should face the consequences.

After that, Augustus had prayed that the gods would be swift and merciful when they struck their damning blow, but guilt came nipping at his heels once more. He had been neither quick nor merciful, and he would receive what he had given—or so the mystics taught.

He had prayed for Elsie, after that.

That she would discard the draught of fear and find peace.

But she had not, on either front, and so, he had ceased to pray all together. This caused him much conflict and strife, for the mystics had taught him not to abandon his prayers—but in leaving them aside he grew closer to the teachings and the paradox was ripping at him.

It must've been almost two in the morning, he judged, sitting in the darkened cell. The guards would dim the lamps as the sun fell, lighting them when the sun arose again, and it was singularly depressing, being imprisoned in the winter months when the sun hardly deigned to peer over the mountains.

A piece of parchment and a stub of graphite sat on the stone floor before Augustus.

With a heavy sigh, he toyed with the spike of metal in his fingertips, worked diligently from the cot frame, sharpened to a point against the stone itself.

He did deserve the godless death that would find him.

He would never be burned on the pyre—the pyre that had been his one comfort, once, because at least his soul would find its place among the stars—but anymore, it was doomed to rot, cold and alone beneath the dirt.

Even if he'd succeeded, he would have deserved this.

Even if he'd managed to rip the magic from the descendant of Death, as he had believed was possible, if he'd managed to gift his warriors with power over dying, if he'd managed to summon Death herself to fight for them, as the Master had claimed...

There was a price to pay.

Such magics did not come without a consequence.

The metal spike clattered gently against the stone floor as Augustus set it down, picking up the graphite nub instead.

Fletcher.

She's using. She told me herself, and I see it, in her reddened eyes.

Stop her. Help her.
Please.

    -A.

He folded the sheet of parchment neatly up, and rising, set it on the small ledge where they deposited his food twice a day. The guard would retrieve it in the morning.

Then, returning to his place on the floor, he picked up the spike.

Rolling up his sleeves, he ran his fingers across the scars that ran elbow to wrist, evidence of his capture just over a year ago. Matching scars graced his thighs, though only Isa had ever seen those.

Isa.

He had not deserved them. With every punch they threw, every blow they gave, he knew.

The enormity of their love was best given to another.

It had been better to take the pain than admit that he wasn't capable of reciprocating such kindness.

"Gods below, hear my prayer." His voice was a whisper in the night. "Cora, cross our threads. Lucia, foment this chaos, I beseech you. Stell, take my icy heart, take it, Hadri, let me give her the starlight that I will never see." Tears were welling in his eyes as he said the words, fumbling through a prayer of his own making. "Gods above, hear my prayer. Kiran, she is the light, surely you must recognize this, Ignata, your fire can release the soul, and you—you must release mine, to protect her, Natali, you are order, and you must see to it that she has a future, Asa...heal us all." Saltwater trenches burned hot on his cheeks. "I am no longer my own. And I know that this is meaningless, I know that, but..."

Augustus gave a quick exhale, bracing himself.

The spike nicked through the palm of his hand, the too-blunt tip painful as it tore across the skin.

"This is mine." He clenched his fist welling with blood. "This is all of me. They tried to tear it away, and I have fought with every ounce of strength I have to defend it. But the gods willed it away. And so, this must be their will." With his other hand, he drew a swirling figure on the stone. Her given name did not translate into the Dradan characters, and so, he'd written one of their own figures to invoke her, *elle*. The moniker of a friend.

He placed his bloody palm over the letter, and closed his eyes. "Elizabeth Faulise, my soul belongs to you. Thus, this vow of fealty. My days are numbered and marked as yours." His voice broke. "Loyalty before amity. My soul is yours."

There was a sharp pull in his chest, knocking the wind from him—and with it, a trembling thread, white and shining. It twisted around, a gentle warmth filling the cell. Augustus's eyes were wide, terror overtaking him as he rose on shaking legs. These cells were encapsulated by iaculic grating that drank up the elven magic just enough to immobilize their hostages, and his magic, it seemed, had been called to war with the force keeping him at bay. His body began to ache, vision tunneling, for the bloody rune on the floor had drawn forth a deep magic. He could feel the grating, the wretched grating and the magic iaculic, trying to tear it away from him, he could feel his own soul lurching, reacting in turn, delving deep to draw forth every mote of magic it could summon, and in a burning wave of discomfort, he fell to his knees, slumping to the stone, unconsciousness at last winning out.

SAM

"We love those of questionable moral standing not because we're unaware of their misdeeds, but rather, because we hope.

We hope we're wrong.

We hope, in the end, they will rally, and prove us right."

~Mariann Bell

Darkness shrouded the velvet parlor, the dim lamp barely reaching the wallpapered corners as Sam sat, stewing in the wingback chair. Too tired to rise, too angry to go to bed, he'd found what little peace he could here. The parlor was meant to be filled with cigarette smoke and whiskey—a breeding ground for brooding if there ever was one.

"It's late." Mattie's voice preceded the man himself, his features set into relief as he leaned against the doorframe.

Sam spared him a single glance. "What of it?"

Mattie only sighed. "Walk with me for a bit."

At the invitation, Sam found the strength to rise, following Matt through the winding corridors of the manor out to one of the garden doors. Things had changed. *Matt* had changed. They'd managed to grow up, and this grief...Teddy simply didn't understand. He couldn't—he wasn't a merchant.

The life of wards and secrets and scandals was, to Teddy, nothing more than a column in the social pages in tomorrow's paper. To Sam, it was his life, whether he wanted it to be or not.

The winter night was frigid, the moon only a scythe above them as they met the overwintered garden.

And Clark was buried in the frozen earth.

The sight of Commissioner Johannsen's body was still burned in the back of Sam's eyelids, the bright red blood all he could see.

"I can hardly believe it." Sam's voice was soft, his breath frosting on the chilled air as they walked past the deadened shrubs. "Johannsen..."

Mattie sighed. "Poor bastard." His looked at Sam askance. "It was in bad taste, doing that. None of us pretend blood is never spilled, but that? I—I have so much anger, Sam," he hissed, "it wasn't right—"

"No! It wasn't! I saw her pull that blade, and I was just—I was in disbelief," Sam gushed, eyes tearing, "Matt, he deserved better than that!"

"Clark? Or Johannsen?"

"Both! I don't understand why she must be this way, and—skies, it's one more thing." Sam paused, glancing back towards the manor, up to the second landing. Somewhere, beyond the glass and stone, Teddy was waiting. "And now," he said quietly, "now, I've got a husband up there, distraught at what a display the burial turned into, furious that I'm here at all, that I'm grieving..." He trailed off, looking back to Matt, feeling guilty. To complain about his husband to an ex-fiancé felt too close to a betrayal.

"And I've a wife with blood on her hands." Matt pursed his lips. "Do you—well, you'll pardon the question, but do you ever wonder what would've become of us, if we'd...gone on with it?"

"With what, the engagement? Matt, I—I spent years wondering." Sam let out a bitter laugh, shaking his head. "I loved you, you know. I could picture our life together. Still can, if I'm being honest." His gaze lingered on Matt, heart aching ruefully.

"I know that today never would've happened, if you were standing in her place." Matt bunched his mouth to the side, quizzical. "I find it hard to believe that Theodore is so unsympathetic."

"It's not that he's unsympathetic, he's...he's just not one of us.

"There's much he doesn't understand about what it means to be rich and famous. There's expectations to it, expectations that aren't so easily cast aside. It's always easy to be moral when you're poor, that's what my late father used to say, rest his soul."

"That's precisely it," Sam said quietly. He felt a sense of calm starting to wrap around his anger with Matt's validation. It had been so difficult for his complaints to find purchase in Caelaymnis—how could they? Everyone there was on Teddy's side. They only saw the quiet Healer trying to reason with his emotional, out-of-touch boyfriend; they didn't see the unworldly husband failing to keep pace with the complexities of an ex-merchant.

"You'll forgive the suggestion," Matt said quietly, giving him a small nudge, "but do you think you've perhaps made a bit of a mistake?"

"That's unfair."

"That's not a no."

The rosebushes about them were dormant in the winter's chill. Come spring, they'd be a fine display, but the sight now was more than a bit depressing. Rubbing his hands together, Sam gave an exasperated sigh. "It's cold, Matt. Why're we out here?"

The velvety night seemed to wrap around them both, everything a wash of silken navy and stars, and Matt put a hand on Sam's arm, his touch warm against the chill. "I'm sorry. I did what I had to do to survive."

"I think we both wish that were true," Sam said quietly.

Matt gestured ahead down the garden path, towards the carriage house glowing some ways beyond. "I could use a whiskey—the good stuff Clark was hiding in his desk, not that swill Cele set out for the wake. Join me."

An echo of a smile tugged at Sam's lips as he nodded, following Matt as he wound his way towards the carriage house. It was warmly lit, reeking of excess and familiarity.

Just before the door of the carriage house, though, Matt paused suddenly. His eyes were twinkling, meeting Sam's, the two of them pressed close to the door in the abruptness of the gesture. "I wonder," Matt said quietly, "if you would permit me one favor. For old time's sake."

"What is it?"

And leaning in, Matt kissed him, lips lingering for one long, sweet moment.

Time stopped, for Sam, for that soft kiss made his heart melt, stirring within him affection he'd thought had long-since died. But of course, the rest came crashing into him soon enough, for his affection condemned him.

Guilt was rising, hot and uncomfortable, growing each second he didn't pull back from Matt. Disgust bit viciously at him, feeding on the guilt, urging him to stay locked in embrace, for he could hardly deny how good it felt—and the longer he stayed like this, Matt pressed against him, the more he saw how deeply unworthy he was.

Not of Matt. Never of Matt.

Of the man upstairs in the manor, waiting for him.

The kiss was something else, now. It was all the ways he'd failed Teddy, laid out in a single gesture. It was every moment of anger Sam had felt towards his husband, every harsh word, every second he wished he could simply be alone, and to break the kiss presupposed that Sam was entitled to go back after such indiscretions. Theodore Mirabeau deserved more than a faithless man, savoring kisses with an ex-fiancé in the carriage house doorway.

It was Matt, who withdrew. Wordlessly, he pushed the carriage house door open, waiting for Sam to follow.

If I were to go back to the manor, what would I even say? What would I do? How could I look my husband in the eyes, knowing what has just transpired between Matt and I? It is his worst fear, manifest. It would shatter him entirely.

Dejected, Sam stepped across the threshold, and Matt closed the door gently behind him. "You look sad."

"I am." Sam's brow was knit, his voice hardly a whisper. "I am desperately sad. I loathe who I am, and though I have tried so very hard to love myself the way my husband does, I cannot seem to." He closed his eyes, tears pressing onto his cheeks. "He would be better if I departed this world. I think it often, of late. I rebuke his comfort, I try his patience, I bring him here, and I..." He blinked, the carriage house watery before his eyes. "Despite his comfort, I have complained of him, selfishly, angrily complained, only to accept your gesture of affection with more pleasure than I ever wanted to admit? What have I done, Matt?" His shoulders were shaking, stomach clenching with nausea.

It wasn't just the kiss, sending him reeling. It was this place.

The carriage house was too full of memories.

Matt pulled a cigarette case from his jacket, giving him a look of sympathy. "Breathe, Sam. Here—have a smoke. Steady your nerves, a bit."

Conflict gnashed at Sam's heart, watching as Matt withdrew a slender roll. "Teddy hates it—"

"You've got to do what you must, Sam. There's no shame in that."

The paper of the cigarette caught on Sam's lips, phosphorus on the air as Matt held a match to the end. "Easy, now."

The ways I disappoint my husband never cease. Sam took a drag, hating how right Matt was, for as he exhaled, he could feel his heart begin to steady.

"Do you really mean that, Sam?" Matt moved for the bar, watching him with curiosity.

Sinking down on to the smooth leather sofa, cigarette still in his shaking fingers, Sam tried to dry his tears, willing them to stop. "I dunno. Maybe."

"You don't really think he'd be better off without you?"

"I think I might die of heartbreak if we parted ways," Sam breathed, "but yes. I think he'd be better off."

"If that is truly how you feel, you'd be sensible to do just that."

Sam was at a loss for words, their conversation taking a dark turn. "I—I'm too much of a coward to leave," he whispered. Death was frighteningly permanent, and painful, if it went wrong.

"We shared a kiss, Sam. That didn't mean nothing. How are you going to explain that to him? That you kissed me?"

"Matt, you misunderstand—"

"You talk so passionately of what could've been! If not to yourself, then you...you owe it to me to find out," Matt pressed. "Cut ties. Come with me, back to the Capital. Let us play out what I've thought endlessly on—"

"How dare you suggest that I cut ribbons with Teddy?" Sam asked, frustration overtaking the disconcertion stewing in his chest. *So much for being understood.*

"It is hardly my place to say—"

"It is not your place at all! When I told you I thought he'd be better off, Matt, I meant that sometimes, everything felt so wretched I just wanted to die! And forgive me, but how is it that I owe *you* anything?" He rose, glaring, suddenly alert. The hairs on the back of his neck were rising, an uneasy feeling overtaking all else.

"I—you said—"

147

Sam flicked his cigarette in the fire, scowling as he turned for the door. "I said much, none of which you seemed to understand! It was a mistake, Matt, thinking I could be friends with you. Thinking that you'd ever be any different." He stopped, fingers on the door handle, glancing back. "And one more thing—we didn't share a kiss! You asked me for a favor, you didn't—didn't even say what it was—"

"And would you have said no, if I had?" Matt was watching him, brown eyes warm in the firelight.

"Eat dirt, Matt. Eat dirt and grow up. You're not seventeen anymore, these games aren't clever. They're just stupid." Sam threw open the door to the carriage house—

A man with flaming red hair was blocking his path, though, leaning against the brick just beyond the doorway. His intricately embroidered vest atop his bare chest was nothing if not gauche, his high-waisted trousers dated and loose, and he grinned, coming face-to-face with Sam. "Going somewhere?"

"Matt!" Sam's heart was pounding, his head starting to feel somewhat dizzy. "What's the meaning of this? Mercs?"

"I asked you," Matt said quietly. "I asked you if you wondered what it would've been like if we'd gone ahead with the engagement. I asked, because I've wondered. I've spent every gods-damned day since wondering what could've been. And now, we're going to find out."

A cold laugh behind them made Sam start.

A rather harried woman with a manically wide smile was leaning against the wall, her hair wild, streaked with white, her charcoal skirts ripped and ruined. She pushed herself off the back wall of the carriage house, deeply amused. "Oh," the woman breathed, meeting Sam with deep, wide eyes. "Oh, he looks just like Kiran."

No.

No, the last thing he wanted thrown about were the names of the gods, not in these times, not with the bloody hunt afoot for their heirs—

Sam took a breath, trying to steady himself. It did little good, though—panic was setting in. He'd been cornered again and again in this damnable carriage house, and right now, there was no way to extricate himself. *It's just Matt. He's jealous and probably drunk.*

"He *does* look like Kiran," the man put in, at last giving up his post at the door, closing it as he came inside. "He's got the eyes. And the build. Delicate, but still muscular—though Kiran might be taller. I remember him taller." The man glanced to Matt. "We'll make him bleed, alright."

"He shares a resemblance, then. I always wondered," Mattie breathed. He looked nervous, circling them all, shooing the two away to get a look at Sam, like he'd never really looked at him before.

"I don't look like Kiran." Sam swallowed hard, mind racing. "Don't even say such things—not in these times—Matt, this isn't funny. Whatever you're upset about, we can work it out..." His eyes locked on Mattie's, desperate. "What do you want? Just tell me, Matt. I..." He trailed off, steeling himself. *No matter the cost, I must get out of here. No matter how high, I can pay the price, as long as it means that I get out. I can deal with it later, but to do that, there has to be a later.* "Matt, I'll do anything. Tell me what you want," he breathed, voice low.

"I told you what I want. Come with me to the Capital. Let me show you how things would've been—"

"I'm not leaving, Matt. Just tell me—here, now, in the carriage house, what it is you want from me." Sam forced his voice to be steady, forced some degree of composure over himself, forced himself to believe it'd be alright if he just stood firm.

"I want things as they should have been—"

"I don't love you, Matt!" Sam's voice echoed in the carriage house, anger overtaking him. "We're not playing hypotheticals—"

"I don't need your love, I'm not after your love, I couldn't care *less* about your love," Matt snarled, taking a step forward. "Clark knew who you were. And the moment he realized I knew, too, he pushed you out of my reach, because he knew I'd do whatever was necessary. I knew, even then, that you were dangerous. Having the son of Kiran, God of Life in our house was not something I would've stood for then, and I don't stand for it now, so when I say, *Sam,* that I am going to show you how things ought to have been, I mean that I will let these *gods* drag you back to some pitiful basement where you can finally be out of our way! When I say that I want things as they should have been, I mean that it has always been you or Aerdela, and I will not risk the Guild! Not when giving up one man can save all. Even—especially—if that man is you."

Quiet filled the carriage house, Matt's words still ringing in Sam's ears.

The prospect of Mattie's love had always tormented him, confused him—but his malice always had clarity.

"You expect me to believe you knew," Sam breathed, anger getting the better of him. "You expect me to think that you figured it all out? That I—I'm the son of a god? I'm no one, don't you get it?"

"Perhaps. But it's a gamble I have to take," Matt whispered, brow knitting.

Tears pricked at Sam's eyes as he gave a bitter laugh. "So, that's the game, then. You're making deals with the Master, thinking it's going to protect Aerdela. Why bother with your games, then? Because that's all it was, wasn't it? I thought I was confessing to a friend, I thought you cared for me—but of course, that isn't true. Why bother, then?" Hopelessness was sinking in, horrid and heavy. "Take me now, if it's so important! That's what they did with Elsie, isn't it? Ambush me! Have your so-called gods seize me this very minute! Why your game about cutting ribbons? Even you, Matt, wouldn't be so cruel."

On the precipice of ruin, and still, Sam couldn't help but cling to straws.

What he does, he does of love. A lie he told himself many times, and nothing would've made him happier than to hear such an utterance tonight. It was better to be hurt by love than harmed by malice, for at least in love, there was hope of better days.

Matt considered Sam's questions, pacing back and forth. "It's curious, you call it a game. I call it...adumbration."

"What?" Sam hissed the word, thoughts whirling.

"The truth is, Sam? You *are* going to leave him. That's always been the plan." Matt pursed his lips in resignation. "I can't have anyone asking questions about where you've gone, or what our dealings with the Master are. There's been enough inquiries. The last thing we want is anyone crawling around, sniffing out trouble."

Sam's shoulders sank, the word *no* poised on his lips. But protestation would get him nowhere.

He'd lost the game the moment he'd followed Matt into the garden. Before that, even—the moment they'd embraced in the foyer. The moment he'd proposed, all those years ago, the moment he'd fallen for the Fieldson boy, the moment they'd met, the *moment they'd met,* he'd been damned.

Matt was moving his playthings across the stage, just like always, indulging dramatics and flights of fancy, having his fun at the expense of others. And Sam had been a fool to think that for one moment, Matt would've made him the exception to this.

The son of a god.

He hardly felt divine, standing there, trapped.

Above everything else, he felt helpless, helpless and used. Not once, had Clark thought that the truth would serve better than a lie—not once, had Mattie felt it prudent to share what he knew. Not once had anyone stopped to consider what might be best for Sam—anyone, that was, except for Teddy.

Teddy, who I feel I have betrayed so deeply tonight. Teddy, who deserves better.

But that had rather been Matt's point, hadn't it? To illustrate to Sam the breadth of his love? He hadn't misunderstood Sam, that much was apparent—Sam said that sometimes, he felt such a burden on those he loved that he wished to die, and Matt was prepared to grant such a wish.

"I fancy a little wager," Mattie said quietly, shoving his hands in his pockets. "I bet that you *are* going to leave your husband tonight. I bet that you're going to walk right up to your suite where he's waiting for you, and tell him that it's over—and you're going to do it so sincerely that there's no doubt in his mind you're telling the truth. And I bet," he pressed, voice dropping as he took another step towards Sam, "I bet that you're not going to say a damn word to him about anything that's happened here tonight. I bet that you're not going to tip him off, or give him cause for concern, or send him to get help, and if I lose? He'll die. They all will. Ignata and Lucia will make sure of that." He gestured to the man, who spread his fingers, fire rising between them.

Three little figures danced in fire, recognizable even in flame.

Elsie twirled, collapsing into a burst of fire, and Ignata laughed. Teddy's head popped off, his body crumpling into flame. Fletcher's body shook with arrow shots, falling—

Sam's eyes flicked to Mattie.

As there was an inescapability to Matt's betrayal, so too there was inevitability about Sam's choice.

From the moment he'd tied ribbon with Teddy over the sink in their apartment, from the moment he'd confessed his love, from the moment Teddy had offered to kiss him in the meadow, from the moment he'd seen that gorgeous man standing at the general store counter, his blue dress making his eyes shine fierce, his hair wrapped in a crown of braids atop his head, before he himself had known he was the boy Sam was going to love until the end of the world, it'd been written.

Never, Sam thought, never would it be said that he put himself above those he loved. Never let it be said that he thought he was worth more than Teddy or Elsie or Fletcher, any of them, for he'd sooner break their hearts than let his own fear and ego lead them to their deaths.

"Fine." Sam breathed the words, the surrender painful all the same. Tears carved his face like a red-hot knife. But he'd have courage. For the ones he loved, he'd have courage. "Fine, Matt. You win."

TEDDY

*"Darling, it is never as simple as an errant fancy
here, a lustuous glance there. The heart is too often a
battlefield, and we ourselves are the victims, if we're not
careful."*

~Matthew Fieldson

Sam's manor bedroom was chilled, no one having bothered to strike a fire in the fireplace.

After the abysmal display at Clark's funeral, Teddy had washed himself with a towelette over the sink before drawing a full bath in the oversized tub of Sam's suite. He could hardly stand the thought of stewing in someone else's blood—yet, to a degree, it was unavoidable, for it had become sticky and oxidized beneath his fingernails, not to mention the splotches he kept finding from where it's soaked through his suit.

Needless to say, fresh clothes and skin scrubbed raw had been welcome, after that.

His plan was to go down to the kitchens and find a bite to eat, maybe some tea, and bring it upstairs. But Teddy had lost himself in thought, curled in the armchair near the darkened hearth. It was unwise, probably, to lock himself away in the cold, forgotten room, surrounded by memories that belong to someone else—to a Sam that Teddy hardly knew at all, he realized. The books on the shelf, some tawdry, others elevated and in Old Vernacular; the art hanging on the wall, oil paintings of horses and sailboats—did Sam even like sailing? He must've, for several miniatures sat on the mantle, but he'd never said a word about it to Teddy. The dusty cabinet of liquors and tablets and opium—Sam must've indulged as much as any other merchant, but he'd given the impression of a man who was as clean as a whistle in his years with Teddy, save for his cigarette habit. They were nasty things, Teddy thought bitterly, looking at the silver case left on one of the side-tables. He'd probably have to tolerate a night of stale smoke, too, for there'd be no question Sam would want to sit by the fire, chain-smoking the rolls until dawn.

Sam had lingered at the burial long after Johanssen's body had been dragged off, long after Clark had been entombed in the earth, long after everyone else had left, and Teddy couldn't stand it anymore.

He'd done what he could. It was on Sam, now, to deal with his grief.

At last, the door to the bedroom clicked open, and Sam appeared, eyes red.

He'd been crying.

Teddy pursed his lips, letting out an exhale of exasperation as he rose. "Oh, Sam."

"Can—can we talk about all this?" Sam's voice was shaky as he came to sit on the sofa, gesturing Teddy back into the armchair.

"Sure," Teddy said hesitantly, sinking back down, "only, I was about to grab some food—maybe we should have a bite? You don't have to talk about any of this, Sam, just give yourself a chance to rest—"

Sam winced. "You haven't eaten dinner yet?"

"No. I—I meant to, just...lost track of time."

"Teddy." Sam pinched the bridge of his nose, looking pained. "For fuck's sake—please, I've reminded you a thousand times, you mustn't forget—"

"—to eat something, I know," Teddy frowned, annoyed, "that's why I was about to...what's going on with you? You're being strange."

155

Sam made a sound of frustration, glancing about the room, like he was trying to gather his thoughts. "No one lit the fire, either? I'll—I'll say something to Cele about it on my way—"

"Sam!"

His reddened eyes flicked to Teddy. Wordlessly, he reached inside his jacket, withdrawing the chain with his golden wedding band. His lips were drawn into a line as he set it on the coffee table before them.

"You're fucking kidding me." Teddy grabbed the chain, scowling. "You are *not* doing this. We can talk about this tomorrow—or next week—"

"Teddy. I don't have a choice." Sam's voice was low as he rose to leave. "I'm sorry—"

"Sit down!"

Sam fell back to the sofa, hands shaking. "I need to end this. I have to, Teddy. I'm so sorry that I dragged you along. It wasn't fair to you—"

"No, what's not fair is that you're—what, exactly?" Teddy's gaze pierced Sam as he dared him to say the words aloud.

"I'm leaving you."

"Like hell you are—"

"Teddy." Sam glanced up, tears in his eyes. "I mean it. I'm not playing around. This isn't me, being a way about it. I just can't, anymore."

Unease was filling Teddy's chest, adrenaline making his lungs constrict until his voice was a whisper. "You're leaving."

Sam nodded.

"Why?"

"Because if I don't, it's going to be the death of us."

"I don't want poetics, Sam, I want answers!" Teddy snapped, tears threatening as he rose abruptly. "You—you come back, you tell me you're ending us? Can't—can't whatever this is this wait until morning? Please—"

156

"It can't, I—I can't—"

"So, you're going to—what, exactly? Go find some guest room, go pout for a few days, and then what? You can't just ditch me when it gets hard and then expect to reconcile once you're finally feeling better—"

"That's not it, Teddy!" Sam was on his feet, face red, voice sharp. "I mean it! Asking you to marry me was not something I did lightly—why would it be any different, ending it?" His cheeks were streaked with tears as he took a step back. "When I say we're through, I mean it."

Teddy wrapped his arms around his middle, the Thread burning, the unfeeling mountain of dissociation inside looming, his heart twisting and squirming amid the fire and the stone. "Please don't." There were tears on his cheeks, his chest tight. "Please just—if you need some time, take it, Sam. But please don't mean it."

"Trust me, Theodore. I wish I wasn't. I wish I had some other choice," Sam breathed, "but I don't. There's no future together—for either of us. It's never been plainer than is now."

"I don't understand—"

"I..." Sam swallowed, tears on his cheeks again as he closed his eyes. "I am a merchant. And you are not. And we both deserve better."

"It's a class thing?" Teddy watched him, incredulous.

"No—I mean, yes, but not entirely—"

"I've been a good husband." Teddy took a step towards him, gesturing at himself tearfully. "I know I have been—and you have been too—except for this, Sam, this is cruel—"

"I'm not trying to be cruel! I'm trying to say that we need to part ways! Teddy, Matt kissed me." Sam was watching him, cinnamon eyes pained.

"He kissed—oh gods. It—that's why? That's why you...it's him. It's always him." Reeling, Teddy tried to steady himself, anxiety making his knees weak. "It was always him—"

"It's not." Sam threw his hands up in resignation. "Believe me, it's not. But it—it only affirmed the feelings I've been having. That I've got to go."

Teddy watched him through saltwater streams. "Do you love him?"

Sam shook his head.

"But you're still leaving me."

"Yes," Sam breathed.

"Honestly? You're really, truly going? Our marriage is over, we can't—we can't be together, there's no apartment, no family, no future, nothing at all?"

"I am really, truly going, Theodore." Sam wiped his cheeks with the back of his hand, shaking his head. "It's what's best for both of us. We—we had a good run, you and I. For the rest of my days, I will look back on our time with such fondness. But look at us. Look at how awful this has all been. And it's only going to get worse," Sam pressed, voice resentful. "Clark's gone. I—I can't be with you, anymore. That's just how it has to be."

Teddy couldn't breathe. The world was caving in around him, and there was no solid ground to stand on. He was on his knees, trying desperately to fight back the waves of panic that threatened to overtake him.

Sam was crouched in front of him, eyes flooding. "Teddy. Teddy, please. I can't stay. I wish this had worked out, you have to know that. I wish that us staying together wasn't—wasn't..." His voice was choked off, and his face crumpled. With deft care, his hand was on Teddy's cheek.

And more than anything, Teddy wanted to scream.

To fight.

To make Sam stay, because they were meant to be. Weren't they? Hadn't they spent years falling in love, hadn't they confessed their hurts and their affections, hadn't they healed and mended and started anew?

But he was frozen, shoulders shaking, face hot, tears carving canyons into his skin, fingers clawing at his arms. He didn't know anything, not truth, not affection, not his own name. Perhaps the room was spinning, if he could see anything beyond cinnamon eyes before him.

Over.

It was over.

Years of anxiety—years of jealousy—and he'd been right.

It wasn't meant to last.

"Teddy." Sam's hand was still cradling his cheek, his voice low. "Teddy, I know you're panicking right now. And I'm sorry," he whispered, face wrinkled in pain, "I'm so sorry. I can't pick you up this time. But I need you to listen to me."

There was no sound in all the world save for the blood, pounding in his own skull.

"Please don't go." Teddy let his head rest gently against Sam's, shoulders shaking. "Sam, please—wait until morning. Wait with me until then—"

"I'm sorry, Teddy." Sam was crying, too.

"Just a few hours—"

"That's not how it works, when people part ways." It was Sam who was begging now, Sam who let his head fall into the crook of Teddy's neck as Teddy held him tight. "You must let me go—"

"I won't." Teddy breathed the words as he clung to him, unable—unwilling—to let him rise. "Stay, please!"

Sam pulled back to look Teddy in the eyes. "I cannot. Teddy, whatever future we have together would be short and painful, and you don't deserve that."

"And what if I want that?"

"I don't!"

"Just give me an hour," Teddy pleaded, desperate. "Talk to me—"

"I can't, Teddy. I have to go."

Terror, lonely and oppressive, sat heavy against him, making it difficult to catch his breath, tears following unceasingly. "And there's nothing I can say or do to change your mind," Teddy pressed, trembling on the precipice of total loss.

Sam shook his head.

Panic roared in Teddy's ears. The room was spinning. Every passing second felt intolerable, the pain physical as he was forced through the moments.

Teddy, listen."

His eyes locked on Sam's at the command, not wanting to obey.

But nine years of trust and love compelled him to, anyway.

"Do not come after me." Sam's hand was holding fast, his voice hoarse. "Don't. This is over, okay? This is the end of the road. Theodore, I love you so much. And this is breaking my heart. But you have a long life ahead of you, and..." He broke off, fighting back tears that scarred his cheeks anyway. "And I need you to live that life, okay?"

Teddy couldn't breathe.

Sam's hand on his cheek was the only thing holding him up, and when it vanished, he would crumple.

His skin was aflame.

I am a mountain.

I am a mountain.

I am a mountain.

"I love you, Teddy." Sam let go, making to rise. "I will *always* love you, Teddy, please understand that."

But mountains knew neither love nor grief.

Sam was gone.

And the mountains did not care.

160

Teddy couldn't say how long he'd lain crumpled on the floor, ribs aching as he cried.

But he knew that Sam didn't come back.

Morning broke, and Sam didn't come back.

Eventually, he'd found the strength to rise, more or less. He'd dragged himself into bed, only to dissolve into tears again, Sam's wedding ring still clutched in his fist.

And Sam didn't come back.

He convinced himself that by lunch, Sam would come to apologize. He didn't. Then, it was by dinner—surely by dinner, Sam would be back—but of course, he hadn't.

Trays of food were brought to Sam's room for Teddy, and resentfully, Teddy replayed Sam's words each time he forced himself to pick through the offerings. *Please, I've reminded you a thousand times, you can't forget to eat,* and Teddy told himself that by tomorrow, Sam would be back. He just had to get through to tomorrow.

But tomorrow became the next day, and the day after that, and eventually, there'd been a light knock on the door of Sam's suite, and Cele Carson let herself in.

Her lilac gown was at odds with her dark expression, Teddy thought, the color too light for such depressing times. Sam could enlighten him on what would be appropriate—he'd ask when he returned.

"Theodore." Cele's voice was soft as she closed the door behind him.

He forced himself to sit from where he'd been curled in bed, eyes red and pained, his cheeks raw from trying to blot the salt water away these past days. He tried to smooth down his mussed hair, tried to summon some degree of composure, just in case. "Is Sam back?"

"No. Teddy, he...isn't coming back." Cele's expression was oddly sympathetic, her voice gentle. "Honey, he's gone."

Teddy laid back down, eyes distant. It felt impossible. But the new wave of grief coming over him said otherwise.

He was drowning.

"I can't imagine how difficult this must be." The bed gave, Cele sinking down beside him. "You are welcome to stay as long as you need."

"Here," Teddy breathed, "in this house of murderers—"

"Here, in this house where I protect the ones that matter," Cele corrected. "Though I am sorry you had to see that. You're a good man. You shouldn't be dragged into our messes." She took his hand, giving it a squeeze. "For what it is worth, I have purchased the lease to your apartment and forgiven the debt. I am aware that Sam had more funds than you, and that alone, you are not able to maintain the rent."

Teddy pushed himself up on his elbow. "Cele, you didn't have to do that—"

"I did." She rose, withdrawing an envelope from her deep skirt pockets, placing it on the nightstand. "He was an ass, leaving you with no plans."

So it was, then. Sam was really gone.

"Mr. Alderton?" Chim was peering through the door, waiting in the hall. "Can I come in now?"

"I'll leave you to it." Cele rose, giving him a small nod. "This is a conversation I need not be privy to."

The door clicked shut behind Cele as she left, and Teddy swallowed, beckoning Chim forward. "Hey. C'mere." She obliged, and he drew her onto his lap, giving her a tight hug. She was not their child—not close, having a good number of years on both of them—but just as she swore to guard their hearth, they'd promised to provide for her.

"What happened?" Even now, she was fidgeting, eyes darting about the room.

162

"Sam, um…left." The words were a searing knife through his gut. Even still, he could hardly believe the words. "He's gotta move on to some other stuff, now."

Chim stilled, eyes snapping back to him. "When is he coming back?"

"Never, I don't think."

"He…decided he didn't want the hearth anymore?"

"That's what it sounded like." Tears were welling in his eyes again. "I'm so sorry."

Chim's face crumped, shoulders starting to shake. "No!" Her face was red, cheeks wet as she screamed, "No, no, he can't! Those aren't the rules, that's not fair! It's not fair, not fair!" Her small arms clung tight to Teddy as she buried her face into his shoulder, crying. "Tell him to come back! Tell him—"

Cradling her, he just shook his head, eyes burning.

"I'll find him, I'll…" She pulled back, gaze locking on Teddy, and her inky eyes were distant as a look of horror passed across her face. "Why can't I find him? Where are the lines of chaos to follow? Where are the threads? *Why?*"

"He said to let him go."

Chim dissolved into tears once more.

She'd taken their hearth. And one of the hearth had commanded her not to follow.

Perhaps in the back of Teddy's mind, some last drop of reasoning had latched onto the paradox.

But the profound sense of wrongness blended into the reality of grief that had fallen down around the last twenty-seven years.

It had been a long life.

And he was a mountain.

EZRA

"Bonds of blood will forever be our shackles. This is the curse of family."

~Proverb of the Padri Dragone

Ezra had intended to sneak down to the kitchens somewhere around two in the morning to get a snack, but his plans had been undermined by what sounded like a violent struggle happening in the servant's quarters, and being a man averse to conflict and terrified of pain, he had simply slunk back upstairs.

He'd decided to try and write to his sister instead.

It was really weird, realizing he wasn't alone in this world—and more than that, realizing that someone else had the same story as him. Elizabeth had been left with a family, and that family had, too, been the victim of Factionist vengeance, and they were both carrying royal blood in their veins—not to mention godly blood—and even though Anscip had called her horrible names, Ezra was very curious about her.

A whole mess of crumpled paper on the desk proved, however, that Ezra's good intentions were not easily translated to ink.

It was probably a mercy that a knock came on his door just as he'd crumpled his third sheet of paper.

"Ezra?" A muffled voice called out, apologetic.

"Come in." Ezra rose, face heating, painfully aware of the mess of paper he'd made.

The door cracked open, and the Master stepped in, plate of food in hand. It was piled high with cold cuts and slices of cheese and fruit and bread and he smiled warmly, closing the door behind him. "I saw you come downstairs. It looked like you were going for the kitchen?"

Ezra nodded, the red flush on his cheeks only deepening as he went to take the plate. He sank down onto the bed, cross-legged, and he'd thought it was probably polite to wait for the Master to leave, but the rumble of his stomach urged him to dig in.

To his surprise, the Master did not make to go.

He instead came to sit beside Ezra on the bed, and with a youthful grin, reached for one of the figs. "These are hard to get here even when the weather is good," he explained, tossing it once into the air and palming it before taking a bite.

"You—you didn't have to do this." Ezra was tearing off a hunk of bread, inhaling the yeasty warmth greedily.

"No, but I wanted to. The staff said that you didn't have dinner, either." The Master quirked an eyebrow, daring Ezra to argue.

"Can...I ask you something?"

The Master drew a handkerchief from his pocket, wiping the fig juice from his mouth. "Shoot."

"What's your *real* name," Ezra edged, fidgeting a bit.

The Master clicked his tongue. "Ezra. We don't know each other well enough for that." But his gaze lingered on Ezra all the same, cheeks flushing faintly pink. "I'm sorry. It's for safety. I want to trust you, Erza, I really do. But a lot of people want me dead. The gods, for one."

Erza nodded, thinking about this point. "You can, though. Trust me, that is." He'd thought a lot about this, lately. About who he could trust.

The Master said nothing. Only glanced over at the pile of crumpled balls on the writing desk. "Do you write, Ezra?"

"I...thought maybe I'd write to my sister."

"Oh." He considered this, looking thoughtful. "To what aim?"

Ezra shrugged, mouth full of cheese. "Dunno. Just...wanted to know more about her, I guess. We're in the same boat, her and I. At least, it sounds like it, after you told me about her."

The Master looked amused at this. He took a cracker from the plate, snapping it in two and began to nibble on one end. "You are not. Though if I could do this over again, I would have offered her the same as I have offered to you."

Ezra paused. "To live here?"

"Perhaps," the Master chuckled.

"You really won't tell me what your name is?"

"No. I won't."

Grinning, Ezra looked away. "It's silly to be so personable and have such a grandiose moniker."

"You don't think it adds an air of mysteriousness and elegance," the Master asked, and he was smiling brightly, voice playful.

"No, I think it's dumb," Erza laughed, picking at a piece of orange. His gaze flicked up to meet the Master's, soft brown eyes gazing right back at him. "It must be very lonely, thinking you're so important you can't even tell people your real name."

The Master's smile faltered. "It is. It is very lonely, Ezra. I...have not had such an authentically enjoyable conversation like this in a very long time. In my daily life, I pretend. I play the part of the dutiful husband. I try to honor my father's legacy. But at night, I *must* maintain a strict façade, for it is serious work, and...you see those who are drawn to this. They all have their own selfish aims."

"I would imagine so," Ezra said softly. "You...really control the gods?"

"Some of them." The Master shrugged, a mischievous smile on his lips. "You ever pray?"

Ezra looked away. "Not really."

"Why not?"

"I mean, who's even listening," Ezra laughed quietly, picking at the tray.

The Master's eyes were bright, his fingers brushing Ezra's arm. "I'm listening. Now, anyway."

"So if I were to pray, you'd hear me?" An incredulous smile was dancing at the corners of his mouth.

"I wish." The Master was snickering, cheeks flushed. "Truly, I wish, Ezra."

"But the gods...you could do something with that. Big things," Ezra nodded, catching the Master's point, even if he couldn't really hear prayers. "No more sitting on the sidelines. You're putting them to work, right?"

"You," the Master grinned, "are an exceptionally bright young man. That's precisely right." His smile faltered. "I used to pray. And...nobody listened. Nobody answered. What a terrible thing, Ezra. To have such power and to sit on the sidelines. What a waste. How could your life have been different, if you'd sat down to pray and someone answered?"

"Maybe Nan would be alive," Ezra said quietly, looking down.

"If I could bring the God of Death to heel, I could bring her back."

His eyes snapped up. "Really?"

"Absolutely." The Master crossed his legs, ankle on his knee, and he looked like a kid, planning something forbidden and exciting, leg bouncing. "I know I could. Course, it'll really be *you,* bringing her back, I'm just a conduit for it." His voice was hushed, excited. "The world is full of possibility. You are full of possibility."

His words made Ezra's heart feel a little wobbly.

Taking a bite of the orange, Ezra sank into his thoughts. He hardly dared to hope. Forget the sugary words he drank up like a starved humming bird. To see Nan again—to bring her back, and they could live here, comfortable...

And all the Master was asking for was a bit of blood. Blood, and Ezra

167

could keep his gold, could live safely, comfortably, could see his Nan again.

Ezra's eyes were misty as he began to shred his orange peel, the acidic tang of citrus making his tongue burn.

"Are you alright, Ezra?"

He nodded. "Yeah. I'm fine."

The Master moved, sliding off the bed. "I should go. I am intruding."

"No—"

"Yes. It is late. Eat, and enjoy the comforts of this house," the Master said softly. "We shall speak more on this another time." With that, he left, closing the door softly behind him on his way out.

And Ezra wished he hadn't gone.

He didn't want to be alone.

ELSIE

"We assume 'evil' means stupid, incompetent,
worthless—we forget, though, these are measured traits,
allotted precisely in those with dark hearts. Just enough
to wreak havoc; not too much so as to stay the forces of ill
will."

~Elizabeth Clement Faulise

Elsie's conversation with Augustus lingered like fireplace smoke on cold morning air, inescapable and inevitable. When they'd talked, he'd urged her to start with Clio, her source of dhacrym.

It was a simple matter, rifling through Fletcher's desk for the form when he'd slipped out that morning.

She'd make them pay, one by one, and it started with the man delivering dhacrym across the continent.

"You can't be serious," Clio hissed, eyes now fixed on the parchment.

Beneath them, great hunks of ice drifted lazily across the deceptively calm surface, idly bumping into each other as the current played them. They'd started to glisten and gleam in the mid-morning sun—not enough to melt, though. Just enough to become blindly slick.

"I have business with the Master," she said softly, trying to look bored. As if it was every day she conscripted the services of a blood magic connoisseur.

The Master had haunted her thoughts since her last visit to Augustus.

The unknown elements of him gave a fiery urgency to Elsie's actions. *If not the lard-haired man, then who? Why the secrecy, why stay hidden when he's capable of such terrible things? Why the discretion when he can seemingly bring anyone to task?*

She'd been surprised at Augustus. How quickly he folded. How almost-soft he was, when he was sober, devoid of the blood magic.

Elsie had quietly wondered which one of them was most insane. Whether it was her, in her dhacrym dreams, needing second eyes on everything that'd happened from the moment she'd been taken to confirm veracity amid the hallucinations. Whether it was Augustus, in his fervent belief that he had done his duty, done the right thing, even while pridefully admitting the wrongness of it all.

Between the two of them, though, there'd been a bit of truth.

This unsettled her.

Truth was supposed to live in other people. Better people.

Not people like them.

Not in books with broken spines, and not in the hands of page-rippers.

"I want a pardon, as well," Clio breathed, reaching for the paper.

Elsie snapped it back, raising an eyebrow. "I don't pay before delivery," she warned, voice low. "You take me to him. Then we'll talk about pardons."

Clio swallowed hard. "I don't know why you're so keen on the Master. If it's expertise you're after, you'd be better asking Lys—"

"I'm not after expertise, I'm after the Master."

His eyes were darting about the bridge, down to the ice, to the streets beyond, to the town taking refuge in their mid-morning prayers, and here she was, making deals with the ungodly at the advice of sinners.

Funny, how the world worked.

"He's in the south." Clio's eyes flicked to hers. "In the Capital. I have a runner leaving tomorrow, she will escort you."

Elsie scoffed. "And find myself at the mercy of your lackey? I think not. Where in the Capital?"

"I would not risk the Commander, nor a pardon, toying with you—regardless of how ill-conceived this plan is." Clio turned, gazing out across the city, folding his arms beneath the cloak.

"Ill-conceived?"

"You presume to seek justice against the Master?"

"That," she snapped, "is *no* business of yours."

"And what," he challenged, raising an eyebrow. "Do you hope to storm his facility? Seek some personal revenge? Your story sweeps the city, I do not believe you wish anything but a reckoning, naive—"

"You believe *wrong*." She was nearly nose-to-nose with him, now, finding the blade in her pocket. It gave a satisfying little *click* as she flicked it out, giving him a poke in the gut for good measure. "My business is my own. And if you value your future in this line of work, you will not question it. I have tolerated your continued existence, and if you prove useful, I may deign to keep you at my heel a while longer. But mark my words, I will not hesitate to cut you from this scheme if your compliance is compromised."

Augustus's words.

He'd made her repeat them back again and again and again, until her voice had stopped shaking, until all anger had been leeched away, until there had been nothing but a cold, steady flow of threats.

Made her.

Well.

He hadn't *made* her do anything.

She could've walked out, and that was something that had splintered its way into her mind.

That she didn't.

She could've, and she didn't, and that...maybe that was an ending.

The first one her broken-spine-book-of-a-self had really written, after him. And maybe it would've tasted sweeter, if he hadn't been a part of the ending at all.

He hadn't tried to stop her. Hadn't admonished her for the dhacrym. Hadn't looked at her with that pitiful expression of someone that *loved* her, of someone who was so blinded that they couldn't see the person behind the pain, and he'd asked if she was *alright*, but not because he thought she was broken or fractured or falling to pieces. He'd asked it like a fighter, seeing another felled.

Like he hadn't expected her to stay down for long.

"Look." Clio was starting to panic, eyes growing wide. "I don't know where he lives. Probably for reasons like this. My runner meets one of the lackeys, who still doesn't know, who meets one of the higher-ups in the ring—there's procedures in place, it's not like I have a—an address I can hand over, it isn't that easy—you don't think I know what's at stake, selling to the Commander's lover? You don't think I'd risk that lovely paper you've got there that gets me my Fitla back? You don't think I know better than to pull something—"

"You sure as hell thought you'd pull something when you tried to sell me swill," she snarled, edging the blade into his gut.

"A mistake, an honest mistake—had to make sure you know what you were doing—"

"Clio," she growled.

"I—I will guarantee your safety personally," he blubbered. "Please, just—Fitla, she didn't do anything, she deserves that pardon—"

She gave him an extra jab for good measure.

Funny, how sweet the cardinal sang, knowing how far there was to fall.

~ • ~

"Elsie." Fletcher's hands were braced on his desk, and it was occurring to her, watching him stand there in agitation, she'd never actually seen his office before. It hadn't even occurred to her that he *had* an office, here, in the Acadamae compound. He'd spent so much of his time just working at home, either beside her in bed while she had been recovering, or else downstairs where he could properly spread around the reports, and— *"Elsie."*

"Sorry," she breathed, eyes flicking up to his. The cold gray walls around them were draped in mountain tapestries, but there were no personal affects here, and maybe that was part of why it was so disorienting, thinking of this as his. It wasn't his space. Not really. "What did you say?" The exhilaration of wringing a way forward from Clio had made her giddy, her thoughts racing.

"How do you know you can trust him? If he's Augustus's lead—"

"And what if we can't? Worst case scenario, he's lying—"

"No, the worst-case scenario is that you end up dead," Fletcher said quietly, brow furrowed. "These are dangerous people—"

Elsie scoffed, crossing her arms. "You don't think I know that? You don't think I've seen that, first-hand?"

"That's not at all what I'm saying. I just...we need to be careful. Elsie, I know we need a way forward."

"We have to find where the Master has headquartered himself," she interjected, voice low. A nudge of guilt set her ill at ease, because these, too, were Augustus's words. But he wasn't wrong. "We must find this house. Everything rides on it. His operation here got dismantled, and he's spooked—"

"You're not wrong." Fletcher was coming around the desk, worried. "Elsie, I don't disagree, but—you kind of did all of this without me—"

"I *need* this." Irritation was rising. "I need to find him, and—and find answers, and find some closure—"

"El, what's going on?"

"What's going on, Fletcher, is that I am *not well.*" Even as she said it, she could taste the tang of iron on the back of her tongue, blood welling as her heart began to race. "I am hurt, I am tired, I am sick to *death* of not doing anything. You are all off doing things, important things, and the Master is still out there, doing this to other people just like me!"

He reached for her, but she took a breathless step back, glaring.

"We need to get to him," she whispered. "And I will do this with or without your help. If Clio is as unreliable as you say, then help me prepare for that. But don't tell me not to fight."

Fletcher was quiet for a moment. "How are you even going to get to the Capital, El?" His hazel eyes were searching her.

El's jaw clenched. Courtesy of the dhacrym, she was anchored to the earth, at least for the time being. Neither evanescing nor Risa's clever discs from the City could cut through the draught of fear. Maybe it was intentional on the part of the brewers, trapping their victims. Maybe it was simply incidental, a nice little treat for the barghests, making sure their fear-packed snacks couldn't run. But whatever the reason was, Elsie could no more leave Caelaymnis by magical means than she could cut a hole in the sky and step through the stars to get back to Aerdela.

The empty glass dhacrym vial stashed in a pile of undergarments at the back of the wardrobe wasn't helping matters, either.

She was supposed to be resting, giving the dhacrym time to clear itself from her system—which it wouldn't sufficiently do if she kept dosing herself.

The alternative would require her to confront an existence where she could neither argue with the imaginary ghosts of dhacrym dreams nor live in a constant state of anxiety, though, and she wasn't sure she knew how to do either—or that if she did manage to find some stability, that it would endure in any capacity.

Fletcher was watching her, waiting for an answer. "Elsie?"

"Try now," she breathed. Her words came out as a threat.

He wrinkled his nose in irritation, coming around the desk, and when he took her hand, it was not with the delicacy of affectionate touch. He gripped her tight, hand starting to shake, eyes closed, and a faintly shimmering mist began to edge around his boots, curling up around his legs, hugging his chest, making his hair whisper in an unseen breeze—

But there was simply nothing.

Elsie could feel the dead weight of herself. Could see how the tinges of Fletcher's golden magic avoided her, brushing against her skin only to recoil—

Fletcher dropped her hand, taking a step back to catch his breath. He slumped against the wall, gazing at her. "How are you going to get to the Capital, El." It'd turned from a question into a verdict.

"I'm getting better," she said quietly. She couldn't look at him any longer.

"Slowly." A pause. "Too slowly, El."

"It's going at the pace it's going."

"I'm worried for you, El. Maybe it's time to seek some other opinions. Risa could bring in a proper Healer, or we could get someone from Thallassas, or hell, maybe even Vaestias..." The concern in Fletcher's voice was going to drive her to tears.

"I'm going to be fine. It just takes time," she pushed back, voice low. "I was in there for weeks."

His sigh was heavy as he pushed himself off the wall. "I have to go."

Elsie glanced up, tucking a strand of hair behind her ear. "I'll see you at home?"

"Yeah." His eyes met hers. "Teddy and Sam back yet?"

Elsie shook her head.

"Risa?"

175

"Busy, I assume."

"Then go see Isa at least, please? And get some rest." He brushed a kiss against her cheek. "We've got to get you better."

Better. Whatever that even meant.

FLETCHER

"A liar, burdened with kernels of truth? Or an honest
man with burdensome sins? How does one differentiate
such things in the face of a world falling apart?"

~Fletcher Nist

The mountains had conspired with winter itself to plunge Caelaymnis
into storms of snow and ice, and if the grumbling on the street corners
were to be believed, upon Stell's promise the city of lights had not yet
seen a winter so bad.

Fletcher had no difficulty believing this, shuffling down the slick
compound steps. Glancing back, the rest of the city was obscured in
white, the occasional crack of lightning the only thing that broke the
darkening sky above.

Gods, below, have mercy.

The guard was waiting at their station, though this time, fiddling with
an envelope clearly authored from within one of the cells. "Commander
Nist." Their lips quirked to the side, envelope thrust out. "For you."

Fletcher swore under his breath, pinching off his frosted gloves.
"What's this?"

"From your brother." The guard gave a quick nod, a look of
apprehension in their eyes.

Scoffing, Fletcher tucked his gloves beneath his arm, and snatching
the letter, slit it open.

She's using. She told me herself, and I see it, in her reddened eyes.

Anger, cold and sharp, curled through Fletcher's chest, and the parchment dissolved into ash and ember in his fist. What a childish taunt, from the man who had himself given her the dhacrym that made her eyes go red and her nose bleed. How *dare* he place that blame on her.

The slips of singed parchment flitted to the ground in quiet wisps.

He had counted Elsie's heartbeats.

Blood had tinged the air, her quiet sobs lilting through the house, because she had been afraid. The dhacrym had brought everyone she loved before her in the cell, but they came as figments and fears, and Elsie said that all the love she'd ever gotten was a lie. All of the good times were a fiction written by a fool, because didn't he know, she'd screamed, didn't he know that life wasn't that kind.

She's using.

Gods damn that horrible man.

Would that his head roll on the senate floor.

"My sister," Fletcher growled. "Open her cell." Something about her insistence had wormed itself under his skin. *You let him take my crown,* she'd claimed, and the accusation rang in his ears long after he'd left her.

He *had*. He'd given up his inheritance, and what other option lay ahead if the Praequintelya family name was to continue?

But another thought had prickled up, a much darker one. Bowyer was in fine health, this—this was a problem of future decades, but there was an urgency to both Cormalum and Cam's insistence, one that deeply unsettled Fletcher.

"Your sister?" The guard looked nervously to the floor. "Ah, she...has been moved, did—my apologies, Commander Nist, you were not informed?"

Fletcher turned on his heel, glaring.

"Prince Cormalum—er, Prince Praequintelya, pardon me, felt it was unwise to keep her in such a, er, known location."

"A known—he thought it was unsafe for me to know her whereabouts," Fletcher hissed in disbelief. "Augustus—my brother, he—"

The guard bit their lip. "He's still here."

"What? What's that look for?"

"It's just...I asked the same, Commander, and Prince Praequintelya—he said that the sentence would be passed soon enough, that...well. In his own words. There isn't cause to spare Augustus from the wrath of his people, for his guilt is plain for all to see."

"Augustus...oh, Stell's ice."

Fury curled inside his chest, hot and conflicted, making his heart go pounding into his ears. Cormalum hadn't been suspicious of a jailbreak—he did not fear that the youngest Praequintelya daughter would subvert the watchful eye of the mystics in their high mountain village to claw away the bars as she'd done once before.

He feared his wife would face assassination before the hearing.

The newest Heir Apparent had, in a single stroke, delivered his own judgment. One of them was worth saving; the other was not.

What do I do.

What do I feel.

Two minutes before, hadn't he wished Augustus's head to roll?

Yes, yes he had, but in due course, not...not from neglect or the righteous anger of a single impulse of vigilante justice. But perhaps that was just posturing, because did it really matter, how life got taken? Really, there was no moral high ground, here, pretending like it was better if Augustus lost his head in the Senate chambers instead of getting a knife through the gut at the hands of an enemy, either Fletcher wanted vengeance for what his brother had done to Elsie or else he didn't, either he wanted blood or he didn't, and...

Fletcher brushed prickling tears from his eyes, staring at the floor, tracing the lines between the stones.

Perhaps I should seek the advice of the mystics.

In another life, he'd have asked Augustus, for all the wisdom that sack of shit could've given.

She's using.

The words tugged uncomfortably in the back of Fletcher's mind, and he turned for the stairs to leave.

He had been tasked with investigating, when he had been given his promotion to Commander.

And so, that was what he'd do.

In this mess of lies and schemes, he'd find the truth.

RISA

"Live the life of the rose. Bloom vivaciously, in the summer sun. Die away in the winter, for the cold deserves not your trust.

And make them bleed.

Gods, will you make them bleed."

~*Quinn Teleya, Founder of Caelaymnis*

The clatter of someone fussing about the kitchen roused Risa from uneasy sleep. Risa lay curled under her pink floral quilt, wedged up against the wall in her lumpy bed, her stiff body and raw eyes evidence that she had, in fact, cried herself to sleep once more. The curtains were drawn, though the light of mid-day filtered through the splits, and to be honest, it didn't really matter what day it was, anymore, whether it was morning or night, whether that woman had lingered a few hours or a few days, because time had no meaning, anymore.

Dragging herself to standing, Risa trudged out of her tiny bedroom, quilt trailing half on the ground behind her from where she'd wrapped it around her shoulders—or, tried to, in her groggy haze. Risa let herself flop onto the pale blue sofa, the springs pinching and groaning as she did so.

The kettle began to whistle with hollow shrieks, silenced only by the clank of Cora shifting it off the metal coils.

"How long've you been up," Risa asked dully, eyes fixed on the reddish wood floor.

Cora's soft steps and the gentle clatter of a cup placed on the side table followed. "A few hours." She sank down onto the sofa beside Risa. "Are...you hungry? You probably need some food, no?"

Risa glanced over, quiet. Cora's dark hair was pulled back, her green eyes deep with concern. The teal blouse must've been borrowed from Risa's own wardrobe, but she didn't recall having anything quite like that, though she must, for the alternative was...what, exactly? Cora, God of Death had been lingering about for days, and it seemed she'd brought a change of clothes. "Where'd you get that?"

"The...shirt?" Cora was watching Risa, expression unreadable. "I conjured it." Then, perhaps seeing the concern, she added, "It seemed rude to dig through your closet, though in a pinch, I would have." Carefully, she passed the cup of tea to Risa with a tiny smile.

"Why."

"Why...would I dig through your closet? Because I have no qualms about—"

"Why are you still here?"

Unless Risa was very much mistaken, a look of pain passed briefly across Cora's face. But it was gone a split-second later, replaced again with a centered but unreadable expression that could've only been tempered through years of practice.

Cora brushed her fingers across Risa's cheek with a soft sigh. "Why am I still here...you asked me to be, dear. My...duty is to tend to souls, is it not?"

Risa gave a quiet huff that might've been a laugh, had she not recently murdered a political rival, had not the subsequent guilt burdened her with the inability to taste joy. "How would I know what your duty is?"

"Fair enough," Cora chuckled, settling back into the sofa. "Drink your tea, you gentle soul."

Lifting the cup to her lips, Risa took a sip. Smooth and hot, it sent a tremor of warmth through her chest, a sweet aftertaste on her tongue.

There is work. Qualifying exams are coming up. Studying to be done, and Elsie—the world is unraveling while I sip tea with Death.

"Things are crumbling," Risa said quietly, staring into her teacup. The steam clustered just above the pale pink surface, dancing gently against the ripples. "Things have been set into motion that...I am inextricably part of."

"That is the way of the Tapestry." Cora moved closer, watching carefully. "It is beautiful and lonely and overwhelming."

"And I—"

Cora laid a finger on Risa's lips. "This is enough." Her eyes were glittering as they met Risa's, and she drew her finger away, leaving goosebumps prickling sweetly down Risa's chest.

The space between them felt warm and electric.

Perfect for Risa's ex-girlfriend to worm her way in.

And what of Lea?

Risa pushed the unwelcome thought from her mind, hairs rising in discomfort on the back of her neck, like she was being watched. Lea was gone. They'd parted ways, albeit messily, and why did it matter, that there was an oppressive guilt, hanging onto Risa's heartstrings? Sure, she'd toyed with the idea of getting back together, but that was absurd. And this—it was only tea on the sofa with...with someone Risa hoped to call friend. If a god could be called such a thing.

Cora watched her, rosy lips quirked into a smile, her knee resting warm against Risa's leg.

It is beautiful and lonely and overwhelming.

This is enough.

"This is enough," Risa echoed.

With a nod, Cora made a quiet sound of agreement.

She had held Risa through the night—the first night, and any nights since, because perhaps it had been a day, perhaps it had been longer, who was to say—and she'd been correct in her assertion it'd been at Risa's behest. *Do you wish me to stay,* Cora had murmured quietly, thumbing away Risa's tears.

Yes.

Perhaps Clark Carson had, even in death, complained so loud the gods had grown tired of it, but Cora did not linger because of the complaints of a tired old bastard.

"Enough." Cora smiled the word, her hand resting on Risa's shoulder.

And gently, Risa leaned in, giving her a soft kiss.

Enough.

CHIM

"There is a trick some dockmen play with shells and cups. We do this in life, too, but with less expertise and much more loss."

~Sam Alderton

It was a dastardly game, Sam was playing.

Chim did not care for it, but it did present a specific set of challenges, and as she was inclined to do, she rose to the occasion.

Perhaps one of her hearth had told her not to follow, and maybe the boys did not specifically know this, but they were all bound to each other. She could no more disobey Sam's wish not to be followed than she could organize a filing cabinet with the diligence of Natali's adpare, wretched little creatures of order.

But, Chim thought, strolling through the moonlit field, Sam hadn't told her she couldn't join him. He'd said he didn't want either of them to go after him. He'd said nothing about going *with*.

This was not a mission to retrieve a hearth-mate.

This was a decision to accompany, pay no worry to the fact she'd change her mind later and bring him back with her, for that was a decision not yet made.

"Oh, my child." Mother Chaos lingered in the frosted grass, her charcoal cloak snapping and snarling about her ankles. She reached out her arms, the gesture stiff and unfeeling, remembered in the body but not the heart.

Chim took a wary step back.

This feint was a clever move, but a dangerous one, too, for there was only one who had dominion over the *kobalde*.

The old hearth magics were a small mercy, though. Mother Chaos may have held sway over some of the *kobalde*, but the magic of old ran deeper—ran faster—than the Master's puppet.

"You have been abandoned, my child." The eyes of Mother Chaos were gray in the moonlight, the whites swallowed up by the stony irises. "It is time to come home."

"Never. I shan't be doing that, not now not ever!" Chim shrieked, and she stomped her foot on the frozen ground, an inky wave of magic swirling forth with a *boom*.

But Mother Chaos stifled the burst with a wave of her hand, a murky slate wind sending the wave melting like smoke in a summer breeze. "Naughty child misbehaves. We can't have that, now, can we." She clicked her tongue, sauntering forward.

Chim turned, ready to run.

But where she willed her body to move, it only stayed stuck, sticky, sticky, sticky—

"Oof." Teetering over, she hit the ground with a hiss. She'd been swaddled in a blanket of that itchy, chaotic magic, squirming and wriggling as it held her tight, eager and frankly rude, as far as magic went. "Let me go, let me go, let me *go*—"

"I will not." Mother Chaos had turned her lips down into a look of disgust. Her brown hair had been streaked with gray, the curls dancing in the wind, nothing more than puppet strings, Chim knew.

"Not this, no, I WON'T—"

"Hush. I have yet another task for you." Mother Chaos knelt down before Chim, head cocked to the side. "And this time, do not think you can play me with your tricks and turns of phrase." She gave a shiver. "Do not think you can play the Master with your tricks and turns of phrase."

"It is—*ermph*—your own fault for being—"

Mother Chaos sent a hand flying across Chim's cheek, and Chim let out a shriek, skin smarting. This was all wrong. All wrong, Mother Chaos would never swaddle her in suffocating magic, let alone lay a hand on her precious children—or chastise one for being clever, this...

Tears were on Chim's cheeks.

This was the wolf's belly, all over again.

Mother Chaos drew a knife from somewhere behind her back. "I have learned much, since you last swindled me." Mother Chaos gave a jolt, knife falling from her twitching fingers to the ground. "I have learned much, since you last swindled him. Your hearth magic cannot save you."

Chim tried to grasp onto the feeling, the tugs, the loopholes of magic she'd been so sure of when she'd set out, the pull that drew her to protect those boys, the insistence of them to protect her, the sense...the sense of family, that at last she had begun to cling to.

This wasn't fair, and Mother Chaos—the Master, more like—was a fool if he thought invoking blood would snap the narrative.

"You are required to do as your Mother commands," Mother Chaos whispered, leaning close. "So it has been. And you have been told by your Mother to stir only the Chaos, but no more. It is time you earn your keep in this world."

Mother Chaos tore away the magic bindings, milky magic fading as she grabbed Chim's hand, resurrecting the knife from the ground.

Squirming, Chim tried to break free—

The blade pricked Chim's finger, a drop of blood hissing as it hit the ground.

"Your hearth will be lured to bone and blood," Mother Chaos murmured, pricking her own finger and letting the blood drip, sizzling atop where Chim's had fallen. "The mortals' time has passed."

It seemed that Chim was not the only one who had turned to the old magic, then.

The gods of old had been bloodthirsty bastards, and as the ground drank up the bubbling concoction, the bones of the old ones were satiated, lending their magic to the ones above.

"Those who partook in your hearth are sentenced to die by your bloodlust," Mother Chaos purred. "Tear them limb from limb and devour their flesh in sacred honor of this pact. The Master tells me how he loathes them both, tells me of his distaste of your betrayal." Her eyes flared in the dark. "I ingratiate myself to him with this offering. Wait for the Master to have his fun, and when he has finished, bathe in their blood. Rip them apart, before their very eyes, listen to their screams of anguish. When the Master finishes with the boy of light and life, bring me their bones, little one, and we will revel in his glory."

ELSIE

*"What else was there to do, but walk into the belly of
the beast? Don't answer that, it's s rhetorical question,
and I do so loathe being proven wrong."*

~Elizabeth Clement Faulise

"You're sure you can use the disc?" Fletcher asked for what must have been the tenth time, leaning against the bedpost. This was his perpetual concern, since they'd talked in his office at the compound.

Whether or not there was still enough dhacrym lingering in her system to prevent her from evanescing out of the mountain city, that was the question taxing both of them.

Elsie had protested, accusing him of being impatient, telling him that the healing process was unpredictable. And quietly, she cut back. She lowered the doses delivered over the bathing room sink until at last, when he'd grabbed her hand, they'd both disappeared as his gentle magic wrapped around them. He folded the fabric of the world, punching through it like a needle, stringing the two of them along like the pair of threadbare souls they were, and when the massive stone bridge of Caelaymnis appeared beneath their feet, Elsie had leaned over the railing and puked right into the Weir.

But at least she could move with magic again—even if it was the magic of others. The elves could use their magic to touch the natural world, and the humans of the Hidden City had been enamored enough—or perhaps reckless enough—to experiment with doing the same, their glass discs working as a small capsule of magic that mimicked the evanescing talents of the elves.

Clio had been supremely helpful with the promise of his beloved Fitla being released from the compound prison cells, it turned out, and he'd followed through, swapping out one of his runners for Elsie herself.

She checked herself over in the mirror once more, unsure if she was recognizable or not.

Lips rouged, and cheeks, too. Hair curled tight and pulled back, eyelids painted dark, she'd pulled on a leather fighting coat over a low-cut camisole, tight-fitting canvas trousers tucked into a pair of knee-high boots borrowed from a spare Caelaymnic uniform. The aim was to look the part—but within the realm of practicality.

Her clothing was her armor.

She needed to be able to take a hit. Fall down, run, without getting weighed down by excess.

It felt oddly empty that Sam and Teddy weren't here, helping her with this. Sam would've tugged at her blouse, seating it as he looked her over with approval while Teddy fussed with her hair. But they still hadn't come back. All there'd been was a note from Teddy.

Caught up with matters here that are taking longer than expected. Be home soon. Love you, El.

They might not be here, but with her switchblade stowed in the arm of her jacket, Elsie did feel ready.

The locket sat in the curve of her chest, the metal warm against her skin.

Elsie traced the entrails of finery down to the gold dollop left below her collarbone, watched the reflection of the filigree heart twirl almost into her flesh itself.

This was left in my possession.
So from mother, to daughter.
And so, to you.

Left in an envelope on her desk in the farmhouse after the autumn festival.

She'd been tangled with Fletcher on the make-shift dance floor of the town square in a borrowed auburn gown, lifted from a dress form in Mulligans, and only now did she realize that Sam had probably made it specifically for her, that it was absurd that she'd borrow something like that, as if it'd be taken by a merchant when it was soaked with the sweat of a gull. And what had she done but toss it back to him in a crumpled up ball, laughing about how it was his mess to unravel, now.

Clark had left the locket for her.

It is, he had murmured, *your inheritance. When you rise—and you will, love—this will be how. Consider it akin to your beating heart. Keep it close. Tell no one. It will be your ascension. The ultimate end to this strategy.*

She found the crevasse, flipping the locket open for the thousandth time.

Nothing.

Empty.

It was nothing short of a miracle, that it had been recovered. When it'd come off...

She hadn't even noticed.

Elsie pressed her eyes closed, the memory vivid.

Augustus, dragging her out of the carriage house before evanescing from the stoop.

Augustus, binding her wrists in satin, and now did she understand what had felt to be nothing short of insanity, the soft shackles. Injury incurred would weaken the blood magic, and they hadn't wanted to risk the slightest drop spilling before she'd been filled with the dhacrym, and so, he bound her in the gentle cords.

Even now, she could feel it.

His hands, rough and callused, trailing her arms, a fight between keeping her still and not damaging the goods.

"Elsie?"

Her eyes snapped open, and she exhaled, pulling the locket off, setting it gently on the dresser. "I'm ready."

She had one aim, in this deception.

One goal.

Ingratiating herself with the ring, gaining their trust, becoming one of them—it was for one piece of information, and one piece of information alone.

Find the Master's house, Augustus had whispered in their quiet confabs. *Find the Master's house, and then, it's an investigation like any other. Don't let him hide his treachery in back alleys.*

Find the Master's house. Find his fortress. And end him.

~ • ~

The Capital was a wretched place.

Packed to the brim with gulls, pecked to death by the pastries and the confections and the tarts, and Elsie supposed she was no different, swirling a mug of something painfully strong. The ceramic stuck to the bar, the wood waxy with dirt and grime, and she tried not to look at the patina of sludge coating the inside of the glass as the whiskey hit her tongue, burning.

Best to play along.

And she needed a drink, after today.

"Oi." A man was leaning on the bar beside her, watching her with interest. "What gods be on your alter, mortal?"

The signal.

"None," she sighed, pushing back the barstool. "I worship the beating of my own heart."

The man gave a nod to the door.

She followed, leaving the bartender wiping down her glass with a filthy rag, though not before tossing back whatever she'd left with a half-hearted shrug.

Ew.

Whatever glamor Sam had spun in his stories of the Capital, she'd yet to see any of it. With the whaynedisc she'd borrowed from Risa—well, *borrowed* might be a generous word for it, because it'd been accidentally left in the drawer of the spare room at Fletcher's where Risa had been staying. It took less practice than she'd thought to get the hang of using the disc, but Isa had been right about evanescing, that it was like being tugged along a single thread—and with the whaynedisc she'd borrowed from Risa, Elsie had evanesced herself into an obscured corner of the Capital, tonight, no problem.

He must've been young, the man she was following down the dark alley. Maybe twenty. Certainly no more.

"You've got it," he asked, not looking behind to see if she was following.

"Nope."

That got his attention.

Stopping, he was eying her with something too much like terror.

If the runner fucked up, he was the one who'd pay, after the runner. At least, that was what Elsie assumed, based on Clio's information. Runners were at the bottom, then the liaison—which was presumably this man before her—then a bunch of other lackeys, people running the individual rings, then at the top, the Master himself.

"I got something better." Digging into her satchel, she pulled out a black bottle, corked and waxed, and then another.

"You fucking with me? This is the order," he snarled, making to snatch the bottles. She was quicker, though, dodging his grasping hand with a step back. "Two quarts, that's what we asked for, that's what's here."

Clicking her tongue, she shook her head. Then, letting a faint smile crawl across her lips, she passed him the bottles, her movements slow and deliberate. "And," she said softly, "something else." She held his gaze as she withdrew a vial from her pocket, holding it up to glisten red in the lamplight.

His jaw clenched, eyes lingering on the vial.

He knew what it was.

Knew, and wanted it.

"It's yours," she said softly, not moving to give it to him. "If you can help me."

"What do you want." His voice was low, hungry as he watched the vial between her fingers.

"I'm looking for a change of scene. Not very fond of my current employer. And there's something about seeing the world, I think. Heard you all like to travel."

His eyes narrowed on her. "How do I know it's the real deal."

"It is."

"Or maybe you're trying to poison me. Don't know you. Don't much like you. And you seem the type."

"Poisoning a future employer is in bad form," she remarked, raising an eyebrow.

"But knocking out a potential competitor isn't." He nodded to the vial. "You first. Then, we'll talk."

The street felt suddenly very quiet around her, the air much colder as it pressed in. "Me," she breathed.

"You."

Exhaling, she popped the vial.

Steady. Nice and easy.

Something pungent and sweet met the air.

A big, fat, sickeningly saccharine dollop hit her tongue, and she had to hide a grimace, swallowing. It tasted like port gone sour and mixed with sugar, because that was more or less what it was—wine, borrowed from the alter of Stell in the temple of the mystics, but it was distilled and infused with magic. This man wasn't getting top-shelf blood magic. He was getting wine, and who knew, maybe a godly experience, to boot.

But it'd be a transcendent experience anyway, and if they got lucky, he'd think he stumbled on some exceedingly fine stores, less the unpleasant side effects of his usual supply.

"Alright," the man nodded. "You got yourself a deal. Here, tomorrow."

He'd taken the vial and his two bottles of dhacrym and left her standing there.

She was one step closer to the Master. She didn't even need to meet him face-to-face, all she needed was to find where he was hiding out, pulling his puppet strings, and Fletcher and the rest could strike. *Second time's the charm, eh?* The first attempt, when they'd thought Clark had been running the whole production circuit, had been abysmal.

It was almost laughable, now, thinking he could've been the Master.

Tomorrow.

Here.

Here, tomorrow.

The words felt thick in her skull, her stomach burning, and she had to hold herself up against the brick, lights blurring in and out of focus as she tried to find the end of the alley.

He just has to go.

Give him time to go, and then you're next.

The disc was whirring, alive beneath her fingertips, and it was like the earth had swallowed her whole, enveloping her as it disappeared in mist and sparks.

ISA

"What lovely sins are available for purchase along
the corridor lined with vendors. And they say our age is
crumbling—why, you can buy any transgression you
wish! Is this truly the symptom of failing times?"

~Anscip Xavishia

Images of the fallen, collapsed in bloody snow, had graced Isa's dreams since they'd returned home.

Mornings found them in a panicked sweat, and the nights, cold and alone.

There was only one thing to do.

Peace was brokered one person at a time. To believe otherwise was to succumb to the isolated lie of the kingdom.

Isa's gray medics' tunic was belted about the waist, the silken cord knotted in specific loops and turns to signify that they had called upon the gods to aid in healing, and it was fitting, that they'd steal packs of medical supplies dressed as such. Asa, God of Healing, would find no crimes in this.

A satchel was heaped onto the desk, and Isa had been strategic, pulling the supplies from the infirmary inventory. They'd have bandages of their own, so there was no use wasting space with rolls of cotton strips and the wads used to stem the flow of open wounds. Instead, Isa could bring tonics and poultices and oily spreads, supplies coveted now by Aerdela, too, perhaps a testament to their abilities. They weren't like the medical supplies of the Hidden City, which had been crafted from magic themselves—the humans were nothing if not clever, blending what little magic they had into every little thing—but the Caelaymnic supplies had stood the test of war time and again.

With a quiet sigh, Isa tossed their jacket on before slinging the now-stuffed satchel over their shoulder. Sixth bell had rung some time before, marking the end of their shift, and they could hear the night medics back in the infirmary proper, shuffling about. Nobody would question the satchel. They'd assume Isa would simply be restocking their triage vest, or else perhaps tending to the darling human that the city of lights had become so taken with.

Even so, their heart was in their throat, leaving.

Like every night since they had returned from the ambush, Isa did not make for the barracks after their shift. They did not turn for the compound showers, did not go for a round or two in the training hall, and they certainly did not slink into the dining hall in the hopes of a quiet meal that would inevitably be disrupted by whispers of *whore* and *traitor.*

Isa's leather boots crunched the ice that should've been cleared already from the palace steps, satchel straining on their shoulder, digging in painfully to sinew and tendons.

Augustus's now-rumpled bed smelled like him, the soft blankets heavy, and in the dark, they could pretend they were not quite so alone. Not quite so cold.

Winding through the cold marble corridors, Isa came to a stop, voices drifting distant even amid the tapestries and carpets that lined the stone halls. They wouldn't be out of place, per say, except their unbuttoned jacket and medic's trousers were a dead giveaway that they hadn't been on the palace rotation that evening—and that was to say nothing of the massive bag on their shoulder, chock-full of medical supplies.

Fuck.

This section of the palace, dedicated to the children, had been reasonably empty.

And yet, now, an apparent argument raged on just around the corner.

"It isn't there," a voice snapped, icy. "What are you playing at?"

"I'm playing at nothing," Cormalum's voice retorted, furious, and there was the sound of shuffling, like he'd tried and failed to push past whoever he was arguing with and escape the interrogation.

"You assured me—"

"You expect that treacherous fool of a prince to have delivered honestly, after all that has transpired?"

The ripping of stitches groaned from Isa's satchel, and their heart skipped a beat, moving to hold the bottom of the bag. *No, no, no—*

"Did you hear that," Cormalum asked, voice clearly panicked.

A pause.

"You're pathetic," the icy-voiced one retorted a moment later. "You best be as competent as rumor suggests, for when the moment comes, there is no room for ineptitude."

Footfalls scurried off, and Isa let out a quiet breath.

A moment later, the sound of fabric tearing and tins and bottles clattering and clanking together filled the hall, the satchel at last giving out.

Swearing, Isa slumped against the wall.

"Oh, dear."

Isa's head snapped up, heart skipping several beats. A man had rounded the corner, pale blue hair pulled back in a bun, an opalescent tunic shimmering in the torchlight where it was tucked into azure pants. He seemed vaguely familiar, Isa thought, but couldn't quite place him—though that was true of most who kept court.

"Given up, have we?" The man's voice was light and jovial as he

198

quirked an eyebrow.

"No, I—I've been lugging this around, and..." Isa trailed off, pushing themself off the wall, heart pounding. "I...am new? And I'm looking for the palace infirmary, but I think I'm going the wrong way."

"Yes. You're a bit off-course." A firm, but gentle warning.

Isa sighed, gesturing helplessly to the pile. Alone, they'd go grab a pillowcase from Augustus's room and reclaim the haul. But a would-be cadet wandering the halls wouldn't. "I don't suppose you've an extra sack, do you?"

The man gestured for the broken satchel, and wiggling his fingers through the split, frowned. But as he continued to fiddle with the split seam, something glacial seeped from his fingers, and a white needle began poking and prodding at the fabric, binding it together with shimmering loops of turquoise. Then, raising his eyebrow, he tossed it back to Isa. "Best be on your way."

"Thank you," Isa whispered, clutching the bag as they knelt down before the mess of medical supplies. *Can—can a Drada do such a thing?* Surely, they could, Isa simply wasn't practiced in the skills of creative magics, like mending or sewing.

The man offered no directions, no clarification, no anything as he walked away, save for a small chuckle. "That's right, on your knees, *ro,*" the man simpered, brushing back his icy blue hair. "You should recognize the face of one of the gods you defy."

Isa froze, a vial of cruor tonic half into the satchel.

A slight at Isa's unconsecrated nature, an exercise of ego, or—

Isa's heart was still pounding uncomfortably hard when they pushed open Augustus's bedroom door. They let the satchel slide off their shoulder and onto the floor, Isa themself sinking down against the door as if to barricade it closed with their body, an armament for this refuge frozen in time.

Oh gods.

Isa's fingers found the mended seam on the satchel, panicky. The fabric was wet where the frozen stitches were already melting.

Exhaling deeply, they closed their eyes.

Stell's ice.

CORA

"Love is that thing where you both agree you would commit crimes for each other. Either that, or where you both have already committed crimes, and you keep each other's secrets. Honesty, amid the lies. That's love."

~Elizabeth Clement Faulise

"I don't *care* what kind of hell he is raising, you are a gods-damned warrior, *deal with it,*" Cora hissed. Standing in the tiny mortal apartment, she was struggling to keep quiet as the insolent and somewhat outraged First Soul stood before her.

"There is a culling of the Guild," Yara bit back, hardly daring to keep her voice down, "never, *never* in all my years have I seen such vitriol at the gates of the Underworld—"

"I am busy, Yara—and you should not be here—"

"Busy doing what? Coddling a mortal? Since when have you coddled *anyone?*"

Cora thrust a finger towards the bedroom. "She is in *pain,* Yara. And this is what I do. I tend to souls. Hers is hurt—and badly!"

"She's a murderer."

"Who among us isn't? Or have you forgotten who I am," Cora snarled.

Yara scoffed. "It seems *you* have forgotten who you are, Rose."

"Don't you dare call me that—"

"You're an imposter, and a poor one, playing at being a god. I thought you were returning to deal with the matter of the quays, not—not share the bed of another woman!"

And there it was.

The truth.

Cora sniffed, eyes flitting around the small apartment. Hand-me-down furniture and a kitchen hardly big enough for one...it was no Palace of Souls, with gold-gilded obsidian décor and lavish, overly indulgent comfort at every turn. But this place called back to mortal days.

Days when she had called herself Rose.

Days before she'd taken this mantle.

Stolen, more like.

"Are you in love with her," Yara breathed, eyes glistening.

But Yara was the First Soul. She knew Cora's heart, knew her inclinations, knew her very thoughts before they could be made into action and spun into the tapestry.

"I asked you a question—"

"Of course I am," Cora snapped, turning away. She couldn't bear to look at Yara, delivering the confession.

Of course, she was in love with Risa.

Those blue eyes had been so tearful, that voice so small, and Cora's heart had been breaking as she'd drawn Risa into her arms, for what a travesty that someone so brave could feel so afraid. Her wit was sharp, her intellect lethal, and her compassion as vast as the cosmos torn to shreds by Fate herself.

These days in this apartment had been an answer to a question asked for six hundred years.

Already, Cora grieved the loss.

The threads were cruel, tying her heart up like this.

Risa was twenty-six. She would have sixty or seventy more years, perhaps a few more if she were lucky, and then Cora would take her soul, too—take it, regardless of whether Risa loved her back.

"This is Beca, all over again," Yara warned.

"It isn't."

"I was your lover, once. I am your lover, still, when you are not busy with this foolishness—"

"This isn't Beca. Nobody can be Beca. Nobody could betray me like that again," Cora breathed, eyes watery. "Will she threaten the heirs I was tasked with protecting? Will she steal and whore her way across the continent with a false god? Will she come to me, heavy with child, only then telling me that she is no longer mine? Kiran is chained beneath the Palace, and Beca is long dead." She sniffed, wiping her damp cheeks with the sleeve of her shirt. "So no, Yara, this isn't Beca, all over again."

Yara scoffed, her ghostly armor rustling as it brushed against the corporeal realm of the living. "You fall too fast."

"It is not my fault that I have loved the wicked," Cora snapped.

"What of me?"

"What of you, Yara? You take to my bed when neither of us can find another way to grieve."

"So that's it? As always, I am pushed aside when someone more alluring comes along—"

"I am not pushing you aside, Yara, I simply do not love you. You have known that from the start," Cora hissed, "I do not love you, you do not love me—"

"Oh." Yara gave a bitter laugh. "I don't? I didn't know you knew hearts as well as souls. You're dense, Cora. I've been tied to you since before you were a god. We were mortals together. I have followed you into this folly. I did not have to stand at your side, I did not have to nest myself inside your heart all these years. But go off, then. I don't love you."

A sick feeling blossomed in Cora's gut.

Yara couldn't possibly have loved her. They were bedmates of

203

convenience. Friends, unquestionably, but this—

"Even now, it's an impossibility to you." Yara shrugged. "It's fine. I'll be fine. I've seen you love others. I watched you fall for Beca. And I'll be there for you when this goes to shit, too. You cannot call yourself a god and love like a mortal, Cora. It's not right, and it's not fair. You love Risa because you've seen her thread weave through the tapestry. You *know* her in a way she can never know you. I don't know why I'm surprised, though. You're too much of a coward to be honest," Yara breathed, brow knitting. "You will go on loving her, knowing all the secrets the tapestry has whispered, but you won't even tell her your real name. You won't even tell her why you're here."

And without another word, Yara was gone, the faintest opal whisps lingering for a second before they too dissolved.

Cora sank to the sofa, chest shaking as tears ran down her face.

Too much of a coward to be honest.

The bed gave, floorboards creaking. "Cora?" Risa was standing in the doorway of her bedroom, chestnut hair mussed, eyes tired.

"I—I'm sorry, I didn't mean to wake you," Cora said softly, drying her tears as she rose, hands shaky.

"S'okay. What happened?"

Cora only met her in a gentle hug. Risa was warm, her pajamas soft with wear, the faint smell of salted pears about her as Cora's arms wrapped around her waist.

I love you.

Risa's fingers were gentle, brushing Cora's hair back behind her ear. "Tea?"

"I'm okay. Really." Her tearful voice muffled in Risa's shoulders seemed to offer the opposite impression, though.

"Talk to me."

Cora's heart was racing, the truth on her tongue. *I know someone is after the gods. I know that, above all else, if I can close the Quay of Death, I must, no matter the cost.*

"There's only so much loss a heart can hold," Cora breathed, cursing herself for the half-truth. "And I can hold no more."

There would be no confessions tonight.

THE BURIALS

I'm livid.

That bastard had no right to leave. I only meant to make a few notes, and somehow I've taken over these damn letters!

I'm going to infiltrate the ring. That's the only way to do this. Last time, our mistake was guessing on outside observations, and I'm not going to risk that again.

Bury me in conspiracy and show me the secrets, and I'm going to end them.

That's what I do, right?

~ELIZABETH CLEMENT FAULISE,
EXCERPT FROM A LETTER DATED FEBRUARY 10TH

SAM

"I did love him. It killed me brutally, to love him, and
I wish I had decided not to. But I was young and
believed the lies they told me: that love wasn't a choice.
That I, in loving him, had no alternative."

~Mariann Bell

A sliver of moonlight cut through Sam's cell.

I am a good man.

Hadn't he felt that, through his twenty-four years? That the men in his life had lacked the propensity for self-sacrifice, and had they given up their own desires, life would've been better?

Even so.

Sam would die with his husband believing their marriage had crumbled. He'd die with Elsie thinking that when it mattered, he wasn't there. He'd die with Fletcher watching a true friend disappear.

But they'd go on living, and time would fix those wounds, eventually. Better to have a heartbroken life than a loving death.

Nobody here had bothered to strip him of the waistcoat and cravat, of his once-pressed ivory tunic, of his bespoke trousers painstakingly tailored, and it would've been easier if he'd been clad in prison ware than in something so ordinary.

He was under no pretenses about what was coming.

It was only a matter of when, and how.

The dhacrym was cold and bitter, and the eyes glittering across the cell from him moved back and forth, a great beast pacing the length, waiting. So this went. He could recall Elsie's explanation, the anticipation of terror making him that much more uneasy.

Sam wondered what his mind would deliver when provoked to bleeding fear. Elsie said that her fears had been unexpected. She'd thought old wounds would be resurrected, but her mind had conjured horrors she hadn't anticipated, for there was comfort in the familiar, she'd said, comfort in old anxieties, for the heart at least knew its way around those worries.

Blood could be given in vow or pact, a magic knot tying promise to action; but, too, it could be taken to seize the will of another.

The act of taking was a terribly powerful thing, Sam reflected bitterly.

Such magic that came from the violation of *taking* was only concentrated through this horrendous process. He had been given the dhacrym to amplify his fears—fears the barghest would feast upon. This act, this feeding upon the emotion of another, it would agitate the magic in his own veins, making it powerfully concentrated, and the first bloody tears he'd cry would be rich with the magic of...of Kiran's line.

If he truly is my father.

Maybe it *was* Kiran, God of Life. There'd been a lot of questions in his life that had been unanswered, and after all he'd seen...

It explained why Clark would've taken Sam as his ward. The son of a god, Sam would be a prized addition to the collection. Somehow, this just made him angry, because if his father was a god, things should've been better. A God of Life, and his mother shouldn't have died.

"Perhaps you were an unworthy son," a quiet voice snickered, and Clark Carson emerged from the shadows. A worry that must've been buried deep in the recesses of Sam's ashen heart—that in the eyes of a god, much less his father, Sam had been found wanting.

And so it began.

EZRA

"We are most ourselves when we are hiding. Thus,
the allure of masquerades."

~Matthew Fieldson

A familiar tap at Ezra's bedroom door heralded in midnight, and Ezra grinned, rising to meet the Master. "You're early."

"Yes, and I don't see you complaining," the Master grinned, sliding into his usual spot on the bed with his usual plate of food. "You are getting spoiled."

"By you, a man who will not tell me his name, or anything about you—save the fact that you are married, very busy, and fond of figs," Ezra laughed, sinking down beside him.

"Oh, sure, leave out that business about the gods—"

Ezra snorted into his hunk of bread, crumbs flying. "Well, that's just run-of-the-mill fascination with mythology. And maybe a god complex."

Laughter filled the room, bright and youthful, and both were fighting tears of delight.

These nights had become something of a relief to Ezra.

Precarious and beautiful, like soap bubbles, these nights were moments of respite and relief. A chance for two men to shed the anxieties of adulthood and revel in the silliness found in adolescence. At 19, Ezra could still claim to be on the cusp of these two worlds, albeit in age only.

He'd been running since he was 16.

The Master was some five years his senior, and it had a way of seeming like oceans of difference—until one of them made a joke, and the two of them dissolved into giggling laughter on the bed together.

"You—you are ridiculous," the Master was laughing, and Ezra didn't really *like* to think of him as the Master. It was incongruous with their informality.

"And you are cagey," Ezra countered. "What is your name?"

He asked this every night.

And every night he got the same reply.

"I cannot say," the Master said, smile faltering.

"Why?"

Though each night brought a refusal, each night also brought forth a different reasoning.

"I fear that if I tell you, you will not like me anymore," the Master said solemnly. "What if the spark of fondness and friendship we have found disappears? Perhaps it is only alluring because of mystery and anonymity."

"Or perhaps you're full of shit, and I'd like you just the same," Ezra countered. With a soft sigh, he slid off the bed, going to fetch a letter off the writing desk. "I finished the letter to my sister. But I'm garbage at writing, it's terrible..." He passed it over to the Master, who looked it over thoughtfully.

It made Ezra nervous, watching the Master read it.

Not because it was particularly personal—how could it be? He didn't know Elizabeth at all, and anyway, the Master seemed to know a great deal about him, so there weren't really any secrets worth keeping.

"I...had a thought," Ezra added, wringing his hands. He'd been thinking on this point for some time, now. "I could send the letter. But if you'd let me, I'd like to go and maybe try to find her instead? Maybe I could bring her back here. That'd be good for you, right?"

The Master's head snapped up, eyes wide. "You want to leave?"

"Not permanently, or even for very long," Ezra breathed, anxiety rising. "I just—I want to meet her. You said if you could do this over again, you'd do it differently, right? You said you'd offer her the same."

"I...did say that, yes." The Master rose, expression no longer one of youthful joy. His eyes were serious, mouth pursed into a line. "What will you do if she says no?"

"I dunno. I don't know why she would," Ezra shrugged, looking down at the floor.

"Ezra." His voice was serious, low. "Ezra, you know that her chance at this has passed. I have told you this. I was undermined, her Ruby Tears were never even collected on account of the malicious agents working against me. She has no reason to pledge herself to this cause."

"But maybe she wants to know me. Maybe she'd want to live safely and comfortably with me in the Capital," Ezra edged. The hope sounded childish, vocalized. It'd been a quiet dream, a soft vision with which he let sleep find him every night.

He could find his twin, and they would not be so alone.

"This is a serious matter."

"What...what if I said that I wouldn't let you have my blood until I found her." Ezra's voice was hardly a whisper, quavering as the fire in the hearth was roaring, and the Master took a step closer.

"What did you say?"

"I—I said, what if I don't give you my blood until I try to bring my sister back here," Ezra echoed again, voice breaking. Tears stung his eyes, and he looked up, face pleading as he met the Master's gaze. "Please. I am so alone, here. You won't even tell me your name. I want to help you, I do, and I'm so fond of our evenings, and I just want to meet my sister. I didn't know she existed, and now...she's all I can think about. There was another part of me, another half, and she's out there, and I—I know that I can get her back. She's *mine*, don't you see? We belong together!"

The Master's glare softened, brow furrowing into worry instead. "Oh—oh, you poor thing." Gently, he drew a handkerchief from his waistcoat, passing it over, and his hands were on Ezra, comforting. "My boy, I...you understand, time is of the essence, though. It is of critical importance to gain control of Cora, for she leads the gods below..."

Ezra sank down to the floor, leaning against the bed and drawing his knees against his chest, burying his face in his hands. He didn't hear the rest of the Master's explanation.

But he was surprised when he felt someone sit down beside him.

The Master.

My friend, so terrified he cannot even tell me his name.

"Ezra. Darling, please."

Shoulders shaking, he felt inconsolable.

"Ezra, I...oh, please, do not cry—"

"How can I not," he demanded, looking up at last. Eyes red and puffy, he blinked, trying to clear his vision to get a good look at the Master. "I am not trying to betray you, or—or sideline your plans! I just want to see my sister! I am fond of you, I have found an ally in you—and you are so terrified that our friendship isn't real! You say you cannot trust me, and yet do not give me a chance to prove my trustworthiness to you!"

The Master reached over, soft fingers brushing Ezra's tears from his cheeks. "Not an unjust criticism."

"I understand that this effort is of critical importance to you—"

He leaned his head against Ezra's, voice soft, breath warm and sweet. "What would I do, though, if I lost you?"

The question knotted something painful in Ezra's chest, something that shouldn't have hurt nearly as much as it did.

"What if she returns with you," the Master breathed. "What if I lost you to a life with her?"

Ezra moved, gazing at the Master with a pained expression. "You are my first friend in three years. How could I give that up so easily?"

The Master's hand fell, brushing against Ezra's, and he laced their fingers together, the feeling in Ezra's chest knotting up all over again. "And you are perhaps the first real friend I have ever had," he breathed. "I cannot risk losing what your blood offers—but more than that, I cannot risk losing you."

"So, that's it, then." Ezra jerked his hand back, pushing himself to standing with anger. "I'm nothing more than a prisoner, here."

"No," the Master said hesitantly, rising too. "No, I...I am not a daft man, Erza. I see that forbidding you would break what affection exists between us. We will go together. I have business in the Valley, anyway."

"You—you'd go with?" Incredulity was rising in Ezra. He could hardly believe what he was hearing.

"Someone must look out for you," the Master breathed. "The Valley was her home. Search for her there, for that is where she was last known to be. If...you are not successful, we may return to the Capital together, and pursue her another way."

Ezra couldn't stop himself. Throwing his arms around the Master, he hugged him tightly, and holy gods did it feel so good when his friend hugged him right back, and hearing the smile in his voice felt like it might almost be enough to make the tears cease.

"Very good, Ezra," the Master breathed, gentle voice easy. "You would do well to pack. We depart tomorrow."

AUGUSTUS

"A soul bond is made by blood, and jokingly called
'forced empathy,' for never do you truly understand until
you feel someone's pain."

~*Alva Praequintelya*

Augustus awoke with a start. The dim light of torches beyond his cell said morning was near. He pushed himself up, stone floor cold beneath him, his palm crusted with dried blood and stinging—

The Dradic letter, *elle,* written the night before on the floor, had bled like rain had fallen, the letter itself fading, streaks of oxidized rust-colored blood running long across the floor.

Deep in his chest, something constricted. Sinking onto the cot, wrapping his shivering self in the itchy wool blanket, he forced pained breaths, disoriented.

And in his veins, something burned, hot and uncomfortable.

It was a dream that had awoken him, he decided, but he couldn't recall what it was. It must've been horrible, though, for the tears on his cheeks would not lie.

This was loss.

Pain.

Grief.

And beneath it all, fear.

Whatever it was, whatever these feelings were—they did not belong to him, but they drew him all the same. The restlessness of inaction made any more rest impossible, though he did not know what he could do.

Something is wrong with Elsie.

Tears pricked at his eyes as the thought persisted.

So much for a symbolic gesture. The Vow of Fealty had taken hold.

He'd sworn loyalty to one in the throes of crisis with his own blood. Her pain was his, now.

~ • ~

The cell door clattered open late that afternoon. Elsie.

And in his veins, that familiar burning, the one he'd awoken to that morning, the one signaling the Vow, flaring.

What have I done.

The fiery grief he felt when she slammed the door behind her—it wasn't ordinary.

It was her soul, calling to him. To his heart.

Here's your Fealty, soldier, it seemed to say. *Your soul is tethered. When I am in pain, you will be called to answer.*

Elsie said nothing.

She tucked a strand of hair behind her ear, and she rolled up the sleeves of her cable-knit sweater, and she slumped up against the stone wall, slowly sinking to sitting. Holding her head in her hands, the unmistakable sound of a tear hitting the stone resounded. The light caught the gold of the locket as her shoulders shook, the godly relic acting like a beacon to her grief.

"Elsie." Augustus's voice was quiet as he came to the bars.

Oh, shit.

Seeing her like this hit him hard. *Feeling* her like this, feeling the tug of magic in spite of these iaculic bars around him that were supposed to dampen such things—

"Elsie," he edged, panicking a little, "what happened."

She looked up, eyes glistening. "Same thing that always happens. I get my fucking heart broken just trying to build a gods-damned family." Elsie shoved a palm of her hand against her eyes in turn, forcing away the tears. "You know, I used to think that it was me that was broken? That I was just...incapable. But it isn't me. It isn't. I see that, now. It's the whole notion of family. It's fucked. Doesn't matter who it is, family will always break you. That's just how it is."

"Elsie—"

"You don't understand how it is, not being able to trust anyone." Her emerald eyes were damp, face crumpling in heartbreak. "I...I should be home. I should go back. Teddy..." Her voice trailed off, and she shook her head, tears overtaking her.

"Loyalty before amity," Augustus breathed, brow knitting. She was wrong. So painfully wrong.

Elsie glanced up, glaring. "What did you fucking say?"

"Elsie, I...did something."

She was on her feet a moment later. "What." Her voice was dark, her damp eyes shadowed.

There was a tug inside Augustus's chest, and the words tumbled off his tongue, uncharacteristically unrestrained. "I have been thinking long about your words, and...I have pledged my soul to you—"

"Gross." Elsie grimaced, crossing her arms. "I don't want it."

"I—I don't know that you have a choice, it didn't go as I planned—"

"Rejected."

"You don't understand, I was praying and I said the Vow of Fealty—"

"Well, that seems like a dumb thing to do—"

"It's an old symbolic ritual, and now, you don't customarily use blood, but I thought it was probably only fair—"

"Oh, gods," Elsie swore, glaring. "What happened?"

Augustus scowled, an uncomfortable apprehension in his heart making it pound against his ribs. "I could ask the same for you. Who broke your heart, this time?"

"Bold to assume it wasn't you."

"I..." His voice faltered, momentarily distracted by the accusation. Turning, he clenched his fists, callused fingers of his left hand catching on the bandage still wrapped around his palm.

"You *what,*" she demanded.

I fucked up. And I tried to make it right, and I am now inextricable from the grief that you won't share. But Augustus said nothing, turning to pace the length of the cell.

Elsie's voice was firm as she met him at the bars. "Explain to me why I own your soul. *Now.*"

"I have been praying," he said with resignation, sinking down to sit on the edge of his cot. "I...have been praying a lot. For forgiveness, at first. For my soul. But it's all shit, Elsie. I've fucked myself over too many times for the gods to care. And what else can one do with a perfectly damned soul, if not try and wring some use out of it before the end?"

Elsie put a hand to her mouth, horrified, eyes welling with tears.

"I did not intend to—to involve myself in your life like that," Augustus went on. "I apologize. I never intended to be privy to...your pain. But I feel it. I woke up this morning, and I felt loss and grief that wasn't mine, and...I never intended to pay mind to your misery like that. All I know is that it calls to me, and I want to answer." His eyes flicked to her.

Maybe the bond had lent him some softness. Maybe the magic gave him some borrowed kindness.

Or maybe you're a coward and you just needed an excuse to care.

"What happened," he asked again, gaze unbreaking.

"Sam left." Elsie's face crumpled. "Teddy's been gone for days, and, he came back, and—and Sam's left. He promised he'd always be here, and he fucking left. And now I find out that you—you trespass on my feelings?" Her look of sadness turned to disgust once again. "Why is it that none of you can find your place with me? You are all either too close, prying into my life with letters and soul bonds, or you lie and deceive and abuse your position, abuse your trust—is it so hard to get this right?"

"Apparently so," Augustus growled, rising. "Sam left?" The news should not have infuriated him so, for he did not know the man hardly at all.

"He didn't say a gods-damned word to me. My brother came home in tears. That's how I found out. Seeing the one person who's been there for me come home with his heart shattered into so many pieces I—I don't know how he'll put it back together. Ever." Elsie shook her head, wiping her tears with her sleeve.

With an exhale, Augustus came to the bars. "Come here."

She met him, glaring. "What."

"Your...brother will put his heart back. He's radiantly uncontained. He is made in the likeness of the stars. It is not so easy to extinguish such a thing," he said quietly.

"And me?"

Pursing his lips, he slid his hand through the narrow grating, offering it to her. "Tear through this world without apology," he said quietly. "When Fate had her heart broken, she pierced the sky itself."

Elsie hesitated for a moment. Then, cautiously, she brushed her fingers against his before taking hold of his hand, her eyes closing with more tears. "Tell me," she whispered. "Tell me about Fate. Tell me what drove her to cut the universe to shreds."

ELSIE

"And he wandered the ice, ever looking, ever
protecting the mountains of his friend. Such is the life of
a god."

~Dradic Legend of Ignata

Augustus was a fool.

Souls and fealty, gods below...

Part of her hoped he wasn't lying. Part of her hoped that he would suffer every ounce of pain and hurt she did.

Another, smaller part of her took comfort in knowing that her pain had a home in someone else's heart, too.

She sighed.

Sam's letters to Clark lay spread across the floor of the living room.

Elsie had read them a dozen times, it felt like, these pieces of unequivocal proof that Sam had fought for her the best way he knew how.

She'd cried with Teddy. Had screamed and sobbed and they'd let themselves be torn apart together, in a way they hadn't since they'd both shared a roof in the now-ashen farmhouse.

Their life without Sam was inconceivable.

They'd more or less grown up together. Sam one of the few bright moments of consistency she'd clung to. Even when she'd spent those weeks raging about these very letters that now lay before her, she'd known it wasn't forever. She'd still slept on his sofa, still shared a table with him, still saw him fuss with his golden hair, still met his cinnamon eyes every morning, and that was safety—being allowed, even despite her anger.

He left. Elsie frowned, fingers peeling through the letters.

Sam was a lot of things, but he wasn't flighty. Right? He was loyal, to a fault, he would fatally give those around him the benefit of the doubt—

With a deep sigh, Elsie rose, legs stiff. There was one among them who'd deliver an unapologetic dressing down of Sam's flaws. Someone who wouldn't pull punches about the cold, hard facts.

Smoothing her mussed braid, she paced the length of the floor once, twice, considering.

I will consult the dhacrym. That was the phrase that had needled itself into her head, and she winced, the words still drifting in her mind as she fished the bottle from a chaotic drawer of undergarments in the wardrobe. *Face my fears.* What other way was there to be, really, if not persistently haunted.

~ • ~

Commissioner Cele Carson was seated at her desk in the study, her wintry plaid skirts elegantly falling over crossed legs, her high-collared blouse stiff as she moved to rise. "Ah. Chancellor." She removed the pair of reading spectacles, studying Elsie with interest.

"Just...Elsie. I'm not a Chancellor." Elsie edged hesitantly into the room, letters bundled in her arms. "Do you have a moment?"

"For you, always."

Elsie gave a small nod of gratitude. Her stomach was still roiling from the whanyedisc, the adventure of evanescing to the Carson manor a deeply unpleasant one. "These," she said quietly, setting the letters on the desk, "were Sam's. He gave them to me, and I wanted to know what you made of them."

"Mm, diving through memories, I see," Cele mused. She scooped up the bundle, flipping through them. "Ah, the last part of the dossier." She snickered, eyes sparkling with amusement. "Sam, Sam...always one to make waves." Cele perched herself on the edge of the desk, tossing the letters down once more, seemingly uninterested in their content. "Risa told you about the dossier. I'm not sure what I can illuminate that she is unable to, though I'll do my best."

"Risa's been busy, I guess. Dunno. Haven't seen her in a little." Elsie's brow knit. "Sam—he said he was told I'd die if he didn't. Was that true?"

Cele scoffed. "Sam is malleable to the highest degree when it comes to matters of the heart. The unfortunate truth is that my father's grab for power was more a risk to you than anything else. Though he was a man who wanted to be in control—so who knows. Perhaps to him it *was* life or death." She rolled her eyes.

Elsie sank down into the damask chair across from the desk, frowning. "But Sam didn't know that it was for Adrian?"

"If he didn't say anything to you, I presume not."

Quiet fell between them.

"So...Sam left." Elsie almost whispered the words, looking up to meet Cele's dark eyes.

Cele pursed her lips. "I know. I felt awful for your brother. He's a stranger in this place, he doesn't know us. Mattie told me what happened, and I gave what sympathy I could to Theodore. I did almost call for you, but he wanted to be the one to tell you. And truth be told, Elsie, I don't think he wanted you to see him like that. Depressed and beaten down."

Elsie sighed. "I still can't believe Sam's gone. He gave Teddy...his wedding band back." Her eyes drifted to the floor. She wasn't supposed to know, but Teddy hadn't even let go of the band clutched in his fist as he'd sobbed into her shoulder, as he'd held his chest, and it didn't take long to see that what he was holding about his neck was the band of his own. It probably should've stung, but it just made her angry.

How dare Sam make those promises so casually.

So haphazardly.

"It's frankly the biggest load of bullshit that I've heard." Cele rose, shaking her head. "My brother would never."

"He did, though."

"You surprise me." Cele clicked her tongue, taking her seat behind the desk once more. "What happened to" —she paused, rifling through the stack of letters— "The *unapologetically bold woman who has, to the highest degree, decided to seize whatever she wishes?*"

"How—"

Cele quirked an eyebrow. "Sam waxes poetic unceasingly. But he's not wrong, you know." Her eyes lingered on Elsie. "I knew my father's death hit Sam hard, but this is surprising, even for him."

"I don't know what to do."

"I know if I were you, I'd want answers—directly from the horse's mouth, too, as the expression goes."

"You're counseling me to, what? Run after Sam?"

There was a long pause. "No," Cele said at last, hesitant. "We don't know what transpired between closed doors. Allowing him room to breathe—albeit dramatically, as is his style—is not the same as giving up on him altogether."

Elsie nodded, sinking back into the chair. "There's a lot that went on that I wasn't seeing, apparently." The realization rather felt like a dagger of betrayal in her chest, and that wasn't fair, because her brother and Sam had a right to their privacy.

Just because Teddy had more or less raised Elsie as his own child didn't mean she had been granted unequivocal and open access to the details of his life—much less, his heart.

"You say that giving him space isn't the same as giving up," Elsie said at last. "You think he's coming back?"

"I don't know. What I do know, though," she went on, tucking a piece of hair back into her updo, "is that Sam has a bad habit of storming out when he doesn't get his way."

Elsie frowned. "The introduction."

"One instance of many."

"He's not flighty, though."

"Isn't he? How many would swear off a life of ease for a cramped apartment and long hours in a dress shop," Cele countered. "He changed his name, for fuck's sake."

"He—he ran to Teddy, that night. I was there. Mattie broke his heart, and he ran to Teddy and me! We were there for him, no one else was—"

"Elsie." Cele rose, raising an eyebrow. "Just because you were the person he ran to once doesn't make you—or your brother—the one that makes Sam stay. You know one side of Sam. You didn't see the boy who would storm out of fine dinners to pout when he didn't get his way. I'm not saying he doesn't love you or that he isn't coming back. I'm merely saying that he makes mistakes, and you owe it to him as much as yourself to see him as the flawed man he is."

She had a point, Elsie thought bitterly. Flawed, indeed.

"Try to remember that it's Sam, not you." Cele's gaze met hers. "You weren't worth leaving. Sam simply doesn't deal well with this sort of thing. He's a bit of a bastard, Elsie. It's perfectly fine to rage about when the men we love act like bastards."

"I should go." Elsie rose, reaching for the letters. "As much as I would love to grieve for Sam, the Master waits for no one." An unfortunate truth, and even so, her eyes pricked with tears.

Everything was fucked.

Rage changed nothing. Her family was falling apart.

RISA

*"She was the string around my finger, never letting
me forget who I really was. What a blessing, to be
reminded of yourself in the throes of love."*

~Rose Morris

Cora's fingers were laced through Risa's as they walked the chilled
streets of the City in search of a dinner not brought forth by the hands
of Death. "I've been watching the tapestry. But that's at best a
generalization of goings-on, particularly in this moment."

A faint smile tugged at Risa's lips. "Watching the tapestry?"

"I'd show you, but you'd have to be dead," Cora winced, pulling her
hand back to gesture in the air. "It's—well, I'm the Cutter of Threads.
People's lives are floss, intertwined together, and the conglomeration of
those are...the tapestry. Souls are a familiar language to me, and I can
read what has happened, but only on a large scale. To that end, perhaps
the words shared between us are recorded in the tapestry, but if they
are, it is beyond me to see them."

"How beautiful."

"If not at times uninformative," Cora added.

Risa sighed, shoving her hands into her pockets. "So, you really
founded this place?"

"I did," the God of Death smiled, glancing up at the high rises. "It's
come a long way since I was last here."

"I'm surprised the myths are factual. I always assumed the monikers
of the Foundress were political taunts."

Cora's eyes sparkled in the streetlamps. "They were. Both can be true."

"This means the lines of chancellors *are* your descendants."

"It does."

"I have been tasked with watching your great-great-great—"

"Ah, let's please skip over that, it makes me feel old—"

"Granddaughter," Risa grinned.

Cora's expression was a bit placid, and Risa wondered if she'd seen that in the tapestry. Or for that matter, had seen Risa herself, and the way her thread must have crossed death often, in more ways than one. Maybe she already knew all this.

"I...should be there with her, now, probably." Risa's smile faltered, going over her failed obligations. Her bones felt tired at the thought. She just wanted to sleep. To go home, back to the apartment, and curl up, and wait for Cora to draw a bath, to bring her tea, to snuggle in close and whisper old stories and comforting words—there'd been so much blood, there, when Risa had played the part of medic the first days with Elsie, so little sleep, so much panic, and perhaps the blood had more or less subsided, but the rest had stayed—

"Risa?" Cora's voice was quiet, eyes worried.

"I want to go back. I don't feel up for this," Risa muttered, already turning to go home to her shoebox apartment.

Cora nodded, taking a couple quick steps to catch up to her, and gently, she took Risa's arm, holding close. "That's fine. There's plenty in your apartment, I...well, let me get you settled, and then I can step out to bring something back. I suspect you're rather tired of broth and bread."

"I did a bad job."

"What—"

Risa's eyes drifted down to the salted sidewalk, crumbles of ice crunching beneath her boot. "I failed. I was supposed to—to be her

228

advocate."

"Sorry, who—"

"Elsie." Risa let her name fall to the ground. "She got hurt. And it's because..." She trailed off, unsure of the blame. It'd been easy to fend it off in the midst of crisis, but she'd been distracted at the masquerade.

Cora paused, watching Risa. "She's hurt?"

"Doing better, now, thank the gods, but...she was arrested—wrongly—on the pretense of treason—"

"Unsurprising, given the state of things here," Cora said quietly, quirking an eyebrow. "Nevertheless, I am sure you did all you could."

Risa glared. "That's a bit of a cold approach, first off."

Cora merely sighed, tucking a strand of midnight hair behind her ear. "You know who I am, right? You know I'm the God of Death? The Keeper of Souls, the Cutter of Threads? Risa, I have harbored the aching souls of countless dead. This City has been in conflict as long as it has been in existence. I would know. And for Elizabeth, I would know better than most. Who do you think carried that child from this place, anyway? What you've just told me is a confirmation of what I have seen woven in the tapestry—she's better now, she *was* arrested, past-tense, meaning it is no longer the case—you seem to have done your job adequately."

"I got lucky. If you can even call...it that..." Risa's eyes narrowed. "You took her to the Valley?"

Cora gave a curt nod.

"I...just always assumed it was Margaret."

With a quiet sound of amusement, Cora shrugged, resuming her walk towards the apartment.

"How—wait, you can't just walk away—"

Cora glanced over her shoulder, and even as she carried on, she stretched out a hand, wiggling her fingers in anticipation of lacing them through Risa's again. "Then hurry up."

A faint smile tugged on Risa's lips, and she had to jog a few careful steps to catch up. "Explain."

"My preference was to keep to myself. My duty was to tend to the souls of the dead, not the living." Her eyes flicked up and down the street, taking it in. "So, of course, when Jon and Margaret arrived at the gates of the Underworld, who was I to ignore their request."

Risa's heart sank at the realization. She...she had known that they were dead. Jon Clement's body had been found in the Archives, but Margaret—Risa had been holding out hope that maybe, she'd made it. That she'd hidden herself away, that she, the inimitable Chancellor who had shaken the City to its core, had cheated death.

It was an honorable last maneuver on Maggie's part, though, begging the God of Death to intervene on her children's behalf. Maybe her death had been inevitable. Maybe she'd been in the wrong place at the wrong time. But she'd taken it, presumably in stride, and invoked a god to protect her children.

"The last time I saw Clark Carson alive," Cora mused, opting to wrap her arm around Risa's waist despite the promise of her hand, "I handed him a screaming child and swore to him that if he fucked this up, I'd take his soul." She sighed, smile faltering. "That is unfortunate, Elizabeth was arrested. I had hoped that she would forsake this place for a better future."

"It had nothing to do with the City. Caelaymnis," Risa remarked bitterly, "has a blood-magic problem."

Cora stopped, scowl etching into her brow. "What?"

"They must've figured out who she was. One of the generals—one of the princes, no less—well, they're deep in conflict with the Woodshades, and he told her that possessing the blood of the Daughter of Death—"

"Fuck."

"Oh, what, you didn't see this in your tapestry," Risa queried,

230

eyebrow quirked.

Glaring, Cora turned, running her fingers through her hair. Her eyes were disappointedly furious as they met Risa's. "It is not a book to be read, it's at best a synopsis. Caelaymnis is going after the gods." She scoffed, and there was a flash of anger in her eyes. "Tell me *everything*. Leave no detail behind."

CORA

"We played the people in our lives by trying to get the upper hand. I had the letters. She had the tapestry. Two people who did not want to cede control."

~Risa Barrett

Risa had spread the dossier out on the floor of her Chancery office, her blue eyes focused as she flipped through folios.

"You're cute, when you work," Cora said quietly, reaching for a stack of papers.

Risa snorted.

"What? I mean it."

"You say these things," she snickered, "and I hardly believe it. You're a god."

"And yet," Cora mused, thumbing through the letters, "I have not in all the ages seen someone looking so adorably focused whilst they sit on the floor of a government building in their pink pajamas."

Flushing crimson, Risa was grinning as she scooted over to sit beside Cora. "These are the first few years. Clark had a fair few in his pocket over the years. He started with a neighbor, who ended up passing, and then moved on to the woman who ran the schoolhouse, with a few supplements here and there."

"These accountings get long and excessively poetic," Cora frowned.

"Ah. That would be Sam."

"Sam?"

"Someone to everyone. He's Elsie's friend, but he's also her brother's boyfriend," Risa explained, "and Clark's ward, too. Sam Alderton, son of Rebeca Alderton and a mystery man he's never mentioned—in one of the letters, he says he doesn't know the name, in another, he claims Clark does but won't disclose it—"

Cora tensed.

Rebeca Alderton.

Gods-damned woman. *She's going to haunt me from now until the end of time, isn't she.*

That wretched whelp—at least he'd taken to looking after Elsie. Perhaps time away from his parents had given him a favorable temperament.

"—and of course, Sam knows who I am, I'm sure," Risa was saying, tucking a chestnut curl behind her ear, "he's stupidly clever, it's annoying—"

"Who you are," Cora echoed, brow knit as she tried to bring her focus back to Risa and only Risa. "I—did I miss something? Who are you?"

"Oh." Risa swallowed, looking down at her cuticles, suddenly very focused on them. "I mean, I'm me. But I'm also Teddy's sister."

Cora tried to summon a look of surprise, though she did not know if she did a convincing job. Mostly, she suspected it was a look of guilt, for Yara hadn't been wrong. She had the high ground, having seen Risa's thread weave its way through the tapestry—more than that, having been quintessential in the swap that landed Risa in this very City.

I helped take you away from your family.

I helped you survive.

It was the height of arrogance on Cora's part, thinking such things, and guilt was on the heels of her pride a moment later.

"There was an accident. I hit my head on the table—it was bad, we didn't really have a good physician, or funds...and you know that Clark had Elsie—"

"Ah." Cora nodded, her interruption making Risa fall silent. It wasn't really a truth, nodding along, but it wasn't deception, either. "You were sent to the City. And Elsie took your place." Sure, she had cadenced it to be a realization, but the words bore no untruth, so it couldn't *really* be a lie, right?

"Exactly." Risa shrugged. "I got replaced."

"You're irreplaceable." Now these words—these ones came without thought, without hesitation.

Risa laughed a little, relaxing somewhat. "That's sweet, Cora."

Maybe it was. *Sweet* was never really something the God of Death had aspired to be.

"Must've been difficult, reading about your brother all these years."

"I didn't know it was him at the time." Risa gave a bitter laugh. "But Clark always knew. I must've re-read these letters dozens of times, after I found out. And of course, it made perfect sense, when I put it together. The subtle remarks about me, coming back to the District—and of course, he was forthcoming about seeing me out of the Valley, all under the guise that our Healers could do what the physicians could not—"

"He wasn't wrong." Cora looked away. "I am the God of Death. Cutter of Threads. Keeper of Souls. I know that much, anyway. He...wasn't wrong."

Silence fell between them.

Cora thumbed through a stack of letters—the girl's life in ink and parchment. "It's a shame about Elsie," she said softly. What she meant was, *it's a shame about the blood magic,* because there was no question that someone was using it to chase the gods, and there was only one reason someone would want *all* the gods of this pantheon together and submissive to their master's will.

She did feel bad for Elsie, though, getting caught in the middle of it—the girl hadn't had an easy life, and she still had difficulty yet to face.

"Elsie's getting there." Risa looked thoughtfully over the pages spread before her. "It was awful. I'd never seen someone who'd taken dhacrym before, let alone that much. I was so scared she wasn't going to make it through that first night."

"But she did. And—and the dhacrym's out of her system," Cora added, hesitant as she gauged Risa's reaction. This was critical—dhacrym notoriously insulated its victims from most magics, effectively isolating them in their fear.

"I think so? If not yet, soon," Risa mulled. "Maybe a couple more weeks at most, she was still symptomatic last I saw, but that's a generous estimate. Why?"

"No reason. Merely curious."

Cora had to be sure. She had one chance with Elsie to close the Death quay—she couldn't risk it going sideways because she'd been hasty. The threat was imminent, and she had to move with alacrity, but that'd get them nowhere if Elsie was drowning in dhacrym, inert and unable to open the quay anyway.

The Master's aim was to control the gods, and sure, maybe he just wanted prestige or the power—as if that wasn't bad enough—but Cora couldn't risk inaction on the chance that he knew what sat beneath the quays.

Or worse, that he knew Alder and her fucked up.

Alder and I were never supposed to be gods.

And they were never supposed to open two of the quays.

If the Master saw that part of his job was already done and two quays were already unlocked, everyone—gods and all—would realize she was an imposter. They'd see that she'd lied, that she'd covered for Alder, that she'd jeopardized everything she and her friends, allies, had worked so hard to protect. They'd see that her name wasn't really Cora, and that if they hurt her, it was not godly blood she'd bleed.

She couldn't risk that. Not now, not when the tapestry showed that it could be prevented. It wove a future where Elsie experienced an impermanent death, and to Cora, the message couldn't have been more plain.

Cora rose, padding to the window to look out across the City. It wasn't hers, as much as she'd laid claim to it in her conversations with Risa. Each window like little stars, suspended in the high rises, each street lamp glowing warm below, each avenue fading into darkness towards the edge of the City—it belonged to another.

And someone was after the gods.

They'd be disappointed, for Elsie's blood would summon no one.

Someone had pieced together the genealogy well, but they'd failed to account for a pair of arrogant mortals and two dead gods.

I can close the Death quay. I just have to make sure that once I do, it can't be opened again.

"I would like to meet Elsie." Cora leaned against Risa's desk, trying to be casual. "I think it would be wise to warn her that she is not my only heir." *I think it would be wise to get the children together, in one place, so they can be guarded together.*

So that there's no loose threads to tie up.

There'd be nothing worse than for the boy to fall into the Master's hands, for there's nothing to stop the Master from killing him to open the quay after I've so carefully closed it.

That'd just be the icing on the cake, wouldn't it? I, posing as the God of Death, undo the mistakes of my past, so carefully avoiding the very thing I claim to have purview over, only for it all to fall apart.

Risa's blue eyes narrowed. "You want to meet Elsie, and tell her about the boy?"

"Margaret Faulise had one request, when she met the Underworld," Cora said softly. "Save my children. Protect the twins."

TEDDY

"Matters of the heart are the heart of what matters.
It's a stupid saying, but alas, a true one."

~Sam Alderton

Teddy's back ached, curled in bed. His eyes were fixed unseeing towards the window, the oppressive silence heavy around him as golden motes drifted up to the ceiling, twirls of Thread gliding up from where his hand lay limp, palm up before him.

Sam was gone.

The moment of leaving in and of itself had been horrendous, but he wondered if Sam knew that it'd been the first in a chain of heart-breaking moments.

Sam was gone. Chim had wanted to know why, and sure, she was a little demon child with a penchant for chaos, but hearths were her currency, and she had loved this hearth, that she'd made no secret of. She'd scampered off, teary and furious, and Teddy hadn't seen her since. Then, of course, there was the telling.

Sam hadn't given any of the rest the courtesy of a farewell. He'd up and gone, leaving Teddy to break the news. The anticipation had left him locked in sorrow in Sam's old bedroom at the Carson manor for weeks, for the thought of facing them all—well.

Saying that his best friend of nearly a decade walked away meant reliving the rejection each and every time he breathed the words.

He'd said the words to Elsie, and they'd cried for hours together. And he'd wanted to tell her everything—tell her they'd been married, that this wasn't just a fiancé or a best friend or a companion walking away. But those words felt fetid. Poison, even.

There was a knock at the bedroom door, and Teddy let out a deep sigh, unmoving as the door clicked open.

"I hope I am not disturbing you?" Isa's quiet voice was gentle, the bed giving as they sat down.

He shook his head. "No."

Of anyone who understood this, it would be Isa. He felt dumb for not realizing that sooner.

Isa brushed back Teddy's hair, resting a hand on his forehead. "Not feverish. That is good, at least." Isa's skin was still cool against his own, though, chilled fingers a relief in the suffocating isolation. Teddy pushed himself to sitting, and Isa drew him into a hug. "I am so sorry," they breathed.

"Me too." Teddy felt tears prickling in his eyes once more, gently wrapping his arms around Isa's waist.

The moment was still and full of heartbreak.

Isa at last pulled away, hand lingering on Teddy's shoulder to give it a squeeze. "My visit is multi-purposed. I have a plan. And if you're willing, I'd like your help."

"What is it?"

"Ever since my commission was reinstated, I...can't fight. Not anymore." Isa's expression was somber. "It wasn't right, and I can't run from that any longer. I've been stealing supplies from the infirmary—I've got enough, now, I think. I want to help the Woodshades."

"Help, as in—"

"As in, they've got a lot of sick and wounded, and I'm a medic. And importantly, you're a Healer." Isa gave him a small nudge. "It'll help us to have a human in the mix—and it'll take your mind off everything here."

Suddenly, the vastness of the world was beckoning. He'd forgotten how wide it all was, in the smallness of his grief.

"You've been saying for ages how much you want to learn to Heal," Isa added, a smile at the corners of their mouth. "Now's your chance. Come with me. Be our human emissary, and let me teach you what I know."

~ • ~

The word *settlement* was, in Teddy's opinion, a generous description for the Woodshades.

A conglomeration of lean-to shacks and dilapidated shelters, they were nothing more than outcroppings of survival, sprinkled through the forested edges of the plateaus before great white mountains jutted up to the sky once more.

Easy. Deep breaths.

Snow crunched under boot, and already, a dog was barking somewhere from within the camp.

Hands up. Nice and easy.

"Who're you," a man snapped, knife already drawn as he skittered through the snow. Beard frosted, he was draped in a crude half-cape still in the shape of what had once been an antelope, Teddy supposed, or maybe a deer, whatever it was they had so far north.

"My name is Theodore...Alderton," he said slowly, voice pitched low as he left the Drada behind to approach the man. *Alderton.* Teddy wasn't giving up that easily, but the name was still an icy knife in the gut. "My friends and I have come to trade."

"Trade, eh?" The man gave Teddy a once over.

"We have medical supplies. And I'm a Healer, I've come to look at your sick and wounded." Healing, with a capital *H*, was a strictly human skill, and one that would likely be more trusted here than anything else.

The man's eyes narrowed. "Come from where?"

"Caelaymnis."

The man gave a derisive snort, crossing his arms. "Caelaymnis. A'right, then. A human, from Caelaymnis. As if those gods-damned vora would take in one of us."

"We want to trade," Teddy pushed, veering the conversation back to where it was salvageable. If Isa was to be believed, the Woodshades would've been happy to extol the sins of the Drada until the world ended, and they didn't have time for that. Not today, anyway.

"Trade?"

"Medical supplies, and we'll tend to your ill as best we can."

"And what do you want in exchange?"

Teddy met the man's gaze, shoulders tight. "Don't kill us." He could hear them, moving through the snow behind him. The man's expression had soured, teeth bared as he watched Isa trudging through the snow to join Teddy.

"We're here to help only," Isa said, their accent somehow thickening with—was it nerves?

"Why."

A particularly reasonable man, Teddy thought, listening to him demand answer after answer instead of gutting them on-site. Though a clash wasn't seen as favorable by the humans without blood-magic on their own tongues, Isa had said, so as long as the supply was low, or none of them were dosed, they'd be safe. And most of the humans didn't use, anyway—it was a few encampments closer to the border who got up-in-arms about it all, and in the heart of winter, dissent was easy to cool.

"We have much," Isa said simply. "If you do not wish to trade—we give you supplies, and you give us our lives—we can take the bargain elsewhere. Yours is not the only settlement—"

"We accept."

Walking through the camp reminded Teddy, in an odd sort of way, of home. People, trying to make the best they could with what they had. Trying to survive against the odds.

The man—who was presumably the leader of the camp, or at least had taken on the mantle for the duration of the visit—brought them to his own tent first. This, he said, would be where the gods-damned vora and their human pet might make the trade, under his watchful eye.

And so the hurt were brought.

It proved an exercise in finding the limits of the Thread, Teddy quickly realized. Healers could use their magic to provoke the natural healing response of a body, which was well and good for cuts and scrapes and bruises and broken bones, but in other respects, it could be dangerous.

A fever was one's way of fighting off infection—a natural response, and one that could be further agitated, with a careless bit of Healing magic. It had been a horrific realization that the wrong bit of magic in the wrong moment might prove fatal. *Cooked to death with their own fever.*

But circumstances such as those were rare and easily preventable, Isa had explained.

And magic was not the only tool Teddy had.

A child with pneumonia—not much that Teddy's own skills could do, but he'd given the mother a tonic. A grandmother with arthritis in her back—he'd given her a tea and salve. After that, though...

It got weird.

It wasn't like the other times he'd healed, where everything had been freshly wounded.

There'd been the cut, festering for weeks, putrid with rot—he'd nearly lost his breakfast, and it'd taken Isa's assistance to mend the whole thing, start to finish.

A thumb, separated from a hand for nigh on a month—why in the name of anything holy they'd *kept* the damn thing, he didn't know, but there'd been little to do but shrug and apologize and explain that it wouldn't do to reattach the shriveled, blackened digit deposited in Teddy's palm.

And he'd never seen *actual fungus* growing on someone's foot, yet there it was, stinking up the place, but it turned out, there was a tonic for that, too.

There was a lot of that sort of nonsense, he found, as the day passed on. Things gone untended for too long, problems too healed up already to really be fixed—the exception being the poorly set leg, which Isa had re-broken and set with a grimace—and when at last Isa tapped him on the shoulder, he'd been nearly ready to collapse.

It was only noon.

"You're doing well," Isa grinned, sinking down by the fire at the center of the tent, pulling their bag towards them.

Teddy followed suit, his knees aching as he crossed his legs.

"Helps, having him here," one of the other medics put in, joining them. "But everyone I tend to keeps asking if he can help them instead."

"Tell them no," Teddy muttered.

Isa passed him a waxy parcel of food. "What happened to the idealistic 'help everyone' nonsense you were spouting about?"

"It died," Teddy sighed reluctantly, pulling a hunk of bread off the roll. "It died, when someone dropped what used to be a thumb in the palm of my hand, and said, 'put'er back, why doncha.'" His eyes flicked up to the medic. "I'm kidding. But seriously, what the fuck was that?"

"Oh, that's nothing, I had this woman—"

"That's enough," Isa snickered. "I'm trying to eat, over here."

Another medic was pushing through the tent flap, though, frowning as she made a beeline for Isa. "Sorry, Captain, but lunchtime's over. We need you across the settlement."

No rest for the wicked, that was the saying.

But to Teddy's mind, the wicked at least got a decent lunch break.

As it stood, the medics were afforded no such luxury.

And he found, curious enough, he didn't quite mind.

ISA

"The bond of another who is radiantly uncontained
is deep. We understand. There's no caging of words
when we talk, there's just relief and relaxation, knowing
that we are home."

~Isa Mirestva

The showers were empty, the dinner bell having rung not ten minutes prior.

It was a small blessing, though—Teddy was human, and regardless of talent, humanity would be unwelcome in such a vulnerable place.

"Towel," Isa muttered, tossing one at Teddy from the cubby of clean linen, reaching for a basket of tiny rectangles, "and soap." They gestured to the stalls. "Have at it. You can leave your clean clothes on the hooks, dirty ones in the hamper, they'll...make their way back to the infirmary eventually." Then, shrugging, they turned, fingers making quick work of the buttons on the uniform jacket.

After the settlements, a hot shower was more than welcome.

Teddy cleared his throat, hanging up the infirmary-ware on the hook. "Thank you. For today."

"I'm glad you came with," Isa shrugged, tossing the jacket aside and peeling off their undershirt. "You were the difference between success and failure, today."

Teddy made a sound of skepticism, pulling his shirt over his head. "I dunno about that. Heartbroken boys aren't exactly the best of company."

"How are you doing with all that?"

He shrugged, bundling the shirt up, studying it like it was a fascinating puzzle. "Oh, absolutely shitty."

Tossing their uniform haphazardly towards the bin, Isa sighed, eyes flitting back to Teddy. "Fair enough." Their eyes flicked down to the scars on his chest, the double scars blessing him.

Teddy made a face, looking down, and then back to Isa. "What," he asked hesitantly.

Isa swallowed, turning their gaze to the empty hall. "I'm...unconsecrated," they said quietly, their own voice nevertheless sounding thunderous as it reverberated off the stone. It was a truth that'd been whispered back by the city itself. "It means I have to live with myself in a way you don't."

The silence was pressing in, interrupted only by the distant *drip drip* of water on tile.

"*Ro* means to be uncontained, right?" Teddy asked softly.

It meant that Isa was one of a thousand stars set into the sky. That Isa had found one of a thousand holy ways of being that transcended definition, unbound by expectation.

"Yeah. Uncontained." Isa glanced over, tears pricking in the corners of their eyes. "And I'm as contained as a wax-sealed bottle of bitter wine." Sniffling, they pushed the damp away with the back of their hand. "I will never be able to buy my way into consecration. I think I realized, a couple years ago, that not being able to buy uncontainment didn't change how I felt. And I *felt* uncontained, Teddy," they breathed, tears welling. "But I'm so tired. I will never be enough, in their eyes. I have not paid the tithes, I have not cleansed myself through their trials— forget my own struggles! It—it's a bunch of rich kids that have to manufacture problems to feel holy, and they like to stand up on their hill and tell me I was wrong for loving Augustus, wrong for using their

245

words, wrong for fucking *existing*, just because I couldn't afford to buy my way into their club—and then there's you, and I look at you and I am so *jealous* of what you have, but if my heart continues to shift, and I continue to drift my own way, then they'll say that I am betraying the gods and the consecrated alike, even though I can never be one of them anyway..." Exhaling, Isa dared a glance at Teddy.

He only pursed his lips, sighing, eyes pitched midnight.

"Sorry," Isa breathed, turning for the stalls.

"Doesn't sound like you're the one that needs to be sorry, to me," Teddy offered.

Isa scoffed, pausing. "I'm not sorry for crying. I'm sorry for me, because it's fucking unfair."

"Yeah." Teddy's expression fell. "It is. It's really fucking unfair. I..." His eyes wandered thoughtfully across the empty room. "I remember feeling that lost. The moment I said the words aloud—it was funny, Isa," he breathed, a faint smile on his lips, "because we were just sitting in the meadow, and Sam was talking about kissing boys, and something clicked into place. And I had been happy, until I realized I wasn't. I saw how big the world could be. I saw who I could be. That I could be comfortable. Myself. And I was so unhappy that I'd spent so long trying to be someone I didn't love."

Isa crossed their arms, tears of relief pressing at their eyes once more. "So, it's not just me, then. Feeling trapped."

"No. No, of course not," Teddy said softly, brow knitting. "I—I love stories, Isa. I felt like a damsel locked in a tower. The room was nice, I was pretty, and I felt like I was being ungrateful for saying it wasn't enough. But it's not. It's not enough, not being yourself. And...I couldn't get out. I couldn't have, not by myself."

"But you did," Isa pressed, sniffling.

"Yeah, because my knight in shining armor unlocked the door."

246

Teddy's eyes were glistening, and he gave a bitter laugh. "Sam was talking about kissing boys, and all I could think was *that's me. I'm that boy.* And Sam—he was so wonderful. He just looked at me, beaming. Not— not an ounce of hesitation." He ran his fingers along the scars. "He paid for these. More promises about *always.*"

"Augustus always loved the ways I was uncontained, too," Isa breathed, and they turned for the showers. To cry unseen.

Quiet drips of water echoed and Isa's soft footfalls against damp stone filled the hall as they met one of the alcoves, partitioned off with enough privacy to justify slumping up against the wall and letting silent tears run while hot water gushed from the faucet.

He's like me.

There was something so comforting about finding another soul that had broken free, Isa thought. Something hopeful.

They'd walk different paths, for how could they not, having different souls, and that—that brought them comfort, too, for what better armament to going one's own way than to see someone else go theirs.

"I...felt like part of my life was over, when Augustus opened the door, and Elsie was sitting there." Isa's words were quiet, and perhaps they did not carry over the sound of water hitting the stone floor to the human ears somewhere in the hall, but the words needed to be said. "He forced me to lay some part of myself to rest, this—this idyllic, haphazard part, and I had to stop being reckless and full of passion and had to start fighting, right then, in that moment. Because it wasn't just Augustus, being an ass, it was Augustus, tossing around life the way a shopkeep hurls overripe fruit into a rubbish bin, and...I am grieving for that. For the bits of radiance that he stifled in everyone he touched."

Silence met the words, the harmonics of voice swallowed into the stone and water, then—

"Because he made you shine," Teddy's voice whispered, torrential.

"Like Sam did with me. He brought so much light."

The Drada believed that fire could release the soul. That once the body had expired, a funeral pyre would ignite one to take their place amongst the stars, and maybe love had been kind of like dying, Isa thought. Still a loss in the end, but one draped in beautiful poeticism.

Until the fire died and the ashen bones lay cold in the dark, and Isa was left to clean up the mess, knowing it was all bullshit. Some mausoleum, this love was.

~•~

It was a poor night for solitude.

Isa watched Teddy dunk a sachet of tea in a cup of hot water now blossoming honey-brown, warm and smelling sweet. They'd sat in Fletcher's kitchen a fair number of times, and Teddy must've seen it in their eyes, the look of despair as they'd dragged fresh clothes onto still-damp skin, trying to hide the tears.

"Why do you use a sachet," Isa breathed, elbows on the counter, chin in their hands. He'd made a full pot of tea that now sat before them, strainer of tea leaves soaking in the hot water, so the separate cup was curious indeed.

Teddy's eyes flicked up. "It's fennelclover tea. If you're keen on whiskers and voice-drops, I'll make you a cup."

A bright smile split across Isa's face. "Tempting."

"I didn't think you'd mind. I usually sit and drink it alone, but the company is nice," Teddy grinned.

Isa chuckled, moving to pour themself a cup of tea from the pot. "I don't mind at all. It's wonderful, actually. I don't often partake in rituals like that."

"I don't know that it's a ritual, but it's certainly a habit, and one I hold close." He took a sip, shoulders relaxing down as he did. "It's lonely,

248

without Sam."

"He's an ass." Isa straightened up.

"He's hurt," Teddy breathed, smile giving way like the temporary respite it was. "And that's so much worse, Isa. Being an ass, I can forgive. Being hurt? All I can do is grieve for him."

"You've a way of getting to the heart of it, don't you," Isa grimaced.

"I'm a bit older than you. It comes with the territory." His eyes flicked up. "You've got your own wisdom, though. I do recall you sitting with a boy, not terribly long ago, telling him he did not have to carry the weight of grief alone."

Isa snorted, shaking their head. "Well, it's because I'm holy, you know," they retorted, sardonic. "I defy the gods, which means I'm rife with logic and reason."

"That's beautiful, that being uncontained is sacred defiance," Teddy said quietly, looking down into his tea.

"How is it to you?"

"I dunno. It just is. People are just people, and from time to time, someone says *Oh look, a baby girl* when what they mean to say is that it's a boy. A clerical error. You correct it and move on." He shrugged, taking another sip of tea.

Isa slumped onto the counter. "I can't decide if I like that better or worse." Their gaze flicked to his. "You're not tired of me complaining about this?"

"Tired? No. It's complicated. If you need to complain about it for a bit, then do. It doesn't make you less radiant—nor does it make you less uncontained," Teddy frowned. "There's a—a delicacy about it. This sort of notion that if parts of this journey are hard, then it isn't worth making."

"Yeah, well, it wouldn't *be* hard if I was taken seriously," Isa bit back, glaring. "Being uncontained isn't hard. It's dealing with everyone else that makes it difficult. So what, that I can't pay the tithes? So what, that my parents weren't devout? That doesn't change how I feel!"

"If you need money—"

"Teddy, I love you, but *stop trying to fix everything*. My point isn't that I'm poor. My point is that being poor shouldn't *matter!*"

Teddy pursed his lips, quirking an eyebrow. "And perhaps *you* could soften up a bit. I'm not trying to fix *everything*, I'm trying to ease some of your discomfort. Sam sure as hell wasn't trying to fix me when he put up gold to buy my scars. He was loving me, Isa." A grimace of pain flashed across his face.

Isa leaned back, softening in guilt. "Sorry."

"Likewise."

"Augustus thought it was all bullshit. He—he would've paid, if it could have made a difference." Isa sighed heavily. In spite of themself, a faint smile pricked at the corners of their mouth.

"What," Teddy breathed, eyes glinting.

"It's so funny. I get so mad, and—and then I'm sitting here, with you, and I think about myself, and how the words themselves make me feel. *Radiantly uncontained.*" They grinned, shaking their head. "What's your word for it? You humans and your Vernacular?"

Teddy laughed, cradling his teacup. "Oh. It, uh. It depends. My grandmother would call me kaleidoscopic. She's old-fashioned, but I always kind of liked it. Anymore, people don't particularly call it out. It is what it is. You are what you are." His gaze was a bit distant, looking across the kitchen. "I remember Sam putting me in a button-down, the fall after I told him. Before the Festival. I felt so nervous. I was in that awkward in-between of second adolescence, and I felt so handsome," he grinned, "and I remember Elsie walked up to me—I will always remember this—she said, *Sir,* and I thought I was going to die of happiness."

"The first time I bound myself, I almost passed out. Not from euphoria—well, not *just* from euphoria. There's such an art to it," Isa chuckled, "I put it on way too tight—"

"Oh, I did that too! It depends on the time of year, too, I always liked it looser in the summer—"

"Skies, same! It gets too hot," Isa laughed, nodding along. "Sometimes the heat of the Thallassas beaches just—just burn away the discomfort. I'll be sitting in the sun, baking on the sand, and my body feels so free. That's so much of the beauty, how many ways of feeling free there are, too."

"I do miss binding, a bit?" Teddy shot a look askance across the table. "It's odd, but it felt so familiar. It was one of the first moments I realized how at home I felt in my own skin, and that's an incredibly powerful thing. I was reticent to give that up, even for greater comfort."

"It's holy. It's...it's illuminating yourself. It's like this armor. We always bind in yellow," Isa went on, serious. "Like the stars. It's symbolic. You wrap yourself in the starlight of the one you follow, and I remember feeling so much less alone, with that. It isn't just binding. It's reassurance. It's knowing someone else walked your path before you, and knowing someone will again once you're gone."

"A beautiful way of being," Teddy said softly.

Isa's eyes flicked up, meeting his, gently blue. The gods ought to tremble, two kaleidoscopic, radiant, uncontained, *are-what-we-are* mortals bolstering their spirits across a kitchen table.

Teddy set his teacup aside, rising, fingertips poised on the table in pause. "I can grab something stronger, and we can continue this in more comfortable chairs? There's still a fire in the living room, I'm sure."

A tempting offer.

Isa rose too, biting their lip. "I...better not."

"You're not imposing if you do."

"No, it's not that. It's...if I stay, and we start drinking, you and I might end up regretting it," Isa said quietly, cheeks flushing.

Teddy let out a sound of amusement, head dropping to study the floor. "That's not what I was suggesting."

"I know it wasn't. But I know me. And I know that if I'm sitting by the fire, drunk, with you," Isa breathed, "you, who is being so kind and gentle and sweet...I'm not going to respect whatever line you draw. So, I have to go."

Quiet fell over them both.

"It wouldn't be the worst thing," Teddy said softly, after a moment. He glanced up.

"Maybe not. But why risk it. I love you as my friend. That's not worth gambling with." Isa came around the table, clapping him on the back before drawing him into a hug. "Thanks for the talk."

"Same to you." Teddy gave them a squeeze, drawing back. "Rest well."

They nodded, waving as they left.

Rest well.

A nice thought. A distant, nice thought. Maybe someday they would—but not tonight.

CHIM

*"Blood pacts are curious things. We like to think
we're static beings, but when the very force of life in our
bodies is commandeered, when wants are molded, when
desires are shifted...we must reckon with the death of who
we once were, and face the person pain has made us
become."*

~Chim, Purveyor of Chaos

To Chim's dismay, Mother Chaos had beckoned her back to the house
of the Master.

"I don't wanna," Chim was whining, stomping up the stairs of the
house, "I don't wanna—"

"That is enough," Mother Chaos hissed, dragging her to the stoop.
"The Fallen Gods have been called to assembly. As my child, you must
answer to the Master."

Chim wrinkled her nose in disgust.

There'd been *nothing* in the blood pact about having to scrape and
bow at that stinky man.

Scowling, Chim squirmed out of Mother's grip, darting down the
stairs and into the flower bed, muddy with slush from the recent snow,
and with a screech, she dove into the filth, covering herself head to toe.
It was a shame, she'd really been partial to this particular apron, and her
red hood would have to be carefully cleaned, but there had been nothing
in her pact saying she couldn't muss up the Master's house with garden
mud.

She only had to wait for the Master to finish with Sam, and then kill him, and Teddy, too.

Mother Chaos didn't say anything about not ruining the upholstery.

~ • ~

"This. *This*. Is the most obscene demonstration of disobedience," the Master breathed, pinching the bridge of his nose in frustration, "that I have ever seen in my *life.*"

"I apologize, Master," Mother Chaos whispered, a mortified look on her face—though it was not an expression that belonged to Mother, this much, Chim could be sure of.

Mother Chaos would have never apologized for soiling the living room of a merchant.

"You have this under control? I cannot use more of the Tears, my stocks are precariously small to begin with, do you understand," the Master hissed, taking a step towards Mother Chaos.

Chim was sitting quietly by the hearth, finger pricked and vow made and she *had* to behave in the Master's house now. Dimly, in the back of her mind, she knew it was no fun to sit still, and yet, in her heart, the overwhelming desire to be polite and quiet overtook all else.

She didn't think this was a particularly fair way to play the game.

Ignata, God of Fire, came to sink down beside her, fiery eyes bright. "*Kobalde.*"

"You *know* who I am," she snapped, crossing her arms. "And I know who *you* are."

Ignata blinked, and some sense of self seemed to come back for a moment. "Chim."

She nodded.

"Do you like arson," he asked quietly, eyes glossing over once more, and he was not himself. None of them were, tied with these blood pacts

254

and Ruby Tears to the Master.

"Of *course* I like arson. But I shan't light this house on fire, I don't want to do that, I want to behave." Chim heaved a sigh, small shoulders sinking. She didn't know if that was true, anymore. Maybe she *didn't* like arson. Everything was muddy, with all these pacts.

"This is enough." The Master was clapping his hands, calling them all to attention.

Stell, God of Ice, was sulking in a far corner, and at the Master's beckoning, straightened to join them by the fire, and Natali, God of Order—Auntie Order, to Chim—she glanced up from where she'd been sitting on a divan. Hadri, God of Night, had been lurking in the shadows, and it was only a pair of starlight eyes that gazed out of the darkened armchair.

"As you know," the Master began, "I am close to gaining control of your pantheon. I lack three gods. Cora. Kiran. Asa. Cora—we have found another heir, and he is securely held. Dhacrym, barghests, and the Xavishia, and we will soon welcome Cora to our ranks, as soon as the heir bleeds."

"Did you nearly bring down a chandelier on this one, too," snickered Ignata, leaning back to rest on his elbows as he stretched out.

The Master's head snapped to the God of Fire, eyes furious. "I told you. That had nothing to do with me. Why on earth would I bring down a chandelier?"

"You owe them no explanation," Mother Chaos drawled, examining her fingernails, and it was to Chim's eyes like a glimmer of someone familiar peering through a dirty window. "No need to explain away the love of blood and destruction and...*chaos.*"

"It's true!" Chim was nodding excitedly. The chandelier drop had been her *favorite*, there'd been glass *everywhere* and she'd been so excited to hear everyone screaming—

255

"I disliked that girl, anyway," the Master was mumbling, gesturing to his arm, and the conversation, it seemed, had carried on without them. "But of course, that Mirabeau boy had to step up and play the hero once more..."

"I'm going to eat him," Chim volunteered helpfully. "I'm supposed to eat him and the other one, as soon as you finish right up with him! I'm going to hunt them down and devour them limb from limb, I am going to crack their bones and suck the marrow, I will—"

"See, this...this is very good work." The Master was nodding, gesturing to Chim. "This is the level of execution that I expect from all of you."

The starlight eyes of Hadri, God of Night, stirred in the corner. "And then we may be at peace?" she asked softly, voice velvet.

The Master nodded. "And then you may be at peace."

ELSIE

"There are parts of ourselves we keep private, for we owe the world nothing."

~Unknown

Tying her hair back into a high ponytail, Elsie's eyes kept darting to the vial of dhacrym on the dresser.

It felt wrong, leaving it out so brazenly, and she had to remind herself that it was not the incriminating piece of evidence it would have otherwise been.

This vial was for the ring.

Even so, she couldn't resist uncorking it, giving it a small sniff.

The familiar earthy tang of the dhacrym met her nose, and she inhaled, eyes closing. It was comforting, in an odd way.

A friend she knew.

And it made her feel such recognizable feelings. Feelings she knew what to do with. Love, excitement, calm—these were not things she was equipped to handle.

Fear? *That* she could deal with.

It was easier to be afraid than to be...well, than to be anything else.

"Elsie?"

Starting, her eyes snapped open, and she was fumbling for the cork, which had rolled off the dresser and onto the floor.

Fletcher stooped down, picking up the cork with a frown. "What are you doing?"

"Nothing," she breathed, setting the vial back down with shaking hands, wringing them as she watched Fletcher seal the bottle back up. "I—I dunno, I was curious what it smelled like..."

He looked like he really, really wanted to believe her.

"I should go." Elsie slung a satchel across her body, touching the locket on the dresser before scooping the vial of dhacrym up. "I can't be late."

"Be safe." Fletcher brushed a kiss across her cheek, eyes still worried.

"I will be." She paused, and somewhat awkwardly, took his hands in hers. "Hey."

"Elsie—"

"You need to trust me."

"I do," Fletcher said quietly, squeezing her fingers, "I do, El, I—I'm just afraid for you. This is so dangerous—"

"And so necessary. There's no other way to get to the heart of this. Night does not welcome the embrace of torches," she quoted, heart aching. Sam had loved that story.

He sighed. "Then go. Be the night. But Elsie?"

She glanced back, already half-way to the door. "Yeah?"

"You're...you wouldn't willingly take the dhacrym again, would you? Even out of curiosity?"

"No," she lied, voice soft. "Of course, I wouldn't. It's not like I want to be afraid all the time." *I just don't know how else to be.*

~ • ~

Roscoe, the boy that had met Elsie in the bar and brokered their first trade in the alley, was waiting for her outside of a seedy little shop on the outskirts of the Textile Quarter of the Capital. "You're late," he sighed, taking a drag from a cigarette.

The air was bitter with tobacco as he exhaled, and it made Elsie miss

Sam that much more.

"Fuck you, I had things to do," she bit back, smoothing the satchel, nausea from the disc still dissipating. "If you can get Clio off my back, you'll find that my services are nothing if not prompt."

Roscoe flicked the ash from the end of his cigarette. "What kind of services," he asked, a faint smile at the corners of his lips, quirking his eyebrow with an *if you know what I mean* kind of lilt.

Elsie cocked her head to the side, hand in her pocket, and in a seamlessly comfortable movement, she flicked out her switchblade and stabbed him in the gut. "These kinds of services."

After that, the trade went a bit slower.

But it felt good, being in this element again. Being honest.

Runners never did a trade alone, even for something like dhacrym, and Roscoe's partner in the shadows came running out. "Roscoe!!"

"He's fine," Elsie snickered, wiping the blade on her pants. "We've learned an important lesson, haven't we, Roscoe? Mind your own *damn business.*"

"You." Roscoe's partner snarled the word, glaring daggers at Elsie as he heaved Roscoe to standing. "Come with me."

Elsie rolled her eyes, sighing as she gave the satchel a pat. "Got this, anyways."

Muttering, the man walked Roscoe down the alley towards the side-door of the shop, propped ajar. "Name's Everett, by the way."

"Do I look like I give a fuck," Elsie bit back.

"Polite thing to do is tell me your name."

"We're not polite people, don't kid yourself."

Everett glanced back, eyes alight with amusement. "You know, I was skeptical, when Roscoe said some girl was looking to run with us."

"Some girl? I should stab him again, that's rude," Elsie quipped, and she had half a mind to now, because she'd learned that boys like Roscoe spoke only one language.

Everett just chortled, flinging open the side-door with one hand.

"Please don't," whimpered Roscoe, eyes flicking to Elsie as they stepped into the shop.

It was surprisingly well-lit, and Elsie blinked, eyes adjusting. They'd taped over the windows with paper, she realized now, blacking them out so it looked abandoned—or at least, too run-down to draw much notice.

To the left, by the front window papered with faded newsprint, there was an elaborate curl of glass piping rich with what *had* to be blood, curling through as it distilled, the large vat on one end agitated to an unsettlingly sluggish simmer, the vial on the other end gleaming as fat drops rolled into the glass.

To the right, shelves of...well, what, Elsie wasn't entirely sure. Some of it was clearly the by-product of blood magic, but then there were also a lot of dried herbs and crushed powders and burlap bags, one of which Elsie could *swear* she saw move.

"Not too bad," Elsie nodded, looking around appraisingly, and she wandered over to the counter, setting the satchel down gently. Quirking an eyebrow, she then made a beeline for the register amid a pile of junk, a smile tugging at her lips. *Just like the one at the general store.* She'd seen Teddy work a register just like it a thousand times, and it was supposed to be a marvel of simple mechanics but gods below had it always been a piece of shit.

She gently pressed down a worn key with *S.c.* on it, and then gave an unceremonious bang of her fist atop the register. The drawer popped open with a mechanical *clank,* and she grinned, palming the gold, all the while making a show of pulling out the coppers.

"Excuse you." Everett was helping Roscoe into a seat, giving Elsie an intense side-eye. "What, are you just helping yourself, now?"

"Just making sure I get paid, since you're so distracted," Elsie mused, pushing the drawer shut.

"I'm only distracted because you stabbed Roscoe," Everett bit back, grimacing.

"Yeah, fuck you for that," Roscoe hissed, face pale, "what the fuck—"

"Hush." Everett was pulling a bag of medical supplies from the stacks of junk heaped against the walls, pushed out of the way to make room for this operation.

Elsie leaned against the counter, watching. "Next time, don't make fun of prostitutes." She watched Roscoe, moaning as he pressed the gauze to his gut. Gross bastard.

"My run," Roscoe whispered—

"Oh, did you have business? Then maybe you shouldn't have been running your mouth—"

"You hush, too," Everett scolded, shooting a look at Elsie.

"Tell you what." She crossed her arms, smiling faintly. "Since you're down a man, I'll cover his run tonight with you. Free of charge."

Gods, she'd missed this.

Being back in dingy shops and shady alleys and mouthing off full-well knowing that if there were consequences, she'd be fighting back, and gods, it reminded her of Percy.

Well.

The *good* times with Percy. The times they'd been stealing and laughing and divvying up the loot, and whenever they managed to get coin without getting caught, Elsie had always tried to bring something home to Teddy, to make up for the trouble she knew she caused, and together, her and her brother would sit on his bed and nibble at a slice of meat pie or share a fancy pastry, and his eyes would light up, his cheeks would be full of laughter and color—

"Fine." Everett was rising, brushing his hands off, eyes still worried on Roscoe, who was clutching his gut, face wan. *"Ginger!"*

Something crashed above them, and angry stomping followed as a woman appeared at the base of the stairs that had, until now, gone unnoticed amid the clutter against the wall.

A very angry woman with very red hair appeared, lips smudged black, eyes smokey, pants tight and blouse low-cut, and *holy gods, she's gorgeous*

"Who's this?" Ginger stopped at the base of the stairs, glaring at Elsie.

"Clio's runner, who stabbed Roscoe, who was being untoward and deserved it," Everett mumbled, fingers brushing against Roscoe's cheek.

"Untoward, what are you, a fucking tart," Elsie quipped, amused.

"Ginger, you and..."

"Dosia," Elsie said quietly, eyes flicking to Ginger.

"You and Dosia go cover Roscoe's shift," Everett instructed. "Dosia here is looking for a...career change, anyway." His eyes flicked to Elsie. "Consider this a test run. If you fuck this up, you'll regret it."

"Good thing I don't fuck up," Elsie breathed, a smile dancing at the corners of her mouth.

Ginger stared at her appraisingly for a long moment, and then, looking pissed, stormed out the side-door.

"Best go," Everett mumbled, sinking down to tend to Roscoe again.

And in spite of it all, Elsie was grinning, following Ginger into the night.

FLETCHER

*"I have loved a thousand versions of her and
mourned the loss of a thousand more. Our bond was
dynamic, ever-changing, as it should be."*

~Fletcher Nist

"Here you are. One cup of hot chocolate." Fletcher was grinning, proud as he passed Elsie the goblet before sinking down beside her with his own. The living room of his Caelaymnic house felt particularly cozy tonight, he mused, eyeing his love bundled in soft blankets on the sofa. She was home. Safe.

There was a half-smile dancing at her lips. "This is fancy, Commander Nist."

"Ah, well, you are a Chancellor, after all," he teased gently, watching as she tossed a blanket over his legs. "I—I am so relieved, El, that you're back and you're alright and everything went well..." His smile faltered as he glanced over to her. "When are you going back?"

"Day after tomorrow." She looked pleased, watching the shaved chocolate melting atop the cocoa. "They trust me. Clio gave me a beaming recommendation. He really wants that pardon for his fiancé."

"Well, he'll get it, if this goes well," Fletcher muttered. He pushed his worries—and Augustus's accusation that Elsie had been using the dhacrym—from his mind.

She had assured him she was not.

The fire was roaring, the house darkened save for the flames that danced against the grated fireplace, fat snowflakes hitting the blackened windowpanes with gentle *thump thump thwumps,* and Fletcher let his eyes close, exhausted.

Da-dum. Da-dum. Da-dum.

The ever-present beat of her heart kept time to the soft clicking of the mantle clock, gears shifting beneath the bell jar as the mechanisms turned, the hands gently guiding the day to a close.

Everything felt temporary.

This house, with the snow piling dangerously against the windows, obscuring the view of the city beyond. This moment, peaceful and calm, and it was like they were back in July, by the fountain, and he loved her so fiercely. Eventually it would all fade away, and they would be back in the cold chaos, the future uncertain.

"You told me," Fletcher said quietly, putting his arm around Elsie, "that you wanted a cat." The thrumming of her heart was in his ears at the query, because hadn't that been another lifetime ago that he'd wanted so desperately to know what their lives held?

"I did say this, yes," Elsie smiled. "After your investigation had concluded, I believe the plan was to acquire a cottage and a cat and live the most boring life the two of us could possibly muster." She hugged the mug of cocoa in her hands, sinking into him as she let out a sigh. "But that was when things were different."

"You don't want that anymore?"

"I do." She paused. "I...don't particularly see how we're going to get there, though. There's no end in sight. I am living my life one day at a time, because there is no choice. What piece of this world will begin to crumble next? What tragedy will the next sunrise bring? I don't know how to plan for peace amid crisis. That's never been my life, and so, the cottage and the cat...they're a nice dream, Fletcher. They're a nice dream."

A ball of something cold and wretched was welling in his chest, tears pricking at his eyes. "No."

Elsie nestled in, leaning on his shoulder. "No?" The word was almost hopeful, when she breathed it.

"This—this is more complicated than we thought. We're in this now, and we will see it through. But we will find our cottage. And I don't understand why this is a sequential order of operation, Elsie. Before— fine. I get that. I...was not forthcoming about my own life, and I had it in my head that was going to be the next step. That's not how it's gone, though, and it was a desperate way of looking at the world." He was shaking a little as he drew her close, kissing her hair. "We will find our peace, despite it all. We must."

Elsie was quiet for a long moment, taking a sip of cocoa. The crackling fire overwhelmed them, the soft rugs and long window dressings and the blankets draped here and there across the furniture, the upholstery itself, all of it drinking in the remnants of Fletcher's voice.

This, then that. It was his way of life, first in the palace, and then at the Acadamae.

One accomplishment led to another, and it was a ladder leading up to a funeral pyre.

"We must," Elsie echoed at last, voice soft. "But...it depends on so much. Where would this cottage even be? Here? Aerdela?"

"The human settlements petitioning Aerdela for districthood," Fletcher suggested, snickering. "For a fair bit of irony, if you like."

Elsie was silent for a long moment. "Or...the Hidden City."

Ah, the place that had been looming over them both like a storm cloud.

"Do you think you might take it," Fletcher asked quietly. "The Chancellorship?"

She let out a tired breath. "I dunno, Fletch. I was born there. But I don't know it. I don't know the people. What right do I have, thinking I can make decisions for a place I've never even seen?"

"But you are considering it."

"Maybe. Just a little." She set her cocoa on the side-table, stretching out of his arms for just a moment to do so.

"Do you not like it," he asked, worried.

"It's good." Elsie shifted to face him, legs tucked beneath her. "But I can't do this with it." And deftly, she leaned in, kissing him deeply, her hands cradling his face.

He let his eyelids flutter closed, his shoulders melting as something warm prickled sweetly through his bones. Her skin was deathly soft, the faint scent of roses about her, and he could hear her heart, the gentle *da-dum da-dum da-dum* running beneath her ribs, and his hands were about her waist, drifting beneath her sweater to brush against her.

And the storm raged on.

~ • ~

Laughter filled the kitchen, Elsie leaning against the counter, eyes sparkling with delight. The tin of occlusive tea leaves shook in her hands in her bouts of rib-aching levity, the tea leaves themselves mostly littering the counter and the floor.

In his undershorts, a blanket wrapped like a shawl around his bare shoulders, Fletcher chuckled brightly, moving to brush some of the bits of tea from her hair. "I was about to say," he grinned, "it's a bit tricky to open—"

"Too little, too late," Elsie accused, peering into the tin. "There's about a third left?"

"That's plenty." He took the tin from her. Kettle merrily chirping, he took it from the heat, splashing it into the small glass teapot before sprinkling two heaping spoons of leaves atop the steaming water to make the brew, a carapace against children. It hissed and steamed, trails of teal bleeding out as the little bits and pieces started to sink to the bottom.

Like the aurora that illuminated the night sky.

He moved for the pantry, for the broom, smiling quietly to himself.

"How long does it steep for," Elsie asked, crouching down to watch the spiraling tea leaves drifting through the hot water.

"Until it all settles to the bottom." The broom scraped against the floor, little bits of leaves making quiet whispers as they got brushed up.

He loved her, in this house. Loved the waves of sweet relief that seemed to wash over him, realizing how badly he'd needed these moments.

"We could stay here, you know," Fletcher offered quietly, leaning the broom up. "This...isn't a cottage, but..."

Elsie glanced over, emerald eyes sparkling. "We could." A pause. "I want to talk to Teddy." She rose from where she'd been crouched before the tea pot, smile faltering. "I don't know what he's going to do, now that Sam...anyway. But I want to be close to him."

"He's always welcome here," Fletcher said quietly.

"Well." Elsie pursed her lips, crossing her arms. "I know. And I think he knows. But tonight, he's back at the apartment, and I—I don't know if he plans to stay, or if he's just trying to tie up loose ends."

Fletcher nodded. He was fond of this idea, of holding their family close.

Their family, because it was his, too, he'd begun to realize.

Sam leaving had been disappointing, more than anything else. Fletcher had prayed with him, had many a fascinating conversation with him, and Sam...

"Do you think Cele was right, about Sam just needing space?" There was a hopeful tinge to Fletcher's voice as he asked.

Elsie only shrugged. "I hope so, Fletch. I hope so."

THE RECALL

What's curious about the phenomenon of discovering is that it bears a strong resemblance to remembering.

I am sifting through these waves of realization, and it's right. I don't say that often in my life. It's one of the few things of late that I can rely on—that the more I learn, the more I recall that I am whole.

~Elizabeth Clement Faulise,
Excerpt from a letter dated February 12th

THE BEAST

"Do not mistake mercy for hope. Even the darkest
hearts have mercy, but it would be foolish to think there
was hope for such a soul."

~Elizabeth Clement Faulise

"I wish to have Caelaymnis, once and for all." The Master paced the plush burnished-ochre rug before the hearth, the Fallen lingering about. "We will move within the fortnight."

The Beast lay curled at the feet of the Fearless One. Shifting, it reached up, nuzzling its head into her hand for additional scritches. The Fearless One gave very good scritches.

"Caelaymnis is already buried in ice and snow," the Cold One said. "Its people are immobile, at best, and public sentiment is fragile as it is."

The Chaotic One studied her nails. "And the dissenters will be taken care of. I have ensured that."

"Then go." The Master smiled. "Take your kin and release yourselves on our precious city of lights. Let the faithful see their gods, and therein, their folly."

The Beast sighed, resting its muzzle on the Fearless One's leg.

On...

On Mariann's leg.

The Beast knew that was what the Insidiae called her, and it had been a senseless word until now. In the wash of satisfaction, the absence of deep hunger that came with her gentle fingers against its head, it could take the word.

Mari.

The Chaotic One vanished in wisps of charcoal powder, the Cold One gone in a swirl of ice, and the Insidiae was left, watching the places they'd stood before looking to the Master.

Jaw clenched, the Master turned for the game board he'd set out on his desk. Five pieces red as blood sat atop a map, tokens of war scattered across the carved stone board, and hands poised against the edge of the desk, Anscip joined him to study the set, red eyes already focused on the spread.

The Beast merely looked up to Mari, giving a little whimper. She resumed her scritches with a faint smile. "Ani," she drawled, glancing over to the Insidiae. "Does this creature have a name?"

He gave no reply, other than a grunt of frustration at having been interrupted.

"Hm." Her fingers found that sweet spot under the beast's chin. "We shall have to fix that. I think...I will call you Howard."

"You are a fool," the Master hissed, patience thin.

"Careful." Again, the Insidiae's warning.

"You are the ones who should be careful," the Master whispered, running his hand through his hair in anguish. "With the gods in hand, there is no telling what I might do."

Later that night, the Insidiae and Mariann whispered alone, the Beast standing guard to their borrowed guest suite.

"His arrogance is getting out of hand," Mariann frowned.

"I do not disagree. But his talent is too great to leave unattended," the Insidiae mused. "If he were not so unbearable, I would commend him. Anyone can dose a mortal with dhacrym and stick them in a barghest cage. It's a rare soul that can dabble in desire and blood to possess the next-of-kin. Transference of control up a blood-line is difficult and temperamental."

275

"Do not kid yourself, Ani."

The Insidiae scoffed. "I don't. I am regrettably at his mercy. Though it is curious he failed to mention he is in possession of another heir." His apple-red eyes darted to hers. "As he coddles his Heir of Death, he keeps two more downstairs. He will have Asa, soon enough—but Kiran, too."

"And yet, his fixation is Cora."

"He's enamored with the boy."

The Fearless one nodded thoughtfully, gaze distant. "He's moving on Caelaymnis faster than I thought."

"He wants the Dagger. He's rightfully seen that the mystics stand in the way."

"You think it is folly?"

"I don't think one way or the other on it." The Insidiae reached into his pocket, drawing out a leather roll, glass clinking as he unrolled it to show Mariann. Five medium vials of deep, rich red lay securely therein, vials larger than any the Master would've ever seen. "When it's right, the gods are mine. The boy can play at this all he wants. I doubt he knows he's playing into bigger schemes—"

"If that is what he is doing," Mariann put in skeptically.

"Your doubt and caution are appreciated. If I am wrong, then I've been exercising an abundance of caution for nothing. If I am right, every single soul that has ever walked this earth will owe me a debt of gratitude." The Insidiae rolled the leather up.

"You can seize them?"

"With ease. The Master has very little of his supply left, and his control is weak. His temperament does not suit possession of a pantheon." The Insidiae shrugged his jacket off, hanging it on the bedpost. His gaze flicked to the Beast. "I cannot believe you are calling that thing Howard."

"He's precious."

"You don't fear him?"

"He's just a dog, Anscip," Mariann laughed, sinking down into bed, hand on her belly. "I always wanted a dog."

"He's not a dog. He's a mortal who committed heinous crimes and was cursed to beasthood."

The Beast didn't know what that meant. It only knew that if it hopped up onto the bed, Mariann would coax it up and give it good scritches.

The Insidiae watched with dismay as the Beast did just that, Mariann's hand finding just that perfect spot behind its ears. "This situation is precarious, love. I think sometimes you ought to leave this. Go back to that husband of yours. You're persuasive. You could convince him to raise the child as his own."

"And miss such excitement? Hardly. Yelena's hemomantic texts have only been partially transcribed—and Tom's an ass." Mariann gave the Insidiae a piercing glare. "Don't counsel me to run back to a loveless marriage. Not when I'm carrying your child, and certainly not when I've dipped my fingers into blood and seen what I can do. It's more than barghests and dhacrym and fear. Blood runs through this world, and in Yelena's texts, I see more beauty than I knew one life could hold. I am making pacts with the setting sun, I can prick my finger and paint myself to the top of mountains, and Anscip Xavishia, don't you dare try and take that away from me. Tom's mistake was trying to pigeonhole me into submission. Don't follow in his footsteps."

The Beast laid its head on Mariann's knee, listening. It wasn't sure what she meant, talking about painting herself to the tops of mountains. But maybe she was right. Perhaps there was more than barghests and dhacrym and fear.

Not that the Beast would know it. Beasts did not know such things.

Howard might, though.

Howard might.

EZRA

"He was a drunk. Lecherous, too—dirty, unkempt, a disaster...but he was kind, and that, I think, gave me hope."

-Ezra Clement Faulise

Ezra Hollick had never ventured so far north as the Valley district.

Everyone knew all the real action was in the south. The Valley—they hardly eeked out a survival. When the gods had crafted the earth, they'd salted the soil—and the people—of the Valley, that was how the saying went.

It was the truest thing he'd heard in a long time.

We'll go to the Valley. Go to the Valley, and find Elizabeth.

Start in Butterfly Ridge.

You'll find ashes.

He hadn't been wrong.

Her home had burned, just like his. Just as the Master said.

There'd been little to do after seeing it but find the nearest tavern and pray they had a hot meal and something that more or less looked like a bed. Forget the lodge the Master—the title sent a pang through Ezra's chest—but forget the lodge the Master had set aside in Taylor Town, reserved specifically for Ezra and the appointed place they would meet to compare notes. Elsie had been from this back-district hovel, and so that was where Ezra would start. And gods, it wasn't like the cities of the south, with their nooks and crannies and places to hide. It was exposed. And in winter, that meant death.

Ezra picked gingerly at the watery soup that'd been slid before him. He'd managed to find a greasy little table in the back, and it was sort of quiet, sort of warm, sort of...okay, he guessed.

He'd been rather partial to the rafters, himself.

They'd offered better accommodations than the tavern did, too, seeing as how the tavern couldn't offer so much as a barn to bunk down in.

Not many tourists in Butterfly Ridge, apparently. And it was no wonder why. It was desolate. Barren.

He'd been lucky, in the Capital, with the warm southern winters and the blazing hot summers and Nan's sweet jams and her jars of honey and—

Don't. Cry.

He forced down a bite of soup, a slimy piece of cabbage somehow managing to get stuck in his throat, unwilling to go down. Given the film settling quickly across the top of the bowl, too, it wouldn't be likely to stay down, either.

"Wouldn't bother," a stumbling voice mumbled, and a middle-aged man dropped down across the table, mug of ale in hand.

Ezra eyed the man cautiously, letting the wooden spoon clunk back into the bowl. "Pardon?"

"Soup," he slurred. "Don' eat it. 'S not good, not good at all. Same pot since...always. Jus' adds more water, when it gets low. Water, an' cabbage, an'..." He shook his head before taking another swig.

It took a confident man to betray his local watering hole with such eagerness, Ezra thought. Well, either confidence or anger. He'd probably been cut off, and as such, had little to lose at critiquing what one might only generously call a chef.

"Thanks for the tip," Ezra muttered, reaching for his mug instead. Slimy cabbage and sticky film aside, if it hadn't received a glowing

279

review from someone chest-deep in ale, it truly must qualify as something inedible.

"Whasyer name? Don't recall seein' you here b'fore."

The ale went down with less resistance than the soup—though to call it anything more than lukewarm mud was a compliment. "Benny," he lied easily. Probably no need, but he had to be careful.

"Benny," the drunk echoed, drumming his fingers against the waxy tabletop. "Benny, Benny...I don't recognize that. Where you say you livin' again?"

"Nowhere around here," Ezra mumbled. *Send him away.* His eyes flicked around the tavern, too busy to get a good seat, too empty for anyone to stop the loyal patron from robbing him blind with a knife to his neck, and he'd had more than enough knives pressed to his throat for the moment, thank you very much.

"An' why're you here, then? Nobody comes to Buddafly—Bu-tt-ert-fl-ay Ridge, for leisure," he stumbled.

Ezra glanced back across the table.

The drunk was sort of stocky, and in his youth, had probably been called strapping, but the beer belly and sallow skin betrayed years of patronage to this fine establishment. Not a promising liaison for the trip. But this was a small town—hardly even a town, really, more of a village...

"I'm actually looking for someone," Ezra sighed, leaning forward, elbows on the table, mug in hand. "A...friend. Name's Elizabeth? The, uh...address...I was given, it—it's no good."

The man snorted, ruffling his hair. "No good? You mean it fucking burned to the gods-damned ground?"

"Yeah. Something like that."

He seemed a little more sober, after that. "Name's Tom." He took a swig. "Don't remember no friend of hers called Benny, though. You know Thatcher?"

"Er…yeah. Yeah, Thatcher and me, we're real close."

"Too bad," Tom shrugged, gesturing another round from the barkeep. "Don't much like Thatcher."

"Oh. Well, I—I used to be close with him," Ezra fumbled, nodding knowingly. "You know where I could find Elizabeth?"

Tom was snickering, now, shaking his head as he tapped the table, a wordless request for Ezra to pick up the round.

"Something funny," Ezra edged, frowning as he passed a pair of coppers to the barkeep.

"You're not her friend."

"I beg your pardon?"

"If you were her friend," Tom laughed, leaning back, "you'd know she don't go by Elizabeth. An' you owe me, buddy, too, 'cause if you foun' her, and called her that, she'd run a knife through you faster than you could blink."

Interesting woman.

"So, where can I find…her," Ezra pushed.

Tom glared, knocking back another drink. "Prolly with my *whore of a wife,*" he roared, looking around the bar, like he'd see the pair of them lingering nearby.

"And, er, where—"

"She fuckin' left me. Can you believe that? *Me.* She goes and finds some—some tart, starts shackin' up withim, an' next thing I know, she's *fucking gone.*"

"I am very sorry to hear that," Ezra muttered, eyes falling to the tabletop, "but Elizabeth—"

"No." Tom was pushing back the chair, rising on wobbling legs as he shook a finger at Ezra. "No, you—you wanna talk about tarts? Then you'll have to go an' talk to—to El…and tell that *whore* she ain't got no right, runnin', an'…an'…" His eyes were glazed over, unseeing as he

281

turned.

Ezra let his head fall, sighing.

I should move.

Follow.

Best lead I've had yet, and he's stumbling out the door.

The night was biting as he met the dirt street.

Tom, it seemed, hadn't gotten far.

Hand braced against the tavern, he was coughing, dragging a sleeve across his mouth, a steaming pile of sick on the ground before him.

Lovely.

"You alright, there?" Ezra asked hesitantly, keeping his distance.

"Whatdaya want, Benny?"

"To find Elizabeth. And a place to stay, for tonight, anyway. Not much in the way of lodging here."

Tom blew out a breath, pushing himself off the wall. Then, with a scoff, he turned—and promptly ate dirt. Ezra took a few quiet steps forward, offering him a hand, which he took, and together, they drew him to standing once more.

"One night," Tom mumbled, brushing himself off. "And you're gone by dawn."

~ • ~

The morning light was etching its way through Ezra's eyelids when consciousness found him.

His neck ached, back cramping, for the six feet and some change of Ezra Hollick was painfully averse to the borrowed love seat.

People of the Valley were a bit salty, he thought, stretching with a grimace. Unpleasant in large quantities. Necessary, in sparing amounts.

Tom had wanted him gone by daybreak, but then again, Tom was passed out cold, and Tom *knew* Elizabeth one way or another, which made Tom the best lead he had, and that was how Ezra found himself rifling through the near-barren icebox in the kitchen.

There was bacon—it looked a little iffy, but that was nothing a frying pan couldn't fix—and he found eggs and tea leaves in the pantry. Not a breakfast of kings, but it'd go a long way towards calming what was going to be a raging hangover.

It'd been a long time since Ezra had cooked a proper breakfast.

It all came back to him quick enough, though.

"The fuck is this?" Tom's voice was gruff, cutting through the sound of sizzling bacon—the universal sound guaranteed to pull even the most deep sleeper out of bed.

"Breakfast," Ezra said simply. Like it wasn't out of the ordinary to be scraping up a meal from a stranger's pantry after a night of heavy drinking. "There's tea, coming shortly, water and tablets on the table." The tablets had been a hard find—though it'd given him an excuse to rifle through drawers and cupboards, looking for anything that might lead him to the girl.

Tom frowned. And took the tablets. And the glass. And downed the pills and water, frowning all the while. He was disheveled, his brown hair askew, his undershirt riding up a hairy belly as he stood there in nothing but his undershorts. "Did...did we..."

"No." Ezra turned back to the stove, trying to swallow a grin. *As if.*

"I think...I must still be drunk," he sighed. A chair groaned as he sank down. "Fucking boy in my kitchen, making gods-damned bacon..."

"I got hungry."

"So you thought you'd help yourself. What does this look like, a fucking bed-and-breakfast?"

"No, because if it was," Ezra muttered, shoveling the strips onto a plate, "I wouldn't be the one cooking." Scooping up one egg at a time, he split the shells against the corner of the counter, letting them drizzle pleasantly into the bacon grease, a quiet popping filling the air. "Tell me about Elizabeth."

Tom's brows knit. "Elsie? What about her?"

"Where is she?"

"How the fuck would I know? Ran off, I heard," he bit back, rubbing his temple. "Didn't matter, not like she was comin' home anyway."

Ezra's eyes narrowed as he turned for the table, plate in hand. "When did she leave?"

"I...don't know." Tom's gray eyes were bleary. He didn't seem to register the food dropped before him, nor the steaming cup of tea deposited a moment after, as his glossy gaze darted about the kitchen, seeing but not, in search of answers. "Wasn't much of a brother, I guess. Couldn't even tell you the last time I saw my own sister." His eyes flicked to Ezra's. "How's that for fucking nice."

"She's your sister," Ezra echoed, eyes drifting in a state of disbelief across Tom. The word irked him. Pulled him uncomfortably and unwillingly into a state of jealousy.

"Honestly, Ted would know," Tom was saying, yolk running across the place as he sliced open the egg with the edge of his fork.

"And where would I find Ted?"

He shrugged.

"You...don't know either," Ezra frowned.

"Shacking up with a tart, last I knew—'course, he doesn't tell me anything. Thinks I care who he fucks, or something. Blames me..." Tom's eyes flicked up from the plate, mouth half-full. "Why you wanna know?"

Ezra picked up a piece of bacon, snapping it in two. "Told you. Elizabeth—Elsie—she's a friend."

"No she ain't."

"She is."

"I got a younger brother and sister. Don't you fucking bullshit me,

284

boy, I can smell it a mile away. Thatcher, or whatever the fuck he's called, shows up, Elsie starts not comin' around, someone torches the farm, then the four of 'em take off? You ain't no friend," Tom warned, prodding his fork at Ezra. "Spill."

CORA

"Lies on lies on lies. Nothing is more utterly human."

~The Foundress

"Stell's being a particular kind of bastard, this season," Cora muttered, rubbing her hands together. Caelaymnis had grown, since the last time she'd set foot in the mountain city of ribbons in the sky, and with it, the ferocity of its winters. Ice pelted down, the whiteout making the quiet street an impenetrable roar. "Of course, it doesn't help that he is not himself. I'd act out too, if I found myself tethered to a mortal."

Risa spared her a glance before pounding on the door. "Nervous?"

"Hardly." It was, oddly enough, the truth. Cora had found a moment to breathe, knowing the answer was in sight. A thread, cut and retied. An heir, to close the quay. Aside from the slight inconvenience of her pantheon being at the beck and call of the Master, it would turn out fine.

The door flung open, and much ado unfolded, Risa having been missed. Cora shook the snow from her shawl, settling it over her shoulders again with a frown, watching from an awkward corner of the foyer.

The man who had answered the door—elf, Drada to boot, unmistakably a Praequintelya. He had the eyes, for one, and the look of quiet cleverness. Fletcher. Cora knew little of him, beyond what Risa had said, for he had not brushed death.

Soft steps down the stairs, and it was the only man Risa would obsess over, Theodore Mirabeau himself. A faint scruff lined his jaw, concealing the occasional reddish blemish of stress. His ribs were prominent beneath a particularly flat chest, pushing his belly softly out—his build, in this, was similar to Risa's. In truth, Cora thought it had probably taken much deliberate obliviousness on both their parts to have avoided the very obvious relation between them.

And then, there was her.

Her.

She must've seen it, looking at Cora. She paused, fingers on the banister, green eyes burning as they lit on the God of Death, and there was recognition.

Cora had diligently worn the mask of her predecessor, though, so any familiarity was a lie.

Elsie's smile had flickered out, her fingers touching a gold locket about her neck in worry—

The iaculus.

Easy, easy. No need to panic.

This was good, right? This was good, she'd been sure Kiran had lost the damnable thing all those years ago, but it was safe, safe and sound, around...the neck of a mortal, and *skies, this is not good.*

It would be fine. Cora had found it again. This would be as simple as leading Elsie to the quay, taking—and importantly, returning—her life.

"Who's this," Elsie breathed, and the foyer seemed to still.

"I am Cora. God of Death, Cutter of Threads, Keeper of Souls." Stepping forward, Cora put her hand out.

Elsie did not take it.

~•~

As far as welcomes went, this had not been a particularly unfriendly one.

Awkward silence had eased to awkward questions, but Risa's assurances, Cora's explanations and concerns, and the mortals' own conclusions seemed to have yielded a common understanding: Cora was of her own mind to share their worries over the master and the quickly-fading agency of her siblings in the pantheon.

The mortals had taken a few moments to discuss it—fair, Cora thought, though it'd left her alone in the kitchen. Privately, she considered this a lapse in judgment on their part. If she'd had nefarious intentions, being left alone was a prime opportunity to act—but then again, it wasn't like a mortal guard could withstand a god, so maybe it didn't matter.

Ever-scheming, aren't you Rose, a voice in the back of her head whispered.

The kitchen door flew open, Elsie leading the rest back. "It seems reasonable to assume you're being truthful." She began harshly, crossing her arms as she shot Cora a glare. "I can't see why you'd lie if you were already in the Master's pocket."

The elf—Fletcher—looked exceedingly uncomfortable, unwilling to defend a god he must've worshipped, but unwilling to entirely doubt her, either.

"I share your concerns," Cora said quietly. "It is news to me, but disturbing news nonetheless. I rarely leave my realm—I am not permitted to, without Kiran's Blessing—and only the dead may venture below." Not strictly true—but then again, she had a talent and a title her predecessor hadn't.

The old Cora may have been the God of Death and the Cutter of Threads, but only she could be called the Keeper of Souls. That didn't change the fact that Cora couldn't leave the Underworld without the Blessing—a small coin gifted to her predecessor, permitting Death to stand in the realm of the living—but she was fairly confident she could bend the rules about bringing someone Below if she wanted to.

Teddy was fixing a pot of tea, watching Risa's reactions out of the corner of his eye. Cora had yet to divine Risa's purpose in withholding—

denying—who she was to him, beyond the insurmountable sadness that would come with confronting the someone she'd been wishing to get back for a long time. Even so, the man seemed to know well enough.

"So. You share our concerns." Elsie's tone was mocking. She bore a striking resemblance to her mother in that respect, Cora mused.

Cora crossed her arms, fighting a smile tugging at her lips. *She reminds me of who I once was.* "Yes. I'm concerned."

"This is funny to you?"

"No. Your anger is...endearing." Cora brushed her hair back over her shoulder. "What I find amusing is that you'd think I would not find this concerning—"

"You're a *god.*" Her eyes glistened with fury. "Where *were* you?"

The kitchen stilled, tension thick.

Where were you?

If only they knew, she thought, lost for just a moment in memory.

I was at the Denison, a mortal, crying as she held the body of a god to her chest, promising the world to a being of unimaginable power. In those sobbing breaths, she'd sworn to protect the descendants of her predecessor. She didn't know how, but Death had looked her in the eyes, at last confronted with the one thing she thought she had purview over, and the dying god had been scared. And she—Rose, Cora, a woman in flux— she'd promised Death she wouldn't bring harm the descendants.

I was above a grave, a terrified woman carrying the newly-claimed mantle with no idea how to handle it. She'd ransacked the body, taking Kiran's Blessing and leaving Death herself to the elements. Her new mantle had been burning, furious to find the new host, and she'd been terrified of what the others would do if they knew. Alder had been laughing, already testing the limits of his new magics, already taking on the face of his predecessor as a façade. They'd swore to each other, right then and there, that the rest of the pantheon need not know of his failure so long

289

as he left it alone. He was a mortal, vying for the relic—but he would have to be content with godhood. So long as he stopped chasing the gods—so long as he didn't go looking for the iaculus—she'd let it go.

I was Below, a new god, isolated, terrified of being found out. She'd barricaded herself in the Palace of Souls. Once her friends, the six remaining gods of the pantheon were liabilities. To see them was to risk being found out. No, after Quinn had died, it'd been better to forsake it all. Let Alder—Kiran—walk about the realm of the living, drinking and bragging. He'd settled for his consolation prize, the other gods kept mostly to their realms, and the Faulises held the iaculus close.

"I didn't know. I am Death. I am...contradictory to the rest, sequestered to the Underworld. And Risa is the one who let me be a part of the lives of the living." Cora glanced to her lover, sighing. "I'm Death. None of this is my purview. But I'm here, now."

Elsie scoffed, shaking her head.

It wasn't a lie. The lives of mortals were beyond her sight—and if she was being honest, she'd been content to keep her sights on the realm of souls.

"Look." Cora braced her hands on the counter. *Time to lie your ass off.* "My solitude has been our advantage. My descendants are few, and only two remain—"

"Two?" Elsie's brow knit, shoulders falling in disbelief.

"You have a brother. Ezra. At the gates of the Underworld, your mother made one request. *Save the twins.* So I did. I did."

To Elsie, it was catastrophic news. She dissolved into tears, blubbering questions, accusations—her face was red, the kitchen erupting into chaos.

It washed over Cora, the emotion a storm, and she, the eye.

Risa played her lies convincingly, holding that she'd only just learned these details when Cora had appeared to her, holding that she'd come here as quickly as she could to break the news, though of course that couldn't be further from the truth. But there was no point undermining that trust between them, not when it was—as it always had been—life or death. Teddy embraced Elsie, and they'd all clustered around her, comforting her, and Cora was forgotten.

It was fitting, the news made her cry. That was how Cora had met the girl.

Crying.

She'd been red-cheeked, wailing, for though she hadn't known it at the time, her parents were dead and her life was about to become exceedingly difficult.

And now, searching for comfort, her family clustered about her, what was it she clung to but the iaculus about her neck, the gold buried under white knuckles.

Fuck.

So much was riding on what little trust lay between her and Elsie. So much depended on access to the girl—and making a grab at the iaculus, particularly when Kiran was safely locked away Below, would unquestionably betray Cora's intentions.

It's back where it's supposed to be. It's with one of the descendants. That's what my predecessor intended.

But she'd seen too much of the fragility of mortal life to really believe that.

I promised a god I wouldn't hurt her. I need her brother safely out of reach, and I need her to bleed. I need her to spill what little ichor is in her blood so that may we seal the quay, and I need her to do it of her own will.

I am forbidden from harming her. She must come to this conclusion on her own.

There was a hitch in Cora's chest. Elsie hardly let go of that damnable thing, rambling about her mother, her family.

"Plainly, this is a lot to take in," Cora began somewhat uncomfortably. "But as crucial as it was to separate you, it is now imperative you and Ezra stick together. It's the only way to make sure the Master can never—never get a hold on me. And one less god on his side is one more...on yours." Her eyes pricked uncomfortably, threatening tears. It wasn't fair. But she didn't have a choice. "I'm sorry. Elsie, I'm sorry," she breathed, and this part wasn't a lie. "I didn't want you to grow up alone. But I desperately wanted to protect you. And I cannot risk the Master finding Ezra. That would be catastrophically bad, Elsie, do you understand? It would do irreparable damage. It would destroy me, and—and I'm sorry that I didn't know. I'm sorry that I am not prescient, I am sorry that I am a young god on a new pantheon, I am sorry that I could not stop what couldn't kill you."

"I wasn't alone." Elsie pressed the tears from her eyes with the heel of her hand.

"No. No, you weren't." Cora spared a glance at those still clustered about her. "But Ezra is. And I know your paths are set to cross—and soon."

"So where is he, then?"

"I tell you again: I do not claim to be prescient. At best, I glimpse meaning in the threads before they're cut." Cora pursed her lips. "We've tracked down where he ended up. As Clark took you to the Mirabeaus, so Michael Fieldson took Ezra to a woman named Mary Hollick."

"You know about your dossier," Risa affirmed. "Ezra had one, too. Unfortunately, it seems as though Fieldson lost part of it, enough that the Factionists were able to track Ezra down. It looks like he might've been plotting something similar to Clark—or perhaps with Clark's help, I wouldn't put it past him. I confirmed through one of my contacts that Fieldson had inquired about bringing the boy into the City, though, and apparently that was enough. He lost a fair chunk of the dossier, and

Ezra's house burned."

"Just like...." Elsie's brow was knit in pain as she looked to Teddy, trailing off. "But Ezra's okay. You wouldn't just come here if he'd died."

"No. I would not have."

"He's going to be difficult to find independently," Risa warned. "Running from the Factionists for three years? That's a long time to practice deception."

Elsie looked less than pleased at this, but she said nothing.

Cora sighed quietly, oddly sympathetic. She'd been young, once, at odds with the world—and there was no reason for a lamb to look eager for the slaughter.

I was supposed to shepherd you.

Instead, I lead you to your death, however impermanent.

You will see it's for the best, Elsie. Maybe not best for you. But best for everyone else.

ELSIE

"I never set out looking for a crown. I took it, all the same."

~The Foundress

Elsie frowned, shoes scuffing softly against the glossy priory floor. The hall was bright, small alters set aside in alcoves for each god in turn, colorful mosaics on the walls in between.

Fletcher had wished to pray and contemplate all Cora had said in the presence of mystics, before holy icons, and after they'd all listened to the God of Death offer instruction while leaning on the kitchen counter, he hadn't been the only one.

Whether Elsie would find answers in the priory was dubious. Her religion had been utility. But her fears had been confirmed—she was a descendant of Death, sought by fanatics and political rivals alike. They didn't care that she had no interest in the Chancellorship, and they certainly didn't care that she had no lethal propensities herself, aside from her occasional tendency to draw a knife on bastard men.

She'd quickly come to resent Ezra.

It was unfair that he garnered such care. No one save for the demon child Chim had intervened on Elsie's behalf, and now, she was expected to protect Ezra?

Elsie's fingers brushed the icon of Death, a woman cloaked in black and gold. *Where were you, Cora? Where were you when death was on my doorstep?*

She expected Elsie to rally to the cause.

Elsie's fingers found the locket about her neck. The iaculus, by Augustus's word.

She'd been too much of a coward to ask Cora about it. To ask was to risk hearing that she wasn't who they thought she was.

What if the iaculus *didn't* mark her as the Heiress of the Hidden City? What if it *didn't* mark her as a descendant of Death?

Or worse, what if it did?

And anyway, Cora hadn't remarked, though Elsie caught her staring all the same. If it'd been a holy relic, surely the God of Death herself would've either blessed it or demanded its return.

Without a word, Elsie excused herself from the priory. This was a place for people with more faith than her.

To her surprise, Teddy had already done the same and was waiting for her in the small entry hall, sitting on one of the benches. "No luck?"

"No luck. Not for me." Elsie sank down next to him, arm pressed against his. The chill from the late winter seeped in, storm beyond vicious. "It's hard to really get into the spirit of it, given everything that's happened."

"A curious turn, that's for sure," Teddy nodded. He glanced over, giving her a weak smile of reassurance that faltered a moment later. "It's fucked."

"You got there eventually."

"Can I ask you something, El?"

"Shoot."

"Does Risa seem like she's being weird?"

"Weird how? She brought a god back, that's pretty weird."

"Has she said anything to you about—about me," Teddy asked nervously.

"When would she have had the chance? I've hardly seen her lately.

Guess I'm better enough not to need her," Elsie added, bitter. She was much improved, but she liked Risa, and with Sam gone, it was a poor time for her to bow out, too. Looking askance to Teddy, Elsie sighed. "She still hasn't said anything to you?"

He shook his head, turning his attention to the floor. "I know I'm your big brother. I know I'm not supposed to lean on you—"

"You know that's not how this works—"

"Yeah, well, you're my baby sister. I look out for you. Always have, and I always will, no matter what." He took her hand, squeezing it as he glanced over to her. "I just—I have to know. Am I being off-kilter, with Risa?"

"Well, you remember what Sam used to say." Elsie grimaced. "Fucker. But he was right when he said it wasn't conspiratorial if there really was a plot against you. It's not unreasonable, thinking that Tess would've played a part in that."

"The problem is, I saw them take her away," Teddy breathed, brow knit. "I spent twenty years trying to convince myself she was really gone."

Elsie bit her lip, thinking. "I know we don't talk about Tess..."

"We weren't supposed to talk about a lot of things. Shoot, El."

"What happened? What *really* happened?"

"Oh." He looked mildly surprised, straightening up.

"If it's too much, you don't have to—"

"No, no, I suppose I didn't realize you never knew the details. I don't know how you would've, but..." He shook his head, fingers still laced through hers. "The three of us were playing buggle in the barley, and it was my turn to be it. It was late, we'd already been told off twice—of course, I tagged her, and she lost her footing and fell. Smacked her head right against the corner of the table. See," he went on, finding a bit of a pace, "where I get stuck is that Marlene and Greg took her into town. All

296

I know of what happened after is what they told us."

"Oh, they're Marlene and Greg now?"

"Well, I didn't want to say *our parents*, thought you might feel weird about it." He shot her a look that bore the weight of the entire fucked-up situation. "Risa keeps denying that she's Tess."

"So, either she's lying and the conspiracy unfolds further, or she's not Tess. And Marlene and Gregory *were* my parents, as much as Margaret and Jon. For better or worse, they were supposed to step into that role." Elsie shrugged. She'd realized, of late, that putting emotional distance between herself and the people who had helped raise her was almost dishonest. It was one of the things she'd come to, locked in the bathroom with a bottle of dhacrym. Calling them by their names did not absolve them of their parental failure.

Silence fell between her and her brother.

"Cora looks like you," he said at last, softly.

"I know," Elsie whispered.

"It was good of her to warm you about—about him." A glare etched into Teddy's brow. He couldn't even bring himself to say the name, apparently.

"It wasn't good of her. You know what she should've done, instead of following Ezra? She should've made some effort with me. Chim is the only reason that Augustus was caught—"

Teddy made a small sound of disdain.

"What," Elsie snapped.

"It's just—El, you were in bad shape when Fletcher found you. As in, Adrian and Risa said that they didn't know if you were going to make it through the night. You'd bled a lot, Elsie. Isa and I were talking about it. Augustus had time to get what he needed from you. That's part of why it's so curious—and Cora arriving here only affirms that he was telling the truth, even if he did gather Ruby Tears, he didn't hand them over."

Teddy shrugged, giving her a *so there* look.

"So, what? You think that Cora knew he was going to lose his nerve? That's not *better*, Teddy. That means she's being entirely selfish—"

"Yeah, El, that's how gods are. You know that. You're from the Valley."

His words hit her like a brick wall, and she'd been running at top speed.

There was a reason the gods weren't invoked in the Valley, at least not by name. They'd been forgotten, and how many times had Elsie heard someone remark about the apathy of gods?

If they wanted us to remember their names, they'd do something worth remembering, Marlene had said, echoing the common sentiment.

And Teddy was right. She *was* from the Valley. Fuck everything else. That was her home, that was the place that had hardened her off, that was the place that taught her skepticism and doubt were more sure than faith and trust.

"You have that look on your face," Teddy frowned. "What?"

"No, it's just—you're right. She's selfish. Her needs happen to work for us, right now. I'm underwhelmed about the idea of Ezra, and less than thrilled about what his showing up would mean," she went on, "but one god less in the Master's pocket is good for us. I hate that we were right, though. I *hate* that." Really, it was Fletcher, who had been right, though it was difficult to blame him. If anything, that was a bit of a comfort, that either his instinct, his investigatory skill, or both, had led him to the correct—if not absolutely abhorrent—conclusion.

How to stop the gods. That'd be the next question, one Cora would hopefully enlighten them on, though that was dubious, given how close-to-the-vest she'd held her cards.

"Fletcher's taking a while," Elsie muttered, glancing at the priory door.

"Cora matters to him."

"I don't understand how he can pray to her, particularly after inviting her to dinner," Elsie clipped, a smile tugging at her lips in spite of her bitterness.

"I, for one, hope she shows."

"You just want to hang about Risa more. You don't care about the gods."

"I can care about both," Teddy countered, defensive. "It's just—she's been busy, lately," he went on, tone shifting to something more worried. "And I only had a brief moment to talk to her."

"You tell her about Sam?"

"Yeah." He shrugged. "She was pretty harsh on him."

"Fairly so, I think."

"She's coming with me to the apartment tomorrow. At least, that's what she said."

"Oh." Elsie paused, choosing her words carefully. "To get you settled in? Or to wrap things up there?"

Teddy's eyes flicked to hers, unreadable. "To pack Sam's things up." His shoulders sank, watching her. "I'm not going to just take off and leave you, Elsie. Especially now. Neither of us needs to be alone. I don't know what I'm going to do, long-term. I'm not ready to ditch the apartment yet—too much work, anyway, and I'm too depressed to try and sort that out. Cele's very kindly bought up the lease, though, so she said it's mine as long as I need or want." He leaned over, at last letting go of her hand to slide an arm around her, drawing her into a hug. "I'm here with you, okay? I'm not going to just take off."

The words of a real brother—and fuel to her resentment against Ezra.

Whoever he is, he can't compete with Teddy.

Whoever he is, he's got no place here. No place at all.

TEDDY

"What kind of lover leaves you behind, knowing
destruction is on the horizon? Doesn't matter how foolish
it is. You don't leave the people you love behind."

~Festival of Frost

"You didn't have to come with," Teddy muttered, fumbling with his keys to Sam's apartment.

Risa was leaning against the wall, hands in her pockets. With a shrug, her blue eyes were deep in the low light of the hallway. "I did."

"It's early."

She quirked an eyebrow, watching Teddy click the door open. "I should be here. You shouldn't be in enemy territory alone."

"Enemy territory—Risa, this was my apartment too—is my apartment still, actually—"

"Oh, no. No, no, no, Teddy, this is a place of memories—I've broken up with enough people to know that this is hostile bounds—"

"This was my home. Sam's...taking space in the most dysfunctional way possible, but I've thought about it, and he and I...aren't done." In truth, going with Isa to the Woodshades had put things in perspective. It made Teddy feel brave—had made him feel capable and alive, and like the world was waiting for him if only he could move past this oppressive grief lingering around him.

If he could take a risk like that and walk head-long into those tense settlements with elves at his heels, then he could ask Sam for an explanation about why their marriage was over.

His eyes flicked to Risa.

Tess.

The world was unkind to taunt him with a would-be ghost. "I still don't know why you're here," Teddy breathed, trying not to be accusatory. The awkwardness between them had eased somewhat—bringing a god home as your girlfriend kind of did that, and anyway, if that was the kind of personal life she had, it was no wonder she'd been distracted—but even so, Teddy had some difficulty moving forward after Risa's vehement denials. Despite her age, her features, hell, even her name, she was clear: she was of no relation. Not that this stopped her from waxing sentimental, of course.

Risa shrugged. "I'm here because I feel bad, okay? I've been busy with other things, and Sam's gone, and—and I feel bad. It doesn't have to be more complicated than that."

Teddy let the keys clink unpleasantly onto the table in the entry way, his eyes flickering across the deserted living room. This place was rife with memories.

A throw blanket was still crumpled on the sofa, one he and Sam had curled up beneath often in their years together. A book lay on the coffee table, one he'd read several times over, and had spent quiet winter nights re-reading again in this once-safe harbor. The breakfast table bore nothing more than table linens and echoes of meals they'd shared, the kitchen—he put a hand on the door frame, eyes unseeing on the counter where Sam had once left the sweet muffins to cool as he'd sank down onto one knee, cinnamon eyes bright.

He'd been twenty, the first time he'd set foot here.

Sam's eyes had been tired, but bright, jingling the keys excitedly in his hand as he leaned on the counter of the general store, talking as Teddy clerked. *And there's plenty of room, it's right down the street from here, you and El—you can stay whenever you like...*

To Sam, it was modest accommodations, but to Teddy and Elsie, it had felt lavish—albeit a bit empty, at first. Elsie had run around the apartment, oscillating between childish delight as she let her voice echo off the bare walls and the pretense of adulthood as she examined each detail of the apartment with a critical eye, all while Sam and Teddy had sat on the floor, talking about the future.

There'd been a pang in Teddy's heart when Sam reached his hand over, putting it on Teddy's knee. *Thank you for everything,* Sam had breathed, cinnamon eyes warm. And Teddy had wanted to lean in and kiss that boy all over again.

The next two years brought waves of change.

Snowstorms kept the three of them holed up safe in the apartment, had kept Elsie dozing on the sofa and Teddy and Sam in the feather bed as only friends that *just happened* to get all tangled up together, because certainly, waking up with his arm around Sam's waist was simply the quintessential moment of best-friendhood, wasn't it? Sam had spent hours in his sewing room, learning, and when he dissolved into tears once more, wasn't it friendship that had driven him to dry his tears on Teddy's shoulder? Hadn't it been that bond of companionship that had let Teddy spill his thoughts on being so utterly kaleidoscopic, so radiantly uncontained, to be free, here, with Sam? That bond that let them trade their hurts back and forth, that let them get drunk together on this sofa, that let them share meaningful glances, that cultivated between them an unquestionable love?

But friends didn't abandon each other.

Fuck love, this was a betrayal of friendship. His best friend walked out the fucking door.

Matt had kissed Sam. Fine. Maybe it had sparked some kind of lust or love or *whatever* in Sam—evidently, it'd been enough to make him realize he had to go. But that wasn't a good enough reason to throw the whole of their lives away. If they hadn't been romantically entangled, Teddy and Sam would've sat talking, late into the night, dissecting *exactly* how Sam felt about that kiss, crying over what it must've brought up for him.

No matter what, they both deserved better than to just disregard those years of friendship, Teddy thought, anger welling in his chest. The Thread gave a quiver of agreement, hot and frustrated. Sam had always been entitled to his secrets, Teddy had never taken issue with that—but this was different. This wasn't Teddy, prying into something he ought to leave alone. This was Sam, fucking off because he was too much of a coward to stay and sort it out.

Empty satchel in hand, Teddy's jaw clenched as he paced the apartment.

Sam told me not to follow. He said it was over.

That I had a long life ahead of me, and...

Teddy blew out a breath. *And that asshole owes me a better explanation of why that long life doesn't include him.*

In a few quick paces, he was at the bookcase, turning over the silver picture frame to unlatch the back. Sam's sketch of the two of them sat inside, a relic of another time. "Gods. Fuck that guy," he muttered, and roughly, Teddy yanked the drawing from behind the glass, folding it up and putting it in his pocket. Sam needed to be reminded that there was more to them than love.

Glancing around the apartment, his mind was more or less made up. He'd come here to pack up Sam's things—but it hardly felt right. To pile them up in boxes and have Cele's couriers cart them off seemed, to him, just as bad as what Sam had done, because it meant he was unwilling to set whatever fracture came between them. He was a poor Healer indeed, if the best he could do at such a wound was to let it fester.

Best case, maybe we can get to the bottom of this. And worst case, at least I stand up for myself for once. At least I can tell him off for what he's done.

Sam would've gone south, that much, Teddy felt he could say with adequate certainty. Mattie governed the Capital District, and being officially tied by family—and apparently integral to Sam, the two having shared a kiss so profound it sparked in Sam the life-changing realization his marriage was over—it made sense that he'd retreat there, out of the way and back into the life he'd known before.

I will find my friend.

And I will make him answer for this.

"You're going after him," Risa said quietly, a glimmer of mischief in her eyes.

"I dunno if it's a good idea. But yeah."

She sighed, and when he glanced over, he saw she was smiling quietly. "I've seen the way he looks at you, Teddy."

Teddy moved for the writing desk, hitting the side with a *thunk* that opened the bottom drawer, skeptical of what he'd find—

"Huh."

Sam's notebooks sat stacked in the bottom.

"Huh, what," Risa asked.

"Huh, Sam didn't take his sketchbooks with him," Teddy frowned, picking up the top one to thumb through it.

"Guess you can just buy it all new, when you're a merchant," Risa remarked.

"Maybe. I'm...a bit surprised, though," he went on, looking about. "It doesn't seem as though he's taken anything." Sam was painfully material, and though it wasn't necessarily out of the question that he would've simply decided he needed a clean start, it was odd that he hadn't retrieved a single item.

I love you so much, Teddy.

Isn't that what Sam had said? Not loved, past-tense. Love, current tense, as in the feeling that persisted, even as he'd left.

Then why did he leave. If he loves me, why did he go.

The questions only affirmed Teddy's impulse.

"Fuck him," he muttered, tossing the sketchbook back in the drawer. "Fuck him so much, for doing this. What a gods-damned mess..."

"That's right, you tell him—"

"I will. I'm going to find him, and give him a piece of my mind," Teddy nodded, sort of finding his stride. "I am done, Risa, I'm so done with people walking around telling me how much they love me as they strike the match that burns me to the ground! I'm over being told how loved I am by the people who punch down at me—over it! No more!"

Risa met him in a hug, squeezing him tight. "Go get 'em."

"I missed you, egging me on," he breathed, squeezing her right back.

She shrugged, pursing her lips. But she didn't deny it, and that made his heart soar. "I'm serious," she pressed. "Don't be afraid to tell him you deserved better. Because you did, Teddy. You really did."

THE BEAST

"I was told, once, that I was well-behaved. I took it to heart, and none ever made the mistake of assuming as much again."

~Mariann Bell

"She's done. I'm tired of her snooping around the house," the Master hissed, pacing with irritation.

The Beast lay by the fire, listening.

Only that was absurd, because beasts didn't listen. Then again, the Fearless One...Mariann...she insisted that the Beast wasn't a beast. The Beast was Howard.

And Howard listened.

The Master had summoned his gods to his parlor again, and the Beast—Howard—was very glad to not be following the Master around these days, for he seemed to be everywhere, all at once. In the Valley, in the Capital, in his head, in another world—

"Master." Stell, God of Ice, stepped forward, hands laced behind his back. His hair was the palest blue, trinkets of ice set into the twists and turns, matching the elaborate embroidery of his jacket. "What do you propose? She is the Insidiae's, and you have heard his warnings."

"Accidents befall mortals every day." The Master flung himself into a nearby chair like an overtired toddler, wrinkling his nose. "Think of something. But she's in the way. Her and that wretched dog." His gaze turned to the Beast, and with a scowl, he hurled his tumbler across the room.

The glass shattered near the floor where the Beast was laying, and with a bark and a whimper, the Beast was padding across the floor of broken glass, tail between its legs.

Mariann was never so mean. Mariann, as a matter of fact, was never mean at all.

Brushing off his jacket, the Master gave a scoff, crossing one leg over the other. He turned his attention back to his gods as the Beast left the parlor. "I would never employ such a woman like Mari," he added with a hiss. "That blood witch is arrogant. One turn" —the Master snapped his fingers— "and she could be gone."

"Dead." Stell's voice was pleased at this, and the Beast stopped in the hall, spines along its back bristling.

No. Of all the things Mariann could be, *dead* would not be one of them.

The Beast took to the stairs, sniffing about for her. She wasn't afraid, not ever, not of anything, but that was alright, because she felt a lot of other things, and the Beast had started to become very adept at sniffing those out too.

Annoyance. Worry. Excitement—

The Beast nosed her door open. It moved for the closet, and nosing open that door too, it sniffed among the trunks and coats until it found a leather pack Mariann kept her supplies in. Dragging it out gently, taking care not to crush anything, the Beast pulled it from the closet, and then, like the goodest boy Mariann always said he was, he sat right down next to it and started to whine.

"Howard!" Mariann set her book down, brow knit. "What on earth are you doing?" She scooped the bag up, put it back in the closet.

The Beast was not deterred. It dragged it out again, and this time, bag in its mouth, stood with its front paws on her shoulders, pushing the bag against her chest. She had to take it. They had to go. This was important.

307

Stell and the Master, they were planning an accident.

She took the bag, brushing his paws down. "What, How?" Mariann's voice shifted. *Concern. An attempt to understand. Trust.* The Beast gave a whimper as she touched its paw, and she knelt down to look. "Baby, glass? How'd you get glass in there? Is that why you want the bag? To bandage it up?"

The Beast jerked its paw back and turned, padding down the stairs again—and mercifully, Mariann followed. Bandages weren't any good, not right now. She had to go. Had to leave.

Stopping just before the parlor, the Beast sat, tail tucked, looking up at Mariann, who peered around the corner. "Glass?" She stooped down to give the Beast a few pats on the head. "Howard, did he throw that at you?" She didn't sound surprised.

The Beast backed up, rising silently to turn down the hall for the servant's stairs. They had to go.

They means we, and we means me.

An odd thought for a beast.

"Kill the blood wench, and once we've gotten enough, that little demon will be set upon the boy downstairs," the Master was saying, loudly, drunkenly. "That fool Insidiae won't know what hit him, once we open the quays and get the relic."

Mariann put a hand to her mouth. Wordlessly, she turned, making a beeline for the stairs. She understood—

"He fancies himself something of an expert," the Master laughed. His voice drifted to mocking, "I don't see how he's got such expertise if a merchant lad can figure it out, of course. He's worked the magic back through the bloodlines—any fool can do it, with enough determination—it's such bullshit, he's so stupid—"

"Master." Ignata's voice cut him off. "You are overheard."

Mariann glanced back, eyebrow raised. But she wasn't afraid. She looked to Howard, about to beckon him on—

The Beast turned, padding, pacing the hall, beginning to whimper.

Mariann must've understood, for she nodded, departing.

The Beast flopped down, beginning to lick its paw, whining louder, now.

"It's just that pitiful creature." The Master had risen, sticking his head out to look down the hall. "There's no one here, you impertinent fool. No one that matters, anyway."

It was curious.

Those words stuck in the Beast's head. The Master went back to complaining to his gods, the Beast padded off to find Mariann again, and those words wouldn't go away.

No one that matters.

The Beast did not have thoughts. It did not feel. Did not care.

But Howard did, because all he could think was that the Master was wrong.

I do matter. To Mariann, very much.

I matter.

EZRA

*"Brotherhood is such a fascinating notion. Where I
think most would hope that it holds camaraderie, it often
merely holds strife."*

~Blaine Liss Coalition Representative

"I'm not used to seeing you during business hours," Ezra quipped,
watching his friend shrug off his coat. The lodge room was nice—far
nicer than the threadbare couch he'd bunked on at Tom's—and in the
back of Ezra's mind, meeting his friend here had the air of meeting
someone in the midst of a clandestine affair.

"Ah, I'm not usually available during business hours when we are in
the Capital," the Master quipped, grinning. "Here, my duties are
husband above business."

"And how is that going?" Ezra's voice cracked awkwardly at this, and
he flushed, moving to go clear his bedclothes off the back of the sofa.
He didn't mean for it to be such a pointed question.

The Master's eyes were on him, soft. "Well enough."

Ezra's mouth was dry as he returned to sit. "I came back again."
Perhaps their usual patter of reassurance would mend the awkwardness.

His friend smiled, sitting beside him. "Ezra, my heart has been
fortified, running this exercise with you. I..." His eyes drifted down,
cheeks heating pink. "I confess that I look forward to this more each
passing day. Never in my life have I done something so reckless as to
trust another man."

"I told you," Ezra breathed, and he was overcome with the urge to take his friend's hand, to squeeze it, bring it to his lips and kiss it, "I told you that I am with you." It was not a difficult thing to reason through. When faced with the choice of security and safety and the prospect of perhaps even love of some sort—or at the very least, this continued affection—it was no contest.

And that was to say nothing of the intoxicating mythology of bringing the gods to heel.

If there even were such a thing as gods.

It didn't really matter if there were, though. It was about the idea of taking control of their own lives, about not relegating their fate to some force beyond their own will.

Never had anyone trusted Ezra with anything so valuable as his own agency.

"So, tell me." The Master leaned back, looking content. "Have you made any progress, finding your sister?"

Ezra shook his head. "We're going to ask about town today, her brother and I."

"Her...brother?" The Master's expression shifted, wary.

"Tom." Ezra shrugged. "He's...fine. A drunkard, but well-meaning, I think. He's safe, I'm not in any danger."

"Oh." The look of relief on his friend's face was obvious, shoulders sinking down. "Oh, this is good news, indeed. And...and you will continue to be here? At the lodge, every morning? 10 in the morning?"

Ezra nodded. "I promise."

The Master smiled, and it looked like a reflex, the way he moved to brush his fingers across Ezra's cheek. "Your promises are intoxicating, you know."

Face heating violently, Ezra turned away. "Good," he mumbled. "Then I shall keep them coming."

"Any luck?" Tom was shuffling over, hands stuffed in his pockets. He didn't claim to know any of his sister's haunts, but Ezra suspected that his own arrival had sparked the realization in Tom that he probably should care where his sister had gotten off to.

"None." Ezra shrugged. "Either nobody seems to know her, or nobody has seen her in months."

It was a dreary day, clouds hanging low over Taylor Town, a thick tang to the air that was unmistakably the staleness of winter. In fact, every day thus far had been like that, and after nearly a week, Ezra began to think that might've just been life in the Valley. Dreary and gray and stagnant.

The door to the apartment building clattered shut, and Ezra's eyes flicked up at the noise, watching a man in a navy coat shut the door behind him on his way out, a woman close behind him. The man looked over, a faint glare etched on his brow, a glare that only deepened when he looked between the two of them loitering. "Tom?"

Tom's head snapped up. "Ted." His eyes widened, and he glanced up at the building, then up and down the street, and only then did a look of realization dawn across his face. "And..." His mouth twitched into a frown, looking at the woman beside him. But it seemed, for the time being, he'd decided to ignore her. "What the fuck are you doing here?"

"Leaving...my apartment, you mean," the man named Ted inquired coldly, not moving from where he lingered, hand still on the door to the building.

"Heard you weren't working—"

"Things happened." The man glanced between the two of them. "What are you doing here, Tom?"

"Looking for Elsie." Ezra's voice cracked as he answered, eyes on the man. Looking for Elsie, because he didn't really care for this man, for his cold eyes and his bitter expression, for the way he looked at Tom with such derision.

"Elsie." Her name was almost a snarl when he said it, at last turning to face Tom and Ezra. "Why."

"I'm her brother," Erza shrugged. "Why not?"

The woman quirked an eyebrow, crossing her arms. But the man's eyes bore into Ezra, a cold, blue fire deep inside. "Is that so," he demanded.

"Ted, it's..." Tom gestured vaguely. "Complicated."

"Is it, now." The man named Ted readjusted the satchel on his shoulder, jaw clenching. Shaking his head, he moved for the apartment door again. "Come on. Come inside. And you better have a damn good explanation. Both of you."

~ • ~

Sitting on the edge of the sofa, Ezra rubbed his arms, wishing the new fire in the hearth was throwing off more than just a bit of light.

Empty promises, he thought dully.

"So, you," Ted bit, pointing at Ezra, "have been looking for Elsie, and *you*" –he pointed to Tom— "you didn't think to, oh, I don't know, write to Sam's sister?"

The woman whose name nobody mentioned was staring at Tom with a disconcerting stare.

"Sam's sister, she's the Commissioner, is the thing," Tom mumbled, looking down at the floor from where he sat beside Ezra on the sofa.

"Your boyfriend is the Commissioner's brother?" Ezra glanced up, eyes wide.

Tom hadn't been kidding about his siblings running with some fancy people.

"It—he—look, this is neither here nor there," Ted breathed, pinching the bridge of his nose. "What do you want with Elsie?"

"I'm her brother—"

"No, *I'm* her brother." Ted cut Ezra off, glaring. "You expect me to believe that now, of all moments, you've simply decided to sojourn to the Valley? Now, in the middle of *winter,* when travel is unpleasant and expensive—"

"Yes," Ezra lied, voice quiet. "I couldn't wait any longer. I've been running." That last part wasn't a lie, and he wondered if blending them together would make him more convincing.

"Running? From who?"

"From the people who burned down our house and killed my Nan," Ezra breathed.

There was a tense silence in the apartment.

"Fine." Ted was moving for the door, the quiet woman following him. "Don't move. We'll go get El."

Ezra breathed a sigh of relief, leaning back into the soft cushions.

They were going to be okay.

He was going to get to Elsie.

ELSIE

"Two halves of one, and yet, both whole. We were a paradox, he and I, and I knew, even then, that it would end badly."

~Elizabeth Clement Faulise

A vial of dhacrym sat on the stone counter of the bathing room, golden locket beside it. The glass of the vial glistened seductively, the locket glowing warmly as the light touched it.

They didn't even have the courtesy of looking innocuous.

In one was represented the ambitions of a man who wanted the magic of the gods at all costs. In the other, the relic of a god—if Augustus was to be believed, though Cora had said nothing of it.

The thoughts made her head ache.

She popped the dhacrym vial open, taking a mouthful and sinking down onto the cool tile.

Cora's voice was an imagined whisper in the bathing room.

What if I'm right, it simpered. *What if you bled for nothing at the hands of Augustus.*

A sharp knock at the bathing room door made Elsie start, heart jolting.

Real or not

Real or not

It opened a moment later, though, and Teddy stepped in, looking— to Elsie's surprise—supremely pissed off.

She almost asked if he was real, his expression was so unwelcome.

Only in her wildest fears did he find her, angry.

Elsie was on her feet a second later, pocketing the vial she'd been clutching. "What—what's wrong?"

Teddy looked her up and down, pausing. "I'm interrupting."

"No shit. What happened?"

"Sorry—" His face crumpled into apology, brow still knit.

"Teddy!"

"I was at the apartment, and Tom showed up." Teddy grimaced, looking upset. "I'll give you one guess as to who he had in tow."

~ • ~

Elsie pushed open the apartment door, steeling herself.

Gods, it's been ages since I've been here.

Ezra was on his feet, wide-eyed.

Good.

He *should* be scared.

Tom didn't bother to stand. Arm resting on the back of the sofa, his cold eyes met her with a look somewhere between derision and amusement and exhaustion. "So it isn't true. You didn't just run off."

"What's it to you," Elsie muttered, pulling her coat off.

Tom just shrugged.

And that was the extent of the sibling closeness they shared.

Elsie turned her attention to Ezra.

His trousers looked like they'd seen better days, with fraying hems and a few poorly mended rips. His tunic, too, was worn, a simple cotton thing where once, there'd been a pair of buttons at the top, probably.

She paused, hand resting on the back of Sam's armchair, watching him wordlessly. Teddy moved past them both, giving Elsie a sympathetically pained look before turning for the kitchen, probably just to lean against the counter and pretend to give them privacy. He'd

316

probably intended Tom to follow, but he hadn't. He sat there, looking between the twins.

Ezra just stared at her.

You're nothing like me.

Dark brown hair overgrown past his ears, eyes verging on something turquoise...but searching for something familiar, she was left wanting.

Same chin, maybe? It was hard to tell through his stubble.

Twin.

A duplicate. A copy. Two corresponding parts to one.

"You're Elizabeth," he edged, taking a step forward.

"Not to you or anyone else," she snarled. "I'm Elsie to my friends and El to my brothers, and I don't think anyone beyond that needs to be hollering my name, anyway."

Tall.

He was tall—taller than her, she thought bitterly. Some copy.

"I'm Ezra." He held out a hand.

She did not take it. "What the hell are you doing here?"

"Looking for you—"

"I know that," she snapped. "*Why?*"

His hand dropped in retreat. "Why not?"

"How did you know where to find me?"

Ezra swallowed, not taking his eyes off of her. "Chance. Luck. Call it what you want."

"So, you expect me to believe you've been wandering around Aerdela looking for someone named Elizabeth Mirabeau, and only now, you've happened upon me?"

"You don't have to believe it. That's what happened."

"No, you—you must *really* think I'm dense," she laughed, shaking her head as she turned away. "I'm getting tired of asking questions you should already be answering. See, I know that I'm a wanted woman.

317

There are any number of wretched reasons someone would come looking for me, and I don't buy your bullshit."

Quiet swallowed up the room, her eyes flitting out the window.

Irritability became her, today, more than most days.

"Nan told me," Ezra said softly, after a long moment. "Mom left us, that much you must know. Left...me. And Nan got your name. I'd always meant to come find you, someday, but Nan—she needed me. She needed me until she didn't."

"Your nan died," Elsie echoed, pacing idly into the breakfast nook to stare out the window onto the street below. The windowpane was cool beneath her fingers, half-clawed against the glass, fog crawling across the picture of the passersby. Hell of a day not to be numb.

Her eyes flicked to the kitchen, where Teddy was predictably leaning against the counter, arms crossed, blue eyes watching her. Teddy gave a skeptical quirk of his eyebrow, mouth pursed into a line that said *I do not trust him.*

"Nan died in a fire. Just like your family," Ezra offered from where he stood in the living room.

"They weren't my family," she snarled, whirling. "Don't come here, presuming to know my life."

Ezra's eyes flicked to hers, somber. "Tom...seemed to think he was family."

"Tom's an idiot." The name was a brick wall against her, driving her thoughts to a complete and violent stop once more.

Tom was distant.

Hardly there when she'd been younger, almost completely absent later on. A decade her senior, it made sense, and she'd never held it against him. He married when she was ten, and after that, she'd seen quite little of him, which had suited her, because he'd never been fond of her—she wasn't Tessa—and she didn't really like him, either—he

318

wasn't Teddy—making the distance between them decidedly mutual.

He'd never even called her his sister, except as a joke.

She turned, glaring at Tom where he sat, glazed look expressionless enough to tell her that he didn't give a fuck.

"Isn't that what you've always said," Elsie challenged quietly. "I'm not *really* your sister."

Tom shrugged. "You're not. If you're not Tess, you're not my sister."

"He—he's nice, though? Ran into him," Ezra shrugged. "Let me bunk on his couch for the night. Told me to ask around about the Carsons. Said someone named Sam might know where you were at..."

Teddy made a small noise of frustration from his hiding place in the kitchen.

Elsie sighed, tucking a strand of hair behind her ear. "Your...Nan, then. She's the one that told you about me. And she knows because..." She couldn't say the word.

"Mom," he put in cautiously.

Couldn't be.

Maybe that's what Cora told his nan. Or she misremembered. Or maybe that's the lie his nan told him.

But he's here.

Ezra...he's real, and he's here.

"How do I know it's really you? How do I know you're Ezra Faulise? How am I to believe any of this is true?" Elsie bit, ever the skeptic.

He dared a step to where she lingered by the window. "You don't. I think...you have to trust me." He was worrying his hands together in nervous apprehension. Another step forward. "Is that my name? Faulise?" he asked, voice a half-whisper.

There was something like terror in his eyes as he asked the question.

He knew he didn't have the answers.

More than that, he knew that *she* did.

319

Her eyes flicked to Tom. "Get out."

The eldest Mirabeau son obliged, not bothering to bid farewell.

Teddy at least gave Elsie the courtesy of a warm hug and a whispered reassurance that he'd be right down the street if she needed him. He'd never presume to be privy to her private conversations, and though she wouldn't have minded if he stayed, she suspected he had matters of his own to attend to.

With the apartment vacant once more, Elsie turned her gaze to Ezra, thrusting a finger at Sam's old armchair. "Sit," she said bossily. "We need to talk."

RISA

Waiting on the street below the apartment, Risa pushed herself off the brick when the door opened, Tom and Teddy meeting the street.

Tom and his gray-blue gaze and his waxy skin and the way he'd grown up just like their father, a spitting image.

Memory had a way of sweetening the past, and Teddy had risen to the occasion, meeting—exceeding—every one of her hopes.

But her eldest brother had simply failed. Tom had become an apathetic drunk.

He hadn't said a gods-damned word.

The worst part was, he must've known it was her, when he'd seen her earlier. The way his mouth twitched with disappointment, he knew, and he'd found a way to hold it against her.

Just as well.

She hadn't realized she cared so much. Tom had been older by enough to make him disinterested in the two younger siblings, and when Risa had left for the City, she hadn't missed him so much as she'd missed the consistency of knowing the people moving through her daily life.

"How's El," Risa asked quietly, meeting her brothers.

Teddy shrugged. "Fine. You know how she is. Cautious." His eyes flicked to hers with a knowing look.

"She's persnickety," Tom mumbled.

Teddy scoffed.

"What? She is," Tom insisted, glaring between them. "Her first question—she said, 'What the hell are you doing here,' not 'who are you' or 'oh what the fuck I have a brother' or anything like that." It was annoyingly perceptive, and in truth, made Risa just a little bit jealous, if only because for a moment, he knew more about Elsie than Risa did.

She sighed.

Ezra—and Risa's own guilt about not checking in—had been the primary reason for Cora's visit. Elsie, Cora supposed, had a right to know that there was another person out there that carried the same potential. Another heir to the Chancellorship. Another heir to Death, really.

Another risk, Risa had pointed out. If the Master found Ezra, he'd be a step closer to shackling Cora. The realization had struck a deep sadness within her, and she'd locked herself in the bathroom, crying silent tears, trying to pull herself together but unable to summon composure.

But Cora had been deathly calm about the whole matter. She confidently asserted that she wouldn't be taken. That the Master could never seize her.

Why, Risa had asked. *Why are you so out of his reach?*

Ezra, Cora had said simply. *The twins are inseparable. He'll be safe with us, soon enough.*

The tapestry wasn't a book to be read, and motives could rarely be read in action. That a mortal acted was unquestionably clear, but why— even the mortals themselves did not often know.

But Cora saw when paths met.

She wasn't prescient, but she'd seen this coming in the weave.

"El knew he was comin'," Tom muttered, rounding out the thought.

Teddy and Risa exchanged a knowing look.

"Ugh. Nothing's fucking changed, you both..." Tom trailed off, eyes growing distant.

"Us both what," Risa snipped.

Tom's eyes snapped to her, cold. "So that's how it's gonna be. That's funny, Tess. I don't appreciate being fucked with."

Teddy's hands were in his pockets, eyes on the ground. "She's not fucking with you—"

"The hell she isn't. You fucked a lot of things up—"

"Hey." Teddy glanced up, glaring. "Don't blame her, it wasn't her fault—"

"But she's sure as shit standing here now, isn't she." Tom threw his hands up, frustrated. "She's a gods-damned adult, has been for some time, just like the rest of us—"

"I don't know what it is you're after," Teddy bit back, "she's not even Tess! I've asked her a million times—"

"Then she's fucking lying to you, Ted. You always were too soft."

Awkward silence filled the street, and Risa found, much to her dismay, the eyes of both her brothers had let on her with uncomfortable expectation.

"It—it's complicated," Risa breathed. Tears pricked at her eyes, painful. Was it complicated? Or was she just a coward?

Nerene always did say she lacked sight of the story for the words on the page, and maybe, just maybe, Risa wasn't as much of a rebel as she thought.

She liked to believe she could shake things up, upset the status quo, but when had she ever done that? She'd followed the conspiratorial rules, had crafted an entire personality out of being constrained from doing what she wanted, of not disappointing anyone she looked up to—

Tom was glowering, taking a step back from them, hands up in exasperation. "You've missed too much. You've been gone too long. You can't walk back and expect things to be like you left them. You've got two brothers and no parents—and no right to waltz back here like you never left! Some of us didn't do so good, with you gone! And some of us have figured out how to—to stumble around with you not being here, so just...shoo! Go!" Muttering to himself, he turned, stomping off.

"Wow." Risa ran her fingers through her hair, exhaling slowly. "I...think my knees are actually shaking, from that?" She turned, looking at Teddy incredulously. "He yelled at me."

"Yeah." Teddy sighed, ruffling his hair in frustration.

"He's pissed."

"Give him a few weeks, he'll get over it," Teddy breathed.

"And you?"

"I just don't understand why you've been lying, Risa." He looked tired, standing in the street. "Did I have to drag you outside and yell at you, too? Is that what it would've taken?"

"No, I—"

Teddy pursed his lips, taking her hand—

Taking her hand, and shoving her coat sleeve up, fingers tracing her forearm, and the scar at the base of her elbow. "See," he said quietly, "that's where Tom chucked a rock at you." He scoffed, shaking his head, letting her arm drop.

Reflexively, Risa brushed her hair back over the nick in her head. She still had a divot, evidence that even Healers could not erase the past.

Teddy just rolled his eyes, watching her. "I'm not about to grab you and start looking for cracks in your head, Risa. Tess. Whatever you're called, these days."

"Teddy—"

"You really hurt me! I was scared and alone and you lied to me! You made me feel like I was losing my mind! And the only reason you can give is that you were a coward. That doesn't make sense, Risa. Even after everything I told you, all the reassurances—that was so deeply personal, and you didn't even have the respect to be honest with me—"

"At first, it was for El's safety—"

"Oh, that turned out great, didn't it," Teddy snapped, glaring. "And what about after that?"

"It—I—you don't have any right to stand here and yell at me—"

"Yes, I sure as hell do," Teddy bit back. "Don't you dare start. You know what I've been going through. I take it back, when I said I was proud of the adult you turned into. She's nothing like Tess. You're too caught up in your own anxiety to see that you were hurting me. El was sick, Sam fucking left, and now this—"

"Hey. You're making a scene." Tom was glowering, striding back towards them both. Plainly, whatever eldest sibling inclinations were left in him had been struck up, hearing his siblings arguing in the street. "And here, I thought I overreacted—"

"No, you were right," Teddy grimaced, shaking his head.

"Take a breath, Ted." Tom's hand was on his shoulder, chilly eyes flitting to Risa. "And you, too. He's right. At the risk of sounding parental, or like I even vaguely have my shit together, you should think about what you've done. Git."

"Fine." Risa turned on her heel, leaving the boys standing there, tears in her eyes. "Fine. You know what? Not all of us are so lucky as to have reunions set into some tapestry by a fucking god. I'm just some backdistrict kid. What happened to me? It wasn't Fate. It was fucked."

THE PURSUIT

Brothers are a bother.

Always have been, always will be.

~Elizabeth Clement Faulise,

Excerpt from a letter dated February 1st

ELSIE

*"Sometimes, I think I'm punished with nostalgia. I
never want to be so soft. And yet, here I am, missing
what has long since passed."*

~Elizabeth Clement Faulise

The mantle clock ticked impatiently, the fire crackling, and Elsie's
eyes had not left Ezra's for a fair few minutes.

At last, the door clicked open, Isa sidling in. They gave her a small
wave, stooping over to unlace their boots.

"Well," Elsie breathed coolly, rising. "That's my cue to leave."

Ezra stood, eyes wide. "What?"

"I'm going home."

"I thought this—"

"This is my brother's apartment. You can stay here tonight. We'll
figure the rest out. That's Isa, they'll be watching you." Elsie made a
gesture from her eyes to her brother's in warning. "You're not going
anywhere."

"I—"

"It's for your own safety," Elsie clipped, glancing to the dining table
in the nook. Fletcher sighed, rising too, and together they left Isa and
Ezra in the apartment-turned-prison.

Only when the door had closed and they were halfway down the
building stairs did Elsie break the silence. "I owe Isa for this."

"They won't mind," Fletcher said quietly. "They volunteered—I would've, if they hadn't. Do you mind if I skip out on dinner?"

"No. Why, though?"

"Don't much feel like wearing a façade. I'm a bit tired anyway, and it's always a strain."

"Want me to bring you anything?"

"If you don't mind," Fletcher nodded, brushing a kiss against her cheek. "I'll see you at home."

The street beyond was chilled, lamps glowing in the encroaching fog. Turning left, Elsie shoved her hands in her pockets, still prickling with irritation. The temporary sympathy she'd had for Ezra melted away in conversation with him. He had a thousand questions and an eagerness for answers that Elsie found exceedingly annoying, and his continued reference to them being the best of inseparable friends had quickly began to grate on her.

He was all sunshine and holding hands and skipping into the sunset to a happily ever after, and it annoyed the skies out of Elsie. After so much difficulty, he had no right to be that cheerful, because it meant he might just be shouldering hardship better than her, which sent her spiraling, oscillating between intense guilt and sharp bitterness.

A sign was swinging in the breeze, the words *The Magpie* glistening in the lamplight above one of the nicer taverns. Pushing the door open, Elsie skirted the establishment, searching the dark-stained tables—

She spotted them at the back.

Her brothers.

Tom was sitting with his back to the corner, the way men did when they'd wronged one too many folk. Teddy was next to him, talking quietly, and good *gods* it must've been ages since the three of them had sat at a table together. Tom and Teddy and Elsie.

"'Lo," Elsie breathed, sliding into the seat across from Tom.

"Where's the kid," Tom asked, quirking an eyebrow.

331

"He's at the apartment with Isa. That's where he's staying for tonight," Elsie muttered. She sighed, leaning back in her chair, looking for the barkeep. "Risa coming?"

"Doubtful, since she wasn't invited," Teddy remarked, grimacing. "Tom, in a stunning display, told her she ought to go and think about her actions."

Tom nodded thoughtfully, taking a sip of ale.

"It's weird, seeing you two agree," Elsie muttered.

Teddy wrinkled his nose. "Hey! We get on just fine. We went our separate ways, doesn't mean we fell out."

"Here, here," Tom added. His gaze flicked across to hers, eyebrow quirking. "So Ezra's your brother, then. Huh."

"I'm not partial to him. He's annoying."

"He is, but he's a good kid, mostly. Curious, what he had to say. Never heard of the Faulises—"

"Not here, please?" Elsie gestured him to silence. "It's private. But yeah. Curious is the right word."

"Looks about your age?"

"Why are you so interested, all of a sudden?"

"Because everything else is shit, Elsie," Tom breathed, watching her. "And this seems good, ya know? You finally get to know your family."

"Tactless, Tom, very nice," Teddy muttered, ruffling his hair.

Tom just shook his head, leaning back to rest his arm on the back of Teddy's chair. "So, I've heard what's new with Teddy. Sam took off— bastard, I'll sock him good if he shows his face here again. Dunno if you heard, but Mariann left, too. Must be a Mirabeau thing, sucking ass at love."

Elsie had little love of Mariann, but privately felt this was probably best for her. Tom might have rallied to be less of an ass as they commiserated over dinner, but he was hardly a star husband.

"Thing is," Tom went on, almost thoughtful, "I'm still wondering where you all went. You—El, you're a flight risk, that didn't surprise me, but Teddy? He's clerked religiously, and I would've sworn he did it until the day he died." His eyes flicked between them. "And I heard Teddy say you got sick?" His voice was quiet, flirting with worry. "But you're back now."

"I'm not back. I'm here, dealing with Ezra. But I'm still sorting some stuff out," Elsie breathed, looking down at the table.

"What happened?"

Elsie reached for Teddy's ale, mulling over the question—and earning a look of reprimand from her middle brother, though he said nothing. "Once, Tom, there was a fiddle player. One day, a king came to him and said his fiddling would bring all the riches of the world to heel, if only he would join the king far away. The fiddler gave up everything to chase after the king. He left behind his family, his friends, his province, all of it, and when he arrived, he was giddy with excitement. But the king had not been entirely honest. The fiddler found himself in a cage, strung up in front of a bloodthirsty audience. If he did not play his fiddle to the king's satisfaction, the king would drop the fiddler into the crowd to let them tear him apart. The audience did not cheer him on, but rather, gathered each day in the hopes that he would fail and their bloodlust would be sated. They paid dearly for the chance to rip him apart, handing over all their gold to the king. The fiddler played day and night, unceasingly. At first, he knew he could overcome the challenge. But by the dawn of the second day, his strength was failing. By the close of the third, he knew he would have to decide which death he wanted—whether it would be better to die with his fiddle in hand and music in his ear, or whether it would be better to give it up and allow the king to throw him to the crowd. His fingers bled, his muscles began to fail, his bones began to disintegrate, and still, he played on and on and on, hoping he had pleased the king. But it didn't matter. He died, betrayed, and with him, beauty."

Tom was glaring, arms crossed. "I don't understand. So you've learned the fiddle?"

The remark earned him a smack on the chest from his brother. "Idiot," Teddy hissed.

"No, Tom. I didn't learn the fiddle. My friend accused me of a crime, and I ended up in a prison cell up north." Elsie took another sip of ale, sighing. "It made me ill."

"Oh."

Silence fell down around them, the noise of the bar overtaking the table. It wasn't a bad establishment, in the way of taverns, not quite being at the state where merchants cared to frequent it, but not being so low that there was sawdust on the floor. Mostly, it was for the middle-class. Those who weren't quite ready to condemn the merchants, and those not entirely unsympathetic with the working class.

Sam had frequented this place often. Of course, he had a way of sliding into that moral gray space, so he'd be at home, here.

"Ted, when you're around, we gotta talk about the farm." Tom's gaze was fixed firmly on his hands. It sounded like it'd taken a lot of nerve, bringing that up, and for that, at least, Elsie almost felt sorry for him.

"What's there to talk about? Let Cele take it," Teddy muttered. "I don't want it."

"Yeah, well, I do. Thought before Mariann took off, it'd be a good place to raise kids. Now, it's—it's the only option, other than a factory, and I don't want that." He glanced over to his brother. "Thing is, I can't really manage the lease right now. Not if I'm going to try and rebuild the farmhouse."

"For fuck's sake, Tom—"

"No, hear me out. It could be better. It's a chance to be better than

Mom and Dad. It's my home," Tom said firmly. "And I'll find a way to keep it. Just figured since your companion had deep pockets—"

"Sam earned most of what he had." Teddy sighed. "I'll talk to Cele. She's been nice with the apartment, maybe she'll help you out with the farm, too."

It was a nice thought, that Tom could build something better.

Naïve.

But nice.

"What's your future hold, then," Tom put in. The question was to both of them, his pale blue eyes flicking back and forth.

Teddy shrugged. "Dunno. Helping Elsie sort this mess out for now. Then, who knows." He paused. "Risa thinks I should go after Sam."

"And," Elsie breathed, waiting.

"I think I might."

"Why," Tom scowled. "He's not one of us—"

"Yeah, but I still love him. And he said he still loved me, but had to go. That doesn't make sense," Teddy spilled, words flowing fast. Plainly, he'd been percolating on this for a while. "I do think I deserve some answers. I've been afraid that I'm—I'm going to find him having an affair, or that he's going to have some new secret, but I don't know how I'll move on without understanding this better."

Elsie gave him a pointed look.

"Fine," Teddy relented. "I miss him. I want him back."

"Even after he broke it off?" Tom looked skeptical. "I wouldn't want to try it again with Mariann. She's spoken her peace. She's pregnant, for fuck's sake."

"That's you and Mari. Sam and I are different."

"I think," Elsie interjected, "it depends on what you find. Maybe he just got overwhelmed and needed some time, yeah?" She hadn't meant to sound so hopeful, but the ale had gone to her head.

"An oddly patient approach from someone who locked her brother in an apartment," Tom quipped, sardonic.

"And yet, here you sit," Elsie hissed.

"I'm not your brother—"

"Why do you double down on this," Elsie demanded, glaring. "What does it matter to you?"

Tom held her gaze for a long moment, a perturbed look carved into his brow. "Sisters leave," he said at last. "They always go. That's how family is. Temperamental and unpredictable. Better if you're my friend than my sister. Plainly," he added, gesturing to nothing in particular, "seeing as Tess finds it suitable to lie to my face in broad daylight. At least with you, I get the truth."

Elsie was left in stunned silence, guilt rising—not just about Tom, but about Ezra too.

The eldest Mirabeau boy was correct, more correct than he had any right to be. Blood ties led to nothing. It was a tool to be used, and nothing more, and honesty could not come from anyone tied to that way—nor, she contemplated, could she be honest in return, for she'd said nothing of the God of Death to Ezra.

So it was, then.

From the mouth of Tom Mirabeau, truth.

EZRA

"And into the meadow he stepped, and he saw. For
the first time, he saw, and such was the beauty that he
was moved to tears.

Never had he known the world to be so kind.

Never had he known it to be so pure."

~ From 'Tales of the Recently Revived: A Sequel'

The Valley apartment was nearly dark by the time Elsie had left, going
to wherever it was she called home.

One thing above all else was abundantly clear to Ezra.

He had stumbled into her life, uninvited, and she resented it. More
than that, she was angry. Angry with a capital *A*. The whiskey was
smooth across his tongue, growing sweeter with each sip. Hell of a
prison, serving top-shelf liquor.

The apartment was unoccupied at the moment, Elsie had said, and
thus, she told him he'd be staying here while they figured out what to
do with him. He didn't tell her he'd be slinking off, come morning—of
course, he'd have to shake the guard she'd left.

It couldn't have been more apparent that Elsie didn't want him near
her, but didn't want him to leave, either.

Unlike his friend, who wanted him near and safe and happy, in all
the multitudes. *The Master.* Tired and worn, Ezra hated that name,

tonight more than usual.

"You okay?"

The voice made him start.

Not alone.

The soldier sank down on the edge of the sofa beside him, offering a quiet smile. "Sorry. Didn't mean to startle you. You must've been pretty far away, to be yanked back so abruptly." It was an odd accent, lilting with not-quite-right vowels and hard stops across the tongue. Odd. But lovely.

His eyes traced the Drada—because elves were definitely real, apparently. As real as magic.

"Isa," the soldier offered.

"Pardon?"

"You looked like you were searching for a name. It's Isa."

Ezra felt the corners of his mouth twitch upward. "Thanks. Lotta names, today, and it's...just a lot." It was impossible to look away. To draw his eyes from the slash of silver buttons cutting across their chest, to stop drawing lines up the booted legs, to pull his gaze from the dark hair, top pulled into a knot, bottom shaved close.

"Mm, I don't think I know that look," Isa edged, dark eyes narrowing. "You've got the name. So what is it, that you're wondering?"

Who you are.

He gave a half-hearted shrug, lips pursed.

What are you. Maybe that was the question he'd been wanting to ask.

Beautiful.

That was the answer.

A beautiful, intoxicating distraction.

He'd tumbled in bed with more than a few lovers, in the Capital. And running was lonely. Pleasure houses cost coin—coin he didn't have— and anyway, he didn't mind terribly, taking matters into his own hands.

And of course, it wasn't as though the tension between him and his friend was real—his friend who couldn't even share his name. The thought made Ezra sad. They shared a lot of camaraderie. Intimacy, even, a certain flavor of emotional vulnerability that satiated some deep longing in Ezra's heart.

The more he thought about it, the more he wondered if maybe a distraction wasn't simply the answer to his tired thoughts.

A few hours.

Put it all from his mind. Elsie's vitriol, and whomever the Master returned to every night. Ezra was lucky to have a friend in this man so loyal and soft—and that something had broken his trust? Well. Ezra would fix it.

Even so, he envied the bedmate of the Master.

The whiskey had gone to his head, making everything swim, and he forced his mind back.

"How do you know Elsie," Ezra edged, drinking Isa in.

Isa's eyes sparkled out, dulling to disinterest. "Long story."

"Yeah." He dropped his gaze to his glass. "Aren't they all."

Sighing, Isa shifted, leaning back into the sofa, their warm leg pressing tight against his, and it was like feeling sparks against his skin.

When was the last time someone touched you intimately.

Gods.

Years, probably.

"They all are," Isa said quietly. "Long stories, I mean."

Ezra gave a half-hearted snort. "Who has the time."

"I don't," Isa breathed. "I just really fucking don't." Their gaze drifted to his again, eyes deep.

Fuck.

Ezra shifted, drawing his knees to his chest, a would-be casual move.

Isa took a deep breath in, lilting their head to the side in study of him.

"How long have you been running for?"

"Er, three years, give or take, I think."

"Three years," Isa echoed, nodding thoughtfully. "Long time."

"Yeah."

Silence fell across them both. A log shifted in the fireplace, disintegrating into nothing more than embers.

"It was lonely," Ezra breathed at last, eyes lost out the darkened window in the breakfast nook. He wasn't staring into the night, though. It was Isa's distant reflection he was watching.

"I can imagine."

Their voice was soft, like lambswool.

He could've gotten lost in that sound for days.

You're drunk.

You're drunk, you've found a place to rest, and you're being ridiculous.

Somehow, he didn't care.

Glancing back to Isa, he met their burning onyx eyes. "You can imagine that kind of loneliness? Wishing, more than anything, for another voice in the night? Wanting someone—anyone—to hold you, just to feel alive again?"

Isa's brow furrowed under the words. Then, gently, they reached a hand to skirt his jaw. "I understand," they breathed. And with that, their lips were against his, hot and hungry.

Ezra lost himself in those kisses, strong and gentle, let his body breathe, muscles melting to jelly beneath Isa's hands.

And when Isa pulled back, Ezra wanted to scream his anguish.

It was the worst kind of letting go.

"I am *ro*," Isa murmured, fingers tracing the contours of his face. "You know this?"

He shook his head, drunk on Isa.

"*Ro*. To be neither. To be both. To walk between worlds. Not a tart or

340

a pastry, but a confection. You understand, Ezra, that if I welcome you into my bed, you will see a *ro* undone. You seem sweet. But I've been soured on false words, of late. You will accept what you find, between the sheets, because what you will find is *ro*. Neither. Both. And if you do not, Elsie will be one brother less, is that clear?"

Neither.

Both.

It made no difference.

He wanted Isa.

Whatever that meant.

"*Ro*," Ezra echoed, lacing their fingers together. It felt so good, being so close to another living heartbeat. To bear witness to honesty for once in his fucking life. "*Ro* sounds perfect to me."

Wordlessly, Isa rose, pulling Ezra to standing, too. "Then I think," they breathed, hands tracing his waist, "it is time we go to bed."

He stumbled after them down the hall, and he was lost in Isa.

Eyes, perfect and black.

Hair, soft and supple, strands falling to cradle their face.

Skin, so silky and smooth, muscles, hard beneath—

He found the silver buttons with trembling hands, not able to work them apart quite fast enough, and Isa had already undone his trousers, unsheathing him, delivering a few firm strokes in the sweetest kind of distraction.

Isa's jacket fell to the floor, nothing but a pale yellow swath left wrapped around their ribs.

And he paused, the moment seeming to breathe between them as he took in the *ro*.

Boots kicked aside, uniformed pants sitting low on their hips, and they were everything.

The only thing he could see, in that moment. His world, beginning and ending, uncontained. Brilliant.

"Go on," Isa breathed, hands braced on his hips.

His fingers found the wrapping, tugging it loose.

Isa's shoulders sank, eyes closing softly as it fluttered to the floor, and they inhaled deeply, a smile at the corners of their lips as Ezra palmed a supple breast, lips meeting the curve of their neck.

The *ro* discarded their pressed uniform trousers in a deft movement, kicking them aside, too, before letting their body sink easy against Ezra's.

The warmth of another person against him seemed to release a tightness inside his chest, and he hadn't been lying, on the window seat, about how damn lonely he had been, but he hadn't realized *precisely* how true those words were until now, until his arm was wrapped around Isa, until he felt safe, because that was what Isa was, wasn't it? A warrior? And who better than a warrior to stand guard over him after so many gods-damned years of running—

Don't cry don't cry don't cry

Nuzzling his face into the crook of Isa's neck, though, drawing them in close, he was blinking back tears.

I want this.

I want you.

The arousal pressing into Isa was evidence enough of that. And yet, the thought of breaking away from this, where they were right now, this unrivaled embrace, intimate and tender and guarded in the most wonderful way, it sounded wretched.

Don't cry don't cry

His breathing had turned from eager to shuddered, jagged as he tried to fight back whatever was rising in his heart.

Isa's skin was damp against his own, and he squeezed his eyes shut, cursing himself, still not letting go.

"Lover," Isa breathed, moving enough to tilt Ezra's head up, to find his watery eyes.

"Sorry," he said hoarsely, cheeks damp. "I'm sorry, I—give me a minute, and I—sorry, I want you, I really do, I..."

Isa was frowning, though, watching him with a discerning stare. "You did not expect to find me undone so—"

"No!" Ezra snapped the word out, panic rising. "That isn't it—I just...I..." But a flood of tears overtook him as he shook his head.

Isa's frown melted, and gently, they moved, thumbing away the tears. "Then tell me."

"Safe with you." They were the only words he could summon, and even those felt childish and stupid. "I—I don't even know you," he whispered. "I'm sorry. I—maybe this was a bad idea, I'm so sorry, you— you don't need..." He trailed off, mumbled words falling flat to the floor, and he tried to rip himself back, tried to turn to leave.

"No." Now it was Isa's turn to protest. "Ezra, wait."

His name on their lips bound him to the room, the chain he didn't ever want to snap.

"We came here," Isa breathed, tangling themself up in him, "for release. For a night of unfettered vulnerability, to bare ourselves, to come undone, and you..." They were smiling now, so sweetly, eyes glistening, too. "You humans. You misunderstand. We can cry together. Find safe harbor in this bed. And we can fuck, too, and then cry some more, and fuck again, until the morning steals us away, but they—they are not exclusive. Intimacy is found in tears, too."

SAM

*"I remember thinking how I had given up the arms of
the man I loved for this—this unending fear, and even if
I knew I had made the right choice, because it meant my
love would live...I missed him. Badly."*

~Sam Alderton

Sam's eyes were watering with anguish as he blinked back the ceiling.

These ghosts were relentless.

You have to get out of here.

Someone was looming over him, scowling, tossing a tiny vial up and down. Then, popping the cork, the man stooped over. His grubby fingers pinched Sam's nose closed, and something vile, sticky and rotten, was sliding down his throat, sending his insides roiling.

The dhacrym.

Gagging as the man released him, Sam rolled over, willing himself to be sick—

"Restrain him. We don't need any funny business." Someone was shoving him up against the wall, and vaguely, he was aware of the cool glass, pressed against his cheek as bloodied tears rolled hot from the corners of his eyes.

A salacious laugh oozed from the threshold.

"I always liked you free," Clark mused, leaning against the door frame. "Bindings...tsk, it just takes the *thrill* out of it, wouldn't you say, love?"

Not real, you're not real, I watched them bury you—

"See, if I'd simply bound you and had my way," Clark carried on, "then you'd have simply *known* it wasn't right and been on your merry way. But free, you were *culpable*. Free, you could've walked away, could've chosen not to share my bed—and there is something deliciously satisfying, isn't there? Knowing that it was ultimately *you* who brought this about—"

"Stop! Stop it!" Hands pressed to his ears, screams scraping his throat raw, he could still hear the cawing caracara, real as sin and preaching truth.

"The worst part, though, is how quickly he has forgotten me." A woman's voice cut through the din, ripe with disappointment.

It had been twenty-one years, and she was frowning, legs swinging off the edge as she sat atop the servant's empty bed.

"Mm, this—this is true," Clark mused, giving her a nod of acknowledgment.

"My Sammy," Rebeca sighed, shaking her head. "So ready to revel in the riches of someone else's life. I starved for you, sold my body for you, *died* for you, and this is how you repay me?"

Not real, not real, not real

He had to find the world once more, the world of the living, the world of reason and ration.

"What..."

His head snapped up at the familiar voice, unable to look away.

Another ghost.

She was so much more beautiful, here, in the land of fear and death. Beautiful—and pregnant.

Mariann Mirabeau was glaring at him from beside Clark, her hand resting on the gently bulging abdomen. Teddy's sister-by-marriage, and she had wanted a baby from Tom, Teddy's elder brother, or so she'd said a thousand times, and yet, they'd been barren for a decade, and fear

345

did strange things to the mind, twisting thoughts until they were nearly unrecognizable.

Mariann was scoffing, frustration plain across her face. "Fuck me...do you see this?" she snapped, gesturing at Sam, eyes finding a man in the corner. "Do you see what a gods-damned mess you're making? One task. You had *one* task. You bring him the Sun."

"Pardon, m'lady—"

She sucked her teeth, eyes darting back to Sam. "Scram. I'll bind him up. We'll keep him in here—not like he's going anywhere, I guess. And don't," she added, whirling on the guard as he tried to slip out the door, "don't you *dare* tell anyone about this fiasco. As always, I will clean up your gods-damned mess. And then *I* will break the news."

"Yes'm," the man muttered, turning.

Sam's brow was slick with sweat, lungs breathless as he watched them trail out of the room, leaving him alone, alone with Clark, and Rebeca, and Mariann, and gods knew who else as the poison ripped through him.

He would bleed out, before the end.

His thoughts flickered to Elsie.

Elsie, reduced to hardly anything, skin and bones beneath white sheets, eyes bloodshot, craving magic that didn't belong to her.

Mariann knelt down beside him, seemingly unaware of the others in the room. "You look like shit," she muttered.

"Who are you," he breathed.

Her head snapped up. "You fucking kidding me, Sam? It's me. Mariann. Your gods-damned sister-in-law."

"No, that—that's who you look like..." The words were growing heavy on his tongue, his mind spinning out. "You're not..."

"I am."

It was easier to relent to the delusion.

"How...how's Tom," he murmured, air growing thin around him.

What are you doing, making small-talk? You have to get out of here—

"Oh, he's lovely," she remarked, voice dripping with sarcasm. "Completely tickled that I ran off and promptly got myself knocked up by someone who wasn't him. Men love adultery—especially when it ends with bastards." Her eyes flicked up, giving him a glare of admonition. "C'mon, Sam. I don't know. Probably drunk and angry, same as always." She found his gaze. Then, lips pursed, she brushed a hand against his shoulder. "Fancy getting out of here?"

He could hardly believe it. He was on his feet—barely.

The world was spinning, and Clark was laughing, his raucous caws echoing through the servant's quarters, Rebeca pointing and laughing all the while. He was going, though, he really was, maybe finally, in delusion, truth, escape—

But the barghest, it seemed, had other plans.

In a lunge, it sprang for Sam, a low rumble of a growl giving him the unmistakable urge to run. The beast's great jaws clamped down around his left knee a moment later, the sick crunching of bone filling the room in time to Sam's scream.

It was fire, hellish and red, an acidic assault of something dark and dastardly, and this—this was a horrendous way to end, Sam thought bitterly, collapsed on the floor, body clenched in pain.

The *click-clack* of claws running on stone brushed past his head, and he braced himself.

But the next wave did not come.

"Fuck." Mariann's voice was breathy. Alert.

There was snarling and hissing and the wretched sound of flesh tearing, and a whimper.

"Good dog," Mariann was whispering, watching two beasts, locked in combat, one pinning the other to the floor, the latter twitching unsettlingly.

347

Sam's eyes flicked down to his mangled leg.

The cloth was shredded, blood streaked across the wooden floor, soaking into the panels.

Find that. Find the pain, find something real—

There was bone, maybe, poking through the skin. Nausea, real and merciful, was rising in his gut at the sight—

Her hand was on him a moment later. The ripping of fibers sent his skin crawling, and he wondered who it might be, behind the mask of fear. Who was staying to bind his leg. If anyone was really there at all.

TEDDY

"I promised myself I would never chase boys. I'd
never be that guy, running after those who broke my
heart—until one of them did break my heart, and I see it,
now. There was no shame in loving someone so badly
you can do nothing but run and hope."

- Theodore Alderton

It was just before dawn when Teddy heard a soft tap at his bedroom door in Caelaymnis. Sleep had been elusive, with his thoughts so loud and his bed so empty.

"Yeah," he sighed, sitting up a little.

Elsie slipped inside, closing the door softly behind her. "Did I wake you?"

"What do you think," he mumbled. He fell back into the soft pillows with a sigh. "How's the brother?"

"I don't know," Elsie bit back sardonically, "how *are* you, Teddy?"

"You know what I meant."

"Ezra's fine? He's...fine. What he seems, I think—a little lost, more than a little annoying. Isa keeps volunteering to watch him—"

"Isa keeps flirting with him," Teddy quipped.

"Whatever. Can't risk him bolting."

"And you can't risk keeping him at more than arm's length? Why not bring him here? It's not like anyone is going to fuss. It's you. They know if they made a fuss, it's be a political disaster."

Elsie sank down on the bed beside him, crawling beneath the

blankets, not answering. But when she glanced over, hair mussed on the pillow, she shrugged. "It's weird, having...that kind of family."

"Yeah. Yeah, it is."

"So." She was fidgety, curling up to lean on his shoulder. "Today's the day you go get Sam?"

"Today's the day I leave to go find him," Teddy corrected. "It's a long trip."

"Why aren't you using one of the discs?"

"I am. It's still a long trip."

"You're going to take a fucking ferry, aren't you," Elsie frowned.

He sighed, saying nothing. The discs made him feel funny, and if he was being honest, he wanted some more time to think through what he was going to say—wanted time to poke around, too, to ask questions, to listen to whispers.

"Tell him off for me, okay?" Elsie's tone shifted as she settled in, stilling a bit. "I miss him, too."

"I will," Teddy whispered, putting an arm around her, drawing her in to kiss her forehead. Then, with a sigh, he rose.

"You should try and get a little more rest—"

"I'm awake." He pulled the blankets around her, quirking an eyebrow. "You sleep. I...I miss Sam, though. I can't wait. I have to get some closure."

~ • ~

The difficulty in having never been to the Capital before was that Teddy didn't particularly have a clear idea of where anything was, beyond Sam's florid descriptions and the map Teddy himself had purchased. The disc relied on magic of familiarity: to venture out without really knowing where one was going was rather like trying to make a stone float; with the right stone, maybe one could, but you had to have a mess of other talents to approach it.

The frozen woods presumably just beyond Silvercreek stretched out around Teddy, his breath frosting in the air. He'd been here, as a child, when his maternal aunt had passed, and they'd taken a ferry down the Merchant's Vein for the funeral. He'd played in these woods with his cousins, once, and it seemed that the memory had been strong enough to at least resonate with the magic. Even so, looking around, Teddy found a slight panic rising in his chest.

This place looked unfamiliar.

I can always go home. I can always go back to somewhere I know.

The distance between Caelaymnis and Aerdela was vast and treacherous in the winter months, and he'd intended the disc to carry him back into familiar territory.

Frozen leaves and debris crunched under his boots as he took a step, eyes flickering around the woods. Taking a shaking breath, Teddy pulled the compass from his coat pocket, eyes focused on the needle.

Then, turning on his heel, he headed off in the opposite direction than the one he'd been oriented in. His memory placed these woods laying to the west of the town proper, though there'd been no such evidence of any forest on the map. Bad cartography, he'd decided. Either that, or bad memory.

I can do this. I waded through snow in the high plains beyond Caelaymnis to bring supplies to a potentially murderous band of humans. I can take a hike through the woods.

A faint smile tugged at the corners of his mouth at the thought. He'd loved that. The chance to hone his healing skill, the opportunity to talk with those living in the settlements, the whole thing, of traipsing off into the world with a friend...

Isa was a particularly dear friend, and anymore, it felt like there was a *lot* that bonded them.

Another reason he was grateful for those double scars along his chest, for they marked him as uncontained without a single word needing to be said. Isa had seen them, and understood.

It wasn't long before Silvercreek appeared through thinning trees. He'd have to catch a ferry down the river towards the Capital, but the venture had shaved perhaps half a day or more off the journey. Inquiring with a passerby, he found the western harbor, and one silver stack purchased a ticket that would permit him to stand on the deck of the barge in the cold as it worked its way down the river.

Watching the shore slowly drift by, Teddy leaned against the railing, thinking.

Chim would've been helpful, he thought dully. But she'd vanished, and it was near impossible to track a *kobalde* over more than a few miles, so all he could do was hope that she'd return once he'd retrieved Sam, and their family could be pieced back together.

ELSIE

"Take this knife. What's life, without a bit of adventure, my dear? And what's adventure if not the balance of self-fulfillment and danger."

~Sam Alderton

"You know, for someone who promised they'd be prompt, you're showing up late an awful lot." Everett was loading up a satchel with glass bottles, corked and waxed and filled to the brim with a deep almost-black syrup.

"Yeah, well....get over it." Elsie was glowering as she shut the side-door to the shop behind her. She'd left Ezra in the apartment under Isa's watchful supervision, and in truth, she was grateful for this distraction tonight.

Actually, she was surprisingly grateful for everyone here. She was grateful that her anger and vengeance and thirst for understanding—both clinical and morbid—drove her into the arms of this syndicate, because it wasn't really a bunch of masterminds gathered together so much as a bunch of people who were as angry and hurt as she was, trying to make sense of their own survival, and that was something her family didn't really get.

Footsteps heralded someone descending down the stairs in the dingy shop, and Elsie had the words *Hey, Ginger* poised on her tongue, only it wasn't Ginger who appeared from the mess of junk concealing the staircase.

"Is this the new girl?" A pale man with silken lardish hair spared a glance to Elsie before turning his attention Everett's preparations.

"The new girl can hear you," Elsie remarked, curious. She crossed her arms, watching him. "I'm Dosia. Who are you?"

The man looked up. "Lysander Xavishia."

Elsie's smile faltered, arms dropping. "Xavishia?"

"Oh, neat, you know my father," Lysander frowned, looking irked.

Everett made a sound of amusement, rising with the satchel.

"What?" Lysander was glaring.

"Nothing, just…" Everett shrugged. "She's new here, fuck her opinion, right? You're soft—"

"I am not!"

"That's not a bad thing, boss," Everett grinned, clapping Lysander on the shoulder.

"You know, he's right." Elsie was watching Lysander, curious. His eyes were muted purple, and he looked young—though, so did his father, and Elsie had the uneasy feeling both men were older than they'd ever admit.

Lysander made a disgruntled sound, grabbing the satchel from Everett. It looked like it was meant to be a gesture to counteract the accusation of being soft, but it came across as rather endearing, Elsie thought, for Lysander put his hand on Everett's shoulder for a brief moment of apology, even as he took the satchel.

"You. Dora—"

"Dosia," Elsie corrected.

"Whatever. You're with me tonight." Lysander beckoned her to follow, heading out into the night.

Elsie glanced in question to Everett, who only gestured her on to follow.

The street beyond the shop was quiet as ever, lamps flickering in the wind. In the Capital, the lamps burned through the night.

"I thought I was with Everett tonight," Elsie frowned, jogging a few steps to catch up with Lysander, breath fogging in the chilled air.

Lysander shook his head. "I want to know all my runners."

"Your runners?"

"Yeah. Mine. This is my gig," Lysander remarked.

Elsie sucked her teeth, steeling herself to pry. "Didn't realize tenancy was so wide-spread."

"Tenancy? That's quite technical for a runner." He gave her a sidelong glance. "No. As I suspect you already know—but are nevertheless seeking to confirm—most of what we deal in is relegation. Put a little spark into some merchant brat's hands, or let them levitate pebbles in the garden, that sort of thing. Parlor tricks."

"Insidiae are known for—"

"Tenancy? Yes. It's a reputation that's served us well—and has been earned fully. Maderlav sees things differently, even this long after the wars—and I can't say I blame you. Not when your mistrust of all things magic comes from humanity's misuse," Lys said simply. "My father's methods—barghest and dhacrym—are wildly efficient. But I understand that your time with my father soured you on the whole thing."

"I—my time with him? I don't know what you're talking about," Elsie lied, sidling up to Lysander.

But to her surprise, he turned, looking at her. "Don't you? You're Elsie, right?"

She stopped dead in her tracks, heart skipping several beats before falling into her boots.

Lysander just kept going, glancing back over his shoulder. "Come on," he beckoned softly, the way one would have called a feral cat.

Elsie's boots followed, her thoughts kicking into gear again a moment later. "You..."

"Oh, I saw you when that Drada brought you to my father," he said quietly, and to his credit, he gave her a small smile. "I'm glad you're okay."

"I—you knew—and just played along—" Elsie raised a finger in question, mouth falling open, devoid of words.

"Oh, you thought people couldn't care *and* be bastards at the same time," Lysander chuckled, settling the satchel on his shoulder. "I see."

"So you're running a novelty shop? That's it?"

"It's an economy. We pay well, and are highly sought after."

"Fat lot of good money is to someone dying—"

Lys gave her a dubious look. "To borrow a merchant phrase, it's a bad business model to kill a cash cow."

"The bodies—"

"Elsie, the dealings with the Master are not our business in the shop. We run it my way. Discretely, and to the benefit of all. His...inclination to leave a trail of bodies is not your concern. We are dealing with it."

"Dealing with it—what does that mean—"

"I appreciate your curiosity," Lys said quietly, "but you overstep. It's not your concern. There are forces bigger than you at play."

They wound their way towards the merchant's ports, the way they always did, for it was never the gulls that wanted to dabble in blood or magic, but the merchants themselves—merchants, Elsie had found, that either wanted extraordinary power or an extraordinary high—were more than happy to.

"So, you're...not going to tell anyone else," Elsie said at last, glare etched on her brow as she watched the ports come into view.

Lysander shook his head. "Nah. What's the point? They can't try to drain you again. Tenancy is finicky like that." He glanced over. "I don't mean that to be cold. I mean that it's low risk, keeping your secret. But...why are you here? Everett told me his new runner was a dhacrym chaser from Caelaymnis looking for security and a better fix. I admit, we have a certain crowd of regulars that comes back. But what they feel and what you do—there is an ocean of difference between them. A couple spoonfuls, a few hours with a barghest, they've got the adrenaline rush they wanted and we've got a syringe of blood for Everett to run through the distiller. You? You...were for something different." His voice was apologetic. "What they needed from you required suffering, indeed. And now you want more?"

Elsie loosed a breath, looking away. "Guess so. He was right."

She was quiet for a long moment, weighing it all.

"Question," she said at last, glancing over to Lys. "You know anything about something called the iaculus?"

Lys looked at her askance. "Funny question to be asking. As it so happens, I do. Curious, a girl like you is asking about relics." The gleam in his lilac eyes said he knew he was obfuscating.

"And the Master?"

"Stick to running, Elsie. And be careful."

She nodded, stuffing her hands in her pockets. *Careful.* Whatever that meant.

~ • ~

The run went smoothly, and gathered back in the shop, Ginger and Lys and Everett and even Roscoe had gathered, along with a few faces Elsie didn't know just yet.

"And it was *fucked*," Lys was laughing, face flushed with alcohol, "absolutely fucked, he cut me right out of my mother's belly—"

"Bullshit." Roscoe was scowling, sitting on a crate at the insistence of Everett, whose own revelry seemed to be interrupted every few minutes by his concern for his boyfriend.

"It's not bullshit," Lys lectured, "it's factual. Insidiae are like that!

357

There's magic that ties us all to blood. There's a tiny little thread that ties me to my father and my aunt and my grandparents and—"

"Like a hive mind," Everett nodded solemnly. "I read about that in a copper novel once, it was this beehive that worked like a brain—"

"Ech, no, Everett, not everything is a work of fiction—"

"But this sounds like it—"

Lysander snorted. "You're a dolt..."

Elsie was smiling, leaning against the counter, listening to the boys argue.

"Stupid, right?" Ginger gave her a nudge. "They tell the same fucking stories every night."

"Well, they're new to me," Elsie said softly, glancing over.

Ginger just shrugged, and then reaching down, took Elsie's hand and made to move for a dim corner of the shop.

It caught Elsie off guard, and she didn't have time to consider if she wanted to follow, or even why Ginger had taken her hand in the first place, or where they were going, and a flush had started to creep up Elsie's chest, gripping Ginger's hand as she pulled them both into the cluttered storeroom, lit only by a streetlamp spilling through a half-papered window and the bleed of lamplight from the main room.

"I heard," Ginger said quietly, reaching into her pocket, "that you're a dhacrym girl."

Elsie nodded, a faint smile at the corners of her mouth.

"Good. Me, too." With a snap, she summoned a tiny flame in her fingertips. "Neat, isn't it?"

Elsie marveled at the fire, running her hands around it, feeling the warmth. "I've never seen anyone that can do that."

"A little skill I lend out to the merchants." With a rare grin, Ginger popped open the vial and took a mouthful, passing it to Elsie, who followed suit.

This one was thicker than Clio's, smoother, too—

"Oh, woah." Elsie thrust a hand out, blinking as it hit her, heart beginning to race with a familiar apprehension, adrenaline kicking into gear.

Ginger was laughing, nodding. "Fucking good, isn't it?"

There was an edge of euphoria around the sense of panic encroaching, an exhilaration, and Elsie took another mouthful, passing the vial back to Ginger, who gave a soft yelp of alarm that dissolved into giggling.

"Oh—oh, sorry," Elsie breathed, panicked, and somehow, her hands were on Ginger's shoulders, their faces a breath apart, and there was screaming, in the distance.

"Don't be," Ginger muttered, and her hands were on Elsie's waist, "it's...it's just strong..."

The shadows in the storeroom moved, and Elsie pressed herself closer to Ginger, and it was gods-damned intoxicating, touching another living person as the dhacrym worked. It was poison and antidote, all together, and—

It'd been a stray thought.

But Elsie leaned in, and kissed Ginger.

And Ginger kissed back.

Hands started wandering, and in the dust and dark and clutter and fearful shapes menacing around them both, this felt an awful lot like everything she'd wanted with Percy, and anyway, something that felt so good wasn't bad, and gods, it felt *good*.

Ginger's kisses were sweet, and Elsie adored the way her curves felt beneath her hands as they pushed their bodies closer amid the onslaught of imagined specters, each touch a reassurance that this wasn't totally fucked, that they weren't alone.

She remembered crying, after Ginger left, and wishing she could sober up.

And she remembered that Augustus had been there, and he'd once more lifted her into his arms as she'd been awash in dhacrym. Only that couldn't be real.

He was locked in a Caelaymnic prison.

And she was high in a Capital warehouse, alone.

THE BEAST

"We chase love. That is all. A tragic side-effect of humanity, I am afraid."

~Sam Alderton

The Beast bit down hard, the tang of blood and sinew sweet, and it allowed itself to drink in the fear, deep and vast.

Only when the life had gone, and the fear was no more, did the Beast allow itself to tear its jaws from the neck of its kin, bringing matted fur and flesh with it. Teeth bared, the spines along its back were bristling as it backed away, on edge.

What an odd thing, the Beast had done, to attack another barghest.

And yet, the Master had begun to grow tired of the Insidiae, and of Mariann, and this place stank of corruption and side-switching.

"We need to go." Mariann was sliding an arm beneath the prisoner's shoulders, trying to help him. His leg was mangled from where the Beast's kin had attacked, and he was making these odd sounds, rasping, but wet.

The Beast prowled past them and into the hall, sniffing the air. Deserted, for the time being.

It wasn't sure where Mariann meant that they needed to go. But the Beast did know two things: the Master was not a very good master, on account of not giving scritch-scritches, and Mariann had awoken a deeper hunger within the Beast that fear could no longer satiate, and the Beast was ravenous for her affection.

Mariann, being a clever woman who gave very good pat-pats, always knew precisely what to do.

She knew the magic that blood could bring forth, and knowing this, she gave a bit of her own, letting precisely three drops fall into the wooden bowl from her kit. She pulled out a vial, ripped the cork out with her teeth, and poured the contents into the bowl, eliciting a puff of fog to issue up, filling the cell with the scent of burnt honey. Then, with a horsehair brush, she began to paint onto the floor.

It was a picture.

She painted on the stone itself, a picture of—

Yes. Yes, the Beast knew this one. That was a picture of Anscip's house, tall and towering. She was taking them home.

The lines of the painting began to drift up off the stone, swirling in an unfelt wind, turning to threads, then to ropes. Motes of magic were dancing in the air, and it had been a long time since the Beast had seen someone create a path of filament from blood itself. This was old magic. Forgotten magic, until now, when Mariann remembered.

Three ropes had formed, one beginning to circle each of them, and the cell began to drift away. The Beast began to whimper and whine, for darkness pressed in—

Something yanked at them, something hard and painful, and there was a yell, a *thump*, and the Beast was clawing at damp earth, spines on its back risen, teeth bared, red eyes searching the fast-clearing mist.

This was not the Insidiae's house. This was not home, this was—this was nothing, this was a forest, this was a boggy, swampy forest—

A screech cut the air, vitriolic and vengeful. A wretched thing seemed to rise from the earth itself, vile and papery.

The Beast lunged with one thought. *Protect Mariann.*

The flesh was fetid, rotting, chalky with age, quivering with what little life remained as the Beast dragged it away.

Mariann was kneeling beside the prisoner, expression serious. Another screech filled the air—

Mariann was quick with her blade. She was fast to spill her own blood, fast to strike a fire with a solution-soaked moss in one of her bowls, and with blood and flame, she was fast to ward a circle around the three of them.

Motes of ashen magic began to drip down as she poured the bowl out, the blood itself taking the fire, the two bonded, and she was fast, too, to close the circle, for another wretched thing emerged from the brambles.

It lunged, too—

"Howard, *no.*"

The Beast obeyed without thought, motionless and watching as the papery fiend hit the ward and burst itself into flame, disintegrating before their eyes.

"We are safe, at least for now." But the look of concern in her eyes was not reassuring. It was a small circle, not particularly out of the elements, not really on the high ground, and the clouds above them were ominous, moving fast and darkening with each moment. She sighed, hand on her belly. "Those...*things* won't be able to find us. But unfortunately, neither will Anscip." Rising, she glanced around, glare etching into her brow.

She didn't have to say a word for the Beast to know what she was wondering, for Howard was wondering the same thing.

What went wrong?

Where are we?

CHIM

*"Only the weak trust what they can see. Our senses
exist for one reason, and one reason alone: to be
exploited."*

~Anscip Xavishia

On the prowl, Chim sniffed the air. The scent of snow and sweat was
heavy, in the Capital, and she frowned, rubbing at the sore spot on the
tip of her finger from where Mother Chaos had made the pact. Days
waxed and waned, and still, it *hurt*.

Kill the mortals.

So, this was it.

As she tasted the air for the trails of chaos, she considered how this
time, the confusion wasn't as sweet as it had been.

Mother Chaos had once whispered sweet secrets into her ear, and
Chim had happily chased down a home and hearth.

But that was before the Master had truly made use of his puppet
strings, and shackled Mother Chaos to his whims with an unbreakable
vow of blood.

Chim's life was tied to the death of Teddy and Sam.

In the back of her mind, she was dimly aware that she'd rather die
than hunt them, but the thought vanished a moment later like embers
in the cold winter wind.

This was no game.

Games were childish and ineffectual. Her games had tormented the
Master.

This was serious business.

This wasn't conning a bag of candy from a man of naivete or feasting on a dockman whose foul words had hurt the gentle soul in the shop.

A tangle of disorder prickled through the streets.

Chim smiled, fangs sharp, eyes inked black, and humming softly to herself, she began to skip down the street, taking care to splash into icky, half-frozen puddles of street water so as to douse the passersby. "I'm going to kill my hearth, I'm going to kill my friends," she sang happily, and rounding a corner, she found the harbor.

She knew he must have come by ferry, for the trail had gone cold at a harbor upstream, and now, all there was to do was wait.

Chim plucked the bag of candies from her apron pocket, the brown bag crumpled and soft. But to her dismay, it was empty.

Every last candy she'd swindled out of Teddy at the general store had been all eaten up, and glaring, she was about to crumple the bag, to throw it away and scream, for she wanted sweets and she wanted them *now*, only...

Only she thought up a better use for it.

She folded the bag up. Stowed it in her pocket. Patted it for safe keeping.

It was the perfect size for what'd be left of their bones.

A little bag of crunched up bones for the Master. Candy...for a bag of bones.

Not a bad deal, really. Not a bad deal at all.

CORA

*"You can't save everyone. The worst part is, you'll
break yourself either way. Either you'll try to save them
all and end yourself in the process, or you'll simply stop
trying to save anyone and lose the core of who you are.
Damned if you do. Damned if you don't."*

~ The Foundress

"You can't do this."

Cora rose from where she had been perched on the borrowed bed, glaring at Yara. "I'm not *doing* anything. I'm here, trying to remedy Kiran's mistakes."

The conversation with Elsie two days prior had gone well—better than Cora had expected, in truth.

It would all be well.

It had to be.

Kiran's folly couldn't yield such horrors.

"You shouldn't be here, Yara." Cora clicked her tongue. "Go home. Move on. Skies know I am."

Yara's ghostly armor whispered as she crossed her arms. "You," she hissed, "have used your position of power. You are no better than this—this Master. No better than Kiran, either, for what that matters—"

"How dare you—"

"Look me in the eye and tell me you're alright with walking that girl to her death."

"You saw the tapestry," Cora snarled, "you know that death is not lasting—"

"Does she know? Does she know that two gods died to open the quays already? Does she know that you stood over their bloody bodies, Rose, does she know that you stole what little power you have—"

"That is *enough.*" Cora's eyes flitted angrily around Risa's apartment, where they'd retreated once again.

"You are sending that poor girl to her death."

"I swore to my predecessor and to her mother both that I would protect her. I am bound by my blood and—and the blood of the god before me," Cora whispered. "I cannot hurt her. She *must* live."

"And yet, you lead her to the slaughter—"

"It is not a true slaughter! The quay is open, and that she can close it without consequence—"

"But—"

"Yara. Leave. Risa is with her brothers, but she—she could be back at any time. Our time, yours and mine...it's over. It's been over. You are my past. A sweet past—but past, all the same." And with that, Cora gave a small gesture to dismiss Yara.

"You'll be lost without me." With a scoff, Yara withdrew an empty vial from her pocket, tossing it to Cora. "I don't know how Elsie dies. But it isn't closing your damn quay. She's full of dhacrym. Her blood is poisoned."

Cora caught the vial, the act carving a glare back into her brow.

Impossible.

Yara's eyes were full of ghostly tears as she vanished, nothing more than a shimmer remaining in the daylight.

THE RELICS

The gods are no longer relics in our world.

~ELIZABETH CLEMENT FAULISE,
EXCERPT FROM A LETTER DATED FEBRUARY 16TH

AUGUSTUS

*"Gods will rise and fall, and we will forever put them
on pedestals, thinking them more than fools."*

~Alva Praequintelya

A curious thing began to happen to Augustus—or, rather, curious things
continued to happen to Augustus, because ever since he'd taken to his
knees to swear the Vow of Fealty, he'd been burdened with the weight
of pain and magic that did not belong to him.

It'd been a symbolic act, he thought bitterly, laying on the cot in his
cell.

This was the punishment of the gods, though. Clearly, he had not
been prepared to truly commit to this act of pledging his soul to another,
and the gods, seeing this, had sought to teach him a lesson.

He was unclear about the repercussions of this. Ordinarily, his soul
would be released in the flames of a funeral pyre when he died, but he
wouldn't be burned after his execution on the hope that his soul would
remain trapped in the earth forever. But if his soul belonged to Elsie—
well, she was human, and their rites *released* the soul when the body was
entombed in the earth, and so, he was left with a throbbing headache
and no answers.

Rising in the dark of the early morning, Augustus gave a small,
reflexive gesture of his hand to conjure a lucent—which was absurd, of
course, because his magic didn't work in the confines of the cell, except
it did, this time. He blinked, squinting at the bright pulsing orb in his
hand, mouth falling open.

Impossible.

He sank back down onto the edge of his cot, probing. *Danger. I can feel it, she's wary, something is off.* And it was near-instinct, to move, only it wasn't him that moved, so much as his magic, and he felt the cell already beginning to disintegrate into the shimmering mist of evanescing.

Only his shock kept him rooted where he sat.

Oh, shit.

Whatever was keeping him here—well. It seemed to be no match for the soul magic at play, that much was clear. Nothing seemed to be stopping him from leaving, and he had half a mind to follow that pull, the one telling him that Elsie needed a soldier at her side.

On the one hand, that was why he'd done this, right? To repay her?

On the other, he was a wanted criminal, and appearing at her side might not be the safest course of action. He had no idea where she was, but it was doubtful to be somewhere his presence would be welcome.

Augustus swallowed hard, knuckles white as he gripped the edge of the cot. This was less than ideal.

A pang in his chest, though, reduced him to tears, and he had no choice.

She needed help—and he'd sworn his soul to her in a Vow of Fealty.

His obligation written in blood.

ELSIE

"Trust is earned, yes. But sometimes it is demanded
by circumstance, and we have no choice. Trust or die.
Believe or perish. That is not faith, that is being held
hostage by fate."

~Elizabeth Clement Faulise

"Something on your mind?"

Elsie started, nearly knocking over one of the vials she was loading into a satchel.

Ginger was leaning against the doorway to the backroom, watching her with crossed arms. "Ooo, a bit jumpy, too, are we?"

"I've got a lot on my mind," Elsie muttered, annoyed. Annoyed and confused.

What the fuck actually happened, Ginger

"Do you need to fucking talk about it or something," Ginger growled, and it was a kind offer masked by layers and layers of reflexive bitterness.

Elsie shrugged. "Probably."

"Then spill—but quick, while the boys are gone."

"You know anything about a...an iaculus?"

Ginger's eyes narrowed. "Iaculus? Is this one of those fucking jokes—iaculus who—"

"No—Lys made a coy remark about it," Elsie frowned.

"Don't know anything about an iaculus. But I'll poke around."

Ginger's brow knit. "Isn't like Lys to hide things. Not from us, anyway." Her eyes flicked to Elsie, narrowing. "That it?"

"No. When you gave me the dhacrym, did...anything happen?" She glanced up, wary.

"Anything, like..." Ginger made an impatient gesture.

"Did I kiss you?"

Ginger let out a snort. "No. Gods, Elsie, you're sweet, and I think you're beautiful, but I've got a girlfriend."

Nodding, Elsie blew out a breath.

"Hey." Ginger came over to sit beside her, amused expression faltering. "I'm sorry, don't take it so hard—"

"I'm not—Ginger, you're great, but I'm also not looking," Elsie said quietly, leaning back on her hands. "It's all starting to blur. I don't know what's real. And I think I haven't known what's real for a long time—if I ever knew at all."

"Of course, it's blurring. Life is scary as shit. When people first find dhacrym, they think it's all nightmares," Ginger mulled. "It's not. Fear is...complex. It's a net, really, for everything else that we feel. You ever kiss a girl before?"

"No."

"You ever get real fond of a girl before?"

"I...I don't know. Maybe."

"So maybe you're just getting to know another part of yourself, and I'll be fucked if that's not the scariest thing there is," Ginger nodded. "You didn't ask for my opinion, but I'm gonna give it. I think your only problem is that you've finally found a way to interact with yourself in a meaningful way, and you're looking for a problem."

"I'm bleeding, Ginger," Elsie said dully, meeting her eyes. "I'm wearing the evidence of dhacrym everywhere I go."

Ginger's fingers brushed the satchel. "That shit you went through is serious. That's gonna leave something behind. That's bigger than dhacrym. It's a whole vat of trauma." She glanced over, pulling a vial from her pocket. "Here."

Elsie sank into silence, thinking over Ginger's words as she accepted, dhacrym meeting her tongue in bitter familiarity. A comforting electricity set her alert, making her on edge and aware. And Ginger— gods. Ginger and her dhacrym were a soft place to land after a spiraling morning of self-condemnation.

The moment was shattered, though, when the side-door opened, and a familiar lard-haired man entered—

Fuck

Elsie turned, the most gods-damned real panic rising in her chest.

Anscip.

Anscip Xavishia.

Ginger was on her feet. "Sir. I—I didn't expect you."

"Clearly," Anscip drawled, striding idly across the shop. "Ginger, I've told you, darling. Stop taking in the strays." His rough grip was on Elsie's arm a second later, dragging her to standing. "I wondered where you'd gotten off to."

Elsie yanked her arm back with a hiss. "Fuck off. I'm just trying to find some work after you fucked me up—"

"It's true," Ginger cut in hastily, "you really messed her up—"

"Silence." Anscip snarled the word, expression somewhere between displeasure and intrigue. His apple-red eyes flicked to Elsie. "You're supposed to be in Caelaymnis."

"Plans change," she breathed.

"You know," he whispered, taking a step towards her once more, "this could work. Of course, I'm a reasonable man. Lys mentions you are inquiring about the Master..." He trailed off, a malicious smile curling on his lips.

It felt too much like she was back in the carriage house on the night of the masquerade, plans dissolving, everything going sideways. She tried to stay sharp, to push the memory of being thrown before Anscip from her mind, to focus on the now—more than anything, she wanted to know what was real, what wasn't—

Anscip's smile faltered, and he let go of her arm. "Skies. Ginger wasn't kidding."

"What's this?" Lys was coming down the stairs, his light expression faltering to worry as he glanced between them. "Ah—well. Shit."

"Lysander Xavishia—"

"Don't even. She's better than half the dimwits that come through here—"

"Hey!" Ginger was scowling. "I'm right here—"

"Not you, Ginger—"

Elsie squeezed her eyes shut, trying not to lose it. It wasn't the carriage house after a masquerade. She wasn't kneeling on a soft rug before Anscip, watching Augustus lurking.

She was in a warehouse, listening to an argument—

But Augustus's voice whispered through her all the same.

Elsie dared to open her eyes.

It was surreal. He wasn't just there in memory.

He stood before her, as real as anything.

He's actually fucking here?

Anscip was leaning against the counter, looking mildly annoyed, Lys was trying to console Ginger, and—

"Oh, mystic's tit," Augustus breathed, pale hazel eyes wide he rose from crouching in what might've been prayer.

An oddly serene sense of calm had settled over Elsie.

An inevitability of strategy, the foreboding sense of a neat plan, though she could not say what it would be.

The illusion was yanked away, though, when Augustus grabbed her arm and the world dissolved.

Starbursts of white and gold filled her eyes, the dizzying sensation of simultaneously being everywhere and nowhere making her want to scream, which she was sure she must've though there was no air to fuel the sound.

Something fiercely cold cut at her cheeks and the specks of gold began to vanish. She rubbed her eyes, bidding the white to fade and for some semblance of reality to return. Augustus's hand was still on her arm, holding tight, a great roar overtaking them—

A storm.

A split of lightning above them cracked through the misery, the thunder making her bones shiver.

"Stell," Augustus swore, head tilted up at the storm.

"Where are we," Elsie shouted over the howling wind, and her fingers had somehow found Augustus's tunic and were clinging to it. If she let go, he would disappear.

Augustus's brow was knit as he glanced around. "Caelaymnis," he yelled back. "Or, near enough to it." He faltered. "It—I've never seen anything this bad. Something's wrong, and I...I don't know what to do next."

"How did you know?" Her voice felt lost on the roar. "Are you fucking kidding me, Augustus?"

But Augustus's breath was warm as he leaned into her ear. "My soul is pledged to yours."

Elsie was shivering, the chill cutting through her. "We shouldn't stay here. Obviously." Disorientation was closing in, with hardly anything but Augustus in her sight. Snow swirling, it was a surreal void of ice and fear.

Augustus seemed to hesitate for a moment before a spinning

378

sensation began to tear at Elsie's gut, and she couldn't breathe, couldn't be entirely sure if his hand was still on her arm, couldn't...

Quiet replaced the roaring, and the ornate ballroom of the Carson manor pieced itself together before them.

It was darkened, an empty shadow on the ceiling where one of the chandeliers had been, nothing beyond the reflection of the snowy day beyond playing at the shining tile.

Augustus's hand fell away, and he exhaled softly, eyes flickering about.

It was an effort to catch her breath, and maybe it was being here that made it harder.

Real or not?

Ginger had passed her the vial, and there hadn't been that much, but the dissociation of anxiety had set a surreal temperamentality to the atmosphere. Each moment was fleeting. Each moment was permanent.

Elsie glanced around the ballroom as she paced, half-expecting to see her brother and Sam walk down the stairs.

Half-expecting to find herself on that wretched night all over again.

But there was nothing more than a keyboard, lid closed and top covered in a velvet wrap to keep the dust off, a small mechanical box and shell sitting on the bench. Elsie knelt before the box, fingers brushing the smooth wood, peering inside.

A plate was balanced on a spindle.

I've got to be high. I'm still in the store in the Capital. Ginger's sitting next to me, high out of her mind, too.

A little crank on the side was begging to be turned, and she was grinding it forward before she realized she'd done it. It clicked with satisfaction, gears turning, until a little bell sounded underneath the wood, and she let it go—

Snaps and pops began to come from the box, a whining violin and accented plucks of a harp following.

A waltz.

"It's beautiful," Elsie breathed, watching the handle turn.

Augustus's hand was on her shoulder, helping to gently pull her to standing, and she was half in the darkened room, half in the masquerade. She could almost see it, the ballroom, the dancers, the orchestra—

But of course, she couldn't, she was in trousers and her tunic, and Augustus in prison wares—

Or was he? Wasn't he in the waistcoat and jacket of a merchant boy, for his hand was surely on her lower back, their hands undoubtedly together, and she could recall with disbelief his skill on the floor.

The steps came like steady breaths, and the whining violin blossomed into a swell of strings, only to die back down to a tinny piano coming from that metal shell atop the wood platebox. Wasn't it beautiful, the way it all seemed to be a dream, wasn't it lovely, how it seemed as if everything could be anew—

"Are you okay?" Augustus's voice was a whisper.

They hadn't been dancing.

She pulled her hand back from where he helped her up, wiping it on her trousers. "I'm fine. You?"

He didn't answer.

She pulled herself back, the dissociated wonder fading to fear and shame. It must be real. The ballroom was clear, the tile slick where snow was melting, splotches of wet across the floor, the platebox still whining away in the corner.

"Apologize," she bit, voice breathy, anger overwhelming all else. How dare he. How dare he whisk her away, to the stormy battlefields where his guilt and sins were born, to the ballroom where he'd promised to protect her—

"No." Augustus shot her a glare. "I owe you this. I'll guard your life whether you like it or not."

"That's so rude, you think I can't take care of myself—"

"It has nothing to do with you being competent," he snarled, "why do you think that just because you *can* do everything alone that you have to? Hmm? Typical human arrogance—"

"What about you? Thinking you can just pledge your *soul*—"

"Well, it worked, didn't it! I finally get to repay my debt instead of sitting there uselessly in that cell waiting to die."

Elsie crossed her arms, unable to look him in the eye.

He had a point.

"I should go back," Augustus said quietly, relenting as his shoulders sank in defeat. He glanced over, eyes conflicted.

"Why here?" The question tumbled off her lips. "Why did you bring us to the ballroom?"

Augustus blinked. "The ballroom? I..." He trailed off, brow furrowing. "I don't know." He put his hand on his chest, as if to signal to the bond between them. "It felt like the place to be."

"And you should be going back."

His pale hazel eyes met hers, looking pained. "That is correct. But it—it seems that if you need me, I won't be far."

She sighed, leaving the now-melting puddle of snow and ice they'd tracked in to summit the grand staircase. "C'mon."

"Where?"

"Up the stairs, you dolt," she said impatiently, beckoning him on. "I've always wanted a lackey."

FLETCHER

*"Those prayers to Stell were for naught, for in the
end, he destroyed the city he had vowed to protect so
many years ago."*

~Story of Gods

"It was...well, it was a bit fucked." Fletcher shook his head, leaning against the bar, mug of hot cider in hand. Caelaymnis was a snow globe of ice and chaos beyond—but the tavern was hot, lots of other soldiers crammed in, as duties had more than likely been suspended on account of weather.

Rodion made a small sound of amusement. "Alva is, by all accounts, one of the most powerful Drada to have graced our three realms."

"Clearly."

"Did she clarify your apparent crisis of faith, hosting a god?"

"No, and she was at best cagey when I asked her about it," Fletcher frowned. "Faith is fine, but much depends on having firm answers, now more than ever."

The tavern stood overlooking the Weir, the great river that cut through Caelaymnis down from the Dagger itself. Aglow with warm lucents from the lightkeepers—the Drada on palace payroll, paid to keep the city of lights...well, alight—this particular tavern was a favorite haunt.

With honeyed oak trees glossed into tables and chairs and pillars, glistening windowpanes stretching nearly floor to ceiling, and a menu of time-honored Dradan cuisine, it was a second home.

Third home?

Fletcher didn't know. These days, he was feeling at home in a lot more places than he had the first time he'd set foot here.

The street beyond was swirling with stinging pellets of ice hurled down from the gray sky above, the air dense with the roar of wind. "Stell's ice," Fletcher muttered, taking a swallow of cider, apple and cinnamon liquor warming his chest. "This weather, gods below—I have half a mind to never leave..."

"Elsie would be—" But Rodion's remark was cut off by a tremor beneath their feet, followed by the ear-splitting crack of wood and a rush of cold wind—

Fletcher moved, throwing a shield above them both, rubble from the crumbling rooftop hitting the barrier with a loud *thud-dud.*

The shaking sent Fletcher to his knees, boots slipping on the unstable floor. "Gods below—"

"Easy," Rodion muttered, arms outstretched to hold himself balanced. "What the fuck—"

Fletcher scrambled to his feet.

A far corner of the bar had been taken off, a great boulder having nearly rolled the whole damn thing over.

The snow was beginning to clear, a quiet eye in the storm sweeping the city, and Fletcher was already running into the street, trying to get a better look at what was going on. But the thinning snowflakes only gave way to great bruising clouds, rumbling low over the mountain peaks, darkening the sky to uneasy twilight.

Chilling silence fell as a massive bolt of lightning pierced the mountainside.

Fletcher was unable to look away, mouth falling open in horror as he watched a crackling scythe rend away the stone and send it crashing down onto—

"No!" Fletcher shouted, throwing a hand up—but he felt the impact deep in his chest. The jolt of the splitting rock, and the punch in the gut as it fell on that white sprawling palace wedged at the edge of the city.

Fletcher glanced to Rodion, whose look of horror seemed to say it all. Brow knit, his brown eyes lingered on the place the sky had brought the mountain down. "Let's go," Fletcher whispered, and grabbing Rodion's hand, they vanished in mist and sparks.

They arrived in a rubble strewn entrance, the once-smooth white steps carved out with great ruts of mountain, and Fletcher was running through the debris amid distant screams and pleas for mercy.

Ama.

His mother was still in there.

The occasional palace guard rushed through the dusty corridors, but it was too empty, too hushed—

Fletcher crashed through the door to his mother's room, heart pounding in his ears. *"Ama."*

She was wrapped in a pink shawl, looking worriedly out the window at the decimated palace walls, and he could hear the soft click of her nails against each other as she lilted in apprehension. Pale eyes glanced back to Fletcher, question deep in the green. "What has happened? Where has everyone gone—"

"Ama. We must get out of here," Fletcher said softly, meeting her at the window. He wrapped his arm around her, ushering her to the door, but she resisted, gaze lighting on Rodion, who'd been on Fletcher's heels running through the halls.

"Lilleana," Rodion begged quietly, joining them.

His mother's look of recognition broke Fletcher's heart as Lilleana rushed past the son she did not recognize to meet Rodion. "What happened?"

Rodion's eyes flicked to Fletcher once, deep with an apology he didn't need, before he took Lilleana's hand. "I don't know. But Fletcher is right, we should go, we can figure out—"

An ear-splitting crack shook the palace, the skittering of rubble bidding another chunk of stone from the mountainside.

"Go. I'm sure Alva has already heard, she's doubtless going to meet you." Fletcher waved Rodion off, trying to keep the urgency from his voice, and to his relief the pair vanished a moment later. Alva had to know, right? *But even if she doesn't, she will soon enough, and she's protected on the Dagger.* That only left—

Father. An uncomfortable weight balled in Fletcher's gut. It was hard to say, without a proper look, but it seemed the landslide had taken the Senate chambers and the offices therein, where Bowyer had a habit of lingering, as one would expect of a king.

A commotion clattered about the mess of stone and mountain and snow and dust as Fletcher found the epicenter of destruction, tears and blood heavy on the open air.

"Bowyer!" The shout came from somewhere in the chaos, and on the heels of the alert, a figure was stumbling from the wreckage of stone, dusty and bloodied but seemingly fine, no worse for wear.

Fletcher's shoulders melted in relief, his chest loosening to breathe the icy air. Provided his father survived the first wave of this destruction, he would be fine—a wary Drada could only be surprised once, Bowyer had himself said.

Unfortunately, this proved to be a false truth, for as Bowyer brushed himself off, two palace guards rushed to seize him. A third forced him to his knees, magic sparking, but it happened too quickly.

A sword gleamed in the storm, itself a flash of lightning, and the sickening slice of steel through sinew and bone sent a chilling silence across them all.

Fletcher stumbled back in disbelief.

Certainly, that was not what he'd heard.

He did not hear a blade rend his father's head from his body. He did not see his father's head roll into the wreckage. He did not smell his father's blood in the air, did not taste the tang of fear, did not even now hold his own shaking hands to his chest—

Bits of snow began to pelt his hot face, and atop the remnants of the palace, a man of ice climbed, pale blue hair in the wind and glacial blue eyes surveying them all.

Stell.

God of Ice.

And at his side, Cormalum.

King of Caelaymnis.

RISA

"Ah, to follow a lover to the depths of hell and back.
Many qualify this as the ultimate test of love, but when
you court Death, this is just another Friday night."

~Risa Barrett

Cora sat on Risa's bed, knees to her chest, eyes fixed on the cityscape beyond the window. A strap of her gray camisole had slid down her arm, her borrowed sleep shorts wrinkled up about her hips.

These weeks with Cora—they were comforting and quiet and filled with grief, grief that Risa was slowly realizing did not belong to her alone.

It was just as well.

Things had ended disastrously with Teddy and Tom. Risa resented being told off, but more than that, she resented that Tom had been right.

And still, she had no answer to bring back to them.

More and more, she began to wonder if she was losing herself—or if she'd ever really known herself to begin with. The lies came so easily, and more than that, the murder—

But there was no use. She'd been through it a thousand times, and the only conclusion was that she was better off leaving her brothers be.

Better off trying to bring some comfort to the god, mourning in her bedroom.

"What's on your mind," Risa asked softly, sinking down onto the edge of the bed.

"Many souls depart, this evening," Cora whispered. "I feel it." Her eyes flicked to Risa, and she didn't seem to be a god, then. She looked young. Lost. "I don't want to go."

Risa's heart sank.

It hadn't been a forever respite.

"I...am one soul." The words were bitter on Risa's tongue. "If you're needed back..."

"I will need to go, yes." Cora's gaze lingered unblinking, though, and she didn't make to rise. Instead, she turned to gently brush her fingers against Risa's cheek. "Do you trust me?"

Risa caught Cora's hand, kissing it. "I do. Unflinchingly."

"Come with."

Uncomfortable silence filled the room. "Cora. I don't want to die." Risa gave her hand a squeeze. "I—I mean, you saw what a mess things are here, but—"

Cora withdrew her hand with a scoff. "What kind of haphazard parlor tricks do you think I peddle?"

"I—you...run the Underworld, Cora," Risa frowned, scooting back on the bed to lean against the wall. There were certain qualifications that had to be met, to Risa's understanding, to venture there, certain contractual obligations involving secession of life.

Cora tugged the pink comforter around her, sliding over to sit shoulder-to-shoulder by Risa. "I'm fond of you. Immensely so, in a way that..." She trailed off, putting a hand on Risa's leg. "I wouldn't ask you to die for me. And..." A faint smile tugged at her lips. "I like that you wouldn't. It means this isn't desperate or panic. It means the time we spend is a choice. You choose to spend this time with me."

"I do choose this," Risa said quietly, resting her hand atop Cora's. "You, here, with me." Her words were pointed—here, where mortals still lived, where Risa spent her life.

"Come with me." Cora shifted, eyes clear. "Not forever. Just for tonight."

Risa tilted her head back against the wall, eyes lilting to the ceiling in contemplation. "And what's the catch?"

"The catch?"

"How do you sneak a living mortal into a house of the dead?"

Cora paused. "I would have to keep your soul for a bit. Bind it to me, as it were."

"Oh. Well. If you're *only* binding my soul—"

"Shut up," Cora laughed, facade of formality fading, "not—bond, like, an ominous, forever bond, just like...you know the story, about paying the ferryman to cross the river?"

"Yeah, and?"

"This is basically me saying I'll cover your tab."

Risa sighed, glancing over. "Fine." A grin split across her face, heart giving a jolt of excitement. Maybe she wasn't ready to ditch this world, but Risa didn't mind the prospect of leaving it behind for a bit. "Binding my soul to yours. What, exactly, does this entail, Cora, Keeper of Souls?"

Cora had a mischievous grin dancing at her lips as she moved, putting a hand on Risa's chest, square atop her collarbone. "This might be a bit chilly," she breathed, and eyes sparkling, she plunged her hand into Risa.

Risa gasped, something icy spreading through her, prickling sweetly, and it was a reflex to laugh, watching Cora in disbelief. "What the fuck—"

"Ah." Cora withdrew, and between her index finger and thumb, a small thread of purples and maroons and gold flowing from Risa's chest. "Just a tiny thread of your soul." Her voice was soft and gentle as she worked, easing the thread into her own chest, connecting them both. "It will snap right back, I promise. But this way, I can find you, and you'll be able to find me. And most importantly, I'll be able to pull you back out." There were words left unsaid in the eyes of Death, but she gave

Risa a soft smile, putting her hand gently where the wisp of soul sat pulsing in her chest.

Risa felt breathless, fingers shaking as she plucked the thread. Cora's laughter burst out as she gave a shriek, flinching. "That—no, stop, that tickles—"

"Fuck, sorry..." Risa's hand fell limply to the bed, eyes fixed wide on the thread.

"Beautiful, isn't it?"

"Weirdly, yeah," she whispered.

"Are you ready?"

Risa's head snapped up. "What, now?"

"Yes, now," Cora said softly, smiling as she rose, and she made to pull back a hood that wasn't there, only, with the gesture, she seemed to draw a cloak from the shadows themselves, her clothes melting into a gown of glittering midnight. "Do I rather look the part?"

Risa's heart was on her sleeve and her soul all tangled up, and she only had eyes for Cora. This woman who was summoned from the shadows to tend to her bitter soul, who brewed steaming cups of tea and summoned shawls, who held her through grief and cold and had for not one moment flinched in the face of her sins, and—

"I love you," Risa breathed, sliding off the bed.

Cora's smile faltered, eyes going wide. "You...what?"

"You heard me. I said what I said."

"Oh." Cora's hands fell, eyes soft.

"You don't have to say it back. Just—know you are loved—"

"I love you, too." Cora nodded, eyes flicking across Risa, grin on her lips. "Shall we?"

"Yes, let's."

And with that, Death smiled, taking Risa's hand, and they were plunged into the shadows to seek the departed souls.

SAM

"I don't think she ever had regrets about the path she took. She did what she wanted, and it didn't matter if anyone else understood."

~Sam Alderton

Sam awoke with a start.

Another *crack* of sap in the fire sent embers in a burst for the sky, and he couldn't catch his breath, head swimming.

Too hot. He was too hot, burning by the fire—

"No, no, no," a soft voice hushed, and Mariann was stilling his hands as he tried to push the blanket away.

His heart gave a jolt, looking her over with bewilderment.

"We're in the woods," she breathed with the air of someone who'd said it many times already. "I will get you some water, but please, don't try to move."

Sam let his hands fall limp where they gripped the blankets as he tried to make some sense of where he was. She...was not wrong, he saw, deadened trees silhouetted against a starry sky, cold air a relief in his lungs. "We...were running," he whispered, brow knit as he tried to dust off the recollection.

"Yes." Mariann slid a hand under Sam's back. "Help me out, here, on three...one, two..."

With a groan, Sam sat up, wincing as some feeling beyond burning began to return to him. The lip of a canteen was chilled as Mariann tilted the icy water into his mouth in dribbles, little trickles of cool skittering through his insides as he drank. A snap of pain shot up his leg, reverberating through his hip, into his ribs, and he coughed, water burning the back of his throat on the reflexive inhale. "Ach—fuck—"

Mariann frowned, brown eyes watching him. "You alright?"

Sam's fingers dug into the frozen earth, willing himself still, would that the sharp cuts sink into a dull throb. "Am...I?" he asked, hoarse, stomach dropping. Bracing himself, he tossed the blanket back, and this time, Mariann didn't move to stop him.

Tears were welling in his eyes as the firelight danced on the strips of black-stained linens wrapped about his knee, another vibrant shot of pain slithering through his leg. *Breathe. It's not so bad.*

"It's...pretty bad," Mariann said, watching him. "I cleaned it, and dressed it the best I could, but..." She shook her head. "It's not gonna get better on its own."

Sam swallowed hard, panic seeping in. He had vague recollections of being dragged from his cell, and he'd endured it, praying it had been a dhacrym dream.

But the world had not been so kind.

"Sam." Mariann's voice was firm. "We've been out here for days. We've had this conversation many times already. You're fevered and hurt—"

Something rustled beyond the light of the fire.

Mariann sighed. "There's...things, Sam. Things in the wood. You're safe, you're entirely safe, but sometimes, they—they get close. When they do...poof." She made a little gesture with her hands. "Just warning you. They scare you, when they come. But there's wards, and him..." She gestured to the shadow by the fire, and Sam started, reflexively trying to push himself away but only managing to muss the blanket he'd been set atop. "Sam. Stop." She sounded so tired. "It's just Howie. He's my dog, we've been over this."

"You telling me we've been over this isn't helping—"

"Tough shit." Mariann shifted where she sat beside him. She shrugged. "It's what I've got. But I don't know what we're doing next."

Sam laid back down, eyes drifting up to the dark sky, letting it flood with tears. It felt so utterly, so surreally hopeless.

"Mariann." His voice felt weak.

"Yes?"

"Did I once accuse you of sabotaging my napkin folding with unstarched linens at one of the Mirabeau dinners?"

"Yes. You did."

Sam sniffed, palming the tears back. "Great. So, not only is this real, but I'm an insufferable ass, too."

She snickered, moving to put the blanket back over him. "Unfortunately, yes."

"How?"

"Well, you were steeped in an atmosphere of superiority and wealth that hinged on the exploitation of the workers—"

Sam made a small sound of dismissal coupled with amusement. "No, how...are you here?"

"Mm. I could ask you the same. Last I heard, you'd taken Teddy and given up Valley life. Seems like we've both stumbled down an unfortunate path."

Teddy. Sam fought back the wave of grief. If he was not faring well... Well.

Maybe it'd really been goodbye.

"What happened with Tom?"

"Ah, you mean, what happened to me? Tom was always on his usual bullshit," Mariann sighed, pulling her own blanket around her shoulders. "I met a man. He seemed fun, and I was slowly dying, so why not?" She shrugged. "But there's always a catch, isn't there?"

Sam glanced over to her, brow knit. "Seems that way."

"Life's a bitch. But so am I, so I guess it's a wash, right?"

A faint smile etched itself in the corners of Sam's mouth. "Pity we never got on when things were better."

"Ah, you're not so bad yourself, when you're incapacitated." With a snort, she put a hand on a very pregnant belly, eyes flicking to meet Sam's. "What? Why are you looking at me like that?"

"You should go." He swallowed, wincing a little. "C'mon." He nodded to where her hand lay.

"Oh, because I've got a child on the way?" Mariann gave him an incredulous glare.

"Yeah. You have a shot."

"So do you. I don't know what lies are in that head of yours, but this is not a death sentence."

"You said it was bad—"

"Bad doesn't mean the end. It just means you gotta fight like hell."

"Fuck." Sam sighed, looking again to the heavens.

"Yeah."

"Well. Congratulations, I suppose."

"Oh."

"What," Sam scowled, not ceasing his study of the stars.

"We're into a new part of the conversation. That's a good sign, I'd wager. Or a bad one? Time will tell."

"Thanks, Mariann," Sam muttered, relenting to a soft laugh. She'd always had a talent for delivering truths with unflinching nerve.

But beyond that, Sam found himself stuck at how little he knew Mariann.

They'd met—when, even? He hadn't bothered to mark the occasion.

She didn't care for him, and he didn't care for her, and he'd assumed, in his dislike, that he knew her so well. Perhaps she'd done the same, for clearly neither had expected the other to take a road so twisted.

"Are you really the son of a god?" Mariann was watching him with almost clinical fascination.

"I dunno. That's...what I've been told. But my dad died when I was two, and I didn't think a god could die."

"Why not?"

Sam sighed, closing his eyes. A question he'd spared much thought to. "I don't know, Mariann," he clipped. "I don't have the answers."

"I rather think they can." Mariann shifted, leaves and dirt crunching as she did so. "I think the idea of someone being so infallible as to be immortal is a terrible notion."

In the distance, a branch broke with a loud *crack*, and Sam's eyes snapped open.

Stillness followed, unsettling and cold.

Mariann glanced to the great beast she'd named Howie, though it didn't seem to pay the sound—nor its human companions by the fire— any mind.

"What are we going to do," Sam breathed. "We can't stay here forever." Well. They could. He could. And he'd take up permanent residence in a grave.

Even laying here, he could feel the fever of inevitable infection wax and wane.

"For now, you rest," Mariann said quietly, staring out into the darkness. "There is no doubt Ani will track us—me—with all his might."

"And...this doesn't scare you?" Sam asked, marveling at the evenness of her voice, calm and confident.

"Why would it?" She glanced back to him, relenting from vigil. "My fear would do nothing but weigh on me, and so, I will not keep it." A faint smile tugged at her lips. "Ani has a brilliant collection of tomes. He's a Xavishia, did you know that? His books catalogue their history. It's soaked in blood, but it's not horrid, not at all. It's amazing."

"And that's why you left that—that place, wherever he was keeping me?" Sam couldn't help the words tumbling from his tongue.

Mariann cocked her head to the side. "Because my lover has a library? Hardly. The Master is a fiendish man who tires too quickly of his toys but gets terribly jealous when someone picks them up. He has no love of me. But Anscip? Familial bonds of magic tie all Insidiae together, and my child and Ani are no exception. I feel it strengthening with the babe."

"He took Elsie—he cannot find me," Sam breathed, terror rising.

"Yes. Well. That is a bit of a complication." Mariann's smile faltered. "But your Ruby Tears were paid, I can't think of what else Ani would want with you."

"Marvelous—"

"Try not to despair, Sam. The Master will hunt us, but Ani will too." Her eyes flicked to a bandaged arm, linen stained faintly red. "One does not become enmeshed in his world, his *life*, without becoming adept at the uses of blood. We're hidden. It's just a question of how well we're hidden from Ani, too—gods willing, we are not, and he will find us first."

"I don't understand, they are working together—"

"The Master is flighty and unafraid of spilling blood. He'd already summoned two of the gods—and had left a massive pile of bodies behind him—when Anscip came to him. Sometimes all one can do is slow the bleeding, not stop it entirely. Things have been going poorly, of late," Mariann frowned. "The Master is...mercurial. Inconsistent. Arrogant, to a fault." Her words were thoughtful, tone diplomatic. "Ani has little patience for such things." She sighed. "But he is reasonable and relentless. Just a girl from a back-district farm, and it turns out I have a talent for blood magic older than even his ancient tomes recall." A smile was curling on her lips now. "I can keep us safe until he finds us. Or you're well enough to run again," she added.

"Mariann." His voice was tired against his own ears. "I'm not going to be doing much running anytime soon."

Her smile flickered out. "Maybe. Maybe not."

"So I have to hope that Anscip Xavishia finds me before the Master," Sam breathed. An abysmal set of choices with no good answer, and his imagination ran wild imagining the horrors each could bring. "Promise me something, Mariann."

"Depends on what it is."

"If I die, burn my body, and tell Teddy what happened."

The placid expression on Mariann's face did little to bolster Sam's confidence. "I will," she said softly. "But you fight, right up until the end."

"I will."

Tears stung Sam's eyes at the command.

Fight. Until the end.

But he would. He would.

EZRA

"Children are so foolish, with their complaints. 'I don't want to clean my room' and 'No, I won't kill my sister' and 'Broccoli is gross.' Truthfully, I'm quite over them, at the moment."

~Anscip Xavishia

Ezra had taken to spending nights at the apartment with Isa.

This was admittedly what Elsie had intended him to do, as she was unaware of the lodge where he'd sneak out to meet the Master every morning, and surely she had not intended that Isa and Ezra would be sharing a bed every night, but things transpired in unpredictable ways.

He hadn't told the Master about Isa. Or Elsie, for that matter.

It felt uncomfortable to keep that secret, but it felt worse to breathe it into the open. And anyways, he wasn't doing anything wrong.

He certainly didn't fall asleep every night imagining the arms around him belonged to the man with soft brown eyes and sandy brown hair whose laugh was like calm ocean waves bringing in tides of good fortune.

Ezra sighed deeply.

His heart was torn in two directions.

On the one side, Isa was illuminating. Beyond their kindness and affection, they were sharp and perceptive, and Ezra had begun to realize that the Master walked a thin line, fostering a sense of intimacy by sharing his plans, all the while carefully avoiding anything akin to real vulnerability. Isa was quick to disclose details of their heart—and, too, a darkly disturbing story of what had happened to Elsie, unquestionably the fault of that wretched elf-general.

Never the fault of the Master.

That thought always led Ezra back to the other side of things.

The side where he was quietly nursing affection for the man who would tell him no other name than the Master. Someone so hurt and mistrustful must be in need of love, and more and more, Ezra wondered if he might be the man to give that love.

It was an absurd thought. Impossible.

But their nights of laughter over plates of food, their mornings of quiet conversation over tea...

Isa might be the one tumbling in bed with Ezra, but for all their sensitive words and gentle turns of phrase, there was an emotional disconnect.

It was this realization that made Ezra's return to the lodge this morning an emotionally harrowing one.

Ezra, the note read.

Ezra,

Forgive me. I have urgent business in the Capital. I will be back as soon as I can.

I came to find you this evening to tell you in person, but found only your note—thank you, by the way, for I do not know what sort of panic might have overtaken me if I had not found an explanation for your absence.

I return the favor, and in my best efforts, your trust, despite my jealousy—I covet you, and your time.

Keep me in your thoughts, love.

~M.

Ezra's own note had been left lying on the coffee table, a note he'd taken to leaving there every night he'd spent with Isa. *Stepped out for some brief companionship. Be back by morning. E.*

Sinking down onto the couch, the Master's note still in hand, anxiety was rising in his chest.

The middle of the night was an odd time to depart.

In the back of Ezra's mind, he wondered if the Master had perhaps not come to his room with some other aim, and finding Ezra gone...

They could not sustain this tension.

Ezra folded the note, tears in his eyes. He'd stumbled into something much bigger than himself, here.

Moving for the secretary desk, he penned another note of his own.

M,

I am sorry to have missed you. I am near to giving up on this search, here. And I think I am near to giving up on you and I.

I do not know how to characterize our time. I only know that it makes my heart ache and clouds my head and I can't think about anything else—anyone else.

But I cannot continue, not knowing.

Who are you.

How can I love someone I do not know.

-E.

TEDDY

"That bastard lied. He toyed with Sam's heart again
and again, and I know that's what drove him to do this.
All of it. He got convinced that he could play god."

~Theodore Alderton

"He doesn't want to see you." Matthew Fieldson stood on the threshold of the Fieldson house in the Merchant's Corner of the Capital district, arms crossed in the chilling refusal. The house faced the bustling streets to the front, only to back up against the vast, forested estate to the back, an attempt to capitalize on the energy of the large city and the peacefulness of the surrounding area all at once.

Teddy's eyes narrowed. He didn't doubt for a minute that Sam would've refused, but that man was a fool if he thought Teddy was going to just give up like he had the night Sam left. "I've come quite a long way to see him. I don't give a damn what he wants."

Mattie crossed his arms. "I don't relish this any more than you—"

"Why won't you let me in?" Agitation was rising in Teddy's chest at the refusal. "He doesn't have to say anything, he just needs to listen—you—"

"Sam is dear to me," Mattie said quietly. "He's asked not to be disturbed. I respect that." His eyes were tired as he leaned heavily against the doorframe, watching Teddy.

"Please, Matt. I know there's some bad blood between us, but I am begging you." He hardly relished the word—*begging*—but there was no use calling it something it wasn't. "I'm begging you. Let me just see him, talk to—at him—however briefly."

Matt was quiet for a moment, gaze distant. Then—

"I will inquire again."

The door slammed, and Teddy was left standing on the doorstep of the Fieldson house in the freezing cold of morning.

Just my luck. Another roadblock. His ferry in had been delayed by ice in the river, and eventually, they'd all had to disembark. Teddy had been nearly to the point of taking a cheap inn room when he'd been struck by a sort of bitter jealousy at the fact that Sam was probably off in the Capital, living it up, and that was when Teddy had more or less realized who he was.

He was Theodore Alderton, husband to Sam Alderton and thus tied by marriage to the Guild Commissioner herself—and that was a currency in and of itself.

Merchant Rithorse, a merchant on the other side of the river from the Capital, and her family were extraordinarily kind people.

He had announced himself as visiting his husband in the Capital, explained that there'd been ice in the river, and Mistress Rithorse had been touched and in awe, for she remembered Sam from when he was young, and *gods, he's found such a sweet match*, she'd said, *Sam's a good boy, I never was much fond of that Fieldson kid anyhow, you're much sweeter.*

Teddy had flushed red at this, muttering his thanks, and Mistress Rithorse had been more than happy to show him to a lavish guest room—complete with a hot bath—and she had even brought him up a cup of tea, too.

Tea—and words of wisdom.

I haven't heard anything about Sam being in the Capital, she'd said quietly. *Gossip doesn't follow that boy like it used to, but I'm surprised to hear that he's there.*

It was a private trip, Teddy had explained, and he hadn't been able to

403

look her in the eye.

Where is he staying? I can't control the river, but I'd happily lend you transport to get where you're going, my dear. No use having you traipsing about in this weather.

Teddy didn't have a good answer, and he knew his fumbling had been apparent. He'd mumbled something about the Fieldsons, and Mistress Rithorse wrinkled her nose.

Sam was good to marry outside the merchants. But your self-sufficiency is not requisite to prove your affection. It is that you made the journey. That's what matters. Not how much you suffered along the way.

Is it that obvious that I'm not a merchant, he'd asked quietly.

Yes. Mistress Rithorse had smiled kindly at this. *But that isn't a bad thing, my dear.* Her warmth faltered a moment later. *Whatever business you and Sam have at the Fieldsons, be careful. Of course, you're surely aware of the contract scandal—*

Teddy had nodded. He knew what happened with Sam and Mattie.

Well. Just...be careful. I swear, sometimes I think that family is out for blood.

Mattie's door clicked open once more. "Come in." Turning aside, Mattie beckoned him in.

Teddy was immediately hit with the heavy perfume of cloves and vanilla as he stepped inside. Eyes watering, he blinked, and gods *below* he hated how comfortable Sam probably was here.

The entry hall was narrow but elegantly decorated, Mattie having apparently gone so far as to procure fresh flowers in the middle of winter for the sake of filling the vase on a side-table.

"He's upstairs—"

A servant was coming down, though, and Teddy did a double-take at amethyst eyes. "Sirs, my apologies," the servant was saying, "Master Alderton has stepped out for a constitutional in the woods with Miss Mari and the hounds."

"Has he." Mattie's jaw clenched at this. "How...unamusing."

Anger.

Real, tangible anger...at Sam, stepping out.

The Thread in Teddy's chest gave a lurch, uneasy.

"I...would like to leave a note for him, then," Teddy breathed, glancing at the servant. "Show me to his room?"

The servant paused, and then nodded, beckoning Teddy to follow up the polished darkwood stairs.

Teddy's heart was beating against his ribcage, the Thread making him feel hot and feverish in its agitation as he was led down another narrow hall and to a mint green room on the left.

Following the servant into the room, though, Teddy's gut twisted in terror, for something was very, very wrong.

Whoever was staying here—if anyone was at all—it wasn't Sam.

"Stationary is on the desk, sir." The servant was gesturing to a neat writing secretary, a fresh stack of parchment and a pencil amid a pile of crumpled sheets.

But Sam didn't ball up his scrap parchment.

Something is desperately wrong—and Sam definitely isn't here.

Sam folded his scraps into little paper hearts, or tiny little birds, or else, simply let the sheets dissolve into the hearth—the hearth, Teddy noted, which was freshly lit.

"Ah, Sam always was messy," he mumbled, brushing the balls of parchment aside, eyes flicking to a cravat on the back of the writing chair. Teddy wasn't really sure what struck him to do so, other than an intense sense of danger abounding in Matt's deception, but he ran his fingers over the cravat, trying to look wistful. "Oh, I remember this one...I always thought it went nicely with his eyes..."

Matt's expression went from agitation to sympathy in the blink of an eye. "Oh, you poor dear. Write him, and I shall continue to do my best to fix this situation up for the two of you."

Teddy sank into the chair, grabbing the pencil. "Did he say what's wrong?"

What to write, what to write

"He's heartbroken, you know how grief is," Mattie mused.

"Mm, unfortunately, yes." Scrawling out a quick message, Teddy's hand was shaking.

Sam.

I love you.

Please come home.

No use saying much else. This note probably wouldn't be getting to him, anyway.

Teddy glanced back at the messy room, rising.

These were not Sam's clothes, strewn about. That was not his cologne on the dresser, these were not his discarded notes...

"Mattie?"

"Mm?" Matt glanced up, looking somewhat bored.

"I do forgive you for kissing Sam," Teddy said quietly. It wasn't true, of course, would never be true, but he wanted to egg Matt on, just a bit. Fuck him, for whatever part he played in all this.

Matt blinked. "I—I am ever so sorry, Theodore, but I think you have it backwards. Sam was the one who kissed me."

"No." Teddy's voice was nothing more than a whisper, and he sighed. "No, Matt, he wasn't. I know him." He knew what sent Sam spiraling.

I'd put money on Matt forcing a kiss on him in the carriage house. Nothing else would've made Sam panic to the point of leaving.

Matt kissed him, that was Sam's phrasing. Gods, it was so easy to see it now upon reflection—how careful Sam had been with his words, how painfully honest he must've been with each turn of phrase.

Look at how awful this has all been. And it's only going to get worse

I—I can't be with you, anymore. That's just how it has to be.

Teddy, whatever future we have together would be short and painful, and you don't deserve that.

Whatever the reason Sam left, it wasn't because their relationship was over. Sam was in trouble, and he hadn't wanted to drag Teddy into it. And that made Teddy angry all over again, angry and miserably sad that his husband hadn't even trusted him enough to tell him he was in trouble.

"Any chance I could catch him on his constitutional," Teddy breathed, glancing over to the servant. *I have to find him. I have to find my husband.*

The servant looked to Mattie, who gave what was in Teddy's opinion an over-eager nod, then back to Teddy. "Yes, sir. Follow me, sir."

THE BEAST

"Sense of self is a curious thing. We function on
instinct far more than anyone would care to admit—and
lose ourselves to instinct far more often than we suspect."

~Howard Bell

Mariann and the...not prisoner, the not prisoner named Sam were asleep by the dying embers as the pale dawn rose.

The Beast had not slept.

Howie had not slept.

It rose, stretching with a low growl. The air was fetid with infection, the forest mercifully quiet.

The papery creatures had learned quickly that the camp was unreachable. That did not stop the occasional one from trying to get to them anyway, but by and large, they had begun to ignore Mariann and Sam and...and Howard.

The Beast padded once around the camp, sniffing the air for any hint of emotion that would betray a hunter.

But there was nothing.

No papery monsters. No master.

Mariann had driven the former back with her ward, and the latter would have difficulty finding her. She felt no fear. A prey who felt no fear would be difficult to track under the best of circumstances, the Beast thought, and Mariann was not so generous as to give them the best of circumstances.

It would be alright.

It had to be.

Even so, Howard had the impulse to cry, but that was absurd, for Beasts shed no tears, and the Beast would've howled to the stars, but the cry of fear would have certainly drawn the others.

More and more, those strange impulses arose.

To cry. To laugh, once, and even to embrace.

The uncertainty was unsettling.

My purpose had been clear.

That could not be as true as Howie thought it was, though, for the purpose now felt lethally important.

Mariann was good.

She gave good pat-pats and nice scritch-scritches, and affection so satiating that Howie came to redefine hunger.

And…Sam. He tried to not be afraid. He'd tried to give pat-pats too, the Beast recalled, though they had been hesitant and apprehensive.

The Beast set to wandering in an ever-expanding perimeter, as it always did in the morning. Snow was on the air, and they'd soon be out of luck if they didn't move.

But Sam could hardly stand, let alone stumble along, even with Mariann shouldering his weight—and she was tired, too, and hungry, and carrying life, and then there was the risk of the papery demons, and the gods, and it was with a sinking feeling that the Beast realized they wouldn't move. Mariann would make a pact with the snow, and it would not fall onto their camp, but as it stood, they were stuck.

Howard stopped at a half-frozen river to paw at the thin ice to drink—

Oh.

Soft gray eyes looked back from the reflection in the shimmering ice, faint rosy cheeks, a mane of thick, slate hair—

Howard blinked.

And it was gone.

Burning eyes stared back, a blackened muzzle licked with fur, skin hanging from its scruff in patchy, oily wrinkles.

A Beast.

Nothing more.

ISA

"A true friend is one that helps you hide the bloody knife."

~Elizabeth Clement Faulise

The world had a way of changing in unexpectedly unpleasant ways.

Isa had been tangled up with Ezra in the Taylor Town apartment, the fire roaring, both sleepy and warm in the midday lull. They'd savored the warmth of Ezra's skin, the softness of his voice, the smell of soap on his clothes, and it was one of the few times Isa had prayed in gratitude to the gods.

But the world had a way of changing in unexpectedly unpleasant ways, and now they were standing on the street below, freezing their ass off, listening as Rodion talked, each word bringing more heartbreak and anger than the next.

His gray uniform, and Mia's too, was splattered with the blood and grime of battle—only this time, it'd come from the streets of Caelaymnis, and his eyes were glazed with tears as he relayed what he'd seen:

In an unholy storm, the gods themselves had lay siege to Caelaymnis. The mountains themselves had begun to crumble, crushing the palace, the houses on the perimeter, the shops, and someone—a nobody—had rended Bowyer's head from his body. That was one of the worst parts. To be killed by a god, or even a rival—there was at least something bitterly natural about that. But it'd been a nameless guard, eager to be a king-slayer.

And then, of course, chaos had broken loose.

Many tried to flee as word spread and the fighting broke out. Those who protested Cormalum's ascent, or suspected of being loyal to the late king, were punished violently. Houses burned, ash falling with the snow, and a lot of people who had not given it terribly much thought were forced to decide which was more important, their values or their survival.

Fletcher and Rodion and Mia—they did what they could. They helped bring the wounded, the infirm, the young to Thallassas, but others had the same idea, and the island couldn't welcome another realm in its entirety. Already, the beaches were lined with the injured, the shops precariously low on food, the palace itself filled with refugees from their sister city. These, though, were the lucky ones. Those who had not made it out before the gods sealed Caelaymnis with great shimmering wards would swear fealty to Cormalum or face the consequences.

Thus, here Rodion stood, on the verge of tears, begging for help from someone without answers, Mia stoically at his side.

Fletcher was striding towards them, his uniform bearing the stains of battle as much as Rodion's. It'd been brave—an exiled prince, the son of the dethroned king, carrying the sick and wounded out while there was still time. He was talking quickly as he met Rodion and Isa. Elsie, he told them, was nowhere to be found, and it was plain that panic was at last beginning to overtake him.

None of them had been meant for this. They were young, their souls not made for war.

Isa slumped against the brick wall of the Valley apartment, in shock. Words did not come, nor could they really hear the words their friends exchanged, not over the roar of disbelief.

Elsie would be fine. Fletcher couldn't find her because she wasn't here—she was in the Capital, she'd told Isa as much this morning.

And their mother, Kai, she'd been in Thallassas, Rodion said, so that was two for two.

No, it was Augustus that Isa found themself selfishly wondering—worrying—over.

There'd been a coup. Cormalum had crowned himself with the gods at his side—the gods. Surely, they wouldn't look kindly on a man like Augustus. He'd fumbled his role in the Master's schemes, or else deliberately undermined them. He was traitor to past and current kings, an enemy of all.

Mia—she said that Augustus had managed to escape. She'd been in the compound when the coup had begun, had heard the guards sounding the alarm. But even if that were true, even if he'd gotten out of the cell, Isa thought bitterly, it was unlikely he'd make it out of the compound prison. His treachery would not be allowed to persist.

How selfish. The kingdom is crumbling, the pain and loss incalculable, and I cry for a traitor, even as Ezra waits upstairs. They could see Ezra's forehead, even now, pressed against the window, watching. Curious.

Isa's heart was torn in two.

Fletcher leaned against the wall, sliding down to sitting. Hands in his hair, his shoulders shook with sobs. It was over. The battle had ceased, and he had seen things, terrible, bloody things that should've never come to pass.

Isa knelt beside him, holding him. The panic hadn't fully set in yet for them, not really, and in the calm before the storm, they tried to let reason take hold. They breathed a few words of comfort in Fletcher's ear—that his mother, Lilleana, was safe in Thallassas, that Elsie was in the Capital—and Fletcher's wrath erupted.

He was screaming, shoving Isa off, shouting in the street about how none of them could understand what he felt, how none of them prayed the way he did, how none of them knew of his crisis of faith, none of them understood that he'd watched his father's murder, and in his agitation, his words shifted back to the language of those beginning to gather around.

Fletcher slipped into the Vernacular, and for the rest of their days, Isa would recall the words he said next.

My father died. I am an elf, a creature of magic, in a foreign land. I have no home. Our kingdom has fallen, our realm has been taken, and our people have nowhere to go.

So don't talk to me about how it's going to be alright, Isabella Mirestva. I watched the gods themselves betray my homeland.

The words echoed in the street, fading into silence, but they roared in Isa's mind, persisting there, more real than ever.

The street had gone quiet.

The passersby had stopped, wearing looks of concern. A street brawl would've brought this avenue to a halt anyway, but this?

Isa suddenly felt naked, eyes on the four of them. On themselves, on Fletcher, on Rodion and Mia trying to calm to the two before it came to blows.

None of them bore the façade required to walk these streets. None of them had hidden their elven selves. Isa glanced down, their long fingers tipped in almost-claws, their limbs lanky even with the musculature. Multiplied by four, coupled with larger-than-human eyes flashing as they looked this way and that, three in blood-soaked uniforms, their words shifting between the long Dradan vowels and the cacophonic Vernacular phrases.

And Fletcher didn't care.

He shoved Rodion off, looking pissed, embers of magic rising in his fingertips.

This, Isa thought, from the man who'd tied himself in knots over who he wanted to be. This, from the man who'd once wanted to let his magic fade and ossify so that he could spend an eternity pretending to be someone he wasn't, so that he could pretend to be human.

With a snarl, Fletcher chucked the lucent in his fingertips to the ground, sparks flying in his frustration.

There was a collective gasp, the sound seeming to break Fletcher's fury.

His eyes went wide, and he came back to himself somewhat, glancing around.

The humans whispered to themselves. But they were not words of wonder or awe. No, they were words of reassurance—not at the conflict in the street, this town had seen many bar brawls spill onto the cobblestones—but at the sight of something they'd whispered about for centuries.

Each one of them standing there knew someone who could do much the same. Some of them—most of them—couldn't control it. Many denied it. It made them sick, sometimes, to push the magic down— Teddy was proof enough of that. But every single human standing in that street knew what they'd seen at Fletcher's hand hadn't been anything new.

And again, his words rippled through them all.

My father died.

I am an elf, a creature of magic, in a foreign land.

I have no home.

Our kingdom has fallen, our realm has been taken, and our people have nowhere to go.

And now, an apology.

Fletcher whispered an apology, a look of horror in his eyes as he glanced at the onlookers, the embers of his lucent still floating softly to the cobblestones where he stood in the middle of the road.

As for Isa, they thought the might collapse under the weight of the moment. Too long, they themself had been an outsider to Caelaymnis—to the faith, when they couldn't pay the tithes, to the soldiers, when they'd taken Augustus as a lover, and to the ordinary folk, when they'd forgiven him and let him back into their bed, only for his treachery to become known. But home was still home, however unwelcoming, and Isa was not prepared to be chased from one of the last familiar places they haunted.

Maybe they didn't love the Valley like Fletcher did. But this street, that apartment—it was as much a home as anywhere, these days.

In the crowd of humans, someone snapped their fingers. Isa couldn't see who it was, but they snapped their fingers and three sparks rose into the air, drifting in the breeze.

Fire magic.

A sigil of like. A way to say that they understood.

The gods had forsaken these elves—well, the Valley folk understood that, too, for they'd been forsaken long ago by gods and magic alike.

Murmurs rose as the human sparks guttered out, and Fletcher gave a conciliatory nod. His eyes met the ground, and he let a deep exhale out, striding once more for the sidewalk. He didn't summon a façade, he didn't vanish, and above it all, he didn't deny what he'd seen rise from the crowd like the Aerdelean Commissioners had done for centuries. He acknowledged it, met it, and with that, everything had changed for those standing in the street.

Aerdela had always wanted magic.

And they were about to get it more of it than perhaps they'd bargained for.

ELSIE

"And thus, we were all back. Only this time, he was
the prisoner, I his captor, and the world was on its way
to being righted.

~Elizabeth Clement Faulise

Elsie's thoughts quickly overtook her, walking up the grand staircase in the Carson ballroom, Augustus at her heels.

She'd promised herself that there'd be justice.

I'm a liar and a coward, just like always.

She had promised that she would make Augustus pay for what he did, but the truth was, he understood her sins—and it was better to risk another hurt than push away one of the few who saw her as she was: flawed and in pain.

Maybe things would've been different if Sam hadn't left.

Elsie sighed, glancing at Augustus as they came to a pause before the doors at the top of the stairs. "I think," she said carefully, "that you could be of particular use. I also think there is a sizeable chance that Fletcher will try to take you back. Best keep this between us."

Augustus gave a curt nod. "What do you propose?"

"I suggest we find Cele, and see if she will permit you to stay here for a time. Away from Caelaymnis, and *away from Fletcher.*"

"That's going to be easier said than done," Augustus frowned.

Elsie prodded his chest with her finger, snarling. "Then you'll have to exercise some restraint against your habitual need to intervene, won't you—"

"Elsie." His eyes flicked to the door behind her, brow knitting. His posture shifted, one of uncomfortable stillness.

"What," she frowned.

"Listen."

Voices were drifting up from beyond the door, familiar cadences edged with urgency.

Fletcher, and he wasn't alone.

"Oh—ah, fuck—" Elsie turned on her heel, colliding with the door to shove it open. *What in the name of the gods could he possibly be doing here?*

But an uncomfortable prickling sensation made the hairs on the back of her neck stand on end, something almost preternatural about them. Augustus's foolish bond had called him to her. If his task was to protect her, and this above Caelaymnis had been the place the bond had guided him—well, that was an ill omen if she'd ever seen one, and she'd seen more than her share.

The commotion that echoed up the grand stairs from the foyer below, for one, voices and almost shouts rising much to her alarm, for she'd assumed the manor empty.

"What do you think you're—"

"—this is urgent, I need—"

"El!" Fletcher's eyes went wide. "What are you doing here—how—"

Elsie took the foyer stairs quickly, heart racing. "Fletcher—why are *you* here, and everyone—"

Cele's head snapped up. "What is going on—"

But Fletcher met her halfway up the stairs, cold hands wrapping around her waist as he buried his face in her shoulder, chilled cheeks against her jaw. She held him tight, panic rising at the echoes of sobs jolting through his back. "Fletcher," she breathed softly, "what..."

"Caelaymnis has fallen," Rodion put forth quietly, still in the foyer below. "I took Lilleana—his mother—to Thallassas, but..."

418

An icy jolt hit Elsie in the gut.

Isa looked uncomfortably between them all. "Cormalum has crowned himself the new king."

Elsie swore softly, clinging tight to Fletcher.

His arms around her seemed to push all the air from her lungs.

"Bowyer is dead," Fletcher whispered, voice shaking. "I watched his head roll."

~ • ~

"The priority right now is to get as many to safety as possible," Rodion said, glancing up to where Elsie and Fletcher still stood on the stairs. "Though Caelaymnis has been sealed away, I'm confident we'll continue to see a steady trickle of those trying to get out—and as it stands now, we've got the sick and wounded laying in the street, and elves gathering west of here."

An uncomfortable silence had fallen over them, one Elsie was furious had ended.

"Rodion will bring as many as he can to Thallassas," Isa went on, picking up where Rodion had left off. "But they simply can't take everyone."

"You wish to bring them here," Cele frowned, crossing her arms.

Shut up shut up let him grieve in quiet

"Yes," Rodion clipped. "I understand the Treaty stands in the way—"

"Then consider it null and void. The Guild withdraws." Cele glanced up the stairs, then back to Rodion and Isa. "Bring them here, for now. I will scramble to find a more permanent solution."

"Oh, gods," Fletcher breathed, and unless Elsie was very much mistaken, it was as prayer of relief—or as close to relief as he could have, given what had happened.

She felt shaky and sick—maybe these were familiar hurts, but

419

Fletcher might as well have been bleeding out on the stairs, for all she could've done. *Hold him. Tight.* This was the base instinct, because in her arms, he was accounted for, and nothing else could happen to him there. But beyond that...

He was forcing slow breaths, still buried in her shoulder.

"Elsie." Isa's soft voice interrupted, and they were halfway up to meet her and Fletcher, fingers trailing reluctantly on the banister. "I have some news. Mia found me—she came immediately, with a message for you. For us. Apparently, in all the chaos, Augustus...has escaped."

Elsie's heart dropped to her shoes, and she felt Fletcher tense, meaning she'd already given herself away, because of *course* her body would have betrayed her in these precarious moments, turning her over to fear and apprehension.

No privacy in her own skin. Her thoughts were written in her body, words inked on a paper ready to be ripped—

No.

"It's okay," Fletcher whispered. "El?"

She winced, pulling away. "I—I need you to understand, Fletcher that it is complicated—"

"Elsie." Fletcher's eyes were red, his voice hoarse. "We will find him, I promise—"

Someone cleared their throat at the top of the stairs. "I'm here, you snow-brain." Augustus was frowning, beginning his descent with caution.

The foyer had gone deathly still.

"I was running in the Capital, and Anscip showed up," Elsie threatened, eyes darting between them all. "I wouldn't have gotten out—"

"You would have," Augustus clipped. "You're resourceful. I know what you're doing, El, but—"

"Don't." Fletcher snarled the word out, eyes narrowed on his brother. "Don't. Call. Her. That."

Rodion sighed. "Okay, Fletcher—c'mon—"

"Did you say Father is dead," Augustus breathed, unfazed by the tension. His pale hazel eyes were fixed on his brother, hands up in almost surrender.

Fletcher nodded, eyes welling with tears.

Elsie's heart was racing in her chest, face flush with anxiety. This—this was two distinct parts, colliding—

"She's going to pass out," Augustus frowned. "Perhaps we can…deal with this later?"

Fletcher's lip curled. "Deal with this?"

Elsie gripped the banister hard, knuckles going white. *Why do I feel so ill?*

"Okay, you" —Isa thrust a finger at Augustus— "fucking make yourself scarce, but don't you *think* about leaving this house. And Fletcher." Their voice softened. "He's right, she is going to have a heart attack with you two snapping at each other, why don't you go help Commissioner Carson instead?"

Elsie sank down to sit on the step, exhaling forcefully. "I need to sit for a minute—"

"Fine. Fletch, sit with her. We need to go, we'll be back." Isa trotted lightly up a few steps, crouching over in front of Elsie. "It is okay," they said quietly, holding their hands out.

She took them, tears pressing at her eyes. "I feel ill."

"I know. That's to be expected, dear. Back here, with Augustus no less." Isa gave her fingers a squeeze. "But I shall tell you a secret, yes? One I think you may have already figured out. Augustus is not a worry, because he knows if anything happens," they whispered sweetly, "I will literally drag him to the underworld myself."

421

"I—I have his soul," she tried to explain weakly.

"That's the spirit."

"No, literally that—that's how he evanesced out," she breathed, eyes blurred with salt water. "He swore some sort of vow, he swore his soul to me..."

"Even better," Isa smiled, holding her hands tight, still not seeming to quite understand. "Put it to good use, Elsie dear. It is time you had some fun. Have him fetch you tea, or dress very silly, in wonky top hats and silly glasses."

She chuckled wetly, the thought edging the panic aside. "Okay."

"Promise?"

"Promise."

Isa nodded, rising. "Good. We shall have laughs when I'm back."

Elsie swallowed, watching them take the stairs two at a time, vanishing with Rodion in a whorl of gold sparks.

So many dark moments, they had shared together. And so many kind words of comfort they'd traded.

Her body felt shaky and disconnected from itself, and there was a fury behind the panic, because hadn't she been prepared for everyone around her to collide so fucking hard?

Fletcher sank down beside her. "El." He sniffed, arm pressed up against her. "Where are we gonna go?"

The question felt like a punch in the gut.

There were footsteps to her left, and Augustus sat down beside her on the step, too.

"Didn't Isa tell you to make yourself scare," Fletcher bit, voice heavy with tears.

Elsie glanced over to those shipwrecked eyes of her companion. "Where's he gonna go, Fletcher? You gonna take him back yourself?"

Fletcher's expression was unreadable, brow knit.

422

"I'm being serious. Drag him back, and get arrested for treason yourself? Or do you suggest that Cele toss him in the debtor's cells? Force him into one of the suites here, he's so intent on *suffering* and *atoning*, I assume a place of such luxury is his own personal hell—"

"Oh, gods below." A faint smile pressed at the corner of Augustus's lips, though, laughter in his soft whisper.

"What," Elsie prodded, giving him a skeptical quirk of her eyebrow. "Give him soft clothes and chocolates, he'll wither to nothing—"

Fletcher snorted, dissolving at last into damp laughter, wiping the tears of grief from his cheeks, looking over her at Augustus. "She's not wrong, you know."

"I can go." Augustus had a faint smile on the corners of his lips, one that flickered out as he held his brother's gaze. "I..."

"It's fine. As long...as long as El doesn't mind," Fletcher mumbled, voice torn between amusement and annoyance.

"I should mind," Elsie breathed. "But I don't. I'm the one who told him to stay in the first place, on account of my poor judgment."

Augustus gave a small snort. "At least you've got the insight to see that's completely fucked."

"As are you, when Isa realizes you've decided to continue lurking."

Reddening, Augustus looked away.

"We...should go help Cele." Elsie squirmed out from under Fletcher's arm, rising. "If the Valley is about to get an influx of magic—of elves..." Her eyes flicked between the brothers. "We've got our work cut out for us."

TEDDY

"People are intricate beings, and yet,
sometimes...sometimes first impressions are quite
correct.."

~Alva Praequintelya

Teddy was sure he was about to be ill, following Mattie's amethyst-eyed servant down the stairs two at a time. "Does Sam go for a walk every morning?" The question was breathless, but he didn't know what else to say.

It couldn't have been more plain that Sam wasn't living in the room upstairs, and these questions were meaningless, for the answers could only be lies.

He asked them all the same.

"No, Master Alderton does not take a constitutional every day," the servant said thoughtfully, choosing his words carefully.

Teddy glanced behind as they rounded the corner, reaching the main landing.

Mattie was still at the top of the stairs, leaning on the railing, watching him intensely.

But the servant had pulled open a discrete side-door, and was already partway down what was clearly the staff well. "Master Alderton? Are you coming?"

His heart dropped, and he moved on instinct, following. "It's just Teddy."

"Pardon me. The...Master Fieldson told me that you were married."

"Ah. It's complicated," Teddy mumbled. "This is unusual, are there not main stairs to access the back of the property?"

"Well." The servant paused, looking back at Teddy. "Yes. But this is the way that Master Alderton came." With that, he turned, continuing down the rest of the way, bypassing the large kitchen to make a beeline for servant quarters.

For better or for worse, though, Teddy made the mistake of looking down.

They reached an empty chamber at the base of the stairs, and the servant glanced to Teddy, beckoning past the door that would've led them out. The room was bleak beyond all belief, dark steps of oxidized blood smeared on the stones, drips and splatters and big paw prints, trailing about the room.

"What happened here," Teddy breathed, turning back, watching the servant with trepidation. *I did not just get myself trapped.*

The Thread was eating at him, demanding answers, and he had none, only questions, questions and horrible visions of what—and who—had left such carnage.

That's too much blood.

Whoever that is wouldn't have made it.

The servant closed the door, cornering them both in the bleak room.

"Answer me." Teddy's voice was shaking, threatening tears as he took another step towards the servant. "What *happened.*"

The servant's voice was quiet. "Sam is gone."

"And me?"

The servant's eyes flicked to Teddy, wide and uneasy. "I know your sister. El's a friend, Teddy. I've seen her handiwork—and I rather fear what she would do if I let you die."

~•~

The morning was frigid, and still, Teddy had unbuttoned his coat, had stuffed his hat in his pocket, for the Thread was burning in his chest.

He still clutched the disc in his hand, that warm little glass circle feeling like a piece of driftwood in a storm, relief and trepidation all at once.

The disc could not take him somewhere he did not know. It could not take him somewhere that wasn't familiar, and one thing had struck him, looking around that bleak room.

Whatever Sam was—whatever he'd lied about—he *was* familiar.

The disc could not take him somewhere he did not know.

But it could very well take him to some*one* he did.

The man—Lysander—he'd suggested it. The amethyst-eyed man who knew Elsie.

Elsie, who by her own scheming was running in a production ring, and this kid was, too.

Honest criminals, the two of them, it seemed, but Teddy's trust had been fractured one too many times to stick around and test it. He hadn't lingered to hear what else would be said—or see what Lysander would do.

Sam's gone. That could mean anything, but Lys's tone lacked finality.

Sam's gone, and what the hell was he doing there in the first place?

That fractured trust was unrelenting. Was it better to find Sam complicit in these schemes and perfectly well? If he'd been hurt by Matthew *fucking* Fieldson—that was a known crisis. Teddy had spent a long time patching up Sam's broken heart. But Sam had already been hurt once, badly.

Anger curled, and Teddy pressed on, furious. Twirls of smoke were rising before him, the only hint of someone else in these woods, these gods-forsaken woods that the disc had carried him to when he'd commanded it to bring him to Sam. He was running, now, beads of sweat on his brow, dodging branches like punches thrown, feet pounding on the packed-dirt strip, and there were what felt like a thousand explanations for the deception.

Out of breath, Teddy came to a stop, chest heaving, and it was impulse, to rub the scars through the sweat-soaked shirt.

"Mr. Mirabeau."

Whirling, Teddy's eyes went wide.

On the path, Chim. Her red hood was pulled neatly back, curls perfectly set, eyes inked to the darkest black, fangs gleaming in the shadowed forest light, and she grinned, wide and vicious. "Mr. Mirabeau, why are you running?"

"Chim." Waves of relief crashed into him, and he sank to his knees, brow knit. "How—"

"How did I find you, running through the forest?" she interrupted in a sing-song voice. "How does a wolf hunt the child?"

The Thread was pushing him to rise once more. "Chim. What's going on? Where did you go?"

"*Chim, what's going on*—no!" She shrieked out the word, stamping her foot. "No, no, *no*, you *don't* get to ask—"

"I have been worried sick about you," he breathed, voice soft.

I should run.

Something was not right, he had a keen sense for danger, and this *was* danger, make no mistake—

Chim let out a scream, wild and full of fury. "NO!"

And from the shadows of the trees, a low, guttural growl entered. It was a lethal call-and-response, a chant of one predator against another, and Teddy was caught in the middle.

Five seconds.

He closed his eyes, bracing.

Four.

427

His dream was always to run, but his instinct was stillness, for experience had been a cruel teacher.

Three.

No matter what happened, at least he'd gotten to tell Tess he loved her.

Not Tess. Risa.

His sister, Risa.

Two.

He'd open his eyes, and he would face this. He would be strong and brave and all the things other people should've been for him but never were.

He'd be them for himself.

One.

He was a mountain, and he would not crumble.

CHIM

*"Blood pacts know no loopholes. This is their value;
they follow intention alone. It makes them worth much,
and deeply dangerous, for we often do not recognize that
our darkest intentions are outside our control."*

~Alva Praequintelya

Staring Teddy down, Chim giggled, pleased.

She had done it.

Oh, to be sure, it had not been easy.

They played a marvelous game of tag, chasing each other through the Capital.

It was easier this way. Easier, that he had been chasing Sam, for he'd led her right through the woods, and this would save her the effort of tracking two separate hunts, which seemed dreadfully tiring when she really stopped to think about it.

This was an exhaustive exercise in obedience.

"Why, what scared eyes you have," Chim breathed, voice sing-song as she took a step towards Teddy. "All the better to watch me with as I devour you limb by limb."

And there it was again, that low growl from the shadows of the forest, that guttural cry of one of the Master's beasts, cornering them both.

"And look at how you tremble," Chim taunted, flexing her taloned hands, "all the better to surrender to cowardice—"

Teddy merely shook his head, brow worried. "Chim, I know this has been heartbreaking. I know that you are scared and alone—"

"No!" Her shriek sent a flock of birds scattering in the distance, and Teddy covered his ears, wincing.

Leaves quivered, and the thud of heavy paws on packed earth were the violent prelude to a hit in the gut, and Chim was on the ground, wind knocked out of her—

Snarling, a massive barghest was looming over her, and she screamed, for even still, the nightmares found her.

Those large teeth that pricked her skin, the jaw that clenched around her middle, the horrible, sickening waves of fear that made her vomit, the awful, wretched stench of rot and filth that made her tears that much worse, and she was *not* a little girl, she was *not, not not*—

Dully, she was aware of Teddy's shouts.

Her would-be victim.

The barghest threw Chim down, her head smacking painfully against the rocky earth, and only in death would the blood pact shatter, shatter like the bones and body that broke as the beast's jaw wrapped around her once more. It flung her like a rag doll, beating her against the earth.

The Master had not forbidden her to die, and the Mother had not chained her to this earth with blood.

But then again, the Master had not forbidden her to run into the open arms of his own puppet master, for as he controlled the gods, so he was governed by one beyond Time itself. Cackling, Chim dragged herself to her feet, bloodied and broken but not yet finished, for she had fight in her yet. Beyond the gods themselves, did she have fight left in her.

If she was to end Teddy and Sam—and she was going to, the pact sewn with blood told her she wanted this—she would not attempt it with the jaws of a beast around her neck and victory nothing more than a distant vision.

On the threads of Chaos itself did she vanish herself away, far, far away, off to lick her wounds at the feet of one who traded in Chaos as much as any of them.

She was off to court the Prince of Nothing.

THE GHOSTS

We are exhausted.

Turns out, the exhuming of relics takes a toll.

Having Augustus here is like having a ghost trailing about. Fitting, I guess. I'm the heir of Death, right? So of course I'd be haunted.

~Elizabeth Clement Faulise,
Excerpt from a letter dated February 19th

FLETCHER

"I would cling to my brother until the end. I don't
blame my lover for doing the same, even if his brother
was a bit of a bastard."

~Elizabeth Clement Faulise

The Dradan family in the foyer—Echeveria, was their name—were
gardeners by trade, though their youngest was, at the moment, running
about the foyer of the Merchant house, shrieking about fighting that
nasty, no good god that'd crushed the mountains.

"Seta," their mother hushed, looking flustered as she waited by the
stairs. "Enough."

"Listen to your mother," their other parent chimed in, snatching Seta
by the arm to pick them up.

This seemed to displease Seta, for they immediately burst into tears.

Fletcher sighed, counting out the blankets in the nearby alcove with
Desdemona. It was a difficult move, no question—the children were
restless, the parents apprehensive, and with no idea what the future
held...

"What are they saying," Desi asked, glancing over at Fletcher. Eyes
sparkling, she had taken to the task of hostess emphatically, excited to
fill the house—and excited to regale any who would listen with the tale
of the night of her introduction, during which a chandelier had crashed
atop her and taken her arm.

The eyes of the Echeveria mother flicked over to the alcove, having
heard the question.

"They're just asking their child to quiet," Fletcher mumbled. "And Des, if they didn't say it in Vernacular, it isn't for your ears."

Desi just gave the mother a warm smile, seeming to disregard Fletcher's warning. "It's okay! We don't mind!"

The Echeveria mother only grimaced, turning her attention back to spouse and child.

"I want to learn your language," Desi chattered on, not seeming to mind as she looked back at Fletcher. "Do you think you can teach me?"

"Maybe you could find someone here to teach you," he suggested, trying not to let the annoyance melt into his voice.

These massive merchant homes proved satisfactory waystations for the Caelaymnic Drada who sought refuge in the Valley—but that did not change the fact that it was still a land of strangers.

At least those in Thallassas were in the company of familiarity.

"Never, in a thousand years, did I think I'd be standing here," Fletcher breathed. Baskets of blankets sat stacked along the wall, pulled from the massive array assembled by Desi's family, alongside a small table of medic supplies to tend to the minor wounds, and Desi's tiny desk, at which she sat, diligently noting the residents, tallying numbers for food and other supplies.

He'd first come to the Valley in another life, he'd decided.

Augustus had told him that the humans of Aerdela were unimportant, their crimes unproven, and Fletcher had been desperate to get out of the mountain city.

One foot in the Valley, and the slow unraveling had begun. The inevitable fall of an old kingdom.

And the beginning.

The last few days had been a blur, a dissonance, watching worlds collide.

437

~ • ~

Chaotic thoughts had been percolating as Fletcher assisted with the settling of families, but the one he had continued to come back to was the matter of Elsie and Augustus.

He wouldn't have called them friends.

But he wouldn't have called them enemies, either, and that was what bothered him, particularly now, when all places of refuge had been swept away.

It wasn't like they could go back to Caelaymnis, and with Ezra being holed up in the Taylor Town apartment, that left few options.

With a heavy exhale, Fletcher tapped on the door of the manor room Augustus had been sequestered to, which, to his dismay, wasn't really a room so much as it was the sofa in his and Elsie's borrowed room. The other rooms were needed, and anyway, it was best to keep Augustus tucked away out of sight. He was liable to take a knife to the gut if the wrong Drada caught wind of him.

He'd deserve it, of course. But best avoid it if they could.

Fletcher couldn't blame Elsie for finding a discrete lounge somewhere to sleep on—she favored the one in the music room—but it wasn't fair, making her drift just because Augustus got shoved at them.

Then again, it was Elsie who was adamant that he stay, so who was to say what was fair, in the end.

"What." Augustus's muffled voice answered the knock. "Fletcher, I know it's you, I can hear you, why are you knocking at the door to your own room?"

Fair enough. Fletcher pushed the door open, finding Augustus sitting on the sofa, eyes unrelenting on the fire.

His brother hadn't bothered to shed the roughspun wares, at least not until Elsie had snipped at him to put some clean clothes on, complaining that if she had to share space with such a criminal, she would prefer he not stink to the high heavens.

Reluctantly, he'd taken pressed trousers and a button-up tunic—which amused Elsie to no end, seeing him in human wares.

"You look like shit," Augustus growled, rising at last to acknowledge his brother.

"Yeah. Well." Fletcher swallowed, uncomfortable. "I feel like shit."

"Fletcher." Augustus's brow was ceased, eyes falling to the floor. "I'm sorry."

"I know." Fletcher's eyes were pricking with tears as he gripped the back of the armchair.

"Okay." His brother's heavy sigh was followed by the padding of feet, and a hesitant hand rested on Fletcher's shoulder. "You...have not slept in several days. It would be advisable that you sleep."

Fletcher glanced over, his brother a bulking, damp mess of human clothes through the burgeoning saltwater. "Are—are you trying to comfort me?"

"I'm simply stating that—"

"No, you're being nice! Elsie broke you, you actually care—"

"I cared before." Augustus pulled his hand away, wiping it on his trousers. "Go sleep. You're hysterical."

Augustus's quiet steps drifted off to the windowsill, as far away as he could linger.

Sleep. Fletcher scoffed, resentfully falling onto the bed.

Before the founding of Caelaymnis, the mountain Drada lived in ancient stone houses, and stone was laborious to move, so the families of old shared space closely.

Augustus cleared his throat. "You were thinking of the—"

"Stone houses, yeah," Fletcher mumbled into his pillow.

A huff of laugh echoed off the glass panes. "Alva would be proud."

"Alva would very proudly tell you you're just good at guessing."

"Ech, *Ama* at least gave us good intuition." A pause. "Even if I ignored it, often."

"She didn't give us intuition, she gave us the rare suspicion that we know what someone is thinking," Fletcher countered, slightly annoyed. Rolling over, he stuffed El's pillow under his head, glaring.

Heavy silence filled the space between them. "Thank you for getting *Ama* out."

Fletcher swallowed, watching his brother as he studied the glassy landscape. "I...don't think she knows *you* made it out."

"It's for the best."

"Is it? She thinks you are dead."

"Of course it is. Our mother is unwell, and I've caused her so much grief—"

"You ass!" Fletcher flung his pillow at Augustus, furious. "She worries about you—"

"No, she's grieving—"

"Don't fucking to tell me to get some rest and then dump your guilt and—and bullshit on me!" The Vernacular words rolled off his tongue, a sharp break from the smooth Dradan words that had been traded between them.

Augustus's head snapped over, pale eyes wide.

Nothing but an obscene gesture was returned before Fletcher rolled over, eyes burning as he let them close.

Sleep found him with alarming speed, along with the realization amid his frustration: with everything gone, he was actually glad to have his brother near. Sins and all.

RISA

*"And Death crafted her realm to tend to the souls, for
no longer could she hold them inside her heart. Thus, the
land of shadows."*

~from The Collected Tales of the Dead

Glittering black gates opened into a lush expanse from a miraged desert
that seemed to fade into nothing and everything at once. Thus, the
Underworld.

Risa's gown seemed to be made of midnight itself, the soft gossamer
so deep and dark that it looked woven of the secrets of the universe, and
as she stepped through the gate, it moved with her. Dressed as the
consort of Death.

"Welcome," Cora said softly, lips tugging into a faint smile as she
gestured the gates shut behind them.

Sloping hills gave way to a massive gray river to the right, the
opposite bank obscured by both fog and distance, a looming court of
shadows to the left, tall and shiny and black. Down the path, Risa could
see clusters of buildings, houses that—as far as she could see, anyway—
were a mishmash of any and every style, pulled from the annals of time
and placed in little, distant villages.

"I...don't know what I expected," Risa said quietly. She looked up, to
the low charcoal dome of almost clouds above, not quite night but vastly
too dark to be anything close to day.

"Ah, well, this is a waystation for souls." Cora linked her arm around
Risa's, guiding them towards the shadowy palace. "I enjoy the, er, more

grand feel, as do some other souls that dwell here, but many simply seek comfort. Hence, the villages." Her expression seemed sad as she brushed her waterfall of black hair back. "They wish to look for familiar souls, to see if they've waited, or else, they seek solace in memories of home they're not prepared to leave—and of course there...is comfort, in seeing other departed souls." Her eyes flicked away. "I think it's a shame that it's only for the dead. When I was mortal, I think my soul needed some tending to. I'd have loved a place like this to rest it."

Along the path they walked stood guards, faintly glowing—and very translucent—who, despite their best efforts, were letting their ghostly eyes wander to Risa.

"The First Souls," Cora explained in an undertone. "The...very first souls I took. They have stayed with me, all this time." Her voice was warm with affection, eyes flicking to a soul striding down the path to meet them. "And Yara, who is my right hand, was the first soul I ever gathered."

Clad in ghostly armor that called back to the time of legend, the elven woman moved deliberately down the darkened path, hand on the hilt of a massive sword Risa had no doubt would end any who crossed it, dead or not.

"Cora, what is the meaning of this," Yara demanded, meeting them with an air of formality.

"This is Risa." There was a hint of apprehension in Cora's tone. "It's fine, Yara, I've tied her soul to mine."

An odd introduction, Risa mused, watching Cora strum the air between them, the faint glow of soul string letting out a low hum before glistening into nothing once more.

"What are you doing, tying mortal souls to yours," Yara clipped. "You vanish in a fit, and return with this—this mortal in tow—do you not understand that your place is with the dead—"

"You are not my keeper." Cora's voice had gone to stone, stilted and cold.

Yara's eyes flicked to Risa. "No. No, plainly, I am not."

"Last I checked, it was Cora who was Keeper of Souls," Risa breathed, tone even. Yara's anger pulled her all the wrong way. "That very much includes her own."

"Fine. Fine, if this is the haphazard turn—"

"You are dismissed," Cora snapped. "Take your preaching elsewhere."

With a bitter glare, Yara pushed past them both, heading for the gate. "On your own head, be this." Fading into the unreal night, the soft whisper of her translucent boots sounded like an agitated breeze against the shining path.

Cora's arm dropped from Risa's with frustration.

An uneasy prickling ran up Risa's spine as she glanced back over her shoulder, watching the faint soul glow fade off. Though perhaps it was just the sensation of being the only mortal in this shadowed realm of death. It was bound to make one uneasy, right?

I feel as though I've spent a long time avoiding this place.

Tall doors slid silently open at a crook of Cora's fingers, and Risa stopped dead in her tracks, mouth falling slightly open.

Warm light bathed the black and gold hall beyond, coruscant detail framing Cora's silhouette as she looked back over her shoulder, and Risa was relatively sure that whatever she was feeling in her stomach was what people in love referred to as *butterflies*, though she'd never experienced them until now. To be touched by beauty was a dangerous thing, but now, oh gods, now...

Never have I seen someone so beautiful.

Never have I seen such beauty in the shadows.

"Come, darling," Cora murmured, giving a coy smile. "There are yet still some hours before morning."

~ • ~

"A tapestry." Risa tilted her head to the side, gown sliding against the smooth obsidian as she took a step forward, fingers outstretched.

"Don't touch." Cora batted her hand away, snickering. "It's not just a tapestry. It's all of reality, woven with the threads of existence. Or, rather, it is what reality appears to be. Reality exists with or without this work of art."

It was a colorful mess, is what it was.

"You looked over your shoulder, and told me that we had hours until morning, and I imagined, uh…not taking a walking tour of the most massive palace in existence," Risa mused, tucking a strand of coppery hair behind her ear. Her legs ached, feet chilly through the thin slippers.

Cora ran a single delicate finger down Risa's spine before wrapping an arm around her waist. "Mm, you don't care for this?"

Chills, delicious and addictive, went shivering down Risa's arms. "I just…Cora, this sort of thing isn't particularly me." Risa sighed, glancing over, her lover's eyes glittering with curiosity. "It's not you. You've shown me all these beautiful things carved of your shadows, but…Cora. Where do you live, when you're here among the dead? Where is your sanctuary that you sneak off to when you're sad? Where do you hide out in the mornings with your cup of tea and get lost in your own thoughts?"

"I live, wandering this hallway," Cora breathed, brushing a kiss on Risa's ear. "I stare at this tapestry, at all the threads I cut, and when I am sad…" She paused, pulling Risa in closer. "I go lurk about my girlfriend's apartment and fix her tea, and we are sad together."

Risa moved, fingers running through that silky dark hair, kissing those perfect lips that confessed their mutual grief, and every nerve was alive. "I love your gown," she breathed, hands wandering, "I'd love to see

444

it on your bedroom floor—"

"I am Death," Cora smiled in between those deep kisses, "you'd do well to watch your tongue."

"You'll be quite familiar with my tongue when I have finished with you—"

"I'll finish *you*," Cora murmured, gently tugging up the skirt of Risa's gown, cornering her against the stone wall opposite the tapestry.

Tracing Cora's collarbone with kisses, Risa palmed her breast, snickering. "I dare you," she breathed. "You never would, not here, not in front of..."

"You don't think so?" Cora's soft hand nudged her thigh, and Risa relented with a grin, bracing herself against the cool stone.

"I think," Risa whispered, tilting her head back against the wall, "you're unaccustomed to—*ah*." Her breath caught, and she let her eyes flutter closed, laughing softly.

"What was that, love?"

Risa just shook her head, and let the moment be.

And what a moment it was.

After the tapestry hall, Cora seemed to relax a bit—a hot shower, a painfully strong cup of coffee, and with no explanation as to how they'd ended up neatly folded on Cora's bed, her pajamas, and Risa had said farewell to Cora as the cloudy sky grew illuminated with chilled light. The souls would not tend to themselves.

There was something casual and vaguely forbidden about wandering the palace in pajamas with a mug of coffee, Risa thought guiltily, padding about bare-foot down the glistening halls.

Cora had tried.

She wanted this place to be grand and beautiful and it was that moment when Risa realized how gentle Cora's magic was. Whatever image she'd tried to build in this palace of shadows, it was betrayed at every corner.

For every hard line, there was a thread in the tapestry, colorful and soft, and for every gilded room lay a patchwork village of posthumous comfort.

Loitering in an alcove, Risa finished off her lukewarm coffee in a single swallow, leaving the mug on a side table with a soft *clink*. Fatigue was beginning to settle heavy on her, in the stillness.

You have so much to do.

Ah. Risa sighed, settling on a cool stone bench, stretching out. That familiar nag that unfailingly pulled at her at the first signs of relief.

She'd been useless, of late.

Adrian had come calling once or twice, worried, but she'd brushed him off. *I need a break,* she'd clipped, and he'd gently reminded her that qualifying advocacy exams could not be postponed, and that she was expected to continue advocating cases in the run up, and she'd shrugged, because that sounded like not her problem, because she *needed a break.*

"Excuse me."

Risa's eyes snapped open, and she sat up, heart opting to jolt her to alertness with a few good kicks.

A woman was frowning in the doorway, very much opaque and not glowing in the slightest—meaning she was just an ordinary departed soul, rather than one of the First Souls. Blonde hair pulled into a ponytail, she was dressed rather smartly, Risa thought, with light tan trousers and a lavender sweater with the sleeves pushed to the elbows— very Hidden City casual, truth be told.

"You're not *alive*," the woman demanded in disbelief. "Cora didn't—"

"Ah. Uh, she did," Risa shrugged, rising. "Risa Barrett." She offered her hand, and the woman took it, still glaring.

"Beca."

"Everyone seems pissed off about my being here," Risa clipped, annoyed.

"This place is for the dead."

"This place belongs to souls that need tending to, and is under Cora's purview. Shouldn't she have the last say about who is allowed here?"

Beca's eyes narrowed. "You're awfully quick to defend a god that deals in death."

And you're fast to assume I'm so innocent.

"I know Cora," Risa leveled, gaze unbreaking.

"Do you, now?" Turning, Beca crooked a finger for Risa to follow. "Let me guess. She dolled you all up, when she brought you through the gates. She proudly showed you this monstrosity of a palace, and was dismayed that it wasn't quite satisfying to you, and only when she had other duties to attend to were you permitted to relax the dress code—"

"I do what I want," Risa snapped, following Beca down the hall. A shiver ran down her spine, though, at being read so plainly. "Cora doesn't have to agree with my opinions, but she certainly respects them—"

"Does she, now." Beca thrust open a discrete side door with a lock that looked jimmied, making her way down a dimly lit spiral staircase. "Tell me, Risa, what dissent have you truly offered up?"

"Why—I hardly see how this is any of your business, I have no idea who you even are—"

Beca snorted. "Ah. Cora failed to mention me."

"I...guess? Maybe you're just not worth mentioning." Risa knew that on principle, she should probably dislike this woman, but it'd been too long since she'd picked a fight with someone, and besides, anyone who knew of secret staircases was probably a decently interesting person to know.

"Not worth mentioning," Beca echoed, giving a sardonic laugh. "Ha. Perhaps. Her endless feud robbed me of my son, in the end. Though

447

what's one more soul to take, really?"

The bottom of the stairs opened to a narrow hallway, and beyond that, a single room.

A dungeon.

Dark stone encased them as Beca stooped before the lock, fiddling with it. Something sinister nipped at Risa's magic, too, abrupt, and she put a hand to her chest, startled fingers strumming the soul thread, making it quiver. *The only other place I've felt my magic dampened like this are the Dradan cells, but this is tenfold what the elves can do.*

What the hell.

What kind of magic does Cora need to suppress?

Beca knocked the door open with a soft *click*.

A man was chained to the middle of the room, great obsidian manacles suspending his arms above his head, ankles shackled to the floor. His dirty blonde hair was pushed back, brow beaded with sweat, and a pair of burning amber eyes flicked up, deep within exhaustion.

"Risa. I'd like you to meet the bane of Cora's existence, the font of her strife, unquestionably a rival to the death. This is Kiran, God of Life, Purveyor of Light, Spinner of Souls, and prisoner of Cora, Mistress of the Underworld. A pair of false gods, the both of them."

CORA

"Nothing is so dangerous as confidence."

~Dradan Proverb

"You know you're playing with fire."

"I'm not." Cora's fingers brushed the bars of the closed Underworld gates, eyes drifting to the straggling few souls being tended to by Yara and her Guards. "I know what I'm doing."

"Not the first time I've heard you claim that," Quinn admonished. His blond hair had been pulled back, heterochromic eyes mismatched as they stared at her in judgment.

"Why are you being so derisive? You know well that if the rest of the quays open, the relics will be vulnerable. We are all at risk."

"You've never been one to cede to Fate, Rose, but maybe it's time. This isn't your battle. You're fighting against forces above you—even as a god."

She scoffed, turning back for the Palace of Souls.

"And what's this, bringing one of the living back?"

"I love her," Cora snapped, "and this is my home, I do as I want—"

"It's not your home. You're living on borrowed time in a stolen palace, Rose—you don't know what the repercussions of this will be—"

"After everything, Quinn, why are you dogging my steps like this? What happened to your quiet afterlife? You were more than happy knitting and playing betsies with the elves right up until the moment I actually try to make good on my sins." Cora paused before the massive doors, turning to look him in the eyes, tone warning. "What do you know?"

"Me? Nothing." Quinn fidgeted guiltily.

"Cut the bullshit. I'm not prescient, and I can hardly read the threads, even after all this time, but you?" Cora laughed darkly. "You are that voice in the back of people's heads. You are that thought whose initiation can't be placed, you are the father of Listeners, Quinn, now *what did you hear?*"

Quinn gave her an obstinate look. "I know that your grand scheme has gone to shit."

That was putting it lightly.

"I have no idea what Elsie wants with dhacrym," she breathed, tugging at her shawl.

"It's potent, and addictive," Quinn frowned. "You could do with a bit more understanding. Poor girl, she doesn't know that she's been spared the fate of following you to that wretched mountain—"

"I have to take the brother, there's no way around it—"

"Mm, truly." Quinn watched her with a wary gaze.

Cora whirled on him. "What."

"Noticed that the brother's thread gets cut, then?"

"I saw."

"That she lives, but he can't?"

"I am Cora, God of Death, Cutter of Threads, Keeper of Souls, of *course* I saw, you fool! It is my business to see," Cora snapped, "I see!"

"And you can't harm them—not that you would," Quinn speculated, watching her with those piercing eyes that saw worlds beyond what she ever could. "But now, of course you're wondering how you're to close the quay—of course, you've seen the lives that are saved because that girl's thread gets re-tied—"

"I thought you had something new to offer. Did I mention she has the iaculus?"

Quinn's eyes lingered on her, unreadable, mouth slightly open in what was perhaps curiosity. "Does she. And did you tell her she's walking about with a well of shadows around her neck? Have you told her that what she has is one half a dangerous weapon?"

"I did not wish to startle her—"

"Startle her? You are as mistrustful as ever, Rose."

"Says you, who lied to me time and again," Cora hissed.

"We both had our schemes. That does not mean I'm not one of your oldest friends. We have seen wars. You stayed at my side as I passed." Quinn's expression softened, and he put a reassuring hand on Cora's arm. "Rose, I have watched you bring powerful men to task, I have watched you shoulder more than you ever wanted to. But you can't fight every fight. Go. Take your girlfriend and go back to the land between, where the living ought to be."

"Where is Risa, anyway?" Cora straightened, glaring. It wasn't a bad idea, returning. She could linger near Elsie, near the children, watch over them both as she'd promised.

Quinn smirked. "Risa? I believe she ran into an old friend of yours. Beca was showing her around—"

"Fuck!" Storming off down the hall, Cora left Quinn standing alone.

Beca would not hold back, and the risk of Risa knowing the truth was perhaps the most terrifying threat of all.

TEDDY

"To become what you feared. In that moment, I knew
I would be faced again with the decision: whether or not
to become my father. When seen so, it isn't a difficult
choice to make."

~Theodore Alderton

Never had the Thread brought so much fury.

Golden motes lifted from Teddy's palm, sweeping off before him, breadcrumbs of pain in this bloody forest.

Teddy was still kind of shit at forming lucents, but the Thread seemed undeterred by this as he strode towards the pair of them. A kobalde wielding wicked words and on the path for blood, and the beast she had collided with.

Losing love, chasing pain, and he knew that had broken him. All of this.

Not broken, as in snapped.

Broken, as in the ways he'd been broken a thousand times before and this time was the one that stuck.

Whatever docility-posed-as-patience, whatever fawning-as-survival had been seared into his heart—it flickered out to give way to the already-kindled rage.

Grabbing the beast's scruff, he pulled it off of Chim, fingers digging into rotting fur already slicking off into his hand. The beast yowled, and he was a conduit, the Thread curling out—

No no no don't mend it—

But the Thread was its own master in this.

Teddy's magic sank deep into the beast as he dragged it back with both hands, and the thing was writhing in pain as he let it drop to the ground some twenty paces back.

Anger made his thoughts clouded, and he'd been nearly set to give it a kick—and likely would've, too, if the Thread rippling about the thing hadn't been so intoxicatingly satisfying.

Scream

Howl

Hurt

He turned, running back to Chim, sliding a bit as he fell down beside her.

But she laughed, eyes fiery, charcoal whisps circling her. "I'm going to get you," she cackled, blood spraying as she spoke, "I'm going to gnaw on your bones, I'm going to devour you all..."

Her words trailed off as she vanished, leaving nothing but a deep, burning anger inside Teddy.

He could not lose any more. He could not watch one more person leave him behind, could not watch one more person torment him and twist him up and lie—gods, the lying, the lines, the deception, the *love* that wasn't *there*—

"Teddy!" A breathy voice hissed behind them, and Teddy's head snapped over.

Through the foliage, he could see someone moving—

"Mariann?" The name was ill at ease in Teddy's mouth.

Her once-short brown hair had grown long, her belly round with child, and her familiar, condescending eyes were judgmental as ever. She was standing still, before a dwindling fire. "What are you doing here—"

"What are *you* doing here?" He bit the words through the woods,

Thread angry.

The great beast rose, limping as it padded towards her. Mariann's face fell, and she gave her legs a pat. "C'mere, boy, what happened?" The beast gave a whine, and Teddy could see where Chim had torn into it, a flap of flesh raw and exposed on its shoulder, its ear half-gone. "You get *over* here, too. Now!" she hissed, glaring at Teddy.

Teddy rose, furious. His body was shaky, trembling with exertion and fever and fear, and he realized that he was a foolish, foolish man.

He had nothing, in these woods.

No food, not so much as a gods-damned waterskin. Nothing more than the clothes and scant few miscellanies tucked into his pack.

"I said get over here—"

"Why should I trust you," Teddy bit back, voice rising.

"Quiet! It's not safe—get over here," Mariann snapped, straightening up as Teddy met the camp, pushing him back. "And hush! You've lost your marbles, paranoid bastard—"

"And you, with that awful thing," Teddy clipped, glaring at the massive dog—and the lump of blankets by the fire, disheveled blonde hair poking out—

"Fuck—Sam?" Teddy's voice was soft, it was all he could do to stumble over to the heap of blankets in disbelief. "Sam!"

Cinnamon eyes blinked back fever, bleary and red. His cracked lips only whispered a faint sound of resignation, eyes searching Teddy.

"His leg is badly injured," Mariann said in a low voice. "It's a long story. But we've been here for days."

Bracing himself, Teddy drew back the blanket.

Oh, gods.

"I hope you've something useful in that pack of yours," Mariann warned.

The bandages were dark and sodden, the scent of deadened flesh

454

lingering heavy about.

The Thread lashed out, hungry for the pain it had been tracking these last days, and laying his hands on Sam's leg, a swell of pale gold light sparked into a glow where he met the fetid bandage.

"Oh." Mariann's voice was soft. "Something useful...not in the pack."

"C'mon..." Teddy could feel the Thread circling, his chest tight, but there was no familiar sterile tang lingering in the air, no burn of knitting flesh— "No!" Breathless, he pulled back, something snarling at the Thread and sending a hiss of pain back, Sam giving a gasp of agony.

Fuck.

"I am so fucking over this—why can I not fix any of you?" Teddy demanded, digging his fingers into his own arms, wincing at the sting. "I have spent my *life* fixing all of your problems and why can't I just..." Swallowing hard, Teddy pulled the medic's kit from his satchel, the same he'd used in the high plains with Isa, more or less. He was fucking useless, trying to help the people he loved. "Water," he breathed, glancing up. "Do...you have water, at least?"

Mariann nodded, moving.

Gingerly, Teddy began to cut away the soiled bandages, fingers trembling.

Do I wish I had found him well and in the company of Mattie?

He swore quietly, eyes flickering over Sam's knee. It was difficult to tell, like this, he had to remind himself. Cleaned up, he could properly assess the damage—

"Teddy." Sam's voice was hoarse, eyes fighting to stay open.

He'd gone over it a thousand times, what he wanted to say. But that'd been before, and now, the words had dried up.

"It can't be you." Sam trailed off. He seemed disoriented, watching Teddy. "Is it? Is it you?"

"Hush. You just rest." Pursing his lips, Teddy set to work cleaning the wound, first with the steaming water, then the antiseptic that sent Sam to tears and yelps of pain.

It was much, much worse than it looked.

The knee was completely shattered, as far as Teddy could tell, the flesh fetid with decay, a horrible black ooze in place of bloodied seepage. A medic's kit could do little more than make him comfortable.

"Here." Teddy's words felt heavy on his tongue as he slid an arm under Sam's back, bringing him to sitting. *Touching him again. I have my arm around him again.* One hand firmly on Sam, helping him remain upright, he brought a tonic to Sam's lips with the other. "This'll help with the pain and the fever, just—easy, there—drink..."

So clinical.

But what else was there to say, right now?

Coughing, Sam brushed the vial away, cheeks ruddy.

"Easy..."

His breathing was labored, eyes glassy, and...

Teddy's heart ached as Sam leaned into him.

"I'm not doing well," Sam whispered, head buried in Teddy's shoulder, and it wasn't a question.

He wasn't doing well.

It was awkward and uncomfortable, Sam leaning into him.

You broke my heart.

"I have so much to tell you," Sam breathed. His weight was heavy against Teddy as he leaned against him, voice groggy. "If you're really here, that is..."

"You need to rest," Teddy mumbled, lifting Sam off and laying him gently down.

Sam seemed unable to stay awake—though in his efforts, he took Teddy's hand in his, albeit somewhat weakly. The gesture hurt deeper than Teddy wanted it to, but he let it pass, lacing his fingers through

Sam's as he drifted off.

Mariann was watching them both with curiosity as she tended to her massive beast, slumped by fire.

"You...said you'd been here for days?" Teddy's voice was hoarse. He didn't know what to do. It felt wrong to sit.

"Not like there's much of another place to go," Mariann put in, gingerly dabbing a ripped piece of cloth against a gash in the beast's muzzle. "Sam is hurt, obviously. I tried once to leave, but something went awry. That's how we ended up here." Her hand drifted to her belly. "And it's not safe, here, wherever here is."

"And your plan is to stay in the woods forever?"

"No. But you wouldn't like my other plan."

"Oh?"

"I was going to sit with Sam until he died, and then go," she said softly. "Or until he got better, but he...is not in good shape." Her eyes flicked to Teddy. "You can't mend him, either."

Teddy glanced back to Sam, but he'd already let his eyes close once more. "Like trying to mix water and oil."

"Barghest bites are bad," Mariann said quietly. "Bet they're poison."

"Barghest?" His voice broke, heart sinking like a stone.

The realization was jarring.

Barghests only meant one thing.

Which one, I wonder? Which divine lineage did they assign you?

Teddy could feel his heart breaking anew. How long had Sam known? And Clark—skies, the man had been collecting bloodlines like they were antique watches.

No wonder he couldn't fix Sam. Loaded up with dhacrym, and he couldn't use the disc to get them out, either—Elsie hadn't been able to evanesce either with elf or disc, not at first, and Sam's raw eyes and blood-stained fingers betrayed a man subjected to something much the same.

"I was as surprised as you," Mari said quietly.

"I don't understand—how are you involved in this *at all*," Teddy breathed, "I'm running through the woods, and I find my sister-in-law. Tom said you—"

"What did he say," she challenged, glancing up.

"He said you had an affair—I don't...how is Sam a part of this?"

"How are *you*?" She was glaring at him, voice sharp. "I think we're nearly found out, and Howard here starts going mad at someone in the woods—"

"Howard? You named it *Howard*?"

"You've got a lot of nerve, Mirabeau—"

Mariann's admonishment was cut off with a hiss and a blaze of fire, a shriek of pain slicing the morning.

Teddy jumped violently, alarm and panic governing, and it was Sam he moved for, Sam he was ready to protect, Sam that already the Thread was reaching to guard—

"It's fine." Mariann watched the burning creature with a placid expression, the thing crumbling quickly to embers, leaving nothing more than an echo in the woods and ashen flakes in the grass. Her eyes flicked to Teddy, and she quirked an eyebrow. "I told you it wasn't safe out there. That's why I've got the wards. I *told* you there was something in the woods."

THE BEAST

"In our dreams, our secrets."

~Unknown

As a rule, the Beast did not dream.

But Howie did.

The gentle man with blue eyes had given him something sweet that eased the pain, and the Beast had slipped mercifully into sleep.

There, he dreamed of a man with gray eyes and long, black hair tied neatly back, who had an easy laugh and played the violin.

He dreamed that one day, malice had crept across the rolling wheat fields, and the gray-eyed man had taken up his scythe and tried to battle back the oncoming evil, but he fell.

He dreamed that the gray-eyed man had been pulled from time itself and stripped of his humanity, and that he forgot himself in the hunger of fear and flesh.

As a rule, the Beast did not dream.

But Howie did.

ELSIE

*"Two emotionally incompetent men, one very
anxious girl, and a ro who was done with the bullshit.
It's not an ideal group of folks to put into a very small
space, that's all I'm saying."*

-Isa Mirestva

Coming back to Sam's old apartment was going to a place that had almost been home.

I hate that things unraveled. I hate that all the promises Sam made behind these doors were lies.

It was worse, now—Sam had left a gaping wound in their family, and now with the production ring out of reach once more and Caelaymnis, she felt like they'd lost any progress forward. They were no closer to finding the Master, no closer to understanding why he wanted the gods, and with his increased brazenness, flaunting them—using them to overtake Caelaymnis—skies only knew what would come next.

Her fingers found the locket, worrying the warm metal.

If it was the relic Augustus claimed, she'd seen no evidence of it. Godly pieces, she reflected bitterly, should be more useful in times like these, and all it'd done was sit there, nothing more than a pretty little target on her back.

"Ezra." Elsie pushed open the door without so much as a knock, half-hoping to startle him with the unannounced visit. A mean thought, probably, but her bitterness was hard to shake.

He reminded her of everything she wasn't.

Her aim in startling Ezra had been successful, because there was a panicked shuffling from the back of the apartment, and Ezra appeared a moment later, smoothing his mussed, dark hair. "Elsie—"

"Is this a bad time," she snipped, crossing her arms.

"It—n-no, it's not *not* a bad time..."

Bypassing him to make for the small kitchen, she rolled her eyes. "Why are you alone here?" She knew the answer, of course—Caelaymnis had fallen, and Isa was otherwise occupied, unable to be on guard duty for the world's most pathetic prisoner.

"He's not alone." Isa turned into the kitchen, pulling on a thick-knit cardigan atop a long-sleeved undershirt.

Elsie set the tap gushing, reaching for the kettle, because that was what she did, when she came to Sam's. Made tea. "Oh, Isa." Her eyes flicked up to theirs as the kettle filled. "Really? Him? You've got the worst taste in men of anyone I've met."

"Oh, fuck off," they snickered, going for the mugs.

Ezra was a deep red, sulking against the entry of the kitchen.

"Couldn't have set the bar a little higher?" Elsie muttered, stove burner guttering to life, blue flame licking the beads of water off the kettle with a satisfying *hiss*.

"I'm right here, I can hear you—"

"Your other brothers are attached already," Isa chortled, though to their credit, they gave Ezra a wink, grinning. "Any word from Teddy?"

Elsie shook her head. "None." Not that she expected any. Short of bringing letters himself, he'd have to rely on the post, which was liable to take weeks this time of year.

"Ech, that's too bad."

"The whole thing is too bad." Leaning back against the counter, she studied Ezra.

Startled, he straightened, eyes wide. "What."

461

"I don't get why you're here." Elsie sighed, crossing her arms. Might as well get straight to the point. Cora had been eerily prophetic about their meeting, but had failed to explain why it had come about. She'd only said that it was necessary, and though Elsie wasn't in a position to disagree, given the presumed bounty on them both, she had no love of mystery.

"I...have a proposition for you," Ezra said. "That's why I came to find you. I've been trying to get the nerve up to ask—"

"What kind of proposition?" She narrowed her eyes, incredulous.

"I—I want you to move to the Capital with me." Tears were welling in Ezra's eyes. "I've spent my whole life being apart from you. I don't want any power, or—or to lead. I just want a quiet, safe life near my sister."

~ • ~

Perched on the edge of the porcelain tub, Elsie's thoughts were roaring, loud and inescapable.

The locket was clutched in her palm, shaking fingers having gently looped it off her neck, knuckles now white around the gold.

What a lonely thing.

She closed her eyes, heart pounding violently against her ribs.

Clark Carson had promised a city beyond imagining, with this locket.

Only, it'd been more a promise to himself. He'd be praised, lauded as a hero by all but the Factionists. It would be difficult not to be impressed by the theatrics of returning a lost heir to the City.

But it felt a little less lonely now, this locket of hers. This iaculus.

I've spent my whole life being apart from you.

Nobody was drawn to Elsie like that. Nobody *chose* to be around her—she just sort of happened to other people, and she'd been okay with that, except now Ezra was here.

462

Ezra, who she'd been tasked with keeping close. Ezra, the apex of her own resentment, Ezra, who...who wanted her as a sister. Ezra, who wanted a safe, quiet life in the Capital.

They were on the same side, her and Ezra.

Two parts of a whole.

It was an intoxicating idea that scared the living daylight out of her.

"Are you alright?"

Elsie started so badly she slipped right off the edge of the tub, falling back into the empty bath. "Fuck—"

Sparks and mist embraced the bulking figure of the ex-general. "Shit—sorry—" Augustus didn't even bother offering her a hand to pull herself up, moving instead to slide an arm under her shoulders, and in a single smooth movement, brought her out of the tub and to standing.

Glaring, Elsie smacked his hands back, adding a good push on his chest for good measure as he stepped off. "What the hell were you thinking?"

The bathing room door clicked open. "Oh, what the fuck..." Isa grabbed Augustus's sleeve, dragging him into the hallway. "Leave her *alone*—"

"I didn't—I felt...danger," Augustus mumbled, not meeting Isa's gaze.

"You felt *stupid* is what you did." Elsie tucked a strand of hair behind her ear, catching her breath. The locket still lay clutched in her fist, chain glittering down.

"Who's that?" Ezra croaked out the question, having apparently decided to risk watching from the end of the hall.

"Ez." Elsie tried to keep her voice calm. "This is Augustus, he..." *How the fuck do I even explain this?*

"I am sworn to guard her." The answer was clearly meant for Isa, regardless of the biting glare Augustus gave Ezra.

"Okay, I—we—we're going." Elsie pushed past the Drada in the hall,

463

making for the damp boots she'd eventually left in a heap by the breakfast table. She looped the locket around her neck once more. No use hanging about here, in this veritable tinderbox waiting to explode.

Isa, too, bypassed Augustus, putting a hand on Ezra's back to usher him to the kitchen. "Leave them be. Tea's bound to be over-steeped..."

"Ez, we'll meet up later, okay?" Elsie glanced up from the still-soaking boot laces. "I—I really need to talk to you. It's important, we have to talk about the Capital—it's such a grand idea, everything just so complicated, but..." She glanced to Augustus. "But I want to talk about it. Just later."

Ezra gave a tiny nod, still looking a bit alarmed.

My brother.

He could be, she considered, watching as the apartment vanished around her. With a little effort, he could be.

AUGUSTUS

"I knew I would love them forever when I saw them
in the arms of another. It wasn't jealousy. It was...relief.
At last, someone to comfort them the way I hadn't."

~Augustus Praequintelya

"What the hell?"

The shimmering mist of evanescing them back was still dissipating as Augustus slunk off to his usual place of brooding by the window. "What happened that provoked such a response—"

"You have *got* to reign that impulse in," Elsie glared, stomping after him. "Fuck the Master, I'm liable to die of fright, with you..."

Augustus turned, eyes on her as she trailed off.

An accidental truth, for wasn't that what he'd nearly done? Dosed her with the draught of fear almost to the point of death?

"At the very least, you're...lucky I didn't concuss myself," Elsie muttered, turning to look out the window, arms crossed.

"I'll try to pull it in." His eyes flicked to the locket about her neck. "You weren't wearing it when I arrived."

"I was thinking."

He shrugged, crossing his arms. "If it's a relic of Death, you ought not to toy with it like that. You might lose it."

Elsie glared. "You should know now that I'm a vehicle of destruction. I am the daughter of a Rescindant anarchist, and my being in the Valley was no mistake. My mother's final wish was that I be placed in sight of her collaborator, and what did he do but wrap this unverified relic around my neck and send me off to fetch him a more powerful post in a more magical city. And I keep asking why this was my fate and not Ezra's. Why do I have to carry the weight of being a troublesome girl while he shoulders the burden of morality and honor? I'm the one that was given this supposed implement of destruction, and my brother has been tasked with the rescue."

Augustus returned to his study of the town below, something tearing in his chest, cold and heavy. "I think," he said softly, "if...I hadn't been such a—a page...ripper, I would have given you a hug right now."

"In another life," she clipped.

There were three times in his life when he'd willingly and of his own suggestion offered someone a hug.

Once, when Isa had been in tears, kneeling on the floor of their room, yellow binding in hand, wanting the love of the mystics.

Another time, when Epherias lay dying in the snow, and Augustus had held that poor boy as he died a quick but painful death.

And in another life where he hadn't hurt Elsie.

"I'm...not there, right now." Elsie glanced over. "It's already a lot, keeping you here. I feel like I shouldn't be okay with it, I..." She sighed. "It's complicated."

He nodded, not breaking his watch beyond the window. "If I have seen anything, Elsie, it is that only fools believe they can master a troublesome soul."

She chuckled a little, turning on her heel as the locket clinked in her hand. "Tea?"

"Please."

The scuffing of sachets and the swish of water into a small teapot met his ears. "You have to warm it."

Augustus turned, joining her on the sofa, where before them she'd set out the tea pot and cups on the coffee table. "I'm not doing it

466

Fletcher's way—"

"Shut up and heat the water, you ass."

A faint smile tugged at the corners of his mouth as he obeyed. He'd missed letting little tendrils of magic touch the world.

"Thanks." Elsie was peering into the steaming pot, watching it steep, and Augustus nodded, leaning back into the sofa. "Augustus?"

His name in her mouth took him aback.

Usually, it was all edges, but this time—this time, it was soft.

He said nothing, no words coming at the moment.

"You say the iaculus is a relic. You say I should be more careful." Her words were easy but withholding. There was something she wasn't saying.

"All I know is what the scripts say. Death, and in her hand, the token of Nothing," Augustus breathed. His gaze met the floor. "So, uh. Are Isa and Ezra..."

"Oh, they're absolutely fucking," Elsie mused, hunched over the tea pot.

"How long have you known?"

"Since this morning."

Augustus sank into silence.

It was an inevitable truth that someone would see Isa for the treasure they were. An inescapable reality that they would find someone capable of better loyalty, better amity.

"Hey." Elsie looked up, green eyes piercing. "You knew this was coming down the road."

Augustus quirked an eyebrow. "I did. I just didn't think I'd be alive to see it."

Elsie laughed quietly, looking up.

"What? What's that about?"

"We...are playing nice right now, you know that? Your soul is tied to

467

mine, we are sitting here drinking tea, and it's all pretend. And we're going to pretend for a while longer, Augustus."

Augustus looked away. "I know."

"I made myself a promise," Elsie breathed.

"I heard it."

"We're going to have it out, you and I." Her voice was matter-of-fact, like she was describing the weather, or a nice flower. "I'm going to learn how to kick your ass."

"Marvelous. I'll teach you."

"Really?"

"Really. I've taught more than my fair share of kids how to deliver a well-deserved ass-kicking."

Elsie smiled at this, looking pleased as she doled them out cups of tea. It faltered, though, when she met his gaze once more. "I feel useless, now that I can't go back to Ginger and Lys and the rest of them."

Augustus growled his agreement. "It's not safe."

"It's just...Lys knew," she pressed. "He recognized me, from when you...anyway." She averted her eyes, uncomfortable. "I dislike not knowing what's going on. Why he was alright with me being there. Why Anscip showed up. Whether I—I could've stayed, if you hadn't interfered."

He straightened up, uneasy. "You wish I hadn't."

"No. No, I'm glad you were there. I saw him, saw those red eyes, and I couldn't stay." She looked at Augustus askance. "You knew that, though. That whatever I wanted, I couldn't be near him. As fucked up as whatever you and I have is, at least I know it's s...something. I dunno."

Safe. He could hear it on the air, she'd been about to say that at least what they had was *safe.*

"Anscip Xavishia is a bastard," Augustus said quietly. "He doesn't really care about anyone but himself or his family. I know that he loves his son. I know that he isn't afraid of a little blood. I know that...that when he was there, he brought terror with him. Not just for people like you, but for everyone—he's exacting, precise in a way I fear and respect. I know that the Master contradicted his instructions at every turn. I know that where Anscip was intent on a clean operation—get what you need and go—the Master was haphazard, messy, happy to leave bodies even when nobody needed to die. I—I know," he whispered, eyes flashing to Elsie, "that the Master had already obtained two of the gods before Anscip Xavishia was even aware this was happening. He bragged about it all the time, about the volume he needed, how he distilled it—the only reason he let Anscip in at all was because the Master saw a chance to make it worse. He saw a tool of precision, where one bloody tear collected cleanly would have been sufficient, and he saw an opportunity to inflict pain." Tears pricked at his eyes now, but he kept his voice low and steady. "I heard Anscip and Lysander talking one night. He has no love of the gods. He'd sooner see them dead than in the Master's hands."

Elsie's brow was knit, emerald eyes burning. "I wondered why he was so involved."

"There was tension between the Master and Anscip, even in what little I saw. I've been the man with blood on his hands, trying to right a catastrophe of someone else's making, Elsie. I recognize it." Augustus blinked, trying to clear the tears from his eyes. "And I know that some part of you has to die to clean up those messes. Anscip's a self-centered bastard whose priority is to preempt the Master. And in truth, Elsie? If I had to choose the lesser of those evils? I would not ally myself with the Master. I would, a thousand times over, choose a man who exacts precise violence with deliberation and calculation than a man who revels in spilling blood for his own joy, thinking himself a savior." Augustus leaned back, rubbing his jaw, trying to compose himself.

"For such a dumbass, you're surprisingly astute." Elsie quirked an eyebrow, taking a sip of tea.

"What did Ezra say that startled you so?"

"He wants me to live with him in the Capital."

"And will you?"

Elsie shrugged. "Everything is too in flux right now. I don't know what my brother—what Teddy—is doing, nor how he's fairing with Sam, but I know that I can't make a decision without them. And Caelaymnis has complicated it even further."

Augustus huffed his agreement.

"Still. Being close to family—I'd like that."

"It's comforting," Augustus agreed. He paused for a moment, listening to the steps come up just outside the door. *Fletcher.* "Fletcher and I have our difficulties," he went on, speaking up, "but I love him dearly, and being near him again has been an enormous relief. Particularly after losing our father—and sister, in her treachery."

Elsie glanced up. "He's right outside, isn't he?"

The door opened, a very tired Fletcher making his appearance. "That's sweet, Augustus. I almost believed that." He brushed a kiss on Elsie's cheek as she rose to greet him. His gaze drifted to Augustus, though, and he lingered for a moment, hand on the back of the sofa. Then, with a forced smile, he gave Augustus's shoulder a small squeeze, gripping it with comradery. "I do miss them. And as much as I hate you, Augustus, I'm glad I don't have to lose you, too."

Augustus put his hand on his brother's, holding it there for a moment.

They were on the precipice, he could feel it in the air. Caelaymnis was in ruins, its people either pledging themselves to tyranny, trapped in the mountain city, or displaced across Maderlav, and the Master stood with his gods by his side, taking what he wanted while Anscip stood in the wings, waiting for his grand finale.

But Augustus and Fletcher and Elsie, they had tonight, that was what he reminded himself. They could toast bread by the fire and pick at the smoked chicken lifted from the pantry, and he could reminisce with his brother, could joke with Elsie, because she was right.

Even if it could never last, they could pretend for a little while longer.

EZRA

*"I loved him. I loved him so much it hurt, and it's
taken a long time to see that if you are in pain? Well. It's
something. But it's not a love worth having.."*

~Sam Alderton

A mournful silence fell in the apartment. The moment Augustus disappeared with Elsie, Isa broke down, silent tears welling in their eyes as they slumped against the counter.

"Hey." Ezra drew them into a hug, heart thumping. "Okay, it's...okay...he's gone now."

"Why was he even here in the first place." Isa's gaze flicked to Ezra, pained.

"I—I mean, I don't—I don't know—"

"I *really* had needed your path not to cross with his. You were both separate, and I needed that space to breathe—"

"It's okay," Ezra whispered, squeezing them tight. "He's gone."

But so was El.

"I have to go." Pulling away from Isa, he moved for the door.

"Like hell you do—"

"I'll be back." Ezra turned, looking Isa straight in the eyes. "Trust me. I was here for days alone, and I didn't do anything. My only crime is wanting a life with my sister. If you want to restrain me for that, then you're not the person I thought you were."

Looking hurt, Isa let him go.

It was just as well. They were dwindling, anyway. The sex lost its fireworks, their conversations fell flat, and Ezra had one man on his mind, now more than ever.

~ • ~

"You came back." The Master's voice was relieved, lodge door clicking closed behind him. Ten o'clock on the dot.

"I always come back."

"Your letter—"

"I found Elsie." Ezra was having a hard time meeting the Master's gaze, curled on the sofa by the fire. "And...I think she's going to say yes."

"You found her?" The surprise in his voice was unmistakable as he sank down beside Ezra.

Ezra nodded.

"Love, what's wrong? You do not seem yourself." The Master had a look of deep fatigue, dark circles under his eyes like smears of berry tart. His hair had been combed, but hastily, the stubble on his cheeks evidence of a sleepless night.

"You don't seem yourself, either," Ezra breathed. "You look tired." His voice was more tender than he wanted it to be. He wanted to hold the firm lines he'd drawn with this man—*let me know you, and I am yours*— but like sand against the sea, he was nothing.

"I am drowning in selfishness and betrayal." The Master sighed, closing his eyes. "I am one step closer, Ezra. We have enough to pull Kiran to our side. That is all that matters. I require rest, and then he will be ours. And anymore, I cannot fixate on extraneous incompetence. I have been counseled to let this one go, and so, I must. I do not have the strength to do otherwise. These gods strain me dreadfully."

Ezra could not stop his fingers from brushing gently against his friend's cheek. "Rest," he echoed, worried.

The Master opened his eyes, catching Ezra's hand before he pulled

473

it away. "You have not answered my question. What's wrong?"

"Why won't you let me know you?" Ezra blurted the question out, panicking.

The Master only sighed, and kissed Ezra's fingers.

"Please," Ezra whispered. The Master's lips were soft against his hand, the gesture sweet and simple and it made Ezra's whole body tense with conflict. "It could be the three of us, in the Capital. You could leave your wife, you could take me instead, I could dine with my sister at breakfast and hold close to you at night, we might be family, just...please. *Please.*"

"I..." His eyes were distant, when they met Ezra's. "I am wary, in light of the news that you have been talking to Elsie." Was his voice colder, now?

"What—what does she have to do with it? That's why we came here—"

"But she is a dangerous person, Ezra. Oh, to be sure, well-intentioned," he added quickly, "but...I confess, I have played a role in her unfortunate path."

"I heard all about how she got hurt," Ezra put in, nodding. Isa had relayed it. How Augustus had been deceptive and cruel, how their family was rife with corruption and devotion to the gods—further evidence that the gods had no place in the lives of mortals. "She's forgiven the elf, I saw them together not an hour ago—I know she can forgive you too."

"I do not want to lose you to a false narrative, Ezra. I am a man with only the best of intentions. And those she runs with seek to undermine me. They make no secret of this."

Ezra blinked. "What—no, that—"

"She has not given you this impression?"

"I know she was curious about you, but she's said nothing—"

The Master dropped Ezra's hand, rising. "What did you tell her?"

"Nothing!" Ezra was on his feet, eyes wide. "Nothing, I swear—I would do nothing to hurt you—I only told her I was curious who you were, too—because I am!" Tears were pressing at his eyes. "You made me all tangled up and I don't even know your name!"

Glancing over, the Master did not move to comfort him, and Ezra sank down onto the sofa, ribs aching as he tried to hold himself together.

Don't cry.

"Has she pressed you about me?"

"No! Why would she," Ezra breathed, jamming the heel of his hand into his eyes. "I told you, I didn't say *anything to her—*"

The Master made a small clicking noise with his tongue, and his hand came to rest on Ezra's shoulder, albeit with an air of hesitation. "If she finds out," he breathed, "I am finished. Did she tell you of the little army she's assembled?"

"Army? What—"

"Did she tell you that she tried to infiltrate one of the Insidiae's production rings to try and get to me," the Master whispered, grip tightening on Ezra's shoulder. "Did she tell you that she is a blood magic runner, hypocrite that she is?"

Ezra's heart stopped cold—probably in metaphor only, but gods *damned* it felt like it might've actually been frozen solid and dropped to the floor.

I've been running, too. That was what she'd said.

Only, she didn't mean that she'd been running, the way he had, from danger. She'd been running *into* it.

"Ah. She has not been entirely forthcoming as to her plans, it seems. Did she tell you that her companion has been hunting me for months? Did she tell you that she is collaborating with terrorists from the Hidden City—"

"What?" Ezra's eyes were blurred with saltwater. "I—I thought she was just recovering? She told me she just wants to live quietly, to retreat—"

"She does not." The Master's voice softened with his grip. "I am sorry, Ezra. I had hoped that perhaps she had given this up. But my most recent trip to the Capital has confirmed they still chase me, doubtless at her behest."

Ezra glanced over to his friend, pained. "What do I do," he whispered.

The Master sighed. "You are not mine to command, Ezra. You are your own man." His hand had fallen to rest on Ezra's hip, the other resting on Ezra's arm. "I fear for your safety. And for mine—though I know that you would do nothing to betray me or this cause. If I only knew what she's planning—"

"What if I could find out?"

Pull me closer. Draw me in, trust me

The Master tilted his head to the side. "And what of your confession," he breathed, voice gentle. "You cannot continue on with me, not knowing."

"I am simply very fond of you." Ezra found he could not break the Master's gaze.

"As I am fond of you. More so than I could have ever thought. I have said this many times, love. I cannot risk losing you."

Ezra sighed, pulling away. "What if I go to Elsie. See what information I can gather."

"You do not have to do this—my mistrust is not your burden—"

"I want to," Ezra nodded, moving for his coat. "For you." His eyes flicked to his friend, pained. *Because I love you.* "And then you will tell me who you are?"

"Once you are safely out of danger, and we are together," the Master said quietly, radiant with joy. "Then, my darling, I am yours entirely."

RISA

*"Life and Death warred, and it was a might battle
over the endings. Death, being inevitable, dragged Life
below, and thus he sat in the shadows, reflecting on his
betrayal of his own powers."*

~ From 'Tales of the Recently Revived: A Sequel'

"Kiran." Risa breathed the name, taking a hesitant step towards the man, strung up in the dungeon of the God of Death. "Kiran, as in the cornerstone?" The relic she'd spent countless hours staring at, contemplating the City and her advocacy and the cases she'd argued, and this—this man...

"They're fakes. Both of them." Beca spat the words with vitriol. "Not that this makes them less petty than the gods they killed so as to take their places. Look upon this, girl, and tell me how much you adore Cora now. Tell me how dear she is, when she can't even be bothered to tell you the truth."

The stale air of the darkened cell closed in, and the chained man was watching her and Beca with burning eyes.

"What are you doing here?"

Starting, Risa whirled, the soul thread shimmering as Cora sauntered through the dungeon door, giving it an irritated pluck. *See,* her fingers seemed to say. *Found you.*

"I told you I was going to wander about," Risa countered, hesitant.

"And you wandered down a *locked* staircase and through a *locked* door into this dungeon," Cora challenged. "Beca, OUT!"

"You can't—"

Cora whirled, face carved in fury, shadows cloying about her. "You have tested my patience for the last time! I have given you all your mortal comforts, and yet your tantrum persists! I have extended my patience and ignored reason, allowing your schemes, and I am done—"

"Cora." Risa breathed her name, fingers grazing her shoulder.

The shadows skittered back, retreating, and Cora's fiery eyes met Risa's. "What," she snarled.

"What happened? Why are you holding another god hostage, here?"

"Because she is a coward and a liar." Beca spat the words out.

"A coward? Hardly." Pushing past Risa, Cora came eye-to-eye with Kiran, grabbing his jaw to hold his gaze. "I was brave," Cora hissed. "More brave than anyone should be at twenty-two, and cleaning up the mess of a man who didn't know when to stop—"

"Rose." Kiran's voice was exhausted, chains rattling. "You can be wrong—"

"You are a god-slayer, a false idol—"

"Beca's right, you're a coward—you murdered your father out of ego and superstition—"

"No." Cora's fingers were white, digging into Kiran's face. "No, what I did was make a series of impossible decisions over and over while you were off playing hero and licking my father's boot, all because you were covetous and arrogant!" She let him go with a sound of disgust. "You trespassed on fragile ground, you slew *gods*, you opened doors that can never be closed and I am left to take the fall!" Cora turned, eyes meeting Risa's. "It's time to leave."

"You've welcomed your souls, then," Risa clipped, uneasy.

"I've ushered in the souls, yes." Cora glanced to Beca. "I'm surprised you didn't come to stand at the gates this time, Beca, as you usually do, to watch for him."

The cry of anguish that Beca let out made Risa's heart chill. "No, please—you can't punish him—"

"*I* won't." Cora turned back, brushing her hair over her shoulder. "I don't simply sit here, clipping threads as I please. Circumstance carries all souls to the gates below, not me."

"Liar! You dragged me here—"

"Beca, you died! It is the unfortunate counterpart to life, and though your husband tells you different, he is wrong—"

Tears glazed Beca's cheeks. "Did you take him?"

"Who," Risa asked quietly, looking between them all.

But the word seemed to give Cora pause.

Like she'd remembered something, and the quiet that fell with the momentary distraction yielded the floor to Beca.

"My son," Beca answered bitterly. "Our son." She gestured tiredly to Kiran.

"Cora," Kiran warned, "you've gone too far—"

Death's green eyes lingered on Risa, ignoring the protestations. "I wasn't the one who went too far," she breathed, the explanation for Risa, and Risa alone.

"Stop shirking responsibility," Beca snarled. "Stop acting as though your stolen godhood absolves you—"

"I have done *nothing!* I am not threatening your son, I am telling you an inevitable fact that you are not prepared to face, that eventually he *will* make for the gates. I am Death." Cora's words were icy, brow carved with refusal. "I do not haphazardly decide who lives and dies, or loves for that matter, like some foolish mortal, or a god who does not know his place! I take the tired souls and trim those painful frayed edges left by mortal life so that they might know rest."

Kiran was glaring, molten eyes burning as they fixed on Cora. "Stop threatening my son to put Beca through her paces. Stop this game—"

479

"It is no game." Cora turned to go.

"He's praying, you know." The chains above Kiran's head gave a soft *clank* as he moved.

Cora whirled on him. "Liar. We don't hear prayers."

"Because *you* don't listen. And who would give devotions to the God of Death, Rose?" Kiran swallowed hard, grimacing. "I'll ask you as I always do. Let me go."

"No." Cora grabbed Risa's arm, dragging her out the door with surprising strength. "We're leaving."

Only once the two of them had ascended to the main floor of the palace did the god let go of Risa, nearly pushing her over in anger as she released her. "Have you lost your ever-loving mind—"

"Have you?" Risa rubbed her arm, scowling. "This is fucked. You're fucked—"

"I'm the God of Death, Theresa, of course I'm fucked! Regular people don't get to places like this—"

"So it's true, then." Tears bloomed in Risa's eyes, making it difficult to hold Cora's gaze with the strength she wanted. "That woman—Beca— she said you were a fake."

Cora's shoulders sank, expression pained.

"That's it? You're not going to say *anything?*"

"What do you want me to tell you, Risa?" Cora's eyes glistened, and for just a moment, Risa could've sworn she had caught a glimpse of someone else beneath the green eyes and obsidian hair.

"I want you to tell me the truth! If you're not real, then…what does that mean? What about Elsie?" Risa's voice was almost a whisper as she took a step forward, glaring. "What about Elsie, Cora? And Ezra?"

"What of them?" Cora shook her head, resigned. "It doesn't matter. None of it matters. They're not my kin. But I swore," she added, pointing forcefully to the floor for emphasis, "I *swore* I would protect them. To their mother and father, and to the god who died in my arms, Risa! You think I wanted this? You think I *asked* for this?" Her voice was rising in anger, filling the corridor. "Why do you think Kiran is chained in the Below? He is a murderer! He is a liar and a coward! I found him," she hissed, "standing over the bloody bodies of gods! I had no choice, taking this mantle—"

"You had every choice, lying to me!" Risa wiped her tears, livid. "So, what—all this has been for nothing? You warned Elsie of her brother for the dramatics of it all?"

"I don't expect you to understand—"

"Try me, Cora! I'm no saint! You, more than anyone else should know that."

Cora smoothed her hair, exhaling deeply, plainly trying to collect herself. "Just because I am a—a false god does not mean the blood magic in the realm above does not pose a threat to us all. The damage has been done. More gods will die before the end, but more than that..." Her eyes met Risa's, tearful. "I need you to just trust me."

Trust.

Such a precarious thing. Easily given, easily broken, and Risa had every reason not to yield.

A false god.

"Promise," Risa breathed. "Promise on whatever it is you love most, whatever you hold dear, promise me, Cora. We're done with the lies."

"Whatever I love most? Whatever I hold dear?" Cora withdrew a knife from her waist, and unflinching, ran it across the palm of her hand. She squeezed it, letting the drops of blood fall to the floor. "It's you, Risa. I love *you*. More than anything. More...than I ever thought was possible." Her green eyes shimmered, tears rolling down her cheeks. "On your soul, Risa. I swear it on your soul. You have my word, sealed in blood. No more lies." Her gaze flicked to the ceiling, exasperated. "And...you

481

wouldn't know it, yet, but where I'm from, that means a lot."

Forceful steps echoed in the hall behind them. "Is my son dead?" Beca's eyes were tearful, her voice furious as she met the corridor where Cora and Risa stood. "Is he?"

Cora stood, fist bloody, glare blossoming on her brow. "How many times must I tell you—"

"You've spent my entire life playing games with me! You're liars, the pair of you, why would I trust you? Just—please, Cora." Beca pressed her eyes closed, trying to calm herself. "Please. Just tell me. Do I need to find him?"

"Not yet."

Uncomfortable silence filled the corridor.

"Why is he here?" Risa let the words fall against the tile, the question burning at her. "Kiran. You said he slew gods."

Cora gave a small nod. "I found him standing over the bodies of our predecessors. The mantle was mine before I had even realized what happened. I...I was a soul collector, Risa. Before, when I was mortal. I was raised in darkness that drew the souls to mine. So it was, with the mantle."

"That's not why he's here." Beca was glaring at them both, her voice quiet. "Lies—"

"He stole the iaculus. The infamous well of cleaving magic guarded by the Chancellors Faulise. One half a dangerous weapon." Cora was wrapping her bloodied hand with a scrap of shawl she'd ripped off, eyes focused on the task with unsettling determination. "Kiran had been after it for ages. The gods sealed half the weapon with blood and the other half with gold. He took the iaculus from Margaret Faulise, and inaction was no longer an option."

"He took me from you," Beca breathed. "That's why he's here—"

"No." The word rang sharp, Cora's gaze snapping to Beca. "You

482

cannot deny he stole the iaculus, you who lie for him still—"

"I do not! It was too late when I learned what he did. He was gone, and I had more pressing matters to tend to—I had a son to care for, and a father relentlessly making my life a living hell—"

"Even still," Cora hissed, "you cover for him. He stole the iaculus, *lost* the iaculus, and you..." She gave a huff of derision, shaking her head.

"The iaculus." Risa breathed the word in disbelief. That was hardly possible. "Sealed in gold—stolen from Maggie—you cannot possibly mean—it's not lost, not at all." If Risa was right, the trinket hanging about Elsie's neck was not just a locket.

Half of a weapon, sealed in gold.

And the other half sealed in blood—it was plain enough why the Master was after the gods, then. He sought to finish what Kiran had started.

And that meant that Elsie was far from out of the woods.

"How widespread is knowledge of what it is," Risa asked, glancing between Cora and Beca. "I didn't realize what it was. Who else knows?"

Beca glanced to the floor. "In truth, even I didn't. Not until Kiran was gone. Before that, it was just Maggie's locket. Just a—a family heirloom. I assumed Kiran stole it out of his petty feud with Maggie. I don't know how the City is these days, but before I died, the—the Factionists loved him. And because they hated Maggie, he did, too. He took it, I knew that, and..." Tears filled her eyes. "I stood by him. I thought she was too blinded by power, and losing the locket that marked her as chosen one might—might give her some perspective. I had no idea what it was—"

"If there is a thirst for godly blood," Cora cut in quietly, "then it is only a matter of time before they go searching for the iaculus, too. The relic will be no good without it."

Beca's wheat eyes found Risa. "Kiran's a bastard. He deserves to be here. But I didn't deserve the hell I got put through just for loving him."

"Tale as old as time," Risa nodded. "Cora, we need to find—"

"I know," Cora whispered, looking apprehensive. "I saw it, too. But I can hardly walk up and yank it off, can I? Not when..." She shook her head. "Though I suppose any trust she had in me is moot. I had hoped to undo the damage Kiran inflicted. But none of it matters. I have no fluency with the tapestry. Even I cannot lock away what he has opened. Even I cannot close the quays."

"The Factionists know well enough who it marks her as, and if Kiran was allied with them, there's a good chance at least one of them knows what it is. Knows that it's...the iaculus," Risa said.

Another mystery, solved. It wasn't just a shiny trinket granting the wearer the right to the Faulise legacy.

It was half a dangerous weapon, and Clark *had* to have known that, when he gifted it to Elsie, Risa reasoned. There was no way he couldn't have, as enmeshed in these schemes as he'd been.

"Do not let her take it, Risa. Not for one minute should a god lay hands on it, real or no," Beca interjected. "Cast it into the sea, be done with it—"

"I was there when it was forged, I will not allow it to slip away into the hands of mortals—"

"That is enough. It is Elsie's!" snapped Risa, voice echoing across the stone. "It—it belongs to her! If she doesn't want to shoulder that burden, then we will help her find a way forward, but I am her advocate! I will not let you step in and start making choices without her! That's how this began, that's how she was found out, that's why she's been through hell!" Something icy worked its way through her, a chill touching her tone. This was what she knew. This was her purview.

I might not be able to do much. But I can stand up for her.

"Every moment we linger is a moment she may be in danger," Risa breathed. "Now let's *go.*"

THE PARTING

Well.

I survived. I...think?

The Underworld has nice stationary, but questionable references to truly determine a metric for living, which makes sense on account of the fact that most of the guests here are dead.

~Elizabeth Clement Faulise,
Excerpt from a letter titled 'Four Weeks, Three Days'

FLETCHER

*"The creatures called vora dwelt long across the sea.
It is said they rode vicious beasts out of the cracks in the
earth when the world was dreamed into being, and with
such terrific legends, the humans took to their swords.
Many made it across the Gray Sea, seeking refuge in the
desert, the mountains, the tropical forests—but many did
not. And so, at the hand of humans, the vora perished.*

Or so we believed."

-An Orated History of Drada, Unknown

"We have a problem." Cele Carson rose from behind the parlor desk, taking off a pair of glasses. "With Caelaymnis under new leadership, the mountain Drada are keen on…how did they put it?" She drew a sheet from the desk. "Ah. 'To preserve the cultural integrity and mutual trust, I take it upon myself to remind you that the Treaty forbids our people to take up residence in your Guild.' Now, we no longer recognize the Treaty, so I can deal with that, but the new king has included…these." Cele passed a hefty stack of parchment leaves to Fletcher.

"Arrest warrants." Fletcher sighed, thumbing through them. "And—ah." He passed a sheet to Isa.

"Oho, one for me," Isa mused. "Delightfully predictable."

The ambient bustle of a now-brimming manor overtook them as Fletcher shuffled through the rest. "Rodion, looks like you're the only one who doesn't get one—El, me, Augustus of course, Mia…"

"That means they plan on courting Thallassas," replied Rodion darkly. Courting Thallassas, indeed—if not arresting the Magistrate's son could be considered courting.

"You are welcome here," Cele put forth, crossing her arms. "But if your people decide a demonstration of force is necessary, and that a select number of wanted persons ought to be removed from this district, you may find yourselves taking up arms against your own kin."

The prospect of bringing more conflict to the Valley made Fletcher feel sick, and the match of mercenary against Drada was, in truth, no contest at all. Valley numbers were minimal anyway, mercenaries being employed at the behest of Merchants not to fight an oncoming army, but to lurk and intimidate and protect investments.

"We should scatter." Fletcher set the stack of parchment on the corner of Cele's desk.

"Draw them away from the Guild and the Valley," Isa agreed, crossing an ankle over their knee and leaning back into the chair. "Cele's got a much better shot of negotiating peace when there's not a mess of traitors camping out in her guest rooms."

"Thallassas would welcome a mess of traitors."

"What of Vaestias?" Isa queried.

Fletcher's eyes flicked to the Commissioner, who listened quietly. "We hear little from the expanse," he muttered. "They took the Treaty to heart. Though, it'd be wise to get to them before Caelaymnis does, they have a strong set-up to argue Vaestias is correct to keep the boundaries."

"And the Coalition," Cele inquired.

A stillness seemed to fall over the parlor.

Rodion shot a glance at Fletcher. "The Coalition is why we have a treaty in the first place. Drawing them in..."

"Could be disastrous," Fletcher finished. "Cele, whatever skepticism of magic the Guild has pales in comparison to the mistrust the Coalition fosters. We seek to co-exist; they will say magic is all that stands in the way."

"Mm." Cele made a small noise. "I have been advised that our last communique was a signed Treaty. You think six-hundred years has changed nothing?"

Fletcher's brow knit. "There's hardly a way to know, and it's a dangerous risk if it hasn't."

But Cele waved him off, returning to her desk. "I disagree. We face a treacherous enemy here, one that threatens our very existence, and we have few choices."

"Cele—"

Her eyes flicked to his. "Either you will go, Fletcher Nist, or I will send another. But I cannot think of a better emissary for our case than a former prince exiled at the advice and guidance of one who controls the gods. Someone will be begging the Coalition for help. And for all our sakes, I hope it can be you."

~ • ~

The bench in the park by the emptied fountain was bitterly cold, stormy gray clouds moving quickly across the sky in the icy wind.

Elsie's breathing was steady, her head against Fletcher's shoulder, a steady *da-dum da-dum da-dum* keeping this borrowed time.

A tense stillness had descended upon Taylor Town, only the occasional *creak* of a shop door opening and closing, hushed whispers of passersby breathing words of strange times, worn coppers being traded for wares that would soon be running low.

There was no point in hiding, anymore. He walked plainly through the streets, no pretense of facade, and every pair of eyes like his that he saw set him at ease. More than ease, it—it was almost excitement, and never before had he wanted to pull someone off the street, to ask, *Isn't this amazing? That we are both here, that we have both survived, that we are walking freely up and down the boulevard, because we're going to build a better future.*

"You really think it'll work," Elsie breathed, nestled into his shoulder. "You think drawing more players will help?"

"If they can be persuaded that this conflict will not stay contained, yes. The...vora—they have kept the ways the Drada have left behind, they..." Fletcher sighed. "El, we need help. No Hidden City. Vaestias is uncertain, the Guild—the Guild has been living with their head in the sand, and Thallassas cannot carry the weight of so many failed moments. If we could stay here—that'd be different, maybe. If we could settle our people together."

"But you know Caelaymnis will be relentless."

"Yeah." Fletcher leaned into Elsie, kissing her hair.

And so, we scatter.

Time was of the essence, and they would need to act quickly to maintain the element of discretion. In twenty minutes time, Fletcher would be on the docks of the Capital and he'd depart across the Gray Sea. It was too far to evanesce, and thus, he'd be confined to a ship, the prospect of which both intrigued and worried Fletcher.

Emissary. Diplomacy had never been his pleasure, but he managed it well enough—better than most, he thought privately. He did not love the idea of knocking on the Coalition's door, but there was some comfort in knowing that if anyone must, it would be him.

Rodion, of course, would return with Isa to Thallassas, with the ultimate aim of pursuing involvement from Vaestias.

The question of Augustus still seemed to be a bit in the air, but Rodion had quietly assured Fletcher that there would be a discrete little cell waiting for his brother on the island, too.

As for Elsie, she'd find Risa and Cora, and venture to the Hidden City itself, Ezra at her heels. Ostensibly, the siblings would be meeting this very afternoon in preparation.

But I'm not there for the Chancellorship, and neither is he, she'd clipped. *They owe us answers.*

"Have you heard from Teddy," Fletcher asked softly, taking a mental tally. He missed them both, Teddy and Sam, now more than ever.

"No. But Cele said Mattie told her he's come to call often, and Matt himself is attempting to broker peace between them." She sighed heavily, fingers giving his leg a squeeze.

He tried to memorize the feeling of her hand on his knee, warm through her thin gloves. But the concentration was consumed in his obsessive mental repetition of the parting, the endless turning over of their destinations in his head.

"Fletcher." Elsie moved, eyes lighting on his—

And he was found, in those eyes.

Words would never be summoned with ease, staring into those eyes, and that was okay, because she never asked for words when she had his eyes, nor his eyes when he gave her words, and in this, deep relief.

Leaning over, Elsie broke his gaze to whisper in his ear. "Of all the beginnings I have had," she breathed, fingers brushing back his hair, "you are my favorite."

Tears pricked at his eyes, and he drew Elsie into a tight hug, breath tight in his chest. "El—"

"It's okay." Her voice broke, too, shoulders starting to shake as she fought off tears of her own. "It's okay, I'll see you again soon—"

"Elsie." He held her tight, feeling sick. "Elsie, of all the endings, you are the best one I could've hoped for."

"I...think I need to go, now. Otherwise..."

"Yeah, no—we'll never go," Fletcher chuckled wetly, pulling away.

494

He thumbed away the tears on her cheeks, giving her a small smile. "It's going to be fine. I'll see you in no time."

She nodded, echoing his smile. "I love you. Be safe."

"I love you too, El." His fingers slid out of her hands as she rose.

This was where he loved her.

As the world fell, by the fountain, in the dead of winter.

Elsie spared a glance over her shoulder as she made for town. She was crying again, her jagged breaths carried on the icy air. "Bye, Fletch." Hardly a whisper, but by the look in her eyes, she knew he'd hear it.

You brought about the end of the world, Elsie.

And you know that the world you ended was mine, that you took a lonely, isolated life and said no more *and that because of you, I found another family. You know that because of you a series of events has been set to fall, and our world will never be the same.*

With a quiet sigh, Fletcher rose.

The fountain and the bench dissolved as he evanesced away, leaving the Valley behind.

The docks of the Capital awaited.

ELSIE

"I would say it was very much an advantage to be
descended from Death herself. Perhaps not initially, but
it is nice to know at least one of the gods had my back."

~Elizabeth Clement Faulise

Elsie jammed the tears away with the ball of her hand, pace fast down the cobblestone sidewalk of Taylor Town.

Not forever. This isn't goodbye forever.

But there'd been a strong comfort, knowing their days came to a close together, and the last nights they'd spent apart had been dark indeed.

Her body felt numb at the prospect. The streets of Taylor Town were awash in people, and it would've been odd, this time of day, except Caelaymnis had fallen, and the mountain Drada needed somewhere to go.

She'd drifted back to a place of unfeeling, her body aching for input it couldn't sense, heart wanting to break but knowing it could not.

Anscip had driven her off the only path she'd had to the Master, and Caelaymnis had collapsed, giving way to tyranny, and the manor had been packed full of elves that would not take kindly to the sight of Augustus—Augustus, who had little choice but to bunk in hers and Fletcher's room, on account of space needed for those fleeing their mountain home, and—

"Dosia!"

Elsie whirled, reaching for her knife on instinct, eyes wide as she scanned the street.

A pissed-off looking redhead was dodging passersby. "I swear to the gods if you stab me—"

"Ginger." Elsie pocketed the blade, shoulders sinking. "How—what are you doing here?"

Ginger rolled her eyes. "Don't get sentimental. I've already had enough of that from Lysander. He's wracked with guilt—"

"Is he okay? Anscip seemed *pissed*—"

"He's fine." Ginger gave a huff that might've been a laugh. "Here." She pressed a slip of paper into Elsie's hand, eyes twinkling. "You were obviously poking around the ring, trying to get some information. So, that's what you get. Information—and a warning."

"What's this?" Elsie unfolded the crisp sheet, a familiar script and haunting message written neatly across the parchment.

Sam.

I love you.

Please come home.

"Lys said to give that to you." Ginger's smile faltered. "Your brother's fine. Lys made sure of it, but Dosia—Elsie." She pursed her lips. "You're in too deep. All of you are. The Master's got an army of gods at his side. You're obviously up to something, you and your friends. Stay out of his way."

"I can't do that, Ginger," Elsie said quietly, "you know that."

"I know." Without hesitation, Ginger drew her into a tight hug.

Elsie let the moment linger, the din of the town around her fading for a moment as she embraced her friend on the busy street, thoughts racing. "Ginger?" She withdrew, frowning. "How did Lys run into my brother?"

"Lys *swore* he's alright, first off—you *cannot* panic, that's the worst thing you can do—"

"Ginger!"

"Lys was trying to clear out the Master's house, on account of the Master nearly coming to blows with Anscip. They're not on the same side, Elsie," Ginger pressed, exasperated. "I wish you hadn't just disappeared that day—you don't get it, what's going on—"

"Ginger!"

"Teddy came knocking at his door, demanding to see...Sam, I think? His husband, Sam? The Master was pissed. Of course, Sam wasn't there, he'd already gone—but it was too much of a coincidence—"

"Sam? Why would Sam be with...the Master...oh, no. Oh, fuck." Elsie's eyes went wide, heart dropping. "No—this is *not* good, Ginger, this is very, very bad—"

"Yeah, that's the general tone," Ginger sneered.

"No, I mean—I know, Ginger," Elsie breathed, voice hardly a whisper. "I know who the Master is."

~•~

It'd all gone sideways.

The Master had been hiding in plain sight, masking his villainy with frivolous slights—at least, that was what Elsie told herself.

She'd seen the signs.

Striding quickly past the general store, bitterness washed over her. Hadn't she leaned there, against the counter just beyond the glass, speculating with Fletcher and Teddy and Sam about how it had to have been a fellow merchant, going after the pastries? How it had to be one of the insatiable capitalists, going after one of their own?

They'd gotten distracted, thinking it was Clark. They'd let their own fury at him guide their investigation, when the real culprit had been standing in his shadow the whole time.

And now, everyone was gone. Fletcher had gone across the sea to treat with an old enemy in the hopes that six-hundred years had bridged the bad blood between them. He would beg for an army, for aid—for any help they could bring against the gods themselves. Teddy and Sam—skies help them, for Elsie had let her brother wander into danger without so much as a second thought.

Sam would never be so selfish. I should've known. When Cele spoke to me about him, I should've known he wouldn't do that, leave Teddy like that.

This left one person, here—one person who wanted to be *her* person, if she'd just let her guard down.

"Ez." Elsie quickened her pace, jogging the last few steps to meet her brother coming down the walk.

He was annoying. He was terrified, he was alone, and he...was her twin.

They'd come into this world together, and that had to mean something. Quite a beginning, that had to be.

A worried look of anxiety was carved into Ezra's face as he met her, Isa a few steps behind. "El," Ezra began.

But she cut him off, wrapping her arms around him, tears welling again.

"Elsie, what's wrong?"

More than anything in the world, she wanted the comforting embrace of her brother.

The gods raged, the Master deceived, and she would not have to face it alone.

"El?"

"Together. We can do this together." She shook her head, and Ezra moved a little, fidgeting. But she wrapped her arms around him in the hug she'd been wanting to give, burying her face in his shoulder, she heard Isa mumble something about Fletcher. "I know who the Master is. We're gonna get him, Ez. I found his house, I know his name. *His name,*

Ezra, it's almost over. I know who he is. It's Mattie. Matthew Fieldson, he's the Master."

Ezra's brow knit. "How can you know?"

"I'm sure of it." She held up the note Ginger had given her. "I've got someone on the inside. Ezra, I—I can't go up against him alone. He's dangerous."

"Matt?" His green eyes were brimming with tears, pain awash across his face. "You're sure?"

"We have to start planning—I don't know what can stop the gods, but maybe we can start talking to the elves? We can go back, fight him from the Capital—I'm saying," Elsie said quickly, gaze locked on her brother, "I'm going with you. Yes. Let's go, let's go to the Capital. Ginger said not to cross him—she's my friend, I'll explain later—but we have to do something, bastards like that don't deserve to draw breath—"

Ezra put a hand on the back of Elsie's head, trembling. "Elsie. I—I can't." And in a single movement, his fingers dug into her skull, yanking her head back. Elsie stumbled against the cobblestones, off balance—

Something heavy hit her square in the chest.

It'd taken all the air from her lungs—couldn't breathe, she couldn't breathe—

A knife gleamed cold in her chest.

Her fingers shook, hot blood against them, and her knees hit the cobblestones.

Impossible.

The locket. He'd pierced the—the locket—and something cold spread through her chest, icy and painful—

Ezra reached down, yanking the knife from her chest, bloodied gold iaculus clattering to the ground. "Sorry, Elsie."

Icy panic was setting in, a deep dull ache coughing through her, the gray sky above her tunneling darker and darker. And she was sorry, too.

SAM

"Crisis numbs all aches. But afterwards, you pay double for the pains you could not feel. This, I know well."

~ Theodore Alderton

Evening approached, and Sam did fight to stay awake, because these were the moments worth fighting for. Even so, he'd drifted in and out all afternoon, each moment of wakefulness a jolt of terror that it had all been a dream, each moment of hazy darkness colored by a desperate plea to stay awake just a bit longer.

"How are you feeling?" Teddy pressed the back of his hand against Sam's forehead. "You're still quite warm, are you too close to the fire?"

"I'm okay," Sam lied. His bleary eyes followed Teddy as he rose to retrieve more water. "Is it still today?"

"Yeah. Still today."

"It'll be okay." Sam breathed the words on reflex, dimly aware that they might not be true.

Teddy knelt down beside Sam, sitting him up once more, tipping water to his cracked lips, saying nothing.

A small sip, and Sam pulled away, looking about the camp.

"What?"

"I want to sit up for a bit," Sam breathed, brow knit. "Back hurts."

With a deep sigh, Teddy set the small tin cup down, and gently, he slid over to sit behind Sam, one leg tucked beneath him, the other outstretched to straddle Sam's good leg. "Lean back," he said softly.

Sam obeyed, deep relief washing over him as he let himself rest against Teddy's chest. "Thank you."

Nothing but silence met him in return.

There was so much awkwardness between them, Sam's own fear only adding to his discomfort, for Teddy wasn't supposed to be involved—and if Teddy knew, everyone else must, and that meant they all were in peril.

And yet, every time Sam saw the silhouette of Teddy's face, every time those blue eyes met his, every touch Teddy gave caring for him made Sam tremendously happy, for he'd been convinced that the last time he would ever see his husband would be crumpled up on the floor, heart breaking in real time as Sam watched.

In truth, he hadn't considered this. That Teddy would find him, that they'd have to rebuild after such a catastrophe—and rebuild in such a short time, if Teddy's pained looks were any indicator of the severity of Sam's injuries.

"Teddy." Sam leaned into him, feeling like he might cry. "I'm so sorry—"

"Don't." His voice was soft, but sure. "We'll deal with this later. Gotta get out of here first."

Sam cleared his throat, trying to summon some additional degree of alertness. "So. I, uh...must not be doing great if we're not gonna talk about what happened?"

A pause. Then—

"If I can't find a way out for you, the last thing we do together is not going to be talking about how you lied to me."

"Oh." Tears pricked at Sam's eyes. They'd gone beyond fighting.

"That was cold, even for you," Mariann clipped.

Teddy ignored her chastisement. "Sam, I am gonna find a way to get us out of here. And then we're gonna have a big fight about this, okay?"

Sam nodded, turning his head into Teddy's shoulder. "Teddy?"

"Hmm."

"I—I didn't leave because I didn't want to be with you anymore."

Teddy made a small sound, moving. "Sam—"

"I, uh..." Sam rubbed his eyes, thoughts foggy. "Matt found me."

Teddy moved, one arm still around Sam, icy blue eyes meeting his. "Please, not now—"

"Or—not him, no Matt, per say. I guess, it was...Lucia? Ignata? They said I was the son of Kiran." It was absurd, saying it aloud. "He...oh, gods, Teddy...I'm sorry. It's lies, I know that, he is a mad man—but he said that name, Teddy. He started naming gods, and I knew none of you were safe. He said if you found out, if you knew, that your lives were in danger."

Teddy's face was carved with pain, brow knit, sinking blue eyes studying him.

And suddenly, a tome's worth of words came stumbling back, this weird, wordless void between them needing to be filled, because Teddy was telling him everything, every moment, every emotion, and it felt like lifetimes had passed since they'd just sat and talked. Teddy was wrong, they *were* going to talk about the lies, because this was what they did.

Swapped heartbreak, no matter how bad things had gotten.

~•~

Teddy paced before the fire, brow creased. "We simply cannot stay here."

The conversation had twisted and turned out of Sam's grasp, and it was all he could do to sit and listen, trying to follow. He'd listened as Teddy spilled every ounce of heartbreak, had tried himself to explain how it had all come to pass—but their words were quickly diverted.

Teddy wanted to know the complexities of Anscip and Mariann, of how they both came to aid Matt. Mari had harshly corrected him, insisting that Anscip was a control to an otherwise bloody massacre, and that he had it all in hand. This, of course, had caused Teddy much distress, and he'd begun arguing with her—which, Sam supposed, was probably easier than trying to fix their marriage before infection overtook Sam completely.

"What do you want to do," Mariann demanded, scowling as she gestured at the camp. Herself, Teddy, a sleeping beast, and Sam himself.

"I...could go get help," Teddy looked over, lips pursed. "Bring back help?" He shook his head, mumbling something, but the words were lost on Sam.

Hot, he was too hot again, beads of sweat welling...

"Lay down," Sam muttered, half to himself, easing back. His chest felt tight, heart pounding out irregular beats. *Fitting, for this irregular time.*

Sam's thoughts were muddy and wild as he blinked back the tunneling dark, trying once more to focus on the stars above, and the conversation unfolding.

Pay attention.

Listen.

But their voices only drifted meaningless against his ears.

Lucia, trickster, stay your hand...

No...not quite...

He could not remember the prayer Fletcher had said with him in the apartment kitchen as Teddy had rested, recovering from seizure.

Ignata, light your lamp...

"Sam?" Teddy's voice sounded distant.

Kiran, restore the day. That much, he remembered...

But it broke him.

Sam fixed his gaze on the one single star above him, still burning bright. *Maybe you're a god to others. But you could've been everything to Mom and me.*

The sky was dark.

A quiet chill had fallen over the camp, the fire having gone, and there was simply nothing but uneasy night.

ISA

"To fight side by side with a foe does not unmake an
enemy. But it is a start."

~Isa Mirestva

Blood was pooling beneath Elsie on the cobblestones, hot and sticky against Isa's hands as they tried to stem the flow. "Someone, stop him!"

Ezra was running, and Isa swore, a deliberately familiar step joining that boy's frantic pace, because the gods were not smiling down on any of them today. Augustus's footfalls were followed by the sound of two bodies colliding, and Ezra gave a shriek as Augustus grabbed him.

"C'mon, Elsie," Isa breathed, eyes searching her. *Not good.* Dradan craft couldn't fix this. They'd triaged enough wounds to see that plainly.

Ezra had met her in embrace. He'd reached his hand into his coat, yanked her head back, and plunged a knife in her chest, clipping a pathetic apology as he took the blade—and the locket. Never had Isa seen someone wield a knife with such ease.

"Gut. Him." Isa snarled the words, eyes flicking up to Augustus. He'd dragged the boy back with ease, fury in his pale eyes.

"I wouldn't do that if I were you." A middle-aged man with salt-and-pepper hair was striding towards them, jaw shadowed with stubble, a weather-stained coat snapping with menace at his heels. "Step away from the girl, vora."

An idle threat, and Isa was unfazed.

"Oh, Elsie—hold on, darling—" Their eyes flicked down, feeling her irregular heart beneath their hands. "Hang on—"

The thud of running feet against the ground filled their ears.

"Always cleaning up someone else's mess—follow the boy, he said—"

Something colder than the winter air whispered at Isa's neck.

A hand gripped their shoulder— "Easy." Risa was kneeling beside them, blue eyes meeting Isa's. "Go. I'll take over."

Rising, though, Isa's eyes flicked to the woman at her side.

Pure emerald eyes, a sheet of midnight hair, and shadows nipping at her heels—

Cora. It has to be her.

Moving, Isa turned to face the approaching force now cornering them. A bloody clash with humans was *not* what was needed.

"Step back from the girl," the grisly man barked. "I'm warning you..."

Bloody hands moving, Isa threw a shield between them, glancing at Augustus, still holding Ezra. *Help?* Curving a shield was something they had not yet mastered, and the single pane left Elsie—and Risa and Cora—vulnerable.

To make matters worse, the salt-and-pepper man moved through the shimmering barrier like it was nothing, and Isa swore, moving to meet him hand-to-hand.

A bad conjuring.

This bastard was fast, Isa realized. They all were, and armed to the teeth—

A *thwack* reverberated as the salt-and-pepper man walked into a neatly domed shield that could've only been conjured by Augustus. But it was followed by the sickening sound of a blade cutting flesh, and out of the corner of Isa's eye, they saw Ezra bolt.

Fuck—

Why aren't they moving Elsie? Why don't they get her out of here?

The dome of a shield fell.

Dodging a swift near-hit, Isa threw up another shield to block the

507

attack of an assailant hurling himself at Elsie—

And this time, it held.

A series of strategically conjured and re-conjured shields should hold, Isa thought, nearly backed into a corner, hands outstretched as they stood before the trio on the cobblestones. Better than continued engagement, provided their magic remained focused.

They glanced behind them just in time to see Augustus round the corner of an alley, a red stain spreading across the side of his cream button-up.

"Hurry," Isa muttered, trying to press extraneous thoughts off, thoughts like *my taste in men is truly shit* and *how badly did he get hurt?*

"I *am*," the God of Death clipped, "I am working—*ah!*" Her cry of effort overtook them. "Risa, I cannot hold her soul much longer—"

"Her soul?" Isa glared, hands working the air, desperately trying to keep the circling monsters at bay.

"I'm going as fast as I can," Risa panted.

"Doesn't have to be perfect, just enough—"

"Get her out of here!" Isa snapped, patience gone. "Stop fucking around—"

"Her soul is tied here, if we move her, I will not be able to pull it back from the Realm of Souls..." Cora's voice was strained.

Isa glanced over their shoulder once more.

A look of intense pain was carved into Death's face, her hands contorted as a single strand of light wavered, piercing itself through the ground, through Elsie's chest and into the air.

"Put that back," Isa snapped, turning their attention back to the street.

In the distance, a girl with ginger hair was striding down the cobblestones, looking pissed, and the sound of a dagger being pulled from a sheath cut through the air.

"This is no time to be toying with a disembodied soul," Isa growled.

"We've got more company—"

But the girl was running for the middle-aged man, and without hesitation, plunged her dagger between his shoulder blades with a shriek of anger. She let his body fall, and eyes locking on Isa, she took up a defensive position before the shield, not saying a word.

There was a stillness rippling out from the man's body.

"She killed Asher!"

"And I'll kill the rest of you, too," she snarled. "Either you're with us, or you're against us. Decide or die."

AUGUSTUS

"What was I thinking, laying there? To be honest,
that I would've been honored to die at the hand of his
twin, because she was the real fighter."

~Augustus Praequintelya

The boy was quick with the blade.

Augustus's side was burning with unnatural fire as he dodged wary onlookers, chasing Erza, anger overruling pain.

His own chest still pricked with the echo of a blow he hadn't taken, but one that had called him into the streets nevertheless, and he'd make that boy pay tenfold for this. Not because of the soul magic, either, he realized, rounding a corner. But because—because—

"Don't." Ezra brandished the bloody knife at Augustus, backed against the brick divider.

"You've made a mistake, boy," Augustus growled, taking a step forward, hands up and ready.

I cannot hold her soul much longer. That was what the woman had said.

Magic sparked ready at his fingertips. "Put the knife down."

"Isa loved you," Ezra breathed. He studied Augustus with jealousy and judgment. "They talked about you all the time. Even when they shouldn't have."

Augustus's patience proved far thinner than he'd thought, and what he'd meant to do was conjure a lucent, hot and lethal, to knock the knife from the boy's hand as he moved to seize Ezra himself. But a stab of pain rippled through him, magic sputtering out.

The stumble was enough of a chance and Ezra took it, moving swiftly. "For Isa," they whispered, plunging the blade into Augustus's gut. "For Elsie. For the pain you *gave them both*." Searing pain flooded Augustus, something unnatural and caustic worming its way through him as he took a staggering step, bracing himself against the wall to keep from falling. He could not keep himself upright, though, for a wave of his own magic twisted through him. Collapsing, Ezra followed him to the ground, kneeling down beside him, each word bringing the blade down again and again and again—

"For *Isa*," Ezra bit, "for El, for *all your sins...*"

What about yours, boy?

Augustus groaned, bones afire.

But it seemed Ezra had accounted for his own sins, too, as he wiped his tears with a bloody hand, crying. "Tell her...I'm sorry. But you gave me no choice." And with that, he rose, sparing Augustus one last look before he turned and ran.

EZRA

"And so, the child ran into the arms of the monster,
thinking him a friend."

~Unknown

In the drawing room of the Master's house, Ezra sat on the floor by the fire, shaking.

I killed her.

He'd replayed it again and again in his mind. He hadn't intended to strike so hard, hadn't meant to summon such anger—

There'd been such resistance, nicking that locket about her neck. But the moment he'd pierced through the gold, the knife had slid through her like butter.

He couldn't bear the way she'd said his name. The Master's name. *Matt's name.*

"Here." The Master sank down beside Ezra, offering him a glass of whiskey. "Ezra, you did the right thing."

"Did I?" He took the glass, downing it in a single mouthful.

"It was her or you. If you hadn't stopped her, I promise that it would've been her, driving a knife into your heart instead."

Ezra set the glass down, hollow, and he glanced over to the Master. "I'm ready."

This was it. The moment they'd agreed upon. Ezra's blood would buy back everything he'd ever wanted. Nan wouldn't be dead anymore. He'd be comfortable, in this house of the man he loved, it would all be as it should—

The Master said nothing. He only rose, and offered a hand to Ezra to do the same, and gently, he led Ezra to a stairwell leading into the servants quarters. "I will stay with you," he breathed, hand on Ezra's lower back. "I won't leave you alone."

"Good."

Down a hall off the kitchen, the Master led Ezra to a sterile-smelling room. It'd been made up, a bed in one corner, a chamber pot, but nothing else.

"It's so empty," Ezra breathed, looking around. "It has to be here?"

"I will not lead a barghest through the house," the Master said apologetically. "It has to be here. Your room will be waiting for you, though. I promise. I know this all must be quite overwhelming. You've been through the wringer, my dear Ezra. But time is of the essence, isn't it, and we must press on." Gentle fingers ran along Ezra's jaw, soft. "Such endurance from someone so young."

Ezra let out a little whimper.

"You poor thing."

"Is—I'm doing the right thing, right?" He was treading water, clinging to driftwood, and he was praying—though not to the gods—that this was the course to right the world he saw was so off-kilter.

"You are," the Master soothed. "I promise. And you are so wonderfully brave for doing these difficult things, Ezra."

"I am?"

"Of course, you are."

Ezra nodded, looking around. "This...is more than a prick on the finger, isn't it," he breathed. "I—I don't want them to win, but I—will it hurt?"

The Master nodded, eyes sad. "I'm sorry. It's not a pleasant process. But I will stay with you. Sit with you. Tend to you."

"Really?"

"Really." The Master smiled, giving Ezra's arm a squeeze.

"Master, I—I would like that, I don't want to be alone—"

"Come now, Ezra. I think we are past formalities. Please," he smiled softly, "Call me—"

"Matthew," Ezra breathed. "Right? That—that's what she said. That's why I..." He trailed off.

The Master gave a nod, eyes searching Ezra. Then, holding out his hand, he smiled warmly. "Let us not have her deprive us of a proper introduction. It's a pleasure to make your acquaintance, Ezra Hollick. I'm Matthew Fieldson, but please." He put his other hand on Ezra's shoulder, drawing him in, voice soft. "Call me Mattie."

EPILOGUE

It had taken days, traversing the barren waste, to at last reach the gates.

Elsie cried a lot, at first.

It wasn't supposed to be like this. Hot and dusty and dry and over.

Her chest ached, and there was a huge gash where she'd been stabbed, and it didn't matter how long she was here.

It never healed.

She was sure it'd get infected as she'd stumbled across the cracked earth towards the ever-distant gates, but then again, she'd also been sure she would be hungry and thirsty and in pain and she was all of those things, but instead of killing her, they seemed to only fester.

It seemed the dead could not be killed.

By the time she got to the gates, she had been delirious with exhaustion. She could recall collapsing down onto the satiny stone walk, breathless and tearful, and she had begged to go home.

But Yara, First Soul, Guardian of the Underworld, said that she was to stay.

Everything after that blurred into numb grief.

Someone had taken her to a bath, had cleaned her up, and in the end, Yara was able to offer up some bandages, which didn't do anything beyond make Elsie feel like she was making progress mending herself when really, she hadn't.

There was a grand hall of black and gold, a brazier roaring, and a single feather bed set before it, a small kindling of home in a hall of lifelessness.

Souls did not need to sleep, but Elsie did, anyway, and her dreams were horrifying. She slept, and when she did not, she laid in bed, staring into the hall, listening to the fire, or else the quiet steps of Yara, coming to check on her, the whispered words of *can I fetch you anything* and *are you okay* so pathetically useless.

Of course, she was not okay.

She was grieving for her own life.

"Can I fetch you anything?" Yara asked the question for the sixteenth time. Elsie had been counting.

"No." She whispered the word into the black silken pillow, tired.

But Yara did not leave.

Elsie glanced up, too exhausted to be annoyed. "What."

"You know, you are permitted to leave this room."

"To do what? To be dead, somewhere else?"

Yara pursed her lips. "You're not dead. You simply are not permitted to leave the Realm of Souls."

"Sounds like the same thing as being dead to me."

"I am just the First Soul, Miss. I leave metaphysical musings to Cora. But you are not dead."

"Why don't we get Cora, then," Elsie said dully. "Let her explain this."

"That's the thing, Miss. I cannot."

Elsie sat up, irritated. "Why not?"

"She's busy, at the moment."

"Doing what?"

"Making sure that your soul stays locked in this realm."

"Oh, is she?" Elsie rose, feet hitting the cold stone floor, a glare blossoming across her brow as she met Yara.

"She is, Miss. But it's tricky."

"And why is that," Elsie demanded through gritted teeth. "Why is it

517

so hard to make sure a soul stays dead?"

"She's not trying to make sure you stay dead, Miss. She's trying to make sure you stay alive."

ACKNOWLEDGMENTS

Where to even begin.

I started this book during my transition year, which was also the first year of the pandemic. I am so grateful that this book accompanied me through an immensely difficult year, and that I've been able to spend the last few years with it.

Thank you to my husband, whose love and friendship remains a safe harbor to turn to. My dear, I am so grateful that you are my companion through this life, and I cannot thank you enough for holding me—and these books—close. When I started this book, it felt as though there were so few good things left, but you will always be one of them. But we made it through the first years of the pandemic, and it's been wonderful, watching how our lives have bloomed.

A special thank you to Lauren; you are such a good soul, and I'm humbled and empowered by our friendship. The space that you cultivate with me is deeply special, and I do not know how I would've made it this far without you. Your fierce wit and unwavering love is everything.

I'd also like to thank my dad for gifting me with a love of books and magic—I don't know that I've ever been able to quite recreate the magic he did, for few things can compare with childhood belief in the fantastic, but I know I will never regret trying.

Thank you to my colleagues, who make me grateful to have a day job, and push me to balance writing and work—I can't imagine having to choose one or the other.

Thank you to my friends, who though we may not talk often, understand that it is the quality, not the quantity, of conversations.

Then, too, I would like to thank all of my characters for once more allowing me to put them through their paces. Elsie, I am grateful that I was able to find you again—your inquisitive nature and fierce passion give me hope, and it has been a delight spending two full novels with you. Here's to many more, my darling MC. Of course, there is Teddy, who continues to heal me in ways beyond words; Sam, whose grief and pain are shared. Fletcher, who helped show me family isn't in a name. Isa, who is always going to sit well inside my soul; Augustus, who is trying his best and really, isn't that what we're all doing, sins and redemption and all? Risa, who will always bridge my work life and home life (I'm shaking my fist at you, because you always complicate my plot); Cora, who straddles wrong and right as she tries to clean up everyone else's mess; Ezra, who is the dumb mess of a boy inside us all; Howard and Mariann, who remind me that love can persist despite it all.

As is the custom, I remind you here that kindness is the ultimate art form, and that we are all better for striving to cultivate it.

Allow what is good and beautiful in the world to consume you. Do not let the sharp edges of others carve away the parts of you that matter; and likewise, do not give gratitude to those who lack the discipline and conviction to remain gentle.

Never do we thank the page-rippers.

ABOUT THE AUTHOR

C.H. Williams is a fantasy author and illustrator living in the Mid-Atlantic with his husband, a very spunky dog, and two troublesome cats. With a repertoire of character-driven high fantasy novels, his writing couples the darker side of fairy tales with the radiance and joy of queer love. When not causing trouble or spending time doing foundry work with his husband, he can be found walking in the woods and listening to music. Before delving into the realms of magic, he worked as a classical musician, actively performing and conducting research about musicians' relationship to gender. He has since pivoted to legal work during the day and writing dark, contemplative fantasy at night.

His writing touches on the soft, small moments of magic made when we cultivate our gardens amid the storms, and on the immensity of experience as he explores character-driven stories that play out realistic decisions and consequences of a fantastical universe.

www.ingramcontent.com/pod-product-compliance
Lightning Source LLC
Chambersburg PA
CBHW030537020726
47494CB00005B/1412